Hitting the Right Note

Also by Rhonda Bowen

Man Enough for Me

One Way or Another

Get You Good

Hitting the Right Note

RHONDA BOWEN

KENSINGTON PUBLISHING CORP.
www.kensingtonbooks.com

DAFINA BOOKS are published by

Kensington Publishing Corp.
119 West 40th Street
New York, NY 10018

All Kensington titles, imprints, and distributed lines are available at special quantity discounts for bulk purchases for sales promotion, premiums, fund-raising, and educational or institutional use.

Special book excerpts or customized printings can also be created to fit specific needs. For details, write or phone the office of the Kensington Special Sales Manager: Kensington Publishing Corp., 119 West 40th Street, New York, NY 10018. Attn. Special Sales Department. Phone: 1-800-221-2647.

ISBN-13: 978-0-7582-8139-5
ISBN-10: 0-7582-8139-0
First Trade Paperback Printing: April 2014

eISBN-13: 978-0-7582-8141-8
eISBN-10: 0-7582-8141-2
First Electronic Edition: April 2014

10 9 8 7 6 5 4 3 2 1

Printed in the United States of America

This one is dedicated to all my single ladies! A word from one single gal to another: Every moment of life is precious—with or without a male attachment. God has an amazing plan for your life. Don't miss out on it. Enjoy every moment!

Acknowledgments

This is my fourth novel. Can you believe it? You would think it gets easier every time, but it doesn't. After three books, there is now a familiarity in the act of writing for publishing, but there is also this personal pressure to do better than the time before. I will confess that there is a lot of me in this novel, which made writing it an interesting experience. But it was an experience I was so happy to have. It was an experience that God needed me to have so he could help me let go of some things that I was still holding on to. So first of all, I have to thank God for not only giving me the opportunity to write this but also helping me through the whole writing process. I couldn't have done anything without him.

I would also like to thank my family for being there for me again. They now know how to recognize writing time and know to give me a wide berth when that is happening. Thanks Vonny, Clive, and Kevin; and extended family Morva, Roydell, Hopeton, Natalie, Brian, Lisa, and Orel for my surprise release party for *Get You Good.* You guys are beyond awesome and I love you to pieces.

Thanks to all my friends from Agape and George Brown College and everyone in between, who keep me grounded, who let me steal their experiences for my plots, and who form the inspiration for so many of my characters. You guys help me without even knowing.

To my editor Mercedes, you are awesome, and the most patient and diplomatic boss I have ever had! Can't believe we've been doing this for four years now. Thanks to you and to the entire team at Kensington Books. You all have made so many of my dreams come true.

To the author and reader communities, particularly the Facebook crew, thank you so much. To Rhonda McKnight and Tia McCollors, who always have a kind word; Jacquelin Thomas, who took the time to share some realness with me; Tyora Moody, Ashea Goldson, Ella Curry, Sharon Simmons, Faith ABeliever, Tabitha Vinson, Vanessa Richardson, Sharvette Mitchell, and all the blogs and book clubs that promote my new releases: I appreciate the time you take to recommend me and my work. Thank you.

And, of course, thank you to all my readers—past, present, and future. Your e-mails, letters, notes, and reviews always come at the most amazing times. You are a source of encouragement to me and a constant reminder that every day spent writing until two o'clock in the morning is so worth it. I hope you have been, and continue to be, blessed and inspired through my stories the way you have blessed and inspired me. Furthermore, I hope that God does in your life exceedingly and abundantly more than you can ask or imagine.

Be blessed!

Chapter 1

"He asked me to marry him! We're getting married!"

According to a recent report on ABC's *Nightline,* 70 percent of professional African American women over the age of twenty-five are unmarried. As JJ held the phone away from her ear to avoid Sydney's screams, she realized that her older sister had joined the 30 percent and left her stranded.

JJ Isaacs set the phone on hands-free and began applying mascara to her lashes. Though the news was not entirely surprising, it was not what she had expected to hear when she saw her sister's number pop up on the caller ID. Not on this night, anyway.

"Ohmigosh, JJ! He wants to marry me. Hayden Windsor wants to spend the rest of his life with me. Can you believe it?"

Could she believe that ex–NBA star Hayden Windsor, one of the first professional basketball players to figure out how to retire from the game and not go broke, wanted to marry her sister? Of course she could. Who wouldn't want to marry her tall, gorgeous, successful-business-owning sister? In fact, if they weren't related, JJ would have married her.

"Congratulations, hon," JJ said, pushing back a thin layer of irritation to find the genuine happiness for her sister that was camouflaged underneath. "I'm guessing you said yes?"

JJ grimaced and reached for her lipstick as Sydney screamed her response in the affirmative. She had never seen—okay, heard—Sydney like this. Her older sibling was usually the sane one in the craziness that was their big, dysfunctional family. Whereas everyone else was content to fly by the seat of their pants, Sydney was always the one with the plan. Getting married to a man she had dated for less than a year was not like her at all. But that's what happened when people fell in love. Or so JJ assumed. Having had no firsthand knowledge of the being-in-love experience, she couldn't say for sure.

"That's great, Syd," JJ said, reminding herself that she was happy for her sister. "Hayden's a prize."

"He is amazing, isn't he?" Sydney said, managing to modulate her voice to a less ear-splitting volume. "JJ, you should have seen his proposal..."

JJ rolled her eyes and mouthed a silent *no, thank you.*

"It was perfect," Sydney began. "He took me to..."

A banging on wood saved JJ's sanity.

"Five minutes to curtain, ladies," a booming voice called from the other side of the dressing room door.

JJ had never been so happy for a curtain call. She loved her sister and really was happy for her, but the last thing she wanted to hear from her sister, who had yet to remember what JJ was doing that night, was how her perfect boyfriend had done the perfect proposal to set off their perfect engagement.

"Syd, I gotta go." JJ jammed her feet into heels and swiped a layer of gloss over her lips as the scramble of women around her picked up speed. "I'm about to go onstage."

"Oh, honey, I'm so sorry! I completely forgot you had a show tonight."

JJ tried to ignore her annoyance.

"It's okay." JJ stood and straightened her dress. "I wouldn't have wanted to wait till tomorrow for this news. In fact, you can call me back later tonight and tell me all the details."

By then she wouldn't be as anxious and cranky as she usually was the last few minutes before a performance.

"Okay, sure," Sydney agreed.

A hand tugged at JJ's arm.

"We gotta go, JJ," Torrina said, nodding toward the door.

JJ picked up the cell phone to end the call. "Gotta go, Syd. Love you."

"Love you, hon. Have a great—"

JJ didn't hear the end of her sister's sentence. She barely got to toss her phone on the dressing room vanity before Torrina, her fellow backup singer, dragged her through the door and down the narrow backstage passageway. Sturdy iron beams holding the stage in place, and swiftly moving black-clothed men and women holding the show in place, barely registered with JJ as she hurried behind the other singers to her place near the second curtain.

"Everyone on your marker Curtains go up in five, four, three, two..."

JJ didn't hear the end of the countdown. Just the drummer's intro as the band started up Jayla Grey's "Sunday to Sunday." JJ was already up onstage with the rest of the backup vocalists as the curtains rolled up. Jayla would make her entrance in only a few seconds as she sang the first verse to one of the most popular songs off her Juno Award–winning album, *Desire.* JJ remembered when the "Sunday to Sunday" single first started blowing up the airwaves a couple years back. She never dreamed that she would be part of the performance for that song, but here she was at the Festival Place with hundreds of eyes watching her perform. Okay, so they weren't really there for her, but she was part of the show.

Jayla's strong, sultry contralto voice came in with the first few lines of the song, about a woman who was willing to slave for her man because she loved him. The crowds began to clap in rhythm and cheer.

JJ's own hips began to move to well-choreographed steps as the song progressed. Beads of perspiration began to dot her forehead and chest as the hot strobe lights shone down on her and everyone else onstage. But it just energized her and set her blood pumping as her voice came in strong for the pre-chorus. Her body began to feel the music, catching its own rhythm, making the steps her own. The sweet melodies curled out of her, blending with those of her fellow singers to bring a rich, lush harmony that cushioned Jayla's flawless voice. The screams of the crowd soaked into her like a light, warm drizzle on a humid day. JJ was in heaven and she never wanted it to end.

But eventually it did. Much quicker than she expected, with the fifty-minute set feeling like only fifty seconds. Her body still buzzed with energy as she skipped down the steps from the stage, her five-inch platform heels clicking gracefully. At first she could barely walk in the things. But after four months of wearing them onstage, she could manage a sprint if she needed to.

"Good show tonight, guys," Coley, the show's producer, said as he met JJ and the rest of the singers at the bottom of the steps. He pushed the mouthpiece of his headset up to his ear. "You guys were awesome, as usual."

"Good to know," Donald, a fellow singer, commented as he uncapped a bottle of water. "Especially since I felt like I was melting underneath those lights up there."

"Yeah," Torrina agreed, with a cheeky smile. "Plus I almost broke my neck on the wires on the floor back there in our little area."

"I guess it's a good thing I work with professionals then," Coley said, returning his mouthpiece to the right position as he began to walk away. "Lesser singers would have complained."

They all laughed as they headed back to the dressing rooms. Jayla, who was already in her robe, met them at the doorway.

"Thanks a lot, guys," she said, hugging each of them. "I was just telling Philip and the rest of the band, everything was almost perfect tonight. Couldn't have asked for a better show."

"Does that mean we get a raise?" Mark, the other male singer, asked with a grin.

Jayla smiled. "You better talk to Todd about that. He's the one signing your checks, not me. I just dish out the praise. You guys enjoy the rest of the night and this week. On Monday we'll start rehearsals for the tour."

JJ smiled but said little. Though everyone had been really nice to her, as one of the newest members of the team of backup singers, she still felt a little on the fringes. Truth was, she was only there because one of Jayla's original singers, Amina, got in a tiff with management and quit. Torrina had shared the dramatic details with her not long after JJ joined the crew.

However, her newness meant she didn't get all the inside jokes and she didn't always get invited to all the social events. But over the past two months, as she spent more time with the team, she was starting to feel like one of the family.

"I'm gonna head out but just wanted to say you were amazing tonight, Jayla," JJ said, squeezing the older woman's arm. She was about to turn away when Jayla grabbed her.

"You weren't too bad yourself," Jayla said with a smile. "I caught you doing your thing out there. You're coming on tour with us, right?"

JJ's eyes widened. She knew Jayla was going on a major tour in a couple weeks, but she had assumed that the main three would be going as backup. No one had talked to her about being a part of that team, and she honestly hadn't even considered it.

"Uh, I . . . I don't know," JJ stammered.

Jayla nodded thoughtfully. "Let me talk to my people and have someone get back to you. But keep your calendar open."

JJ opened and closed her mouth a couple times to answer and just ended up nodding.

Jayla chuckled. "See you next week, JJ."

JJ stumbled through the dressing room, barely able to focus as she gathered her things and exited the building. As soon as she stepped through the door into the cool, dark night, a hand grasped her upper arm, yanking her forward.

"Did I just hear what I thought I heard?" Torrina asked, her voice several pitches higher than usual and her eyebrows arched several inches higher than normal.

"She wants me to come on tour with her!"

Both women squealed and jumped around in the parking lot, holding on to each other. JJ wasn't normally a screamer, but maybe there was something in the water tonight. She couldn't help herself.

"Jayla Grey wants me to come on tour with her!" JJ shrieked again. "She told me she was going to talk to her people. She invited me to rehearsal on Monday. She wants me to come on tour with her!"

"Oh, that's amazing," Torrina said, still bouncing even though her feet were planted firmly on the ground. "It would be so much fun to have you with us. I mean the other guys are great, but it would be great to have a girlfriend on the bus."

"I know," JJ said. "And, girl, I'm gonna need you to have my back. Someone's gonna have to keep me from making an absolute fool of myself when I see Angie Stone."

"Girl, I don't know if I can help you there," Torrina said, slapping a hand on her hip. "Last year I saw John Legend backstage at a show I was doing and I near lost my mind."

JJ burst out laughing.

"I'm serious!" Torrina said, eyes widening and hair flashing in the normal dramatic way in which she told her stories. "I was trying to climb over the barriers from our backstage area to his, nearly ripped my thousand-dollar dress. I almost got to him too, except his security guard got to me first."

"Oh no!" JJ covered her mouth. "That must have been embarrassing."

Torrina grinned. "Just a little. But I could take a little embarrassment for some John Legend. You know what I'm sayin'?"

JJ laughed. Only Torrina.

The door swung open again, letting out a blast of sound and another round of musicians and performers, some of them from Jayla's team.

"JJ, Torrina, you guys heading out with us?"

"Where's everyone going, Sam?" Torrina asked the short, stout guy wearing a spiky Mohawk and sunglasses.

"Probably going to grab a bite to eat in the hotel restaurant, then hit a couple bars downtown. One of the other guys says he knows a spot where they have a live band all night. Wanna come?"

"Sure," Torrina said with a nod. "I could eat. You too, JJ?"

"I'll head back with you guys to the hotel, but I've gotta crash," JJ said. "I'm exhausted. I think my body's still reeling from the excitement of these last couple nights. Plus I feel a headache coming on."

"Not used to life on the road yet, are you?" Donald asked. He threw an arm around JJ, tugging her against him as he joined their circle.

"No, not yet," JJ said with a tight smile as she casually eased herself out of Donald's uninvited embrace. "Still a newbie."

JJ followed the group over to the two huge, black SUVs that would take them back to the hotel where they had been staying for the past two days, making sure to be seated between Torrina and the door. As the vans pulled out of the parking lot, Torrina leaned over and whispered in JJ's ear.

"It's okay. You can come with us tonight. I'll keep Donald out of your way and make sure they lay off you at the bars. No one will give you a hard time."

JJ was grateful for Torrina's concern. She knew that Donald's unwelcome attention created an issue for JJ, especially when they all hung out socially. In any other situation JJ would have just told him to back off. But she was trying to make a name for herself in the industry and didn't want to stir up drama over what might just be a minor issue. The fact that she opted not to party like a rock star already made her stand out. She didn't want to be called a whiner on top of it too.

"Thanks, but I really am tired," JJ whispered back. "Three shows in three days is crazy."

Torrina's lip curled. "I know that's right."

"Plus my sister got some big news today and she's supposed to call me back tonight, so I really want to catch her," JJ added.

"Gotcha." Torrina nodded. "If you change your mind though, just text me and I'll let you know where we are. We'll probably be out till four a.m. anyway. When we finish a set of shows like this, these guys like to go hard and then crash for a couple days."

JJ chuckled. "I can imagine."

The SUVs pulled up to the hotel entrance and they all got out. JJ waved to the others as they split up in the lobby; she headed toward the rooms, they headed to the hotel restaurant.

"Call me if you need someone to scrape you off the bar floor," JJ called.

She grinned as the sound of Torrina's laughter followed her across the lobby.

Pushing the door to the stairwell open, she began her trek up the steps to the sixth floor. She spent most of her life bypassing elevators for the stairs, so her thighs were used to the workout. Once inside her room, adjacent to Torrina's, she slipped off her jacket and sank down onto her bed to take off her strappy shoes. She had just freed her toes from their confines when she heard a knock on the door.

"Room service."

She grinned and hurried to open the door. Her bellhop was dressed in a gray ribbed sweater and leather jacket instead of a uniform, and carried several take-out containers and a bottle of something sparkling instead of pushing a hotel dinner cart. Plus she was sure it was illegal for someone to look that deliciously handsome.

She grabbed the lapels of his jacket and pulled him inside.

"Perfect timing," she murmured before his lips met hers. He managed to kick the door closed and wrap his arms around her without dropping any of his packages.

JJ snuggled closer, slipping into the familiar place where her body fit in his arms. Okay, so she may not be getting married, and her sister may have just abandoned her in the single zone. But at least she wasn't hanging out there alone. Being in the 70 percent might not be so bad after all.

Chapter 2

"Good show?" Rayshawn Forbes asked with a chuckle, when they finally broke away from each other.

"You tell me," JJ said, settling her arms around his shoulders. "Weren't you watching?"

"I got there late from my meeting," he said apologetically. "Only caught the last part of the performance."

JJ pouted, and he kissed her upturned lips briefly. "From what I saw it looked great, though."

He paused, and JJ watched as his deep brown eyes roved over her face. "I'm so proud of you, babe."

She ran her hand over his smooth, nut-brown skin, touching his strong, angular jaw, catching her finger in the dimple in his cheek, feeling the stubble of his goatee and razor-thin mustache beneath her fingertips. She smiled. She had always thought he looked more like an R & B singer than a talent manager. But he was a manager. And he was hers.

"Thank you. I couldn't have done any of it without you."

Her eyes floated closed as his lips met hers again with gentle, soft kisses that she had come to get used to over the past few months. She had always thought it a bad idea to mix business and personal life, but when she first met Rayshawn several months earlier, the attraction between them had been immediate and undeniable. She had met him at Lost and Found, the little jazz bar she used to sing at. That first night, when he gave her his card, she had passed it off as a pickup line. But then he showed up the next night, and the night after that with two other associates, one of whom invited her to audition for backup vocals for Deborah Cox. She never got that gig, but the things she learned through the process were priceless. In a matter of weeks she had signed on with Rayshawn to manage her, and in turn his agency, Franklin and Forbes, provided her with a vocal coach, a demo CD and a press kit and everything she needed to get her foot in the door of the music industry. By the time she got around to auditioning for Jayla's team, she was ready.

During that whole time they had done their best to keep things entirely business. But once she got the Jayla Grey gig, all that changed. All it took was an unplanned kiss at a celebration dinner and it was all over.

He pulled her closer as his kisses deepened. She melted into him, glad to finally have a few moments together. They were both traveling in Alberta, Rayshawn for some business meetings, and JJ for a weekend concert blitz for Jayla Grey. But so far their schedules had allowed them barely any time together. This was the first occasion they'd had to be alone in the past three days.

Rayshawn's hands gently traced her shoulders, her back, the curve of her spine, and then edged lower. JJ gently pulled away, putting some distance between them.

"Our food's getting cold," she said, trying to slip out of his embrace.

"Let it." He pulled her back, capturing her lips for a brief moment.

"Shawn...," she murmured against his lips, pulling away again.

He knew what that meant. He sighed and released her. "JJ, you're going to kill me one of these days," he grunted, releasing her. "Go get some plates."

"You started it," JJ threw back slyly as she headed over to the single cupboard above the sink to look for dishware. "What did you get us?"

"Cheap Chinese food," he said, opening the cartons in front of him. "I know you love that. Plus I picked up two movies. *Do the Right Thing* and *Inside Man.*"

JJ smiled. "Another Spike Lee night, I see."

Rayshawn grinned. "I'll let you pick which, babe."

She brought the plates over and put them next to the food containers.

"I'm gonna let you get away with that tonight," she said, her wagging finger a mock threat. "You're lucky I'm in a good mood."

Her good mood continued to stretch through the evening as they lounged together, watching *Inside Man* and picking at their food. Rayshawn stretched his arm around her shoulders and she snuggled deeper into his embrace. This was nice. This was how life should be.

JJ had just paused the movie as Rayshawn went to refill their drinks, when the phone rang.

"JJ, we have an emergency."

JJ curled her feet up under her. "What kind of emergency?"

She knew her sister Lissandra, and so she knew that she should wait to be concerned until after she got details.

"You will not believe what Sydney is trying to do. I swear, she and Hayden got engaged like two seconds ago and it's like she lost her ever-lovin' mind, do you believe she wants to—"

"Lissandra, get off the phone and leave JJ alone," Sydney said.

"Hey, Syd," JJ said, acknowledging her eldest sister, who had likely just picked up another extension of their home phone line.

"Hey, JJ," Sydney said cheerfully. "How was the show?"

JJ grinned. "It was amazing, Syd. The room was packed and the crowd was full of energy. Jayla was on fire tonight. Oh, and I have news!"

"What news?" Sydney asked, echoing JJ's excitement.

"Jayla wants me to come on tour with her!"

"Oh my goodness, JJ!" Sydney squealed. "That's amazing!"

"Yeah, yeah, that's great," Lissandra said, cutting in impatiently. "But we have bigger issues here. Do you know Sydney wants to move Sheree into the house?"

JJ momentarily forgot her news at the mention of the name Sheree. "What!"

"Now, JJ, before you jump to any conclusions, hear me out," Sydney said. "You know I wouldn't do this unless it was really serious. Plus I didn't say for sure that we were going to do it, I was just saying we should consider it."

"Consider it?" JJ asked, her stomach tightening. "You want me to consider living with Sheree, the woman who lied about being pregnant so she could marry our brother, Dean, then stole his money, and left him so distraught he ran his car into a tree and ended up in the hospital?"

"I know but—"

"Sydney, this is the same woman who almost ran you off the road with her car less than six months ago," JJ continued. "The same woman who left us with debt up to our eyeballs from Dean's medical bills. The same woman who has caused our family nothing but chaos since we met her."

"I agree, but—"

"This woman almost ruined your relationship with Hayden," JJ argued.

"I know," Sydney said, cutting in. "But Hayden is the reason I am asking you guys to consider this. He is Sheree's half brother and pretty much the only family she has left. If he doesn't want to give up on her, how can I? And now that we're talking marriage, I have to accept that she is going to be a part of my life too. Actually, all our lives."

"Oh, hell no," Lissandra said.

"Sydney, you can't be serious. I can't think of anything that would make me be okay with moving Sheree into our home," JJ said.

"Well, maybe—"

"Babe," Rayshawn called from the kitchenette. "You think

they have any club soda? Was thinking of making some of your sangria."

JJ winced and covered the mouthpiece of the phone. But the dead silence on the line told her it was too late. With the mouthpiece still covered, she rushed over to her mini fridge, dug out a bottle of carbonated water, and tossed it at Rayshawn before slipping into the bathroom and closing the door.

"Who was that?" Sydney asked finally.

JJ cleared her throat. "Uh, no one."

"So no one has a deep male voice and calls you babe?" Lissandra asked.

JJ said nothing.

"Don't tell me that Saint Judith has a man in her hotel room," Lissandra said with a laugh. "Oh, this is too good."

JJ's cheeks burned, even though she knew her sisters couldn't see her. She needed to end this conversation now.

"So you were about to say something about Sheree?"

"Uh-uh," Sydney said. "We're not about to skip over this. Do you really have a man in your hotel room, JJ? Please tell me that Lissandra isn't right."

"There is someone here," JJ said. "But it's not what you think. We just had dinner and so he was just making sure I got back to my room okay."

It wasn't a complete lie. They really did just have dinner. But a year ago, JJ would have condemned her sisters if they had tried to pull off a half-truth like that one. However, she had told so many half-truths to so many people over the past couple months that it was almost becoming second nature. She was a better liar than she thought. Or maybe the assumption that people made that she never lied—which had been true up until recently—just made her lies that much easier to get away with.

"I know you're not trying to sell me that."

Except with her sisters.

"Look, are you going to explain about Sheree or not?" JJ asked impatiently.

"And she's catching attitude too, Sydney," Lissandra said. "What is really happening with our little Diana Ross?"

"Sydney?" JJ pressed, ignoring Lissandra.

"We can talk about Sheree when you get back tomorrow. Nothing's happening before then," Sydney said soberly. "Right now, I think you have more important things to deal with."

JJ didn't miss the disappointment in her eldest sister's voice, and it hurt more than the teasing from Lissandra.

"Okay," JJ said quietly. "I'll see you guys tomorrow."

"Alright," Lissandra said. She chuckled. "And remember: no glove, no love!"

She heard Sydney sigh. "Bye, JJ."

JJ hung up the phone, closed her eyes, and rested her head in her hands. Her guilt felt as real as the pressure of her fingers against her temples. What was she doing? Why was she letting Rayshawn stay, even though it was almost two a.m.? Undoubtedly he thought he would be crashing for the night in her hotel room. And why wouldn't he think that? They had let it happen before. And even though nothing other than sleeping had happened yet, it was only a matter of time. Her body had already come close to betraying her more than once.

"J, everything okay?"

JJ opened the door to the bathroom and found Rayshawn standing on the other side, concern marring his handsome features.

"What happened?" he asked.

She dropped her eyes and slipped past him into the room. "You know it's late. I think we should call it a night."

There was a pause, but JJ busied herself picking up plates instead of turning to face him.

"It was your sisters on the phone, wasn't it?"

She nodded. "Yes, but it's not about them." She carried the plates and food containers to the kitchenette. "This is about me. And I can't keep doing this."

He raked his hands through his hair brusquely. "Doing what?"

"Acting like we can sit here together, and fool around at two in the morning in my hotel room, and nothing's gonna happen." JJ dropped the plates into the sink, the crash jarring her senses. "You know I'm not trying to have sex with anyone right now..."

"And you feel like I'm trying to do that?" Rayshawn asked, an edge in his voice. "JJ, we already talked about this. I know you're celibate, and I'm cool with that."

"Are you?" JJ asked, turning around to look at him. "'Cause I don't know too many guys who are..."

"I'm not too many guys," he said, crossing the room to stand in front of her. "I thought you already knew this."

JJ's eyes fell to the floor.

"Babe." He lifted her chin with a gentle touch. "My hands may wander from time to time, and I'm sorry. It's just reflex, and just me wanting to be close to you. But have I ever forced you to do anything you didn't want to?"

JJ sighed. "No."

"Then trust me," he said. "What's important to you is important to me too. And I know this thing, waiting, is important to you. So I'm respecting that."

JJ nodded.

He looked at her a long moment. "You know, maybe if your sisters met me..."

"No," JJ said, moving around him and out of his reach.

"Babe, if they got to meet me, they would know who you're with all the time," he said, his eyes following JJ as she busied herself around the room, picking up items out of place and straightening furniture. "They'd see I'm a good man and I'm not trying to hurt you. Maybe they would even like me."

"It's not that simple, Shawn," JJ said.

"Then what is it?" Rayshawn asked. She could see his frustration, sense it bubbling at the surface. He *was* a good man, and he was good to her. How could she tell him, then, that no matter how good he was, her sisters wouldn't think he was right for her because he was too different? His values were too different. His faith—or lack of it—was too different.

She walked over to him and put her arms around him, kissing him deeply before pulling away. "Thanks for the dinner, Shawn."

He closed his eyes and let his head fall back. "You're kicking me out."

She smiled and stroked the sides of his face with her thumbs. "Just saying good night."

His head came forward and his eyes met hers. "JJ. Sooner or later..."

"I know," she said. JJ followed him to the door as he grabbed his jacket and keys, then tipped up to kiss him briefly.

"Call me when you get in," she whispered against his lips.

She watched him walk down the hall until he turned the corner. Then she closed the door and leaned back against it. Rayshawn was right. Sooner or later she would have to make a choice about them. She had a feeling it was going to be sooner. She just had no idea what that choice was going to be.

Chapter 3

"Honey, I'm home," JJ called jokingly as the pulled her suitcase through the front door and dumped it in the entryway. She looked around at the mid-Toronto house that had been her home for the past seven years but which over the past seven months she had barely seen in the light of day. Everything looked more or less the same. From the front door she could see down the short hallway into the open-concept living-dining area. A wide counter separated the dining area from the kitchen, the place where the sisters spent most of their time.

All of them could hold their own around a stove—Jackie Isaacs, their mother, had made sure of that—but Sydney had a special touch when it came to the oven. She took after their father that way and had followed directly in his footsteps by opening her own gourmet pastry shop less than a year earlier. They all thought she would have inherited their father's store, which she had run for over a year after his death, but things hadn't turned out that way. Thankfully, however, all that was in the past and now Sydney was settled into her own place, still named Decadent in honor of their father's old bakery but fully owned by Sydney and her boyfriend-turned-fiancé, pro-basketball trainer Hayden Windsor. A fiancé who, judging by the size thirteen Nikes at the front door, was in the house right now.

"JJ, we're in the kitchen," a familiar baritone voice called out. "Your sister is trying to give me a heart attack and gross me out at the same time."

"I am not!" she heard Sydney reply.

Grinning, she slipped off her shoes and padded down the hallway, through the living area to the kitchen.

"So I guess Sydney is experimenting again?" she asked as her sister and Hayden came into view.

"Yes, I am trying out a sweet cabbage strudel recipe, but forget about that—you're home!"

"Yes I am, and just in time apparently," JJ said with a grin. "Let me see it!"

Sydney pulled off her oven mitt with a grin and held out her glittering left hand. JJ squealed as her eyes took in the white gold engagement ring which featured a round diamond surrounded by elegant clusters of diamond side stones.

"Oh my goodness! It's beautiful. Congratulations, Sydney!" She threw her arms around her sister.

JJ felt the last bits of the Alberta cold disappear as her sibling wrapped warm arms around her in a giant hug. It had only been a few days but she had missed her big sister. And regardless of how she had felt when she first heard the news, she really was happy for Sydney.

"Good job, Mr. Windsor," JJ said, playfully punching Hayden on the shoulder.

"Thanks," he said with a grin. "Gotta do my best to keep this one happy."

The look that passed between him and her sister was so full of love JJ had to look away.

"It's so good to see you." Sydney beamed when she finally remembered JJ was there. "How was the trip?"

"It was amazing," JJ said with a sigh as she plopped down onto the stool next to Hayden, at the counter. "We did three shows while we were there, including singing at a children's hospital. We shared the stage with a whole bunch of other musicians. I got to meet K'naan!"

"Wow," Hayden said, looking impressed. "Look at you moving up in the music world."

"That's awesome, JJ," Sydney said. "I'm glad it was great. I hope nothing happened to spoil the occasion."

She gave JJ a meaningful glance, which JJ read clearly.

"No. Nothing happened," JJ said, emphasizing the nothing.

The two sisters locked eyes with each other in silence for a long moment. Hayden looked back and forth between the two of them.

"Okay," he said, standing up. "Guess that's my cue to go."

"No," JJ said, standing up and then moving toward the stairs. "You stay. I'm gonna go upstairs and lie down for a bit anyway. Still a little worn-out."

She gave a weak smile and avoided Hayden's and Sydney's eyes as she headed toward the stairs. She was not looking forward to her conversation with Sydney. Her older sister could get water from stone. She would look at JJ and immediately know something was up. JJ was sure she had some kind of special radar. It was scary.

At least she had enough time to take a shower and relax before the interrogation began.

Or so she thought, until she returned to her bedroom from the shower and found Sydney sitting in her chair.

"Geez, Sydney, can you give me a minute to breathe before you start the third degree?" JJ asked as she searched in her drawers for underwear and clothes.

"What are you talking about?" Sydney asked innocently. "I just wanted you to taste my cabbage strudel."

Expectantly, she held out a plate of questionable-looking pastry.

JJ wrinkled her nose as she pulled on a pair of calf-length leggings. "Ugh. As if I would put that grossness in my mouth."

"It is not as bad as you think," Sydney said, rolling her eyes. "Even Hayden said it was pretty good."

JJ grinned. "Love covers a multitude of sins."

"Come on," Sydney whined. "Just try it."

"Sydney..."

"One forkful."

"I don't even eat sugar anymore."

"One bite won't make you put on a hundred pounds," Sydney said, rolling her eyes again. "And if you don't like it, you can spit it out," Sydney finished, holding up a napkin with her free hand.

JJ finished buttoning up her shirt, then plopped down on the bed.

"Alright," JJ said, reaching for the plate. "But if I do this, you can't interrogate me about my trip."

"No deal," Sydney said, immediately moving the plate out of JJ's reach.

JJ groaned and leaned back on her hands on the bed.

"And now that you've opened the door to that conversation..."

"Nothing happened, Sydney."

"Great," Sydney said, taking a bite out of the pie. "So you'll have no problem telling me all about it. Where did you stay?"

JJ reached over and grabbed the fork and plate from Sydney's hands. Maybe the strudel wasn't such a bad idea. At least it would buy her time to think of answers. Or make up ones.

"Crowne Plaza Edmonton," JJ said, putting a forkful of strudel in her mouth. A mix of sweet, delicate flavors that she wouldn't have normally associated with cabbage hit her tongue. Surprisingly, not bad.

"Pretty good, isn't it?" Sydney said with a knowing smile.

"M-hmm," JJ murmured with a nod as she kept chewing.

"Good." Sydney gave a short nod of satisfaction. "Now back to this trip. What was the hotel like?"

"Beautiful. Clean. Expensive. Great service. And the hotel restaurant was pretty good too," JJ said. "We had dinner there a few nights. They had the most amazing amuse-bouche, Sydney. You would have loved it. If you and Hayden go to Alberta, you should stay there."

"Well, it's unlikely that Hayden and I would be staying at a hotel together anytime soon since we aren't married yet," Sydney said pointedly. "Speaking of which..."

"Have we got to the part about who was in her room yet?" Lissandra asked, showing up at the door.

JJ rolled her eyes, wondering how she had not heard her other sister enter the house.

"Just about," Sydney said, pursing her lips.

JJ put a large forkful of strudel in her mouth. She would pay for this later with a few extra laps around the block, but she needed the time.

"Mm-mm-mm," Lissandra said, shaking her head as she folded her arms. "Look at her buying time. Syd, you better take that plate from her."

Sydney shrugged. "There's not much left anyway."

JJ put down the fork and faced her fate. "Guys, like I said, it wasn't a big deal. I had just had dinner. A friend was making sure I got back to my room okay."

"What friend?" Lissandra pressed.

"A friend," JJ pressed back, glaring.

"Anyone we know?" Sydney asked.

"You don't know all my friends," JJ said defensively.

"Especially not lately," Lissandra muttered.

"Look, JJ, if you're dating somebody, that's great," Sydney said, taking on a more coaxing tone. "That's nothing to be ashamed of. We just don't understand why you would hide that from us."

"Unless you're sleeping with that someone," Lissandra said.

"I'm not sleeping with anyone," JJ said more loudly than she intended. She glared at Lissandra. "Though I can't see how that would offend your nonexistent values."

"Hey, I never claimed to be anything other than what I am," Lissandra said sharply. "You know I am all for a good time, no matter how it comes around. I'm not the one who used to walk around here holier than everyone else, condemning everyone else for their mess, acting like she had an alarm system on her chastity belt—"

"Okay, Lissandra, that's enough," Sydney cut in.

"Look, I am a grown woman. Who I see and what I do is my business. I don't have to share that with you. But if I am dating someone and it is serious, I will let you know. Again, for the record, I am not sleeping with anyone. So, yes, Lissandra, my chastity belt is firmly in place," she snapped. "At this point I am not sure if you could even find yours."

"Maybe it's with the man who was in your room last night," Lissandra quipped.

Sydney glared at Lissandra. "Enough!"

"I am done talking about this," JJ said, folding her arms. She could not believe she had let her sisters railroad her like this. Sometimes she wondered if they were for her or against her.

"I agree," Sydney said. "Let's drop this whole thing for now. There's something more pressing that we need to talk about."

"Sheree?" JJ asked, glad to steer away from the topic of her love life.

"Yes," Sydney said. She took a deep sigh. "Now I know I said that we would talk about this together, but things have been happening really quickly and—"

Sydney was interrupted by the sound of the doorbell.

"Who's that?" JJ asked, getting up.

"I don't know," Lissandra said. "I wasn't expecting anyone."

The doorbell went off again. Several more times in a row, with more urgency.

The three women rushed downstairs, JJ making it to the front hallway first. Without checking the peephole, she flung the door open. Before she could say a word, a heavyset man walked in and set two suitcases in the hallway before stepping out and making way for a second man, who brought in a huge, heavy-looking box.

"What in the world—"

"Whose are these?" Lissandra demanded from the second brother who had set down the box. "And why are you bringing them into my house?"

"I'm just following orders, ma'am."

"Whose orders?"

"Mine."

All three women looked up to see a fourth, very pregnant, very tired-looking woman standing in their doorway.

JJ hadn't seen her in more than a month. But there was no mistaking the person standing in front of her.

"Sheree?"

The woman let out a tired breath. With a hand on her back and another one under her protruding belly, she took two slow steps into the entryway.

"Hey, JJ...Lissandra...Sydney," she puffed, taking a labored breath after each word. "Is there anywhere I can sit down? I think...I'm about to..."

And then, before she could even get the words out, she fainted.

Chapter 4

Simon hated hospitals.

It was the first thought he'd had every morning since he first arrived at Mount Sinai Hospital in Toronto, and it was the first thought he'd had again this morning as he stepped through the sliding glass doors. He hated hospitals. It didn't matter whether they were in North America or Northern Africa; whether they had state-of-the-art technology or second-hand machinery. In every case it was the same. And it was mostly because of the smell. Whether it was of disinfectant or dysentery, it was unhealthy. Unnatural. It was not the smell of life. It was the smell of sickness and death. No wonder so many people died in hospitals.

And yet this was where he would have to spend several of his days for the next few weeks. It was for the greater good, he knew. This is where people came for care, and so this was where he needed to be. But the Lord knew that if he could have built a makeshift office on a boat and docked it in the Toronto Harbourfront nearby, he would have. At least that way he might breathe in a little semi-fresh, non-artificial air every now and then.

"Paging Dr. Massri. Dr. Massri to the Maternal Fetal Medicine Unit."

"They musta spotted you in the parking lot, Doc," the security guard in the lobby called out to Simon as he saw him approach.

"Nah. It's that tracker they implanted at the airport, Lawrence," Simon said, tossing an apple to the burly, baby-faced man in uniform. "They always know where I am."

Lawrence caught the apple and nodded his thanks. "They got us all on the grid, I tell you."

Simon chuckled as he entered the waiting elevator and hit the button that would take him up to obstetrics, where he would spend most of his day. He might hate hospitals, but usually the people weren't too bad.

"Dr. Massri, where have you been? You were supposed to be here at ten o'clock. It's a quarter to eleven."

"Good morning to you too, Dr. Sterling," Simon said, trying on his best smile for the acting chief of the Obstetrics and Gynecology Department, who looked like she had been waiting for him to arrive so she could remind him how late he was. Other doctors at his level would have told him not to take that kind of talk from a local staff MD, even if she was the chief. But he had met Dr. Sterling over ten years ago, when he was nothing but a young doctor still wet behind the ears. Before he got a PhD in research. Before he had received any international awards or been called to work all over the world. Before he gave it all up to do what he did now. She had known him then. And she still knew his mother and father. So when it came to putting him in line, she got a free pass.

"Don't good morning me. I have two women waiting to see you since ten thirty, and another one just came in," she said, pinning him with her trademark stern gaze. Though he towered over her, his six-foot-five frame squirmed under her glare. This woman was old enough to be his mother, and there had been more than a few occasions when he felt like she was.

"I had to stop by SickKids," he said apologetically, referring to the Hospital for Sick Children. "Dr. Mason had a case there he wanted me to look at. I've been over there since seven a.m. Up since six. Don't you feel sorry for me?"

"I've been up since four," she quipped. "Don't you feel sorry for me?"

"No, ma'am."

Her eyes widened but then she laughed. "You take these charts from me before I smack you with them," she said.

"Good morning, Dr. Massri."

Simon and Dr. Sterling looked up as a much younger nurse, who looked more like a cover girl than a medical professional, sauntered down the hallway pushing a cart. Simon was about to open his mouth to respond when Dr. Sterling smacked him with the charts in her hand.

"You stay away from those fast-tailed nurses," she whispered quietly for his ears only. "You do what you're here for and get back to what you're really meant for. Without any distractions."

Simon saluted. "Yes, ma'am."

He chuckled as she shook her head and walked away. The few times he had been at Mount Sinai, he could always count on Dr. Sterling to take some time out to check on him.

Glancing at his charts of referrals, he headed to the first patient. Each one took time. Time to get the family history. Time to assess the patient's state of mind. Time to become up-to-date on the situation, do an assessment, and draft a plan of care. By the time he got around to his third patient, he was already feeling emotionally drained.

"Good morning, I am Dr. Massri," he said, stepping into the private room to find a honey-toned young woman with cropped hair propped up against pillows. Her forehead was dotted with perspiration and her eyes were bloodshot and tired.

"You must be Sheree Isaacs," he said kindly, immediately feeling empathy. Without glancing at the chart he guessed her to be about five months along. Pale skin. Shorter than normal breaths. Could be anemic on top of everything else noted in the referral.

The woman nodded, just as another woman, who had been on her cell phone, turned around.

"I left a message for Dean. Hopefully he'll at least call back," the woman said. Then she looked up and Simon felt like he had been punched in the chest.

Her hair was different. Short. Some kind of uneven cut that ended at her chin. Like that black girl he had seen on the cover of some magazine at the nurses' station. It wasn't just the hair though. Her features seemed slightly sharper. But maybe that had to do with how much thinner she was. There were lines in her forehead, near her eyes. Not age lines—she was too young for those. But she had aged since the last time he saw her. The first and last time he saw her. Almost four years ago. So long ago that someone else might not be sure that it was her.

But he was sure.

It was the eyes that confirmed it. Those huge doe eyes. Brown, with flecks of gold. Eyes that didn't really belong on a creamy caramel face, but which fit perfectly on hers. Eyes that showed emotions like windowpanes. Eyes that he used to see in his dreams a long time ago.

What in the world was she doing here? In this hospital? And why had she cut her hair?

"Hi, I'm JJ," she said, holding out her hand as if she had never seen him before in her life. As if for one day—one intense day—their lives hadn't dramatically intersected. "I'm Sheree's sister-in-law."

He stared at her for a long moment. Waiting for her to say something. Waiting for a spark of recognition. Waiting for her to explain why she had cut her beautiful long hair.

Nothing.

Then she was pulling back her hand and pursing her lips, and he realized that he had unintentionally snubbed her. He barely managed to nod in her direction before turning away.

"So, tell me what's been happening with you, Sheree," he said, pulling up a stool to her bedside and doing the only thing he could do while his senses were reeling—focus on his patient.

"She fainted this morning on our doorstep," JJ answered for Sheree, the clipped tone of her voice indicating her annoyance. Probably at him. "I was told her pregnancy was high risk, but I don't have any details. She said she was referred by her OB a few weeks ago but hasn't had an appointment with the specialist yet."

"I've been having these fainting spells for the last six weeks or so," Sheree explained slowly. "And for a time my pressure was pretty high. The doctor says I might be anemic. They prescribed some drugs, but I don't want to be on too many medications while I'm pregnant. I don't know how it will affect the baby."

Simon nodded. "And you've been taking all your prenatal vitamins?"

"Yes," Sheree said after drawing a deep breath. She listed off the supplements she was on and how long she had been taking them. Simon wrote down everything she said, knowing that there was no way he would remember anything, with him being so aware of JJ's every movement on the other side of Sheree's bed.

"Okay," he said finally. "Let's see what's going on with your baby."

He chatted with her casually as he prepared her for the ultrasound. It wasn't long before the sound of the baby's heartbeat was echoing through the room. He heard JJ gasp and looked over in time to see her cover her mouth as she stared at the moving images on the black-and-white screen.

"Oh my gosh, he's so beautiful," JJ breathed. She tore her eyes away from the screen to look over at Sheree and then Simon. "It is a boy, right?"

Before Simon could open his mouth, Sheree spoke up.

"Hush!" she ordered with more vigor than she'd used the whole visit thus far. "I don't want to know until I hold him or her in my arms."

JJ looked up at Simon with pleading eyes, and he had to look away.

"Mother's wishes." His voice sounded gruff to his own ears. But then, he seemed generally out of control of his faculties today.

He cleared his throat. "So far everything looks good. Baby's heartbeat seems normal, there're no signs of distress, things look fine. And your previous tests say your blood pressure is in the expected range."

He shut off the monitor and turned back to Sheree. "Based on your test results from two weeks ago, your hemoglobin was a bit low. I'm going to increase your dosage of folic acid for now, but I'm also going to have the nurse come in and take some blood so we can look at your levels again and make sure everything else is okay."

Sheree nodded.

"I understand your concerns about medications," he said, leaning in. "I much prefer more natural methods myself. But we do need to make sure your hemoglobin count is where it should be, so that you and your baby can get enough oxygen and stay healthy."

Sheree bit her lip, and he caught the scared look in her eyes. He reached out and grasped her hand.

"We're going to make sure you and this baby are okay, Sheree," he said with a smile. "I know you're doing your best to take care of your little one, and we're going to do our best too."

JJ crossed and then uncrossed her legs in the chair across from him. He succeeded in not looking over at her.

"Is there anything else going on that you're concerned about?" he asked, focusing on Sheree. "Any pains, discomforts, irregularities?"

Sheree bit her lip thoughtfully. "Just a little cramping in my stomach now and then. My doctor says it's normal."

"How often do you feel that?" he asked, making a note on the chart.

She shrugged. "Couple times a week, maybe less?"

"Does it keep you up at night?" he asked.

She shook her head. "Not really."

He nodded, made a note on his chart, and then put it away. "If it gets any worse, you let us know immediately, okay?"

"Okay."

The door opened again and a taller woman, similar in features to JJ but a little thicker, walked briskly into the room.

"Hi, I'm Sydney, Sheree's sister-in-law," she said, smiling tightly and offering her hand to the doctor. "How is she doing?"

"I'm Dr. Massri."

JJ coughed as he shook Sydney's hand.

"We're going to run some tests to make sure, but I think she's going to be okay."

He turned back to Sheree. "Either way, I want you to make an appointment to come in this time next week, so I can follow up with you on your tests. And if you have any issues, you can call the hospital and they'll page me."

"That's very reassuring of you, Dr. Massri," JJ said.

He finally braved a look at her and forced his lips into a smile. "That's what I'm here for."

She held his gaze and... what? Was that... recognition?

But before he could confirm it, it was gone. He turned back to Sheree.

"So do you have any questions about your pregnancy?"

He knew it wasn't really his role, since he wasn't her OB and he hadn't officially taken her on as a referral yet, but he knew taking some time to talk to Sheree about her pregnancy would make her feel more comfortable sharing any issues she might be having, which in the long run would make it easier for her to get the right care. Plus, based on the comment her sister-in-law had made when she got off the phone, it seemed like the baby's father might not be readily available. If he could do anything to make her feel less alone and more supported, he was willing to do it.

He chatted with her, answering her questions and occasionally Sydney's and JJ's, until he heard another page for him from the hallway.

"So I'll get the nurse for you," he said, standing up. "And remember to make that appointment for early next week. Until then, take care, Sheree."

Sheree beamed. "Thank you, Dr. Massri."

"No problem," he said with a smile.

"Yes, thanks a lot," JJ added. He looked up just in time to catch a softness in her eyes. "I really appreciate you spending time to answer our questions. This pregnancy is going to be a first for all of us."

He couldn't speak, so he just nodded before ducking out of the room. When he was finally in the hallway, he let out a breath he hadn't realized he was holding.

He had seen her again, and now he had an updated image to add to the one that had floated in and out of his mind for several years. On top of that, he just might be seeing her a lot more often. He sighed.

Heaven help him.

Chapter 5

"You really appreciate him spending time to answer our questions?" Sheree snorted. "Why didn't you just ask him for his phone number?"

"Huh?" JJ tried to play off a confused look, but she was too busy trying to recover from the shock. There was no way that the man who had just walked out of the room was who she thought he was. It was impossible. Even if the heavy thumping of her heart told her otherwise.

"Could you drool anymore over Mr. Doctor man?" Sheree asked.

"Please," JJ said, looking anywhere except at Sheree. "I just thought it was nice that he hung around and took the time to explain things."

"You thought he was nice to look at," Sheree said with a smirk, sitting up as the nurse came in.

Okay, that too. But she would never let Sheree know that. Besides, she had a boyfriend. Sort of.

"Sheree, you're crazy," JJ said, pulling out her iPhone. "Sydney, can you tell her to stop?"

But when she glanced over, her sister was trying hard to fight a smile of her own. "Well, you were kind of staring at him."

"I was not!"

"Oh yes, you were," Sheree said, holding out her arm to the nurse so she could find a vein. "And I can't blame you. He is one fine brother."

Sheree squinted thoughtfully. "That is, if he *is* a brother. All that semi-straight hair and café-au-lait skin. Looks like he got some united nations going on up in there."

"Oh geez," JJ groaned, dropping back into her chair.

"Those were some long dreads he had," Sydney said absently as her fingers flew over the keypad of her phone. "Kinda sexy. You like dreads, don't you, JJ?"

"How do you get that I like dreads?" JJ protested.

"We had a neighbor with dreads, and you used to follow him around all the time," Sydney said. She paused from her typing as if thinking. "What was his name? Mathew? Maizon?"

"Maseen," JJ corrected, rubbing her temples. "And I never followed him around."

"Maseen, Massri, sounds pretty close if you ask me," Sheree said with a little chuckle.

Sydney snickered as well.

"I can't believe it. You two are ganging up on me? Wasn't it the two of you who almost tried to kill each other a couple months ago?" JJ asked, looking back and forth between her sister and her sister-in-law. "When did the two of you get all chummy-chummy?"

"Nobody's chummy-chummy," Sheree said as she held a piece of cotton down on the spot from which the nurse had just pulled the needle. "But since both of us are going to be in Hayden's life for the long haul, we might as well try and get along with each other."

"And when did this peace treaty start?" JJ asked.

"When Sheree wrote the check that covered all Dean's medical bills," Sydney said, folding her arms.

JJ raised an eyebrow at Sheree, who looked away and began to swing her legs off the bed.

"Yeah, well, a lot of good that did," she murmured. "He still won't talk to me. Isn't even interested in seeing the baby's ultrasound pictures."

"Well, you did lie about being pregnant to get him to marry you, stole his money, and ran off with another man," Sydney said dryly. "Can you really blame him?"

Sheree's eyes fell to the floor. "Guess not."

JJ thought she heard a tremor in Sheree's voice, but she couldn't be sure. Over the past year since Sheree had come into their lives, JJ had built up an image of her as this cold, heartless man-eater who was only out to milk Dean and their family dry. Her faith in God and her awareness of her own shortcomings had urged her to try and give Sheree the benefit of the doubt. It had been a challenge.

But seeing her struggle to get out of bed in the hospital room, tears in her eyes as she talked about Dean, was starting to break that image down. Now JJ wasn't at all sure what to think of Sheree.

"Alright, don't try to get up yet. Just sit tight for a couple minutes," the nurse said, easing Sheree back onto the bed. "You might feel a bit light-headed, so we're gonna get a wheelchair to take you down to the front, then your sisters can take you home."

"Sisters-in-law," all three women said at the same time.

The nurse's eyes flew open as she glanced around at all of them.

"Okay. So your sisters-in-law can take you home." She shook her head as she exited the room, muttering something about "dysfunctional" and "family."

They sat in uncomfortable silence for what seemed like forever, until an orderly came in with a wheelchair and helped Sheree into it. Then they traveled down to the lobby, waited for Sydney to bring the car around, and rode all the way back to the house in uncomfortable silence.

JJ sighed. If today was anything to go by, it was going to be a long four months.

Chapter 6

"JJ, five minutes!"

JJ groaned and put the pillow over her head, burying herself a little deeper between the blanket and comforter that sandwiched her body in the bed.

"JJ, get up. It's nine a.m. We have to be in church in an hour."

Sydney's voice was like nails on a chalkboard.

"Go away," JJ whined. "I'm tired."

"Then maybe you should have slept last night instead of creeping in here at four in the morning," Sydney said. JJ could hear the scowl in her sister's voice.

JJ shifted onto her side but didn't bother opening her eyes for her first lie of the day. "I was at the shop," she muttered, referring to the clothing store she ran with their mother. A clothing store that she'd had to squeeze into the few free spaces left in her life since her music had taken over.

"Yeah, and I'm marrying LeBron James." She heard her sister sigh before heading away from the bed. "Whoever he is, I hope he's worth it."

JJ didn't bother to respond, partly because Sydney was already out the door and partly because she had in fact been with

Rayshawn for part of the night before. Instead, she crawled out from under the covers, grabbed her robe, and headed to the washroom.

Fifteen minutes and a hot shower later, she heard a knock on the bathroom door. She found Sheree standing on the other side.

"Sorry, pregnancy bladder," Sheree said, offering an apologetic smile. "Please don't let me do stairs."

Toothbrush in mouth, JJ stepped outside the bathroom and let Sheree in so she didn't have to trek to the bathroom on the lower level. It had been almost two weeks since Sheree had moved into their home and JJ had gotten used to sharing the upstairs bathroom with one more female. After some time she heard a toilet flush. A minute later the door opened and JJ and Sheree exchanged places again.

"So what's all the commotion for this morning?" Sheree leaned against the bathroom doorway as if she had nowhere in particular to be. "Everyone working this weekend?"

JJ spit her toothpaste into the sink. "Church."

She went back to brushing, without noticing the confused expression on Sheree's face.

"Church?"

"Last Saturday of the month, everyone goes to church together," Sydney said as she passed by the bathroom on the way to her room. "Isaacs family rules."

Sheree's eyes followed Sydney, then looked back at JJ as if to confirm.

"Are you serious?"

JJ swished water around in her mouth then spit it out. "Yup. It's our mother's contribution to making sure we're all saved."

"Or trying to make sure." Lissandra's voice floated out from her bedroom.

"So you're saying everyone in your family, all your sisters, even though you're grown, you all go to church with your mom the last weekend in every month? Even if you don't want to?" Sheree asked.

"Pretty much," JJ answered as she rubbed moisturizer on her face.

"Why?" Sheree asked, her face scrunched in confusion. "Why not just say no?"

"You think we haven't tried that?" Lissandra asked, coming to her bedroom door. "Our mother has found creative ways to punish us for our absence."

"Like the silent treatment," JJ said.

"Or the do-my-errands-for-a-month treatment," Lissandra added. "Imagine having your mother call you every single day, several times a day, to ask you to pick up things for her, or drive her here or go with her there. And she's not doing it because she can't do it herself or because she wants your company, but because she knows just how much it will irritate you."

"It's not that we couldn't say no," Sydney said, coming into the hallway to join the conversation. "But it's pretty much the one thing our mother has asked us all to do. And out of respect for her, and to keep the peace, we just do it."

"It's easier just to go," JJ said.

"And everyone goes," Lissandra said, heading back into her room. "Including you, Mrs. Isaacs."

"Me?" Sheree's eyes widened. "You don't think...your mom can't expect..."

"Isaacs family rules," JJ said, leaving the bathroom. She stopped in front of Sheree and dropped her voice. "Besides, everyone will be there. Including your husband."

"Estranged husband," Sheree said dryly as she returned to the bathroom.

JJ smiled when she heard the shower. In a strange way she was starting to get used to Sheree being in the house, kind of like having a racoon in your attic. Sure, you would rather it not be there, but as long as it stayed out of your way, didn't make too much noise and didn't invite any friends, you could temporarily coexist.

They managed to make it to the Granville Park Adventist

Church by ten fifteen, which JJ thought was pretty remarkable given their party of four and a half. JJ helped Sheree out of the car and let the woman lean gently against her as they followed Sydney toward the front steps.

As planned, they managed to make a quiet entry into the church sanctuary, slipping through a side door onto the bench with the rest of their family. JJ's mother was already there—likely since nine, when they first cracked open the church doors. JJ's younger sisters, Zelia and Josephine, sat on either side. JJ let Sydney and Sheree slip onto the bench ahead of her. She'd had an argument with her mother the week before over her singing career, one of several that in the last few months had created a chasm of tension between them. It seemed like every conversation they attempted to have of late had ended with Jackie voicing her disapproval of JJ's new vocation. As a result, JJ was more comfortable keeping her distance.

Unfortunately, in this particular place, she would never be comfortable enough, no matter how far she sat from Jackie. It was ironic because this was the place where she had once found comfort when the rest of her world was spinning in chaos. There was something about being in church that made her feel closer to God, made her feel like he was really a part of her life, that he filled the space in her heart that was meant for him.

Of late, however, that space that she previously thought could only be filled by God was filled with loneliness and disappointment and the discontent of being on the downside of her twenties with almost nothing to show for it. As her sisters conquered their career dreams, got married, and moved forward with their lives, she felt like her life was stagnant. She had no thriving career of her own, just a job in her mother's shop—a shop in which she had no stake, no ownership, and very little control. She had lost a chunk of her savings to the woman with the protruding belly leaning against her, and owned nothing more than a twelve-year-old car and one-third of an old house in Toronto. And then there was her love life, which had been nothing more than a series of unfortunate events that weren't even interesting enough to provide good fodder for a girls' night out. Yes, that had been her life. And though she had wanted to believe all the Bible verses that told her God had a plan for her, she couldn't help but think that if what she was living was that plan, then the plan sucked.

She shifted restlessly in her seat. Discontent was a dangerous thing.

It was what had caused Sydney to go off the rails just a year earlier when Decadent, the gourmet pastry shop she had poured her life into, had been sold from under her, and Sheree had run off with the proceeds. JJ knew what discontent could do, and she knew she would never—could never—do what her sister had done. There was a difference between taking the law into your own hands and taking your life into your own hands. Sydney had done the former, when she tried to get their money back from Sheree on her own and nearly killed herself when a car chase between her and Sheree put her at the bottom of the Kingston Harbour. JJ was just taking control of her life. Making some plans for herself. And who's to say that wasn't God's plan after all?

The slight jolt of her sister sitting beside her after her extended break outside was enough to shake JJ out of her thoughts. She glanced over at Lissandra and wrinkled her nose at the mix of mint and cigarette smoke that tickled her senses. The permanent scowl that always sat on Lissandra's face for church was in place.

"What did I miss?" Lissandra asked.

"Not much," JJ murmured.

Lissandra let out a sigh. "I am so over this church thing with Mom. She's getting one more year out of me and that's it. As soon as I hit thirty..."

"Your butt will still be coming to church once a month," JJ hissed. "You know Mom's not letting you get away with that."

Lissandra scowled. "Maybe if church was more entertaining it wouldn't be a hassle. But honestly, you want me to get up out of bed on a Saturday morning for this? There aren't even any good-looking men in this mug."

JJ chuckled. She couldn't disagree with Lissandra there. Church was definitely lacking in that department.

"Bathroom break," Sheree whispered, getting up.

"Already?" Lissandra murmured as she made way for the woman to pass. "Geez, we just got here."

"Well, it was a long car ride," JJ said in defense of Sheree. She turned to the pregnant woman. "It's on your left as soon as you exit the main doors. You want me to come with you?"

"No, I'm good," Sheree said, waving JJ off. Nonetheless, JJ kept an eye on the woman until she left the sanctuary.

"So what, you're her new best friend now?" Lissandra asked.

"She should at least feel comfortable where she lives," JJ said. "And you are sure not helping with that."

"Just like I said I wouldn't," Lissandra said. "I may be many things, but I keep my promises. Speaking of promises, feel like making things interesting?"

"Huh?"

Before JJ could respond, Lissandra used her bum to shove JJ over next to Sydney and into the space where Sheree had been, leaving an empty space at the end of the pew. It only took a moment for JJ to figure out why.

"Hey," Dean said, nodding at them as he slipped into the pew next to Lissandra. "What did I miss?"

"Nothing," Lissandra said, an evil smile playing her lips. "Things will really get started any minute now."

JJ knew what Lissandra meant, even though Dean didn't. She racked her brain to figure out a way to intercept the inevitable, uncomfortable situation that would unfold once Sheree returned to the pew. She glared at Lissandra.

"Why are you doing this?"

"Why not?" Lissandra hissed for JJ's ears only. "They're grown people. They need to figure their stuff out. And what better place to do it than in the house of the Lord?"

Though there was some truth to Lissandra's words, JJ couldn't agree with her methods. But there was pretty much nothing she could do about it, because at that very moment Sheree appeared at the end of the row. Every pair of Isaacs eyes turned to see the scene unfolding. Sheree paused, a look akin to panic shaping her features as she realized she had nowhere to sit but next to Dean. They all remembered the last time Sheree and Dean had been in the same room together. It was a few weeks after they had found Sheree living outside of town. JJ hadn't been there, but she heard the story. Sheree was at her brother Hayden's home with Sydney, and Sydney had called Dean to come over, without telling him why. He had walked in the door, taken one look at Sheree, and walked right back out. He had gotten in his car and driven away and refused to talk to any of them for the rest of the day.

As they watched him sitting at the end of the pew, looking up at Sheree then down the pew accusingly at the rest of them, JJ wondered if today would be a repeat of that. JJ watched his jaw tense and his brow furrow as he fought with himself over what to do. Then he surprised all of them and moved over closer to Lissandra, making space for Sheree.

The surprise kept Sheree standing for a moment. Then he shocked them again by standing up, taking Sheree by the elbow, and helping her sit.

"Thank you," Sheree murmured, a look of uncertainty and vulnerability crossing her face.

Dean nodded without looking at her.

JJ watched as Sheree struggled not to stare at him. She couldn't imagine what that was like, feeling like the man you loved, the man whose child you were carrying, might hate you. A wave of sympathy for Sheree washed over JJ. Maybe there were worse things than being alone. Like being in a relationship that probably shouldn't have happened in the first place.

They could have told Dean that his relationship with Sheree was a bad idea. But he had hidden it from them until it was too late. Until he and Sheree had gone too far to turn back. Guess hidden relationships weren't a new thing in JJ's life after all. However, her relationship with Rayshawn was nothing like Sheree's and Dean's. For one, she wasn't sleeping with Rayshawn and she would never make that mistake. Sure, he might be outside of her family's comfort zone, but she had a handle on her relationship with him. She would never let him change who she really was on the inside. She was sure of that. She had learned from her brother's mistakes. That was a promise.

Too bad that promise didn't bring her as much comfort as she'd hoped.

Chapter 7

Placental abruption.

Simon was almost sure that was what was happening with Sheree and her baby. In the two and half weeks since he first met Sheree and began to consult on her care he had run the full battery of tests to figure out what was causing the tenderness she complained about and the bleeding that had been observed. He had taken several ultrasound scans, looked at the fetus's growth markers, and everything pointed to abruption. But the dizziness and fainting didn't really match. They were the reason Dr. Brighton, the OB he had consulted with, had been doubtful about his diagnosis. But Simon had seen this too many times, and by the time they saw all the signs that it was indeed an abruption, it would be too late. He worked with his gut, and his gut was telling him this was what was going on with Sheree. He couldn't remember the last time he had listened to that gut feeling and been wrong. He wasn't about to start now.

He sighed as he walked down the hall toward the exam room where she was waiting for her appointment. Now came the task of breaking the news to her, and likely to Judith also, who had been with Sheree during the last two visits.

Judith.

He still couldn't believe she was here, in the same hospital with him, connected to one of his patients. He had come to both dread and anticipate his appointments with Sheree because they almost always brought him into contact with Judith. He looked forward to seeing her, but it was almost painful to stand in the same room, look at her, talk to her, everything that had happened hanging in the air between them. But if she wasn't going to say anything, neither was he. In fact, his approach thus far had been to interact as little with her as possible so as to preserve his sanity. He was content to continue with that approach.

"Good afternoon, Sheree," he said, prepared with a warm smile for Sheree as he pushed open the door and entered the room.

"Good afternoon, Doctor," she said, a tired smile lifting her lips.

As suspected, Judith was standing on the other side of her bed. He was surprised to find her watching him, her eyes slightly narrowed, as if waiting. But for what?

"Hello, Miss Isaacs," he said, nodding to her briefly.

"Please, call me JJ."

Not in this lifetime.

He nodded and focused on Sheree. "So we got back your tests from two days ago, and we think we know what may be happening with your pregnancy."

Worry wrinkled Sheree's features. "I'm listening."

"We think that you may have a slight placental abruption," he began calmly. "Basically, that's where the placenta separates from the uterus. In a severe or complete abruption, the separation would cause the fetus to be deprived of oxygen and nutrients from your body. We would have to do an immediate C-section to save the baby."

He heard Judith gasp and saw Sheree's eyes moisten with fear.

"However," he said, placing a calming hand on her arm, "in your case, the abruption seems to be quite small. So we should be able to manage it and your care, so that your baby can further develop and have the best chance of survival on delivery."

Sheree began to swipe at tears as they rolled down her cheeks. He knew she was afraid, but it would have been unfair to not give her all the facts. He watched JJ perch on the edge of the bed and take Sheree's hand comfortingly. The compassion in her eyes stabbed at his heart.

"Hey, I know this is scary," JJ said gently. "But Dr. Massri said that in your case we caught it. You know what that means? Chances are, everything will be fine. You have to believe that. This baby will be fine, Sheree."

"Your sister-in-law is right," Simon chimed in. "About one in fifty pregnant women will experience an abruption at some point in their pregnancy, so it's not that uncommon. We know how to handle it. So I want you to stop worrying. But we will have to monitor you closely to make sure that everything is going smoothly, and you will have to take it very easy. Your pregnancy is high risk, and so I want you doing no strenuous activity at all."

Sheree nodded. "Okay, I can do that."

"Also," Simon added, "I'd like to see you weekly, at least for the next few weeks, so we can keep track of things. If you have any problems, I want you to have the hospital page me."

Sheree nodded.

"Any questions?" he asked.

They had lots, just like he thought they would, and he did his best to answer them. When they had run out, Simon stood to go.

"Don't worry, Sheree," he said reassuringly. "So far, your baby looks fairly healthy. All we're doing is making sure he or she stays that way."

"Thanks, Doc," Sheree said, a slightly more relaxed look on her face.

He smiled. "You're welcome."

"Yes, thank you," JJ added.

He glanced at her and found himself staring into her intriguing hazel eyes. Beautiful eyes that would draw him in if he stared too long. He tore away from her gaze and hastily exited the room. It was only when he was outside that he realized he hadn't responded to her thanks at all.

He had to stop doing this. He couldn't let one woman unnerve him and turn him into a fool like this.

Get a hold of yourself, Massri!

He gritted his teeth, angry at himself, and headed down the hall.

"Wait! Stop."

There were footsteps behind him. But he didn't pay attention, didn't realize the calls were for him until a hand grabbed his arm. When he stopped and turned around, he was surprised to find a beautiful woman glaring at him. A beautiful, ticked-off woman.

He opened and closed his mouth several times before coming up with an appropriate sentence.

"Miss Isaacs...?" He blinked rapidly to confirm that he wasn't imagining things. "Is...uh...is everything okay? Is your sister-in-law okay?"

"My sister-in-law is fine," JJ said, crossing her arms. "I, however, am not."

More blinking. "Excuse me?"

"Do you have a problem with me, Dr. Massri?"

"What?"

"Do you have a problem with me?" JJ repeated, enunciating every word for emphasis. "Do you have an issue with the way I treat my sister-in-law? Has she said something to you about me that I should know? Do you think I am not taking care of her?"

JJ stepped toward Simon, and he fought the urge to respond with a step back.

"Because I'm getting the distinct feeling that you disapprove of me," JJ continued. "And let me tell you, I have been better to Sheree than all my sisters, so I don't know why you're treating me as if I am a problem."

"I don't think you're a problem..."

"Then what's with the attitude?" JJ hissed, the intensity in her voice jumping up a few notches, her hands finding their way to her hips. He noted her pupils dilating, the veins at her temples pulsing, the pace of her breathing increasing, all biological signals that she was in as heightened an emotional state as he was. Except the emotion at work for her was probably anger. And for him, it was something else. Something he hadn't quite been able to put his finger on thus far.

"Attitude?"

"Yes, attitude," JJ continued, taking another step forward. "The way you ignore me when I'm in the room, the way you barely acknowledge my questions, the way you dismiss me almost immediately."

"I have never been rude to you."

"No, you only act like I don't exist," JJ shot back. "I have been with Sheree for every appointment, but you barely say two words to me. You treated my sister Sydney better on the first day you met her than you treated me today, even though you see me every time Sheree is here!"

"I'm sorry if you felt that I haven't been professional with your family."

"I'm not talking about my family!" she snapped, stomping her foot for emphasis. "I am talking about me. I may not be a patient, but I am a visitor to this hospital. And I deserve to be at least treated with regard. But you have been nothing but aloof with me since the first time you saw me—"

Simon didn't know what got into him. Maybe it was all the frustration of the past few weeks, not talking to her about what was on his mind. Maybe it was the curious eyes of the people who passed them in the hallway. But he grabbed JJ's arm and pulled her into an empty waiting area off to their right. The minute he let her arm go, the words tumbled out of his mouth.

"The first time I saw you, you could barely breathe. You were curled up in the corner of an elevator in the middle of Paris, about to pass out from panic. And if I recall correctly, I did a lot more than treat you with regard."

Time seemed to stop.

He watched her eyes widen and recognition flood in like the tide of a rough sea washing onto the shore. Her mouth fell open as her eyes searched his face, devoured his features. She stopped breathing even as he struggled for a breath of his own.

"Oh my," she whispered, her eyes still glued to his face. "It *was* you."

He took a deep, measured breath.

"Yes," he answered, matching her whisper with a murmur. "It was me. Judith."

It was so liberating to say her name. To finally have it out there. To acknowledge the connection they had, beyond her sister-in-law. Beyond the walls of the hospital. Beyond even this city of Toronto.

She couldn't seem to pull her eyes away. He knew he definitely couldn't, with her looking at him like that. And as he looked down into her hazel orbs, he could see layer after layer of memories float to the surface. The days and events that had brought them together for those few hours so many years ago became real again. If he was honest with himself, he often wondered if he had imagined the whole thing. It seemed like something out of a movie. A man trapped in an elevator with a woman who in their first meeting manages to trigger more protective instincts in him than anyone else he has known in his life. And then she steps on a plane and disappears and it was like it never even happened.

She started to breathe again. Each breath lifting her chest slightly, warming the narrow space between them, tightening his chest. Tightening every muscle in his body. Every part of him was tense, just as it was whenever she was around.

They could have been standing there for five minutes or five hours, for all Simon knew. She never looked away and neither did he. He never heard the footsteps. Never heard the sounds from the hallway enter the small, semi-enclosed area. Only faintly recognized his name. And that was only after the third repetition.

"Dr. Massri!"

He stepped back from Judith and turned around. It took him a few moments to remember where he was. He looked at the woman in aqua-green scrubs, barely registering her.

"Dr. Sterling wants to see you before you leave for the

evening," the woman said. She looked at Simon as if she wasn't quite sure he had heard. Then she glanced behind him at JJ. She raised an eyebrow but said nothing.

Simon blinked and looked down at the charts in his hands. Then back at the nurse.

"I'll go see her now."

Numbness settled over him as, without looking back, he stepped toward the door and out into the hallway behind the nurse. It was a good thing Sheree had been his last patient. He was definitely done for the day. He dropped the charts off at the nursing station on his way to the office where he knew he would find the chief. He was almost there when he heard her voice again.

"Wait!"

He didn't wait. Didn't even slow down.

"Simon, stop."

He stopped at the sound of his name on her lips, and she planted herself in front of him.

"If you knew me, if you remembered me all this time, why didn't you say something?" she demanded.

He shook his head, surprised and disappointed. "Why didn't you?"

She threw her hands up helplessly. "It was five years ago. Who would remember? Or even want to?"

"It was four and a half years ago," Simon said, beginning to walk again. "And I remember."

"Is that why you're treating me like this?" JJ asked as she tried to keep up. "Because you're upset that I forgot you?"

Simon stopped suddenly, causing JJ to almost crash right into him.

"First of all, you didn't forget me," he said, glaring at her. His eyes dared her to protest, and when she didn't he knew he was right.

"And second of all, I am not treating you any differently."

JJ put her hands on her hips. "That's a lie. And you know it."

"Whatever," he said, turning around to leave. "Believe what you want."

"No!" She grabbed his arm and froze him in place with her touch. "Tell me the truth. Tell me why, for some reason, you're mad at me."

He turned back to face her.

"Okay," he said, his brows drawing together. "Honestly? You threw me. This person you've become..."

He motioned helplessly to her form.

JJ looked down at herself then back at Simon. "What person?"

"This person with the short, over-styled hair, and the makeup and the black nails, and those, those...clothes," he said, failing to keep the negative tone out of his voice. "This is not the woman I met in Paris. It's not the woman I..."

He what? Went back to the hotel looking for the day after? Thought about for weeks? Wondered about for months?

"It's not you," he finished finally.

He watched her self-consciously fold her arms around her body. "My clothes and hair are different, so I'm different? Isn't that a bit judgmental?"

He shook his head, his eyes softening as he stared at her. He could see pieces of that woman he'd met in Paris. Flickers that would slip through when she smiled, or when she wasn't being as careful.

"It's not just the hair and clothes," he said quietly. Her eyes fell to the floor and he knew that he wasn't just imagining things. She knew what he was talking about.

He ran a hand over his dreads. "Look, you're right. I have been treating you differently. I was wrong and I'm sorry. I'll do my best to be...professional from now on." He sighed. "I'm sorry if I offended you. I didn't mean to. I was just surprised to see you."

She nodded but didn't look up at him. This was not the way he had wanted this conversation to go. He had hoped they would be able to talk about this. That they both could remember. That maybe she would be even half as curious about him as he was about her. It wasn't supposed to turn into this confrontation, with them fighting and him feeling like a jerk. It wasn't supposed to be like this.

Another sigh, another long look, and he turned and headed back down the hallway.

"Simon."

He stopped. Closed his eyes for a moment then turned around slowly.

"It was a couple hours in an elevator," she said calmly. "It takes more than that to know a person."

He lifted his arms and let them drop to his sides again. "Maybe," he said with a shrug. "But sometimes a couple hours tells you a whole lot."

Several emotions that he couldn't read swept across her face. He tried to figure them out, but she was right. He didn't know her that well. So he just stared. This time she was the first to walk away. When she did, Simon couldn't help but think that unlike their first time alone together, this time he had done more harm than good.

Chapter 8

June came in like a beast, and it was taking everything in JJ just to survive.

With rehearsal for Jayla's tour six days a week and her backlog of orders at the shop, JJ barely had time to take a bathroom break, much less sleep and spend time with her family. She probably wouldn't even see Rayshawn if he wasn't managing half her life for her. Add to that the adjustment of making time for Sheree's medical needs, and most of JJ's days had begun to run into each other. She didn't mind helping with Sheree, though. Her schedule, though packed, was usually more flexible than her sisters'. And once she went on tour she wouldn't be able to help at all, so she might as well do as much as she could now.

She was coming off another one of her run-on days when she found herself stumbling up the steps to her home during the early hours of the morning. She yelped as she banged her toe against the planter near the door. She cursed herself for not remembering it was there, even though it had sat in the same spot for almost twenty years. But the truth was, she was so tired she was surprised she even remembered her address.

"Had a good time at your sleepover?"

JJ had barely caught her bearings after coming through the

front door when she noticed Sydney sitting in the living room. A faint light from the kitchen cast a strange glow on the living room, clouding her sister's face in shadows. But she didn't need to see Sydney's face to know how ticked off she was. The edge in her voice was enough.

"What are you talking about, Sydney?" JJ asked, though she wasn't really that interested. She had spent her whole day in rehearsal and most of her evening at the hospital with Sheree, enduring another awkward encounter with Dr. Massri. After squeezing in a late dinner with Rayshawn, she had gone back to the shop, where she had spent the last seven hours hunched over a sewing machine. All she wanted now was to crawl into bed. Not even a shower would take precedence over some shut-eye at this point.

"I'm talking about the fact that it's four-fifteen a.m. and you're just crawling into the house," Sydney said. "Is this going to be a regular thing now? You spending the whole night out?"

"Sydney, I would really love to have this conversation with you," JJ said, leaning against the door frame as she pulled off one shoe. "But right now, I can barely think straight."

"Yeah," Sydney said. "I'm guessing a couple hours of sleep will be enough to help you get your lies in order."

A couple hours of sleep would be a luxury she likely couldn't afford anytime soon. But her sister wouldn't understand that.

"Okay, fine, Sydney," JJ said, tossing her shoes into the closet by the door. "Since I apparently have reverted to sixteen years old and you apparently have transformed into my mother, I guess you need to know where I've been all night. I was at the shop, working on bridesmaid dresses. You happy? For heaven's sake..."

"Wow. I can't believe you could just stand there and lie to me." Sydney was standing now, and in the light JJ could see the fatigue and frustration on her sister's face. What was going on?

JJ's mouth fell open. "What?"

"And after everything we went through together last year, JJ," Sydney began. She shook her head. "I supported your music career before anyone even knew what you were doing. I never judged you for it and I kept it a secret for as long as you asked me to. And now you turn around and lie to me? I thought you knew you could trust me."

"Sydney..."

"How could you, JJ?"

"I'm not lying!"

"I saw you!"

"Saw me where?" JJ asked, her eyes barely open. "In the back room? Pricking my fingers on needles in the dark?"

"No, at The Grove, last night."

Oh no.

JJ's mouth opened but then closed.

"Nothing to say now, right?" Sydney asked. "Imagine my speechlessness last night when I look up from my meal to see my little sister across the room, practically sitting on the lap of some guy I've never met."

She had seen them. Seen her with Rayshawn. JJ couldn't breathe. Couldn't believe this was happening. What were the odds that she and Rayshawn would end up in the same restaurant as Sydney, on a weeknight? She hadn't even wanted to go to The Grove. She was tired from a day of being on her feet and had ended up dozing on Rayshawn's shoulder while they waited for their food. That must have been when Sydney saw them. She was so stupid. How could she have been that careless?

"Hayden wanted us to go over, but I couldn't," Sydney continued. "What was I supposed to say? Hi, I'm JJ's sister, nice to meet you, man-my-sister-obviously-knows-very-well-but-hasn't-thought-of-introdcing-me-to?"

"Sydney it's not like that..."

"And so I come home and decide to talk to you when you get home, because I'm thinking, maybe she's afraid to introduce me to him because she thinks I won't like him, thinks I'll be too judgmental," Sydney says. "Except you don't come home, JJ. All night."

JJ sank into the loveseat close to the entrance and closed her eyes. She knew exactly what her sister was thinking. And really, she couldn't blame her. If the tables were turned, she would think the same thing.

"I'm not sleeping with him, Sydney," JJ said quietly, her eyes still closed.

Sydney shook her head. "You know, maybe if this was a year ago, even six months ago, I would believe you. But this woman, sitting here in front of me—the one coming in at all hours, hanging out with strange men I've never met, lying about where she's been—I don't know who she is, and I don't know what to believe. I used to be so proud of you, JJ. You were my rock. The one I could count on to pull me back from the edge when I went too far. But now, now I don't even know who you are."

JJ's eyes burned as her sister's words slashed at her heart.

"I am exactly who I always was," JJ said defensively. "Except now, I've decided to have a life of my own instead of living in the shadow of my sisters' lives."

"And this life of your own that you're having, are you proud of it? 'Cause maybe the fact that you have to sneak around to have it should tell you something."

"I am not sneaking around!"

"So why do I have to find out about this by accident, JJ?" Sydney asked. "Is this the guy you were with in Alberta? Have you been sleeping with him since then?"

"Are you even listening to me?" JJ almost screamed. "I am not sleeping with him! And even if I was, is this the way you would treat me? What kind of hypocrisy is that? Lissandra spends her life doing whatever she wants with whomever she wants and you don't bat an eye, but you're all geared up to stone me over this one guy? This is exactly why I never brought Rayshawn around. I knew you would be like this."

"That's not fair," Sydney shot back. "You never gave me a chance to have an opinion because you hid all of it from me. And why was that? If you're not having sex with him and you're not sneaking around, what are you so ashamed of? He doesn't look twenty years older than you. Is he married? Have kids? Unbeliever?"

JJ's gaze tripped away as her sister stumbled onto the truth. Sydney stepped closer, peering at JJ.

"That's it, isn't it?" Sydney said. She shook her head. "What are you doing? This is not who you are. I know you. Your faith is the most important thing to you. How can you be with someone who doesn't share that? The two of you can't possibly be on the same page."

"You don't know anything about me and Rayshawn," JJ said, looking up. "He understands me, sees me. I can be who I want to be with him, and it's okay. And he believes in me."

"I believe in you, JJ."

"Not like that," JJ said, shaking her head. "You believe in me because you're my sister and you're supposed to. But it's more than that with him. He sees what I could be, sometimes more clearly than I can. And he cares about me, Sydney. Really cares about me. I've waited so long for that. For someone to choose to love me. Do you have any idea what it feels like to wait for that? To do all the right things and walk the line everyone says you should, only to watch that happen for everyone around you and not see it come your way?"

"Yes, I do," Sydney said. "It wasn't too long ago that I was exactly where you were. And then Hayden came. And I knew he was who God meant for me. But this relationship, JJ, this man, no matter how wonderful he is, can't be who God meant for you. Not now. Not like this."

"That's easy for you to say," JJ said. "With your engagement ring weighing down your left hand."

"It might seem that way, but haven't you learned anything from our mother's own history? Three marriages. None worked. And now she's alone again."

"Yes, Sydney, you're right," JJ said. "Three marriages, to three men who claimed to be believers. And look how well that turned out for her."

"That doesn't make this right—"

"For Pete's sake, Sydney, can't you just be happy for me?" JJ stood up. "Can't you just say, 'I hope you're happy. I hope this works out. I love you, JJ.'?"

"You know I love you," Sydney said sadly. "And I know you might feel happy now, but this thing is not going to work out, no matter how hard any of us hope and wish for it. Because either this man is going to break your heart or he's going to turn you into someone you're not—someone who loses that one true relationship that has kept her going for years. And the sad thing about it is that I can tell that it's already started to happen."

"You know what?" JJ returned to the entryway and grabbed the shoes she had just abandoned. "I don't need to listen to this anymore."

"JJ..."

"I always thought this place, this house, would be a safe place for me." She pulled on one shoe. "A place where I could be myself. Where I could feel comfortable no matter how right or wrong anyone thought my decisions were."

"You can, JJ," Sydney said, moving toward the door. "Please don't leave."

But JJ knew she couldn't stay. She already had her mother's judgment weighing down on her. She knew her sister would never be okay with her relationship with Rayshawn. But she thought that at the very least her sister would be there for her in spite of it, just like JJ had been there for Sydney when she had been dealing with her own confusion only a year ago. But it seemed like that was too much to ask.

"JJ, please." Sydney's hand clasped her upper arm, and JJ cringed and pushed back tears before pulling away.

"I have to go."

Then, before she could break down, she slipped through the front door and hurried down the front walk to her car. She had to get out of there.

She made it across the city in less than twenty minutes. When she rang the doorbell at her destination, it didn't take long for someone to respond.

"Hey, can I stay here for a bit?"

Rayshawn swung the door open wider and welcomed her in. "You never have to ask."

Chapter 9

JJ stepped inside the dark living room and dropped her purse and keys in the chair near the entryway.

"Babe, what's wrong?" Rayshawn asked, concern filling his voice. He reached for the lights, but JJ grabbed his hand before he could switch them on.

"No, don't," she said, her voice muffled with tears. "Just please. Leave them off."

"Babe, you're worrying me," he said, pulling her into his arms, pushing her hair away from her face. "Talk to me, please."

Even through the slivers of moonlight stealing between the curtains, JJ could see the concern in his eyes. The affection there. How long had it been since someone had looked at her like that? Without judgment, without need, without expectation. Just looked at her, like no matter who she was or chose to be, it would be okay. What had happened to all the people she used to be able to count on for that?

JJ couldn't talk anymore. She had talked enough for the night. She was tired of talking; of thinking. Instead she buried herself in Rayshawn's arms and wished it to all go away. And when he kissed the top of her head gently, she lifted her face and returned the affection with a kiss to his lips.

And then he was kissing her, parting her lips gently with his, drawing her into him with every caress of his mouth. JJ couldn't resist the sensation, didn't want to stop his hands as they traced a path down her back, slipped under her shirt to stroke her flushed skin beneath. The argument with Sydney had turned a bad day into a terrible one. And that just topped the ongoing conflict with her mother and the unexplained guilt she felt for disappointing Simon Massri, a man she had met only once in her life. Nothing in her life seemed to be coming together the way she wanted it to, but this moment felt good. This moment with Rayshawn, who had been with her through all of it; who understood her more than her family or friends; who wanted her—who wanted to be with her—who had chosen her. This moment with this man was enough.

And so when he lifted the hem of her shirt and slipped it over her head, she let him. And when his fingers began to undo the buttons on her jeans, she didn't stop him. And when his hands hooked under her thighs, easily lifting her off the floor and up the stairs, she wrapped her arms around his neck and let it happen. Because that early morning, in that moment, when everyone else in her world had tossed her aside and rejected her, there was still one man who wanted her.

And never had it felt so good to be wanted.

The ceiling fan whirring overhead was the first clue to JJ that something was wrong. She did not have a fan in her bedroom. The hand draped across her bare stomach and the realization that she was not in bed alone was the second, and definitely more startling, indicator that JJ had crossed over into foreign territory.

Panic rushed in to fill the void that familiarity had left behind.

What had she done?

She looked over at Rayshawn, whose head rested on the pillow next to hers, and her stomach clenched. Bolting from the king-size bed in alarm, she wrapped the sheet around her and dashed into the bathroom. She sat on the closed toilet seat, the vague soreness in her nether regions confirming that this was in fact not a dream.

She had slept with Rayshawn. Even though she had sworn she wouldn't, she had broken her promise of celibacy to herself and to God.

She covered her face in her hands as waves of guilt and despair washed over her. They were right. They were all right. She had changed. And she wasn't even sure who she was anymore. She tried to hold back tears as she sat hunched in the tiny room. What was she thinking? How could she let herself slip like this? She didn't remember if they had used a condom. What if she got pregnant or got something worse? And where were her clothes?

A knock on the door broke into her thoughts.

"JJ?"

She wiped her hands hastily over her face. She would not let him see her cry over this.

"Babe, I know you're freaked out about this," he said gently. "Do you want to talk about it?"

"No!" That was the last thing she wanted to do. Especially with Rayshawn. She needed to leave. Now.

She opened the door and found him dressed only in a pair of jeans, holding a mug of hot cocoa. He was smirking.

"I knew you wouldn't want to talk about it." He handed her the mug and kissed her on her forehead. "I know you're mad at yourself. But these things happen. Don't beat yourself up over it. And you don't have to worry about me disappearing like some other guys. I'm not going anywhere."

His words brought a tiny bit of comfort to JJ, but not a lot. No matter what Rayshawn said, it would never justify what had just happened.

JJ looked down, unable to meet his eyes. "I just want to go home. Can you..."

"Get your clothes?" he asked. "Sure. Enjoy your hot cocoa."

He squeezed her arm before walking out of the room. JJ wrapped the sheet tighter around herself and shuffled out of the bathroom, looking around the room for a place to sit. She glanced at the rumpled sheets of the monstrosity in which she had given her body to Rayshawn and looked away. She chose the lounge by the window instead, pulling her legs up under her. She closed her eyes, wanting to pray, but knew that God wanted nothing to do with her. So she sighed and sipped her hot cocoa, and hoped Rayshawn would hurry up with her clothes. When he finally did return, however, JJ could tell that what had happened a few hours earlier between them was no longer on his mind.

"What's wrong?" JJ asked, cutting to the chase.

Rayshawn laid her clothes on the lounge and sat at the foot of the bed, facing her. She didn't like the lines on his face, the way he seemed to be thinking about the best way to say whatever it was that needed to be said.

"Just spit it out," she said impatiently.

Rayshawn sighed. "I just got the call. You've been dropped from the tour."

He might as well have told JJ a meteorite had dropped from the sky onto her house. The news was just as unbelievable and equally devastating.

She stared at him, opening and closing her mouth like a goldfish.

"It's not a personal thing," he continued gently. "Amina made up with Jayla's producer, and Amina's lawyer threatened to sue Jayla's management team if they didn't honor the terms of her contract..."

"The same contract she tore up in front of everyone?" JJ asked, finally finding her voice.

"Yes, the same one," Rayshawn said. He got up and moved to the spot beside her on the lounge, taking her hands in his. "They could have fought it, but I think Jayla wants her back. It's not that she doesn't like you, it's just that she loves Amina. They've been together for years. They understand each other. You're the new girl on the block."

JJ couldn't believe what was happening. In the space of twenty-four hours JJ had gone from being employed with a full-time music gig for three months to not having a stage to sing on. But that was the nature of the business. There was no such thing as stability. You could be a hot ticket-item today and a thrift-store castoff tomorrow. And there was almost nothing you could do about it.

"I'm sorry, JJ." Rayshawn rested a hand on her thigh. "This is the business we work in. These things happen."

JJ moved her legs out of his reach. She got up and walked to the window as she considered her present dilemma. Rayshawn was right. This *was* the business she was in. But is this how she wanted it to be? Getting tossed from stage to stage, artist to artist, like a piece of rental equipment?

"So what now?" she asked, her back to him.

She heard Rayshawn sigh and the cushions shuffle as he shifted. She had never heard him sigh as much as he had since he stepped into the bedroom just moments earlier.

"Now we keep working on your tracks, and we find you something else," he said. "I have my eye on a few things in the pipeline. Lots of artists are going on tour in the next couple months, and if that's what you really want to do, I think I can find you something. Otherwise, we can use this time to get your solo career going. Keep doing the local venues, get you opening for some other up-and-coming artists, see what we can do."

JJ didn't answer. It sounded like a lot of shots in the dark. She folded her arms and stared out at the cityscape. She shouldn't have come here to Rayshawn's home. She shouldn't even be with Rayshawn—for a million and one reasons ranging from professional to spiritual. This was why everything was falling down. This was her punishment for getting entangled in a relationship with a man who was not right for her and doing things with him that she had no business doing.

He came over to stand behind her. JJ flinched and moved away when he rested his hands on her shoulders. She sensed him tense behind her.

"Babe, it's going to be okay," he said quietly. "This is just a minor setback. Don't let it bring you down. You have an amazing talent and the world is going to see that—even if I have to tour you around North America on my own dime."

The sincerity of his words reached out and grabbed her heart, and this time when he reached out and turned her around to face him, she didn't resist.

"JJ, I believe in you with everything in me. That's why I kept coming back to that little dive downtown even after you turned me down three times."

JJ rolled her eyes and bit back a smile. "I only turned you down twice."

The corner of his mouth turned up in a smile. "I'm also counting that time I asked you out for drinks and you said no."

He earned a chuckle from her for that one.

"Listen, babe, I know talent when I see it. But I also know you. And I know you won't give up until you make it. That's what I love about you. And even if you do, I won't." He tucked a lock of hair behind her ear, his eyes locked on hers. "It's going to happen for you. I promise."

JJ sighed, her eyes dropping to the floor.

"I don't know," she began. "I just keep thinking... what if this is not what I'm supposed to be doing? What if this is not the way God wants me to go about things? To be honest, I've made so many decisions I'm not sure about lately..."

She felt Rayshawn tense and pull back from her. She looked up at him, but his eyes were focused to her right.

"Look, JJ." He had that tone that he used whenever she mentioned the G word. "I respect that your faith is important to you. But this is business. You can't expect that things are just going to fall into your lap because you wish for it. If you want this, you have to go after it. You have to do whatever it takes."

"I know that, Rayshawn, but I can't live my life as if it's only about me," JJ said. "Everything I have is because of God. This voice, this talent, even these opportunities, I wouldn't have them if—"

"You wouldn't have them unless you worked for them, or I worked for them for you, or you were lucky enough to be in that little bar the same night I was," Rayshawn said dryly. "Don't make it more than it is, and don't use this religion thing as an excuse to back out of what you want."

JJ felt herself getting annoyed. She hated when Rayshawn became like this—when he was condescending. It was like they were speaking two different languages and it was almost impossible for them to come to any sort of understanding.

"This *religion thing* is important to me," JJ snapped. "It is a big part of who I am. I told you that from the get-go. I won't do anything I feel doesn't fit with what God wants for me."

"Really?" Rayshawn asked dryly. "You felt that way last night too?"

It would have hurt less if he had punched her in the stomach.

JJ felt the air leave her lungs at his words. And as she looked at him, she saw something ugly and mean that she had somehow missed before.

When she finally gathered the words to speak, her voice was so low and cold she barely recognized it. "You are lucky that mug is on the other side of the room, or you would be wearing that hot cocoa."

His eyes closed as remorse washed over him, but it was too late. JJ had already grabbed her clothes and was heading to the bathroom.

"JJ, I'm sorry," he said as the door slammed closed behind her. "I shouldn't have said that. I was being a jerk. It's early, I haven't had my coffee yet, and this thing upset me just as much as it upset you. Maybe more."

JJ struggled to put on her clothes, needing to get out of there. What had she done? Had she really broken her promise to herself and to God for this man? This man who would disrespect her faith and throw her mistakes in her face like that?

But this wasn't even Rayshawn's fault. It was hers. She had gone looking for acceptance in the wrong places, and everywhere she turned she kept getting burned. Now she was walking around with nothing but scars.

"JJ, come on. I didn't mean it." Rayshawn was still going at it on the other side of the door, but JJ was barely listening. "Just come out. We can talk about this."

JJ did come out, and when she did she headed straight out the bedroom door and down the stairs to the living room.

"Where are you going?" he asked as she grabbed her keys and purse from the chair where she had discarded them the night before.

"Home," JJ snapped, swinging the door open. "To think about how I felt last night."

His groan was cut off by the slamming of the front door. JJ got in her car and headed for home. It might not be the most comfortable place. But at least it was hers.

Chapter 10

The town car that picked JJ up was so dark that she couldn't tell whether there was an actual driver or if it was being driven by a ghost. She stared at it for a moment, not sure if she should get in or wait for someone to roll down the window. Before she had to make the decision, the driver's side opened and a thick, clean-shaven man in a dark suit stepped out.

"Miss Judith Isaacs?" he asked with an accent that sounded more New York than Toronto.

JJ nodded.

"The name's Marvin," he said, opening the back passenger door. "I'm here to take you to your audition."

JJ cleared her throat. "Uh, okay."

She reached for her overnight bag, but Marvin got to it first.

"Thank you," JJ murmured, sliding onto the leather-covered backseat. The door had barely closed behind her when she noticed the bouquet of white tulips on the seat next to her.

Rayshawn.

He knew white tulips were her favorite. He also knew she knew they were out of season, and so he'd have had to make some effort to locate them. She shook her head. This was another part of his apology. He had been doing everything he could to make up for the argument they'd had two days before when JJ had stormed out of his place. This audition that he had pretty much pulled out of thin air was the first part. The Victoria's Secret gift basket, delivered to her doorstep with all her favorite items the day before, was another. If his goal was to wear her down, she had to admit that it was working.

She breathed in the light, fresh scent of the tulips before opening the attached card.

I'm a jerk. Forgive me? I want to be there to celebrate with you after you ace this audition.
—Shawn

She held the tulips to her nose again. She would think about it.

Thankfully, JJ was able to see more looking out the windows than she had been able to see looking in, as Marvin took several roads out of Davisville, her Toronto community. Instead of heading north to the 401, the major highway, he headed west until he picked up the 400 going north.

"So, where exactly are we headed?" JJ asked, hoping she could uncover some of the mystery shrouding the whole experience. Maybe Marvin would be more forthcoming with details than Rayshawn had been in his e-mail earlier that morning when he told her to pack an overnight bag and be ready at eight p.m. for an audition.

"I'm afraid I'm not at liberty to say, Miss Isaacs," Marvin said. "But I would suggest you go ahead and relax. Take a nap even. We'll be on the road for about an hour."

She was on the way to a middle-of-the-night audition with someone she didn't know, who lived so far out of Toronto it would take her an hour's drive on a traffic-free highway to get there. She wasn't likely to be relaxing anytime soon.

"Yeah, don't think that's going to work."

Marvin chuckled. "Thought you might say that. In that case, there are a couple magazines on the backseat you could browse."

JJ wasn't in the mood for browsing. She was far too wound up. She must have dozed in spite of it, however, for the next time she looked up, the town car was rolling up a long driveway lined on each side by ground-level lights. Beyond the driveway the thick foliage of tall pines worked with the darkness to keep JJ ignorant of her surroundings. After what seemed like forever, the trees parted and the driveway opened up to reveal a lit fountain surrounded by a stone pond. Behind it stood a three-story monstrosity like nothing JJ had personally seen before. Even in the poor view provided by the floodlights around the front and sides of the property, JJ could tell that the mansion was something out of an episode of the celebrity homes show, *MTV Cribs.*

"Close your mouth, Miss Isaacs," Marvin said, opening JJ's door. "This time of year, you could catch flies like that."

JJ hadn't even realized he had stopped and gotten out of the car. She snapped her mouth shut and tried to pull herself together. She didn't need Marvin telling whoever it was he worked for that she acted like a plum fool.

As she got out of the car and followed him to the front doors, she couldn't help but stare. The brick walkway beneath her feet led straight to the main entrance, which comprised a heavy oak doorway about fifteen feet high, balanced on both sides by thick stone columns that ran from the ground to almost the top of the second floor. Moonlight bounced off the tall arched windows to the side and offered the illusion that one could see inside the home. However, JJ didn't need to peek. As if expecting them, the front doors opened and they were welcomed into the huge entryway.

"Hi, I'm Kate. Judith?"

JJ took the hand of the fresh-faced woman standing in front of her. In her snow-white blazer and slim-fit slacks, with her hair perfectly coiffed and her makeup flawless, Kate looked like it was the middle of the workday instead of 9:25 at night. She suddenly felt underdressed in her billowy sweater-blouse and dark-wash jeans. At least she had worn heels.

"Most people call me JJ."

"Okay, JJ it is then." Kate smiled, but JJ didn't miss the way the woman's eyes flitted over her. "Come with me."

Their heels clicked as they walked over marble tiles past several doors on both sides. Finally, at the end of the hallway, Kate opened wide double doors and stepped aside to let JJ into a large, windowless room with hardwood floors and maple paneling. Several ceiling-level spotlights were aimed at a stage, set up at one end. As she moved closer she saw that there were also microphones and feed boxes on the stage. Scattered around the room were women looking over sheet music, others with headsets and clipboards moving swiftly among them, and yet still others whose specific role she could not determine. Despite their numbers, the sound in the room barely rose above a dull murmur.

Before she could take in any more details, Rayshawn was at her side.

"Hey, babe," he whispered in her ear, giving her a quick kiss on the cheek. "Glad you made it."

"Shawn, what's going on?" JJ asked, forgetting in the awe of the moment that she still might be mad at him. "Who are these auditions for? Are these the only people auditioning? Will I have to sing in front of them?"

"Yes and yes," Rayshawn answered, his eyes sparkling. "But don't worry. You got this. Did you bring the music I told you to and did you practice the new songs?"

"Yes," JJ said. "But you still haven't told me who I am auditioning for. And why would you want me to bring the Deacon Hill songs? I've never sung those before."

"Because that's who you're auditioning for."

JJ's mouth fell open and she felt her heart beat triple-time as the blood rushed to her ears.

"I'm auditioning for Deacon Hill?" JJ was barely able to squeak the words out. She grabbed her chest. "Oh my God, I can't breathe."

Rayshawn put an arm around her and led her to an empty corner. "Easy, babe, deep breath. Relax. You can do this."

The deep breath did seem to help settle her heart rate, just enough so she could punch Rayshawn in the arm.

"Ouch!"

"How could you not tell me this?" she hissed, careful not to draw attention to them. "I would have practiced more, I would have chosen better songs, I would have chosen a better outfit!"

"That's exactly why I didn't tell you," Rayshawn said, rubbing his arm. "You would have overdone it, psyched yourself out, and then been a bundle of nerves."

"You mean like I am right now?"

"JJ, you have got to relax. Deacon Hill is just a man like anyone else. Remember that and you'll get through this audition fine."

Before she could argue, a throat cleared and everyone in the room looked to the stage. JJ gasped. It was him. Deacon Hill. Multiplatinum-selling recording artist and owner of the hearts of 80 percent of the women across the world. He was dressed in black jeans and a gray henley, but he might as well have been wearing a Brooks Brothers suit for how amazing he looked. Smooth, olive-toned skin; dark, close-cropped hair; and darker eyes. Not too short but not too tall. Not too built but not too lean. He was every race, every kind of singer and every woman's type.

"Good evening, everyone," he said in the smooth, silky voice that had invaded JJ's dreams once upon a time. "And thank you for coming here at such an ungodly hour. I know this is a bit strange for most of you, but I am run by my schedule and have to get through this now, so I can fly out midday tomorrow. Kate will give you the instructions for the audition, but I just want to wish you all the best. I am looking forward to working with those of you who are chosen, in the next couple months."

Deacon stepped away from the mike and Kate took his place, giving the instructions for how the auditions would take place. Apparently they were looking for four singers for Deacon's second line. There were eleven of them there to audition. Most would go home tonight. Those called back would stay overnight, and the final four would be determined in the morning.

JJ had never been to an audition like this. But she had heard that this was how some major superstars recruited their musicians and backup, and Deacon Hill was definitely a major star.

From what she saw around the room, it seemed like a female-only audition. She tried to block out the other women as they sang, knowing it would psych her out. By the time it was her turn, she had gone through so many levels of nervousness, excitement, and fear that she was almost numb.

"You got this, babe." Rayshawn squeezed her hand before she slipped through the crowd to the stage. She headed to the musician, and was surprised to find it was a female keyboardist She had been so busy watching the other singers audition she hadn't noticed.

"What you got?" the redheaded, gum-chewing young woman asked.

"'It's My Time,'" JJ said, handing her the sheet music. She saw the woman raise an eyebrow as she saw the markings JJ had made.

"Alright," she said, something that could have been a smile cracking the corner of her lips. "Let me know when you're ready."

JJ took the mike at the center of the stage and glanced down at Kate, Deacon, and three other persons sitting in folding metal chairs in the first row. She closed her eyes.

Okay, God. I know I messed up and I have no right to ask you anything. But if you could have favor on me for a moment and help me through this, I would be so grateful.

With her eyes still closed, she nodded to the musician. She heard the strains of the song open up at the lower key she requested. Then she stopped thinking and started singing. She didn't sing Deacon Hill's "It's My Time." She sang Judith Isaacs's. Every word, every melody flowed through her like it was her own. In that moment there was no one else but her and the music. It *was* her time. And since she didn't know if she would ever again get a chance to sing before someone as powerful as Deacon Hill, she sang like it was the last time she would ever sing.

When she finally got to the last note, she let it hang in the air like the breeze after a strong gust of wind. Then the final chime of the piano, and silence. So complete and so deafening that

JJ's eyes popped open, wondering if at some point the room had emptied. She blinked and stepped back shakily from the microphone when she realized that everyone was looking at her. The busy bees with the clipboards had stopped moving, Kate's fingers on her phone had stopped typing, even the musician's gum-smacking had ceased. The silence hung for a long moment and panic seized JJ's heart like a rough fist. She had overdone it, just like Rayshawn had feared. She had wrecked the song. Totally and completely trashed Deacon's song right in front of him, and now they were about to throw her out.

"What was your name again?" Kate asked.

JJ struggled to speak. "JJ—Judith Isaacs."

"Hmm." Kate looked down at her clipboard and JJ noticed her strike something through. She flinched as if the pen had literally been scratched across her.

"Thank you, JJ," she said, still scanning her list. "Who's next?"

JJ felt her shoulders slump as she returned to the musician to retrieve her music. The woman stared at her, a strange expression on her face.

"Thanks," JJ said, collecting her music.

The redhead nodded. "See you in the morning."

It wasn't until she was off the stage and almost back in her corner that she realized what the woman was implying.

She had made it to the next round!

JJ let out a sigh of relief. Looked like she would live to sing another day.

Chapter 11

The five a.m. wake-up call was beyond unwelcome for JJ. She knew that she should be grateful that she was still at Deacon's mansion as one of five girls who had made it to the final screening, but four hours of sleep had not been nearly enough. Plus she was more than a little annoyed that she hadn't heard a peep out of Rayshawn since her audition the night before. A glance at her cell phone confirmed that he hadn't even left her a text message. This was not the time for him to pull one of his disappearing acts. But that's what you got for having a covert relationship with your manager. On days like this, their relationship was so covert that JJ wasn't even sure it really existed. But she didn't have the energy or time to contemplate that this morning. With her eyes burning, she stumbled to the en suite bathroom, took a quick shower, and changed into her other set of clothes. By the time she got downstairs, it was five forty-five.

She found four other girls in the kitchen. Another African American young woman with short hair and huge, ruby-stained lips was in a corner on her phone. A girl who looked to be a native Canadian, wearing earphones and sunglasses, was hunched over a bottle of water and some fruit. Two others chatted with each other near the refrigerator. None looked interested in talking with JJ. With a sigh she headed to the table where a spread of beverages, fruits, and pastries were laid out. Knowing better than to eat, JJ prepared herself a cup of camomile tea with a touch of honey. Then she settled at the table across from Miss Sunglasses and waited.

"Not eating?"

She was surprised when the woman addressed her.

"No," JJ said finally. "We don't know when we'll be singing, and you don't want to sing on a full stomach."

JJ took a sip of her tea as the woman looked down at her fruit plate of oranges, grapes, and strawberries.

"And it's probably none of my business, but you might want to skip the oranges," JJ added. "The citrus will dry out your throat."

The hiss of teeth drew both women's attention to the corner of the room.

"You do know this is a competition, right?" Miss Cell Phone said, scowling. "You can't be dishing out free advice. They're only picking three of us."

"Three?" JJ echoed. "I thought Deacon needed four backups."

"He does," one of the women near the refrigerator commented. "But little Miss Keyboards from last night is already in one of those spots."

JJ looked around at the other women. All the faces seemed to suggest a common knowledge of this information just supplied to JJ. "How do you already know this?"

"'Cause you learn things when you go through the whole audition instead of coming in during the last rounds," Miss Cell Phone said, before going back to her phone call.

JJ looked down at her tea, heat creeping up her neck. So Rayshawn had slipped her into the final round of the audition. It would make sense that the others were a bit resentful. They'd had to work their way to this point, while she just came in at the last minute and stole a spot. Okay. Maybe she could find a little forgiveness for his current behavior then.

"Forget about her," Miss Sunglasses said. "She's just mad 'cause she had to get up early. I'm Diana, by the way."

"JJ."

After finishing her tea, JJ excused herself to return to her room, where she did a few minutes of quick vocal warm-ups before returning to the main area to find that two other women she remembered from the night before had joined their group. However, before she could join Diana at the table again, Kate entered.

"Okay, ladies, let's go. This morning is going to go really fast."

She wasn't lying. Just a few more rounds of group singing like the night before, and then they were asked to do one more solo audition, with a piece of their choice. JJ watched the other women enter and leave the same room from the night before for their solos. She was second to last, with Diana bringing up the rear.

"Good luck," Diana said, nodding at JJ before she entered the room.

"You too," JJ called back, knowing she probably wouldn't see the young woman again before she went in for her own audition.

It was a much smaller crowd than the night before. In fact, the only persons present were Deacon, another gentleman, Andrew, who introduced himself as being from Deacon's label, Sound City, and of course Kate, whose role JJ still hadn't been able to define. They asked JJ a little about her background and why she wanted to sing with Deacon Hill. For a moment it seemed more like an interview than an audition.

"So, like you were told, for this section we want you to perform something that you think represents you," Kate said finally. "We need to know who you are as a musician—what you think your strengths are and how versatile you are. So whenever you're ready, you can give Sabrina your music and get started."

JJ glanced over at the female keyboardist from the night before, then behind her at the band setup she had noticed when she came in. It included drums, a second keyboard, a bass like Dean's, and several guitars.

"Actually, I was wondering if I could play my own accompaniment," JJ said, turning back to the judges.

Kate and Andrew looked at each other, surprised, while Deacon's formerly blank expression cracked slightly into something JJ couldn't define.

"Uh . . . sure," Andrew said.

JJ chose the acoustic guitar, plugged it into an amp, and adjusted the mikes and stool until she was comfortable. This was her last chance to show Deacon Hill that she was the one he should pick as his backup artist. She knew they were looking for singers, but it never hurt to show them what else she could do, and she knew she could play a guitar like nobody's business.

"The song I'll be doing is 'I'm Yours.' "

She hadn't sung this song in a while, but she didn't need to practice the song that she had composed herself. She had played it with Dean until the chords were imprinted on her fingertips and the melody engraved on her heart. So when she started playing, she didn't miss a single note, and for the most part she kept her eyes on Deacon.

It was a love song. When Rayshawn first heard it, he thought it would make a great ballad. But it wasn't that kind of love song. It was a love song to her Savior. One she hadn't thought about in a long time. And as the words flowed through her lips and crawled over her heart, she remembered when she used to have that kind of love. When God used to be her every breath, her every inspiration, her reason for living and being. When her life was so completely his that she couldn't tell where he started and she ended. She missed that feeling. That place of security, the safe haven of his love. She had wandered away from it, and she hadn't realized how cold it had been outside his love, until embers of it reached out to her through this song.

When her fingers stilled on the guitar, she had to close her eyes a moment, until the emotions welling up inside her subsided. When she finally looked up, Deacon's eyes were the first to meet hers, and as he looked at her, something there told her that he knew the real love behind her song.

"Okay," Kate said, letting out a deep breath. "Thank you again, JJ. We'll let you know—"

"You're in."

Four pairs of eyes stared at Deacon in surprise.

He shook his head as if trying to clear his thoughts. "I'm sorry. I know we're supposed to wait until after and decide together, but I already knew last night that I wanted you on my team, and after this"—he motioned to the guitar—"this just confirms it," he said. "Can you play electric?"

JJ nodded mutely.

"Then you're gonna fit right in with Sabrina. And maybe now we can get that girl band that I've been asking for."

"So . . . I'm in?" JJ asked, slipping off the stool.

Kate glanced over at Deacon, who nodded. A reluctant smile stretched her lips. "Well, you heard the man. You're in."

JJ jumped off the stool and squealed, "I'm in!"

Sabrina laughed, Andrew chuckled, and Kate rolled her eyes. But Deacon was grinning from ear to ear and so was JJ. She couldn't believe this was happening. Maybe she had been wrong. Maybe, just maybe, she was back in God's favor after all.

Chapter 12

She was standing by the nurses' station when he finally showed up. She almost missed him completely, thanks to her nurse friend, Janice, who had been talking her ear off for half an hour. But if it wasn't for Janice she wouldn't have figured out his schedule anyway, so she couldn't complain.

"Dr. Massri!"

He turned the corner and kept walking. But she wasn't letting him get away that easily. Grateful that she had chosen Converses that morning, she took off in a run-walk down the hospital corridor after him.

"Hey! Dr. Simon Massri," she called, drawing eyes to her. "I know you can hear me!"

She noticed someone say something to him. He suddenly stopped, then pulled earbuds out of his ears and turned around.

"Think you can get away from me? Nice try," JJ said, stopping dead in front of him, hands on her hips. "What's this about you leaving? How are you supposed to help Sheree through her pregnancy if you're not here?"

Sheree had shared with JJ the news about the doctor's potential departure the day after she got back from her Deacon Hill audition. With only two days before rehearsals for Deacon

Hill's tour started in full force, she knew she had little time to convince Dr. Massri to change his mind.

His mouth was slightly open, but he didn't answer. Just stared at her. Well, not so much her, but her crown. Then after what seemed like forever, he said, "Your hair..."

JJ blinked. "Excuse me?"

"Your hair... it was short"—he motioned to the mass of curls that haloed her face and escaped down her shoulders—"but now it's long again... like before... but..."

JJ folded her arms and let him hang himself trying to find words. He scratched his head in confusion and she shook her head. Clearly this mixed-race man didn't have many black women in his world.

His brow furrowed. "Didn't you cut it?"

"No, it was just a wig," JJ said with a grin. "It's more convenient for shows to have it that way. You just caught me in between visits to Tracy."

"Tracy?"

JJ rolled her eyes. "Never mind that. Can we get back to the subject at hand? You're leaving?"

He was still staring at her hair. JJ snapped her fingers above her head to grab his attention. She had never seen him act this strange before.

"Oh! Uh... yeah. I've been asked to go to Malawi to do physician-level training with nurses and health care staff who work in rural hospitals."

"So tell them you can't go," JJ said.

His left eyebrow shot up to his hairline.

"You can't just leave my sister like this."

He looked confused. "I thought she was your sister-in-law..."

"She needs you," JJ continued, ignoring his comment. "You're the one who realized something was wrong with her pregnancy and figured out that it was a placental abruption. Without that we might have lost my nephew."

"Look, I understand your concern," Simon said, going into physician-speaking-to-family mode. "But you have nothing to worry about. This is one of the best maternity wards in North

America, with some of the best OBs. Your sister will get nothing but the best care—"

"I'm not your patient. Stop patronizing me."

"I'm not."

"You are," JJ countered, hands on her hips. "And you know it. I know this is a decent hospital."

"Then you also know Mrs. Isaacs will be fine."

"I can't be sure of that unless you're here," JJ said.

Simon shrugged and began to back away. "I'm sorry. I've already made a commitment."

He turned and began to walk away, but JJ wasn't done yet.

"So change it," she said, following him down the hall. "Tell them you have an emergency. Tell them you'll come in three and a half months. Sheree will be due by then. As soon as the baby is born, you can take the next flight out."

He glanced across at her, eyebrows furrowed. "Is this how things work in your world? You just ask people to drop everything to do what you want and they say yes?"

"No," JJ said, stopping suddenly.

When he realized that she wasn't still walking with him, he stopped and turned around to look at her.

"In my world, I never ask anyone for anything," JJ said. "There aren't many people to ask anyway. But this is not for me, it's for Sheree. She's doing the best she can with this baby, but it's hard for her, hard for all of us."

JJ's gaze dropped, the emotion rushing through her making it hard for her to look at him. She had come to realize that the ties binding her family together had lately become nothing more than a single thin cord, and she was afraid that the weight of another tragedy, another disappointment, would break that cord and scatter them so far it would be impossible for them to reconnect once more. Sheree and Dean needed this baby to be okay for their marriage to have even a possibility of working. Sydney and Sheree needed this baby to be okay to cement their tentative truce of forgiveness. They all needed this baby so their family could be whole in ways it hadn't been for a long time. And JJ was afraid that might not happen if this man, who had more giftedness in his pinkie finger than all the hospital staff combined, didn't stick around.

"You can't go," she said, looking up at him. "Please."

Everything was all over her face. She could see it in his eyes as he looked at her, just like she could see him struggle with what she was asking him to do.

"You really love her, don't you."

Love? Sheree?

JJ had never thought about it. But now that she had...

She shrugged. "Yeah, I guess I do."

He tapped his clipboard against his fingers as he chewed on his lower lip thoughtfully. Full brown lips, with the slightest hue of pink underneath. JJ was surprised at how difficult she found it to pull her eyes away from his mouth. Then he turned his intense eyes on her and JJ lost her breath for a moment.

"You have somewhere to be right now?" he asked after a long moment.

She blinked, surprised at his question. "Uh, well, I was gonna run over to the studio to get some time in, then go do some work at my mother's shop..."

He glanced at his watch, then moved off down the hallway. "Come with me."

She scurried to catch up with him, his long legs making it a challenge.

"Where are we going?"

"Wait here," he answered as he ducked into an office. Through the glass window she saw him talk with someone she couldn't see. He laughed for a moment before handing over the clipboard and heading back to her.

"I need to go somewhere," he said, heading back the way they had come. "Come with me and I'll consider sticking around for the next few months."

JJ was confused. "Wait. Go with you? As in leave the hospital with you?"

He glanced at his watch again, prompting JJ to look at her own. It was barely after seven a.m.

"If we leave now, we should be back before nine."

She should ask more questions. Find out where they were going and for what purpose. Because truth be told, regardless of their history and their most recent re-acquaintance, she really did not know this man. How could she even consider going anywhere with him? Especially given how confused her emotions were around him?

"Okay, let's go," JJ said.

She tried to keep up with him as he took off down the corridor.

She really needed to start going to bed earlier.

JJ sat up with a start, momentarily disoriented.

Something was pressing against her chest. She reached up her hand to touch it. Seat belt? As she blinked, clearing the sleep from her eyes, she noticed the open road ahead of her. Nothing but fields on either side and not a house in sight. She looked across at the beautiful man sitting in the driver's seat, his profile highlighted by the morning sun, his long locks like thin ropes pulled back from his strong face. The morning's events came rushing back to her.

The sound of something instrumental whispered in her ears. Her eyes floated over to the console and, after observing the CD player going, widened when she saw the time: 9:21 a.m. She shrieked.

"I thought we weren't going far!" She sat forward suddenly, only to be forced back by the seat belt.

"We aren't," Simon said, his eyes still on the road.

"We've been driving for two hours!"

"We're almost there."

"Where is there? You said we would be back by nine!"

"Yeah. Nine p.m."

JJ felt another scream bubble up in her throat as momentary panic swept through her. "Simon! I have a life, a schedule. My boyfr—I mean manager, is going to be wondering where I am. What if they call me in for rehearsal?"

"It's a Sunday."

"My Sundays are very busy, mister."

"Look, if you want, I can have someone take you back, but you were the one who begged me to stay for your sister, and you agreed to help me out today as part of that deal."

"I didn't know helping you out would require me to go cross-country."

"Not across the country," Simon corrected. "Just a little out of town. But if that's too much for you, I can turn around. It's up to you, Judith."

She turned to look at him. Normally she preferred JJ, but something about the way his faint British accent wrapped around her name made her like it when he said it. Again, the control center in her brain reminded her that she did not know the person sitting next to her. But somewhere, in some irrational depth of her mind, she wanted to trust him, if for no other reason than to learn more about this intriguing man whom she had spent a whole year of her life thinking about. A year that could have stretched into two, had she not managed to convince herself she would never see him again. Sydney would definitely kill her for what she was about to say.

"Okay, fine," she said with a sigh. "But you still didn't answer my question. Where are we going? I don't think we've known each other long enough for you to be taking me long distance."

"But just long enough for you to know my schedule, right?" His narrowed eyes stole a glance at her. "How did you even know what time I started this morning?"

"Nurse tipped me off..."

Simon shook his head. "So much for confidentiality."

"Don't worry. I'm a special case. I used to volunteer there when I was in college. Plus I spent a lot of time in that hospital when my brother was transferred there last year."

JJ frowned as she remembered Dean. Simon noticed.

"This the same brother who's the father of your sister-in-law's baby?"

JJ nodded and looked out the passenger window. Simon whistled.

"Sounds like there's a story there."

JJ grunted. "You have no idea. Let's just say my family is better than TV." She glanced over at him then back out the window. "I don't even know why I'm telling you all this."

"'Course you do," Simon said with a roguish smile that gave her a peek into his personality. "I'm the man who saved your life."

"It was a panic attack!"

"There is some research that suggests prolonged panic attacks can have adverse cardiological effects that can lead to fatalities."

JJ scowled. "Show-off."

He chuckled. JJ liked the sound of his laugh. She turned her head to the window so he wouldn't see her smile.

"So you mentioned studio and manager," Simon said a few moments later. "You're a singer?"

"Yes," JJ answered. "An aspiring one, I guess. But maybe not so aspiring anymore, since I just landed a major contract."

"Congratulations," Simon said, a smile in his voice. "For your own record?"

"Not that, but almost as good," JJ said, her mouth spreading into a grin. "For a tour. I'll be a backing vocalist for a major R & B artist."

"Hmm," Simon murmured, nodding his head. "You sound excited."

"I am," JJ said, sitting up in her seat. "This is an amazing opportunity for me. I'll be meeting people in the industry who can help get me where I want to be."

"Well, good for you, Judith," he said. "When do I get to hear you sing?"

"When you tell me you'll stay and take over Sheree's care."

His lips quirked. "That's a high ticket price."

"But so worth it," she breathed in a husky tone. His eyebrows shot up and his head whipped around. She laughed at the surprised and curious expression on his face. She could have a lot of fun with Simon Massri.

"What about you, Mr. Big-Shot Physician?" JJ asked. "I never guessed I would see you in Canada. Not that I'm complaining, but it wasn't one of the places on your list of work locations. I would have remembered that."

"Would you?" Simon asked, just before he made a left turn onto a narrow two-lane road. "That was a long time ago."

"I have the memory of an elephant," JJ said proudly. "Great for learning other people's songs on the fly."

"Well, let's see it at work," Simon challenged. "What do you remember about me?"

The exact greenish gold of his eyes, the tiny scar right above his left eyebrow, the way his lips crooked up a little higher on the right when he smiled...

JJ cleared her throat and shook the unexpected thoughts from her head.

"Let's see," she began. "You were born in London, but your mom is actually Irish and your dad is Egyptian. You have lived all over the world because your family moved a lot. You have two brothers who live in London. You started out a GP but decided to specialize in maternal and newborn care. You love the outdoors, hate the winter, and hate cell phones even more. You've worked in India, Thailand, almost every country in Africa, Pakistan, Qatar, Brazil...and Ecuador?" She looked at him.

He grinned. "Yes, that is correct and I am impressed—"

"Wait, I'm not done," JJ said, cutting him off. "You're vegetarian, you've haven't owned a television since undergrad, but you've watched every episode of *ER*."

"And I now own the entire series on DVD," Simon said proudly.

JJ let out a laugh. "No way! All fifteen seasons?"

"All fifteen seasons."

"That's crazy." She paused. "But I will admit, when I got home I watched the first two seasons on DVD."

It was Simon's turn to laugh. "You're kidding."

"Nope, true story," JJ said. "And can you blame me? If the guy who doesn't own a TV loves the show, there must be something to it."

"And?" Simon probed.

JJ winced. "I tried, but I couldn't get into it."

Simon groaned.

"I'll admit season one was very good, and season two had some good episodes too. But I kind of got lost somewhere in season three."

Simon shook his head. "You should have stuck it out. It only got better."

"I don't know," JJ said, shaking her head. "It didn't help that my sisters couldn't get into it either."

"See, that's the problem—you had the wrong company. Now had I been around when you were watching it, I would have made sure you saw the beauty of it. Some things, you just have to hold out for a bit to get the best out of them."

"Maybe."

Holding out had not been JJ's forte. Especially not recently. And she was all too aware of that. Before she could fall too much deeper into her thoughts, Simon turned his Jeep Wrangler off the road and drove through two rusted-over metal posts that once could have been a gate. A long, smooth, paved road led them to a sprawling, single-level warehouse-like structure. It rested in the middle of acres of open, flat land that stretched beyond where JJ could see.

"Where are we?" JJ asked, looking around for signs of life. She was starting to regret her decision to go with Simon. This was the kind of place where a girl could get killed, have her body dumped, and not be found for days.

"Private airstrip," Simon answered.

Then, before JJ could question further, he pulled the Jeep around to the other side of the building and stopped short.

"We're here."

JJ didn't hear him. She was too busy staring at the two small planes lined up near what had to be a makeshift runway and the two others parked in the warehouse space that she now knew was a hangar.

Simon opened her door and helped her out of the Jeep.

"We'll be taking the blue one," he began. "It should be all fueled up, but I'm just going to go fill out the manifest and do a few checks to make sure. In the meantime, I'm going to need your help packing the supplies onto the plane."

Supplies? Plane? JJ's head was spinning. A few hours ago she was standing in the hospital in Toronto. Now she was in the middle of nowhere, about to get on a small aircraft that looked like it could fall apart with a strong enough gust of wind. This was not happening.

"Okay, Simon, I'm going to need you to start talking, right now, or I am taking your keys and driving myself back to Toronto."

"That's going to be a bit difficult, isn't it?" His voice floated to her from the back of the Jeep. "I mean, I know you have a great memory, but you slept through half the trip."

"I have a GPS on my phone," she shot back. "I can find directions."

She heard him snort. "Not from out here."

"Simon!"

He poked his head around the side and his brows furrowed when he saw the seriousness of her demeanor.

"I'm sorry." He stopped what he was doing and walked around the vehicle to where JJ was standing with her arms folded. "I should have told you before. We're going to a native reserve community a couple hours north of here, but it's fly-in only, so we have to take the plane."

"Why didn't we just fly in from Toronto?"

"Too expensive on gas and too much red tape."

"Why didn't you tell me this before I got into your car?"

He shrugged. "You didn't ask."

"Who's flying?"

He cracked a small smile.

She turned around and opened the door of the Jeep.

"No way, Simon Massri." She climbed in. "As far as I know, you are a doctor, not a pilot. Where is your license? You don't even live in Canada. How do you even know where you're going? And that plane does not look safe for carrying birds, much less people."

Simon took a step toward her, leaning his elbow against the open passenger window. "I assure you, the plane is safe," he began gently. "It's been used for just this purpose for years, without issue. I myself have been in this plane several times in the past few months and flown it to the exact reserve we're going to. Yes, I am a doctor, but I am also a trained pilot. It was a helpful skill when working with Doctors Without Borders. And if it will make you feel better, I will show you my license. It's in my bag in the back."

"Buddy, you can't just do this. You can't just take me somewhere I don't know and expect me to do something like this with you," JJ said, feeling her body begin to tense up. "We might have spent several hours stuck in an elevator together, and spent hours with each other over the past month and a half, but I don't know you enough to trust you like this."

"Judith—"

"You can't just put this on me at the last minute and expect me to be okay with it," she said, unable to control the rising volume of her voice. "This is not okay!"

"Judith."

"What?"

Simon grimaced at the sharpness in her tone and took a deep breath. "I'm sorry. You're right. I shouldn't have . . . I guess I just feel comfortable with you and sometimes I forget . . ."

He took another deep breath and turned away from her, squinting at some point to her left. When he finally looked at her his eyes were dark with remorse. "I'm sorry," he said simply. He closed the passenger door, shutting her in, then came around and opened the driver's side. "I'll take you back."

JJ watched him as he started the vehicle and did a U-turn to head back the way they came. She sighed. "Stop."

He slammed on the brakes so hard, JJ's purse fell off her lap. She turned to meet his expectant eyes and glared at him.

"Okay, I'll go with you this time," she said. "But you ever pull a stunt like this again . . ."

"I won't," Simon said, turning the Jeep around just as quickly as he had stopped. "But we have to hurry. They've been expecting me."

As if on cue, another vehicle, one much newer and nicer than Simon's, rounded the side of the hangar and two male passengers got out. They walked up to where Simon and JJ were parked.

"You got here quickly," a tall guy in aviator sunglasses said, nodding to Simon. He glanced curiously at JJ.

"Nigel, this is Judith; Judith, this is Nigel and his dad, Bob," Simon said, getting out of the Jeep and making introductions.

"You can just call me JJ," she said, getting out and walking around to shake both men's hands.

"Bob's gonna be our flight controller here. Nigel's coming with us to the reserve," Simon explained. Then he turned to the men. "We need to unpack and do the checks, and we don't have much time. Let's move."

JJ hadn't noticed the bags and cartons in the back of Simon's Jeep until he opened up the tailgate. Most of it looked like medical supplies, but there was also food and water among the load. Nigel had similar booty in his vehicle. Despite the extent of the cargo, they made quick work transporting it to the small craft. While Simon and Bob did the preflight checks, JJ chatted with Nigel. She found out that Nigel was also a doctor and had also been in the Doctors Without Borders program with Simon.

"So you left the program for Toronto while Simon was still in it?" JJ asked as she got into the back of the plane.

"Yup. I believe in Médecins Sans Frontières," Nigel said, the French name for the international organization rolling off his tongue easily. "But I'm not a lifer like our friend here. I don't know many people who are. Asking that man to stay in one place is almost like asking a fish to live out of water."

"How long have you guys known each other?" JJ asked.

"Oh, probably fifteen years," Nigel said as he slipped on a clunky headset and settled into the copilot's seat. "Met during the days at Cambridge. Both of us kids from somewhere else."

"I thought Simon was born in London," JJ said.

"Yeah, well, when you move around as much as he did, I guess you feel like you don't really belong anywhere," Nigel said. "Guess that's why it's so easy for him to move around so much. The man doesn't really have a home, you know? I think the seven years at Cambridge was the longest stretch he ever spent in one place."

Nigel flashed a grin back at her. "But you already know that, don't you?"

JJ frowned. "Why would you think that?"

"You're Elevator Girl."

JJ's mouth fell open. But before she could answer, Simon appeared at the door.

"All strapped in?"

She nodded, still too dumbfounded to answer. He checked her seat belt, then slid the door shut and got into the cockpit. The rush of wind grew louder as the plane's propellers began to spin, and JJ was glad for the earphones that would help the three of them hear each other throughout the flight. She heard Bob give instructions over the airwaves and Simon answer back. The craft rattled and shook as it began its first movements down the runway and JJ gripped her seat, her stomach churning. She was beginning to wonder if her first impressions of the plane were indeed right.

She felt the wheels of the aircraft run over the bumps on the strip as it went faster and faster. She held her breath and squeezed her eyes shut, waiting for it to all fall apart, and then, almost unexpectedly, they were moving up. She felt the wheels lift off the ground and the journey smooth out as they glided up in the air.

"You can open your eyes."

Simon's voice came clearly into JJ's ears, as if he was sitting right next to her, and her eyes popped open. She caught him watching her through the rearview mirror at the front. She couldn't see his whole face but caught the crinkling at the corners of his eyes and knew that he was laughing at her.

"I'm still waiting to see that license, Simon!"

It took a while for JJ to release her iron grip on the seat, but her desire to take in the view as they glided over lush, uninhabited northern Ontario land helped to speed the process along. JJ had never had a view like this. Even when she flew across the country, they didn't fly as low as she was soaring now. She could see the tops of regal pines, the sharp edges of stone-faced mountains, and the white-capped peaks that still held layers of snow. All this beauty in her province and she had never seen it. It took her breath away.

"Amazing," JJ murmured.

"Like something out of a magazine, isn't it?" Simon said.

"I never knew Ontario was so beautiful," JJ said. "It's like an untouched wilderness."

"Is that the birth of a nature lover I hear?" Nigel asked.

"This is nature like I've never seen before."

The ride seemed short. Almost too soon Simon was announcing their descent, and the landing strip for their destination came in sight. JJ braced herself for the contact with the runway, but it was smoother than she expected. Okay. Maybe Simon did have some skills after all.

"So, what's the verdict?" Simon asked as the plane slowed to a stop.

"Seven out of ten," JJ answered as she released her seat belt. "There's always room for improvement."

They didn't have to do unloading at this end of the trip. They were met on the tarmac by a mixed group, including native Canadian First Nations people and several others, who JJ soon learned were members of the support group that Simon was a part of. Several trucks took them away from the airport into the reserve town.

JJ was wedged between Nigel and Simon for the ride, but she could still see out the window, and what she saw shocked her. This was not so much a town as a collection of standing structures; some shedlike buildings made of wood panels and sheets of zinc, others tentlike structures made of tarps, and yet others traditional teepees. None looked stable. None looked like a safe place to live. And yet there were people sitting on uneven steps constructed from wooden slats, standing around in front of their living spaces, peeping through window cutouts where there may or may not have ever been glass. They were definitely far away from Toronto.

They arrived at the health center in less than twenty minutes. It was by far the best-looking building she had seen since they landed, but nothing near as good as the worst walk-in clinic JJ had seen in Toronto. This time she helped carry the medical supplies inside. People were already lingering outside the doors, waiting for someone to come. JJ didn't know why Simon had asked her to come with him. She had no medical knowledge beyond basic first aid, and most of the people here would require more than that. But she was here and she would be useful.

She turned to Simon. "What do you need me to do?"

He ran a hand over his dreads then looked around. "Help Marianne with intake," he said. "We'll need to find the files for everyone who is here and make files for the first-timers. There's an intake form that you can go through with them. For those who don't speak English, Marianne will help you."

"Okay," JJ said, turning to go. Before she did, however, he grabbed her arm and pulled her back.

He glanced around before lowering his voice. "Are you going to be okay with this?"

She met his gaze. "I'll be fine once I get working."

They worked for hours. JJ got to know Marianne, a quiet, middle-aged woman with long, silky dark hair and kind, generous eyes. She reminded JJ of Diana from the audition. She told JJ that she had grown up in that very reserve, moved away, and then come back to work there as a nurse. She had three daughters and four granddaughters. One of her granddaughters had committed suicide the year before. She said it as if it was a tragedy similar to having one's garden of flowers die from frost—sad but not entirely uncommon. JJ soon learned that indeed that was the case. Everyone in the reserve had a family member or knew someone who had died this way.

When the crowd finally cleared, JJ stood up and stretched. She glanced at her watch and saw that it was almost two p.m.

"Is that really everyone?" she asked Marianne.

"Oh no," Marianne said, putting some files that Nigel and Simon had returned back into the filing cabinet. "That is just the morning group. After five p.m, when work is over, there will be more."

"Wow," JJ said, sitting back down. "Is it like this every day?"

"Every day?" Marianne chucked. "No, my dear. The doctors only come here once a week. Sometimes once every two weeks, depending on if they have time. Before Dr. Massri, we only had one doctor. Then Dr. Massri came and brought his friend and now we have three, though the other one was not here today. We are so blessed to have them. God has smiled on us."

JJ's eyes opened wide. "Are you a Christian, Marianne?"

Marianne smiled. "I believe there is a God. I believe that he is everywhere, and that he is in everything— even in us, if we let him. The problem is many of us do not let him. Or we let him only when it is convenient for us. But we must accept the way of God always, even when it does not follow a straight path."

Marianne might have expressed it differently, but the concept was one JJ was familiar with. God's ways were not always easy to understand, but trusting him was our best option. But JJ had been struggling with the trusting part lately. Especially the trusting part that required her to wait on God to do what he promised for her. But why should it be a challenge? Her needs—if she could call them that—were nothing like the needs of the people she had met in the last few hours. She knew that. Marianne knew that. And if Marianne could live in this place and believe in trusting God the way she did, why was it such a challenge for JJ?

Chapter 13

Simon watched JJ eat the sparse meal without hesitation as she chatted with the young woman who had helped serve them. It was lunchtime, and the team had traveled a short distance from the clinic to a place Marianne knew where they could have lunch. The day was warm enough so they sat outside at picnic tables, eating and enjoying the weather in the few hours' break they had before the crowd would turn up again at the clinic.

"See something you like?"

Simon tore his eyes away from JJ to glance at Nigel.

"I see you've regained your energy," Simon said, smiling at his friend as he dodged his question. "Been a while since you worked so hard?"

"You got that right," Nigel said, putting his fork on his plate and stretching. "Feels like MSF days all over again."

Simon turned around, resting his back against the table. "Those were good days."

"They were," Nigel agreed, fishing a toothpick out of his top shirt pocket. "But not days I can go back to. I'm too old for all of that. A brother's gotta settle down, start a family. Forty is right around the corner."

"Maybe for you, old man," Simon said with a chuckle. "Forty is still a ways off for me. And in any case, forty's not old. We have doctors in their midfifties with us at MSF."

"Yeah, but that's too late to start having kids," Nigel said. "I need to be able to run around with my little rug rats while the ligaments in my knees still work."

"Does that mean you're ready to give up your player card?" Simon asked.

"Hold up now," Nigel said, glancing at his friend. "I didn't say all that was gonna happen right away. It's a transition, my friend."

Nigel glanced over at JJ then back at Simon. "You, however, look like you've already traded in yours."

"It only looks that way 'cause I never had one."

"Either way, looks like Elevator Girl has got you by the nose."

"Elevator Girl?" Simon asked.

"Yeah," Nigel said. "The one from that elevator incident in Paris?" He shook his head. "See, that's what you get for staying in those cheapo roach motels. I keeping telling you, Massri, you're a doctor. They pay you those big paychecks for a reason, so you can stay in the Marriotts and Crown Plazas of this world and avoid anything that doesn't have an international name. If that had happened in the Sheraton, do you know how much you could have sued them for, bruh?"

Simon ignored his friend's rant. Despite the fact that he had been close friends with Nigel since his undergrad days, the men were polar opposites. While they both appreciated the opportunities for humanitarian work their jobs allowed them, Simon had always suspected that Nigel did it to assuage his conscience for all the other non-humanitarian things he did, like the revolving door of women he was involved with, the huge sums of money he spent on entertaining himself, and the scant regard he gave to his family—particularly his devoutly Catholic parents. In fact, Simon had given the issue a lot of thought and concluded that Nigel remained so invested in their friendship because Simon's own Christianity—though not of the Catholic type—reminded Nigel of his family. Being with Simon allowed him to support some of the values of his family without his parents' constant pressure to be religious.

"Anyway, I've pieced it together and I am pretty sure that Miss Hot-Bod over there is the girl from that elevator, the one you were sweatin' for months after—"

"I was not sweating her."

"And the one you just ran into the other day," he said. "Now, I don't know what you told her to get her on a plane with you, but..."

"I just told her the truth," Simon said.

Nigel glanced at his friend through the side of his eye. "I've never seen you bring anyone else out here. In fact, I've never seen you bring any other female anywhere since you flew into Canada. So something must be special about this one."

"Stop trying to stir up something," Simon said. "Don't you have enough to worry about with your own love life? For all you know, your girlfriend might be burning your clothes in your car as we speak. Wasn't that what the last one did?"

"And you know what I learned from that, bruh? No one gets the key to my place but me."

Simon laughed at Nigel's light chatter. Their conversation was trivial, because it was the only way to survive trips like this. If they focused on everything that was wrong, all the patients they hadn't been able to help completely, all the people they weren't able to see, it would kill their spirit. Better to keep the mood light so they could make it to the end.

When Nigel wondered off to catch a nap in the back of the truck, Simon went in search of JJ. He found her in an open field across the street from where they had eaten. She had left her jacket as well as her shoes and socks in a pile near the edge of the field, and in the distance he could see her trotting barefoot through the grass, the wind blowing her hair and the grass brushing her legs. At one point she stopped and held her face up to the sun, her eyes closed, and Simon felt his breath hitch in his throat. Okay, so maybe Nigel had a point after all.

"Judith."

He knew everyone called her JJ, but he couldn't get used to it. The first time he'd met her that fateful day in Paris, she'd told him her name was Judith, and she would always be Judith to him.

She looked over at him and smiled a lazy smile, then twisted her head to the left in an invitation. Before his mind even formulated an acceptance, his feet were moving in her direction.

He forced himself to walk easily over to where she had plopped down on the grass. When he reached her, he followed suit. For a while they sat in comfortable silence, the cool afternoon wind blowing over both of them, bringing with it only the sound of the leaves rustling in the trees and the call of a bird or two. Simon sucked in a deep, cleansing breath. You didn't get this kind of quiet in the city.

"How long have you been in Canada?" JJ asked.

Simon let out the breath he had inhaled. "About six months now."

"And how long have you been coming here?"

"The same," he said. "My dad told me about some of the needs on the reserves and connected me with Marianne."

"Your dad?" JJ asked, looking at him. "Is he a doctor too?"

Simon smiled. "Yes. But not the medical type." He paused, squinting at her for a moment. "My dad works with the United Nations."

He watched as all the pieces came together in her mind.

"That's why you moved around so much growing up?"

"Yes," he said.

"Do you think that's why you ended up doing the kind of work you do? You know, working with MSF?"

Simon tilted his head to the side to consider her question. "I've thought about it a lot over the years," he began slowly. "I think some of it must have to do with how I grew up, traveling around the world, seeing the unglamorous side of it, thanks to the job my parents did. But then, so did my brothers, and they are so different. One's an accountant. The other's a personal trainer."

"True," JJ said. "But you also are the oldest. You experienced a lot more of that life than they did."

She did have a point. Simon was eight years older than his closest brother, and ten years older than the next. He still remembered a lot of his life before they were born, a lot of the places his parents had lived when he was a little boy. He remembered the nanny who took care of him when they lived in what was now Myanmar. He remembered when she stopped coming to work and no one explained to him why. He also remembered how he'd had to leave all his toys behind the night they left.

He remembered going to his father's hometown in Egypt and meeting his father's cousins. They had looked different from him, lived differently, and had not had a lot of the things he had been used to, growing up. He remembered the arguments his dad had with his uncle there. They never went back again. His brothers had never met that side of the family. As an adult now, he understood so much more than he had then.

"Our childhood really influences the life we choose as adults, doesn't it?" Simon said.

JJ nodded. "It does. It always makes me wonder what choice we really have in who we become. After all, if our parents raise us in a certain setting or under certain beliefs, isn't it almost inevitable that those are the beliefs we are going to have? The things we are going to desire? It's almost as if they chose for us."

"I think so, to some extent," Simon said. "But if they teach us to be critical thinkers, then, though we might have grown up with a certain set of values, being able to think and assess for ourselves should open our minds up to appreciate new and maybe better ways of thinking and being."

"I am surprised that you think that way," JJ said, looking at him. "Given all the places you have been and all the people you must meet. How many people really end up being different from the way they were raised?"

Simon didn't have much to say there. The evidence seemed to suggest that people were more a product of their environment than anything else. But he couldn't accept that argument as definitive, because that would mean that people couldn't change. And they could. He had seen that.

"Take me, for example. I grew up going to church every week, having devotions with my parents every day. Even after my parents split up, my mother never faltered in her belief in the power of God. There was never room for me to believe anything else, so why would I? But what if I hadn't grown up that way? What if I had grown up in a home where my parents were atheists, or where belief didn't matter one way or another? I probably wouldn't have a relationship with God at all. Who would, under those circumstances?"

Simon shrugged. "I would."

He watched her turn to look at him in surprise. He met her gaze without faltering.

"I never grew up in a religious home," he admitted. "My mother grew up Catholic. She believed God exists but thought that being a good person was enough. My dad? Complete atheist."

JJ's jaw fell. "But how? They dedicate their lives to an organization committed to helping people. How can they live like that and not believe?"

Simon raised an eyebrow. "How? Lots of people do. My parents happen to be two of them."

He could see that she was fascinated. She had twisted around, her body now facing him completely, her deep brown eyes probing him like a newly discovered mystery.

"But you told me you believe. That your relationship with God is the center of your life..."

"It is."

He watched her squint at him in confusion. "How?"

How did he come to know Christ? That was a long story and a hard one to tell because in some ways it was incomplete.

"Short version? I got to know Christ during medical school, and I had experiences not long afterward that confirmed his existence for me," Simon said. "I read the Bible, critically at first, and tried to prove him through everything he said, and found him to be true."

JJ started at him, rapt. "And that was it? That was enough for you?"

He chuckled. "*That* took a number of years. And like I said, it's still incomplete. There are still some things"—he looked away from her—"some things I struggle with."

JJ shook her head. "Wow. I never would have guessed."

Simon rubbed his hands together self-consciously as JJ looked at him, her eyes glowing. It was like she was seeing him for the first time. It was unnerving.

"So what did your parents think?" JJ asked.

He rested back on his palms. "I guess they thought it was a phase at first. But eventually they came to accept it. They both are very open-minded people. How else could a white woman from high society Ireland and a dark-skinned Egyptian from the slums of Cairo ever end up together?"

JJ smiled. "Sounds like a good story."

"It is, and they love to tell it. The summary is, they met at the UN, they met on an assignment, fell in love, and got married. After my youngest brother was born, my mom retired."

"So your parents are here in Canada now. Is that why you're here? To be close to them?" JJ asked.

Simon shrugged. "My mother sure hopes so. She has many plans for me."

JJ chuckled. "Plans to marry you off and have her some grandbabies?"

"Are all mothers like this?" Simon asked with a laugh.

"Most," JJ said with a smile. "My mom is really looking forward to the birth of her first grandchild. It may have been unexpected, but the occasion won't be any less joyful. Speaking of which"—JJ smiled sweetly at him—"can I assume then that you will be staying with us, Dr. Massri?"

"You know what you do when you assume."

"I am hoping this time the rhyme will be less true."

Simon got to his feet and held out a hand for JJ. "The day is still young, Miss Isaacs," he said, pulling her to her feet.

She squeezed his hand before letting go. "Indeed it is."

Simon watched as she turned and headed back the way they had come. He felt his stomach twist as he watched her hair toss in the wind, the sunlight bounce golden rays off her skin. The day might be young, but he already knew how it was going to end—with JJ getting her way and him being led around by his nose. He closed his eyes. Lord, what had he gotten himself into?

Chapter 14

The hospital hallways seemed longer than usual to JJ as she raced through them to the maternity ward. It had taken her almost half an hour to get to the hospital after she got the call saying something was wrong with Sheree and the baby. Thankfully, she had just stepped out of rehearsal or she might have missed the call completely.

"What happened?" JJ asked when she was finally face-to-face with the doctor handling Sheree's emergency.

"Your sister came in with bleeding and pain a few hours ago," the doctor began. "We did some tests and noted that the baby's heart rate was elevated and that your sister's condition was deteriorating fast. Based on what we note in her file, we think that there might be close to total placental abruption. The best option right now for the health of both baby and mother is a C-section delivery."

"C-section?" JJ's head was spinning. "She was fine when I left her this morning, she just had a checkup last week. How can this be happening?"

"These things can turn quickly." He gave her a sympathetic look. "I know it's a lot to take in and it's tough to make a decision like this so quickly, but you are the only one of her two emergency contacts whom we could reach. She's been out for a while and she may not be awake and lucid in time to decide for herself. You have to make the decision on the surgery."

"But how can she handle a C-section now if she's losing so much blood?" JJ protested. "Plus she's not even seven months pregnant. What about the baby's chances of survival?"

She saw the doctor exchange a look with Janice

"There is some risk, but if the placenta has separated completely, then the chances for the baby's survival more than double with surgery. We will take all the precautions necessary and have blood units available."

"No," JJ said, shaking her head. "There must be some other option."

"Ms. Isaacs, I know the surgery sounds frightening but—"

"Where is Dr. Massri?" JJ asked. For what felt like the hundredth time in the past week and a half, she was very glad that he had decided to stay.

The doctor and Janice exchanged another look.

"JJ," Janice began, touching her arm. "Dr. Brighton is very qualified..."

"Do we need to decide now?" JJ asked.

The doctor placed his hands on his hips. "We need to make a decision today about what will happen, but, no, we can keep her stable for a while."

"Then you keep her stable and you find me Dr. Massri," JJ demanded, fixing her gaze on Janice. "He's the one who's been taking care of her. He's the one I want to talk to."

The nurse sighed. "He's off duty today but—"

"Please," JJ said, pleading with her eyes.

"Okay, okay, I'll see if we can track him down," Janice said, holding up her palms as she backed away and hurried down the hallway.

JJ looked at the doctor, who was fully prepped for surgery, and ignored the annoyed expression on his face.

"Can I see her?"

He shook his head and let out a grunt. "We'll move her out of the OR into a room, get her stabilized, and then bring you to her."

JJ nodded. "I'll be waiting."

Fifteen minutes later, another nurse came and led JJ to Sheree's room. As the doctor had mentioned, Sheree was unconscious. Tubes and wires crisscrossed her body and connected to a drip, and various machines surrounded her bed. Pulling the lone chair in the room up to the bedside, JJ sat down and sighed.

"Boy, you sure don't do anything the easy way, do you?" she said to her sister-in-law as she leaned back in the chair.

"Well, you know me," a weak voice responded. "Go big or go home."

JJ sprang from her chair. "Sheree! You're awake!"

Sheree slowly turned her head toward JJ and offered a weak smile. "Yeah, guess I am."

"Oh, thank God," JJ said, sinking onto the side of the bed. "I've been going out of my mind with worry since they called me and told me an ambulance took you to the hospital. How are you feeling?"

"Sore, weak, and ready. Feels like this baby is about to pop out." She winced as she tried to pull herself up.

"Hey, take it easy," JJ said, putting an arm on Sheree's to still her movements. "Let me call a nurse."

"No," Sheree said, grabbing JJ's arm before she could reach the call button. "Just help me lift this bed..."

"I don't know if you should be sitting up," JJ said, surveying Sheree and the cords snaking from her arms, chest, and belly. "They almost sent you into surgery. Just relax, okay? Simon will be here in a minute."

Sheree sighed. "Fine." She leaned back, giving up her pursuit of the button to adjust the bed. "But only if you entertain me by telling me how you went from *Dr. Massri* to *Simon.*"

Even in her weakened state she managed to smirk at JJ.

"He's still Dr. Massri," JJ corrected. "And we've just been coordinating about your care, which we will apparently be doing a lot now that you made me an emergency contact without telling me."

Sheree waved JJ's stern look away. "Ain't nobody talking about that. Has he asked you out yet?"

"What?" JJ protested. "Of course not."

Their little adventure out of town was not a date. And she had barely had contact with him since.

"Well, don't slouch, honey. You can ask him out too," Sheree countered.

JJ laughed. "First of all, I do not do that. Secondly, Dr. Massri is not interested in me."

"JJ, please. I have seen the way that man looks at you. He is definitely interested."

"It's not what you think," JJ said. She paused, considering whether she should mention her past connection to Simon. She hadn't even told her sisters yet that he was the man she had met in Paris. It would just complicate things way too much, and she didn't need that right now.

"Okay, spit it out then."

"Sheree, you should be focused on your health right now, not on some imagined thing you think is going on between me and your OB," JJ said, fussing with Sheree's covers.

"JJ, I'm lying in a hospital bed, bleeding on and off, not sure if I am going to be able to carry my child to term. The doctors could walk in here right now and say that I need to have a C-section. Just thinking about the risks to my child, being born two months premature, is enough to get my heart rate up."

JJ looked up when she caught the serious tone in Sheree's voice.

"So if I make up something between you and Dr. Massri, it's only to distract myself from the less appealing reality of this situation," Sheree said. "And can you really blame me?"

JJ sat down on the chair beside Sheree's bed and closed her eyes. "You're not making it up."

"Spill! Immediately!"

"Only if you calm down," JJ said quickly and sternly. "If I hear that heart monitor speed up or you get overexcited..."

"Okay, okay, I promise," Sheree said with a sigh, but her eyes sparkled in anticipation.

JJ sighed also. "And you cannot breathe a word of this to anyone here, especially not around Simon."

"Quit stalling," Sheree hissed. "By the time you get started, he'll be back."

"Okay, fine." JJ glanced over at the door before she started. "My last year of college, five years ago, I did a study-abroad program in Paris. It was like a French immersion thing, learn the language and learn about clothing, textile, and design in one of the fashion capitals of the world—"

"Yeah, yeah, go on."

"Can you not rush me?"

"Well, you're taking forever."

"It's my story!"

"Okay, sorry," Sheree said. "No more interruptions."

"So anyway, I spent the year in Paris and it was great. I had a couple weeks between when classes ended and when I planned to leave, so I decided to go traveling outside Paris with some friends. The day before our departure, I sent my luggage ahead to the airport and spent the night in a hotel in Paris, planning to go to the airport the next day."

JJ sighed as the memories of that day began to come back to her. "I remember I was rushing that morning because I was running late. I didn't even notice him in the elevator. I just remember the sound when it stopped. It was this horrible grinding sound like metal against metal, then the lights blinked and we stopped moving. I remember I pressed every button. Nothing happened. He tried to get a signal on his phone, but there was no signal in the elevator. We tried the elevator phone; it didn't work. The only thing that worked was the little button that you are supposed to press when there's a problem—you know, the one that sets everything ringing but doesn't actually do anything? Yeah, that one."

JJ took a deep breath. "That's when I started to panic. I hate elevators, Sheree. Always have. It's just something about that small space that I can't deal with, and in Paris—" She shook her head. "Paris elevators are barely bigger than upright coffins."

"So what happened?"

"It felt like I was having a heart attack. My chest started tightening, I couldn't think, I couldn't breathe. I was in the corner like a baby. I felt like I was going to die. And then... he saved me."

"He, who?"

JJ looked at Sheree knowingly. When she woman's eyes widened, she knew she got it.

"Simon?"

JJ nodded. "He calmed me down, got me breathing, got me through the whole thing. He was the man in the elevator, who I never noticed until I needed him." She bit her lip. "I don't even remember everything he did. But I do remember that he prayed for me. It was crazy. This man, who I had just met moments earlier, prayed over me like I was the most important thing in his life." JJ shook her head. "I can't even describe what it was like. I just know I felt... safe. I've never felt like that with a stranger ever before in my life."

"And then what?"

JJ sighed as if reliving the experience all over. "It was like a weight lifted off me. Like I forgot why I was so panicked in the first place. And then he kept me distracted, talking to me about almost everything. We talked about faith, life, what he was doing in Paris, what I was doing in Paris. We were there for hours, and at the end I felt like... like I knew him."

"So what happened when you got out? Did you go for coffee? Dinner? Anything?"

JJ shook her head. "No. There was so much chaos when they finally got us out. Everybody was outside waiting. The fire department, the police, the ambulance, lots of hotel personnel, even a news team. We got separated in the fray. The hotel staff felt so bad, they covered my charges and got me a car for the airport. I missed my original flight but managed to get a red-eye out." JJ shrugged. "It was my last day in Paris. I never saw him again."

"Until now."

JJ sighed. "Yes, until now. There, are you happy now? You have all of it."

Sheree stared at her. "You know what this means, right?"

JJ pursed her lips at Sheree. "And what would that be?"

"That the two of you were obviously meant to find each other!" Sheree said. "You have to explore this, see where it goes. This is fate!"

JJ got up and stretched. "Sheree, stop."

"This man saved your life! How sexy is that? And I know you like him, JJ. You get this wide-eyed, doe-in-the-headlights look every time he walks into the room. You hang on his every word—"

"I do not!"

"I thought it was a bit wonky at first, but now I know why."

"Whatever," JJ said with a laugh. "You're a bit wonky. I can't believe a hard-core girl like you could be such a romantic."

"Hey, ghetto girls can have a soft side too!"

They were both laughing when the door opened. However, the pensive look on Simon's face when he walked in cut it short. JJ's eyes roamed over him involuntarily. He looked dishevelled, his hair barely tied back, his skin bronzed as if he had spent most of the morning outdoors. He wasn't even wearing a white jacket or scrubs, just some track pants and a white T-shirt, which he somehow managed to make look amazing.

"Ladies," he said, stepping into the room. "Tell me what happened."

"She came in a couple hours ago with bleeding," JJ said. "The doctors called and told me to get over here immediately."

"They want me to have a C-section," Sheree said, her voice unsteady. "But I'm only seven months. My baby's not ready."

She tried to look brave, but Sheree was doing a terrible job of disguising the depth of her worry, and JJ could see it.

"You have lost a lot of blood, which can be dangerous for both you and the baby," Simon said, getting straight to the heart of the matter. "We're going to start you on a transfusion to bring you back up to safe levels. But I am worried that we may not be able to manage this on an outpatient basis anymore."

"What do you mean?" JJ asked, confused.

"I mean that if there is another incident like this, where Sheree and the baby are in distress, we will have to perform a C-section if we want to save them both." He sighed. "I'm going to have to put you on complete bed rest and have you admitted here so we can closely observe you. Dr. Brighton was not wrong in suggesting a C-section. Most doctors would already have you in the OR. But I want to see that baby develop as much as possible before we bring him or her into the world."

His brows knotted as he considered the two women. "Can I get you both to agree to this?"

JJ looked over at Sheree, who sighed tiredly before nodding. "Whatever it takes to bring my baby safely into this world."

Simon's face relaxed for the first time since he had stepped into the room. "That's good to hear," he said.

Sheree nodded, but JJ wasn't sure the woman believed what Simon was saying. She was wringing the bed sheets tightly, a look of worry all over her face. Simon seemed to notice it also, because he put down his charts and came to sit on the edge of Sheree's bed.

"Hey, it's going to be okay," he said gently, squeezing her hand. "We had a bit of a scare this morning, but we are monitoring you and the baby and you are both doing okay. Not as well as we'd like, but okay. I suspect that once we get that transfusion going, things will start to improve. Furthermore, having you here means that we can catch anything going wrong as soon as it happens. This is a good thing for you and the baby."

Sheree nodded. "I know, I know. I just..." She trailed off, and JJ felt the pressure on her hand as Sheree squeezed.

"It's okay," JJ said. "I'm here. And I'll be here through all of it. All of us are going to come through this. I promise."

JJ knew she shouldn't make promises she couldn't keep, but she wanted Sheree to know she was not alone. No matter what happened, someone would be there with her.

"They're going to come by and put in the IV anytime now," Simon said. "But I need you to rest, give your body time to rebuild its strength."

Sheree nodded and settled back in the bed, seemingly a bit more relieved.

"I'm gonna go make arrangements for your being admitted," JJ said. "I'll be back in a bit."

JJ followed Simon outside. Once the door to Sheree's room closed and they were a few feet away, she grabbed his arm.

"How is she really?" she asked, concern gripping her heart in a vise.

"Supremely blessed," Simon said with a shake of his head. "I don't even know how she is still alert and focused with her red cell count that low. Do you know if she has been taking on too much at home?"

"She's been mostly resting," JJ said. "But God alone knows what she does when we're not there. She's not used to depending on others, you know?" She bit her lip. "I'm actually a little relieved that she's being admitted. I'm afraid of what might happen in the next couple days when I'm not there to check up on her. My sisters try, but their lives are crazy. Plus none of us has ever had kids, so we have no idea what we should be doing."

Simon smiled. "Don't worry. You're doing fine." He paused. "So you're going away?"

"The tour starts next week, so I'll be all over the States," JJ said. "I should be back in time for the delivery though. I don't want to miss that."

He nodded as he looked down. It seemed to JJ like there was something he would say, something he wanted to say, but nothing came. He was about to turn and head off when she grabbed his arm again.

"Can you do me a favor?" she asked. When he looked at her curiously she dug into her purse and pulled out a business card. Turning it over, she wrote her cell number on the back. "Can you call me and let me know how she's doing?" she asked timidly as she held out the card. "I know you're super busy. But I don't need long summaries. Just an update every couple of days so I know that she's doing okay. It would mean so much..."

"Sure," he said, taking the card even as his eyes pierced through her. "It's no problem, Judith. I'll call you."

She didn't know why his words sent a shiver through her. Why the thought of her cell phone ringing with Simon on the other end made butterflies swarm in her belly. This was only about Sheree, right? Nothing else. She just wanted to make sure that she kept her promise to be there for her sister-in-law, who had somehow managed to sneak into her heart.

And yet, as she stood in the hallway as he walked away, watching him tuck her card into his pocket and check to make sure it was all the way in, she couldn't help but look forward to the first time he kept his promise to her.

Chapter 15

"Ladies and gentlemen, are you ready!"

The screams reverberated through JJ as she stood waiting behind the curtain. Her heart was beating like a drum, pumping hot, electrified blood through her veins. Her fingers slid over the smooth surface of the guitar, idly tracing her initials engraved in the body. She tingled with an exquisite blend of release and tension. This was it. Her first official night on Deacon Hill's ten-city *Satisfied* tour. Their first of twenty or more live performances starting in Los Angeles and ending early September in Toronto. Was she ready? She had no idea. One thing she knew, however, was that this moment, standing on stage at the Staples Center on this hot night in the last week of July, would be burnt into her memory forever.

The curtain went up, the lights hit them full blast, and the LA crowd screamed. JJ met Kya's eyes and they both grinned. The woman she had labeled Miss Cell Phone had become her fellow band member and second on guitar. Her attitude had come along with her for the tour, and that had already put her at odds with JJ. It made JJ all the more glad that Diana had also made the cut. Sabrina, the keyboard player at their audition, was fairly supportive and gave good leadership to the band when she wasn't pissed off about something. But Diana was the only one JJ could consider a friend. Through the deadly rehearsal schedule, the late nights on the tour bus, and the drama that sometimes went down behind the scenes, JJ knew she could count on Diana to be genuine. It didn't change the way she related to the others, however. At the end of the day, they were members of Deacon Hill's female band She-La and they were all in it together. If they wanted to make it through the tour, they would have to put aside their different personalities and perform as one. So far, the music had helped with that. No matter how they bickered off-stage, onstage they were unified. Just like tonight.

Over the crowd, JJ managed to hear Diana give the count with her sticks. Sabrina followed the timing on vocals.

"One, two, three, *four*!"

Diana came in strong and confident on the drums and cymbals, followed by the other women. Kya stepped forward with the vocals for the hook in "Satisfied," the headlining song for the tour. They had practiced that song so much that JJ could perform it blindfolded with earplugs, in her sleep. The other women fell in with the harmony. The whole thing went as smooth as butter.

"And now, the man you've all been waiting for, three-time Grammy-award winner, Deacon Hill!"

JJ didn't think the crowd could get any louder, but when Deacon stepped onstage, the screams jumped a few decibels. As she watched him, she couldn't help but smile. That man was a performer like no other. He never stopped moving once he got onstage and his energy seemed boundless.

Performing was not like rehearsal. Rehearsal was long, tedious, and painful. But performance was fast, electrifying, and exhilarating. The minutes felt like seconds and they flew through the first half of the show. JJ had never taken drugs, but she imagined this was what being high felt like. Being onstage was nothing like she had ever experienced before. And being onstage with Deacon Hill was miles away from singing with Jayla Grey. When you went from crowds of hundreds to crowds of thousands, there was no comparison.

"Oh my God, that was amazing!" JJ screamed to Diana as

they ran offstage after Deacon's encore. They laughed and hugged each other as well as the other members of the band. Even Sabrina-too-cool-for-school was grinning from ear to ear.

"You guys were awesome," Sabrina said, hugging all of them. "I am so proud of you."

"Proud of *us*," Diana corrected. "We all rocked tonight, including you."

"I think we deserve to celebrate, ladies!" Kya announced.

Sabrina nodded in agreement. "I'm all about that! Get your stuff. I think all of us are heading out on the town tonight."

"Okay, just let me change, and I'll meet you guys out back," JJ said.

"Change for what?" Kya asked. "We look hot. These dresses look like the one Rihanna wore at that club in Paris after she ditched Chris Brown."

"These dresses look like the lingerie I bought my sister for her honeymoon, put through a shredder," JJ said dryly. "I'm changing."

She left the other girls laughing at the scowl on Kya's face and headed to the dressing room. She had barely adjusted to the wardrobe requirements of the music industry. All her clothes had suddenly become tighter, shorter, and more transparent, all because—according to Rayshawn—she needed to look the part. Most of it she could handle, but some of it had been a challenge to her values. However, from what she had seen so far, the Deacon Hill tour wardrobe would require her to stretch them even further.

Just one more thing she needed to get used to. But she could handle all of it for this amazing opportunity.

What she couldn't handle was the tour-style partying that had gone down even before they started their first show, and that was about to go down tonight. JJ had experienced a bit of it two nights earlier, and she was still reeling from the experience. Alcohol indulgence at insane amounts, pill popping, magic cigarettes. Anything you could imagine, it was going on. JJ had barely lasted fifteen minutes before she made some excuse to go home. As she changed into something she could sit in, she considered opting out of this evening's expedition also. But it was too early to start acting like a loner on tour. So she would do what she had done the night before: stay fifteen minutes then make up some excuse to leave.

She applied some lip gloss and stuffed all her clothes and cosmetics into her bag. She was barely into week one. They had seven more weeks to go. JJ hoped she could survive it. She looked at herself in the mirror and sighed.

"Dorothy, you're not in Kansas anymore."

Chapter 16

"Where's the fire, man?"

Simon slowed his run down to a brisk walk, allowing Nigel to catch up with him.

"What's wrong?" Simon asked, glancing at his friend with a grin. "Can't keep up?"

Nigel panted as he tried to keep pace. "Not with whatever you're chasing. Wanna let a brother in on what's going on?"

"Not really," Simon responded, his feet pounding the pavement in sync with Nigel's.

"Great," Nigel responded with more enthusiasm than Simon thought was merited. "Now I get the fun of guessing."

Simon took a swig of his water, knowing better than to try and dissuade his friend from the topic. Even if Nigel didn't know Simon as well as he did, he would know that Simon was terrible at hiding his emotions. And right then his emotions were in more turmoil than ever.

"Let's see, is it work?"

"What would I stress about here?" Simon asked, thinking about all the Toronto hospitals he had been to since his arrival, with their modern equipment and sufficient staffing.

"Ah yes, nothing in our civilized world stresses the wilderness doctor," Nigel said dryly.

Simon chuckled and kept jogging.

"How's your mom?"

"She's good," Simon said. "Great, even."

"Still consistent in her efforts to marry you off and start the next generation of Massris?"

"As ever."

"Any potential match-ups rattling your cage?"

"She's too busy organizing Dad's retirement banquet for that," Simon said. "But I'm sure she'll come up with someone by then."

"Then it can only be one thing." Nigel glanced over at Simon. "Elevator Girl."

Simon picked up his pace again and pulled ahead of Nigel. He heard his friend's laugh echo behind him.

"And we have a winner!"

Simon could ignore Nigel all he wanted. But he couldn't ignore the truth. He was thinking about JJ. It had been thirteen days, three hours and twenty-seven minutes since he had last seen her. As she had requested, he was calling her to update her on Sheree's status every couple days. Most times he had to be satisfied with her voice mail. But the rare occasions where he got her on the phone were like precious gifts. They were short conversations, the longest being only ten minutes, and she almost always sounded tired. But the calls helped soothe the irritation that came from not seeing her as regularly as he had before she went on tour. During their last talk, the conversation had slipped away from Sheree and on to how she was doing. She admitted that life on the road was more work and less glamor than she'd thought, and that it was beginning to take its toll on her. He had struggled with what to say to her then. Everything he wanted to express was inappropriate for his position as her sister-in-law's doctor. But the truth was, he had crossed over that line from the first moment he saw her in Sheree's hospital room.

That night on the phone, he felt like she would have said more too, but then she had been called into early rehearsal. He was worried about her. He had a feeling she wasn't doing well.

"You still calling her every day?" Nigel asked.

"Every couple of days," Simon corrected, noting that even though he had not slowed down again, his friend was now managing to keep up.

"Heck, that's more often than I call my girlfriend."

"You, however, are a scoundrel," Simon said.

Nigel grinned mischievously. "You got me there."

"Besides, I only call to give her updates..."

"Of course," Nigel said. "Because there's no way her family could do that."

"She asked me to," Simon countered.

"Of course she did."

"She gave me her number—I didn't ask for it."

"But you were very happy to take it, I'm sure," Nigel said.

Simon reached out and punched his friend in the arm.

"Oww," Nigel groaned, faltering as he grabbed his shoulder. "What'd you do that for?"

"The truth hurts," Simon said with a grin.

"Yeah," Nigel said, rubbing his sore arm. "And it's gonna hurt you if you don't do something about this woman."

"It's nothing," Simon said. "It's just shocking to see her again, after all these years."

"It was shocking two months ago when you first ran into her," Nigel said. "Now it's something else. You're checking in with her every day—"

"Every other day."

"—going in to work on your day off for her, changing your schedule to stay in Canada because she asked you to." Nigel shook his head. "Buddy, this is beyond shock. This is...you know what this is."

"Okay, fine," Simon said, letting out a breath. "I might be a little attracted to her—"

"Try *a lot.*"

"—but her sister-in-law is my patient and she's all over the place, literally. What am I supposed to do?"

"Get over her or get under her."

Simon nearly hit the pavement face-first at his friend's words. He stumbled to a stop and stared at him. "What?"

"You heard me," Nigel said, stopping a few steps away. "And you know exactly what I mean. Hit it, quit it, and get it out of your system."

Simon shook his head and started jogging again. "I can't believe those words just came out of your mouth. You know I don't get down like that."

Nigel rolled his eyes. "Oh yeah. I forgot. You're saving yourself for Wonder Woman."

Simon snorted.

"Okay, let me put it to you in good-boy terms then," Nigel said. "Either you test the waters with Elevator Girl to see if something's there, or you hook up with someone else and get her out of your head. But either way, you gotta do something. 'Cause this limbo you're sitting in is painful to watch, bruh."

"Whatever. You're exaggerating," Simon said.

"Really," Nigel said. "Did you see those two women running, in very tiny shorts, who were just checking us out?"

"What women?" Simon asked, looking around.

"Exactly," Nigel said. He shook his head. "Massri, do something."

Nigel's words were still ringing in Simon's head an hour later as he emerged from the showers in the staff changing room at the hospital. His unsanctified friend was usually the last one he would take advice from, given their vastly differing perspectives on life. But in this case, maybe he had a point. He should at least try to see if there was room for friendship with JJ. Maybe that was why he got the chance to see her again after all these years. Maybe they were supposed to be in each other's lives. He wouldn't know for sure until he explored it.

But first he had to check in with the woman who was becoming his favorite patient.

Fully dressed and chart in hand, he headed down the maternity ward.

"How's mother and baby doing today?" he asked, entering Sheree's hospital room, which with its growing collection of flowers, books, magazines, and DVDs, seemed to look more like a home bedroom every day.

"Doing good, as far as I can see," said Janice, the nurse JJ was friendly with. She looked up from where she sat in a chair by Sheree's bedside. Both women had been peering at a bridal magazine, and several others were scattered at the foot of Sheree's hospital bed. It looked like Sheree had managed to draw the woman in as much as JJ had. He had noticed that about Sheree. During her days at the hospital, she managed to make friends with many of the nurses and staff, even some who weren't involved in her care. Rare were the times when he would come to check on her and not find someone there. The one person he hadn't noticed, however, was the father of her child, and even though she never said much about the man, Simon suspected it bothered her that he wasn't there.

"Did you know that Janice is getting married in a couple months?" Sheree asked, her eyes bright. "I was just telling her that she should get my sister-in-law Sydney to do her cake. She has an amazing gourmet pastry shop—probably the best in Toronto."

"If she's doing well enough by then, Sheree says she could do my hair," Janice added. "So I was just looking at styles with her on my break."

"Well, I hate to break up the wedding planning session, but I thought it would be a good time to check on Baby Isaacs," Simon said with a smile. "What do you say, Sheree?"

Sheree nodded. "I'm down with that."

Janice cleared the magazines from the bed and placed them on the side table. "I'll go get the items for the ultrasound."

Simon pulled a rolling stool up to Sheree's bedside and sat down when Janice stepped out of the room.

"How are you feeling?" he asked.

"Physically? Pretty fine. Not much change, which, given what's going on, is probably a good thing," Sheree said with a forced laugh.

"And otherwise?" Simon probed, sensing there was more.

"Otherwise? Maybe a little anxious," Sheree said hesitantly.

Simon's brow furrowed. "Oh?"

Sheree shrugged and dropped her eyes. "Everything is in flux, you know? Anything could happen at any moment with the baby, and that's a little scary. Plus I don't really have any family other than my brother, and he's away."

"Well, things have been pretty stable over the past couple weeks," Simon reassured her. "Like you said, nothing has changed. In the last few tests your levels have been good, the baby looks good, and if we maintain at this pace, you should have a safe delivery in two months."

"I know, I know." Sheree sighed. "JJ used to tell me that every day. It was nice having that positive support all the time to counteract my negative thinking. I really miss her."

Simon nodded. That made two of them. "It's different not having her around as much, isn't it?"

"Yeah," Sheree said. "She makes sure to call every day, but it's not the same. Plus I get the feeling she's pretty stressed herself with her tour. I spoke with her early this morning from New York, and she sounded terrible—like she was getting sick. I don't like the idea of her being cooped up alone and sick in a hotel, even if it is the Marriott. Do you get that sense too, when you call her?"

Simon was surprised at the question, and it took him a moment to answer.

He cleared his throat. "Well, I talk to her voice mail more than I talk to her. She is a busy woman, and she only asked me to keep her updated."

Sheree looked at him a long moment. Simon could almost see the gears turning in her mind before she seemed to come to some sort of decision.

"Dr. Massri, can I ask you a personal question?" Sheree asked.

"Uh, sure," Simon said hesitantly. He glanced at the door. What was taking Janice so long?

"And I need you to give it to me straight," Sheree said.

He cleared his throat again. "Okay. I'll try."

"You like my sister-in-law, don't you?"

Simon blinked several times, opening and closing his mouth. "Uh... I don't know if I should be..."

"She told me the elevator story," Sheree said knowingly.

Simon closed his mouth. Then closed his eyes. If he hadn't just left Nigel in the staff locker rooms, Simon would have thought that he and Sheree were conspiring together. When he opened his eyes again, Sheree was staring at him expectantly.

"Well?"

He took a deep breath. "Sheree, you're my patient. Judith is your sister—"

"In-law."

"—and it's complicated," he finished.

"But don't you think it's a crazy coincidence that you would see her again? After all these years?" Sheree asked.

Simon cracked his fingers and glanced at the door. Where in the world was Janice?

"I see the way you look at her," Sheree continued. "I know you're attracted to her. And I think there's something on her side too. I'm not asking you to start something with her, but when you call her, can you just... see if she's okay? If she needs something? She won't tell me 'cause she's too busy worrying about me. But she might tell you..."

"Sheree, my relationship with Judith is completely professional."

"Dr. Massri, please," Sheree said as the door opened. "Can you just try?"

Simon glanced over at Janice, who had returned with a trayful of items and was looking at the two of them curiously.

"Please?" Sheree asked again.

Simon had a feeling she wouldn't take no for an answer, and unless he wanted the whole hospital to know about his feelings for JJ, he needed to end this conversation fast.

"Okay, I'll try," he said, giving her a look that told her to drop it. She smiled in understanding.

"Thank you," she said.

He nodded. "Now how about we get to this ultrasound?"

Sheree pulled down the sheet and pulled up her gown to expose her rounded belly.

"Let's go!"

Chapter 17

"Okay, ladies, let's take it from the top. Diana, you need to come in strong at the start. Kya, easy on that bass—you are not the lead for this one. And, JJ, pick it up. Your vocals are strong, but you're falling behind with the guitar."

JJ took another swig of her energy drink before lifting the strap of the electric guitar back over her shoulder. Most days she liked Sabrina. But it was nine-thirty p.m. and the band had been rehearsing since midafternoon, and even her Nitro wasn't going to be enough to get her through another hour. Usually she could cope with the long hours, but they had performed at New York's Madison Square Garden the night before and still had had to get up midmorning to do choreography and a quick run-through with Deacon. After no more than an hour's break for lunch, the girls had gone straight into rehearsal with Deacon, then She-La band rehearsal without him, where Sabrina was pushing harder than usual. She suspected it was because Sabrina had had a fight the night before with Deacon. Anytime the two of them fought, everyone had to pay for it in rehearsal. This is why performers should never date each other.

JJ stretched her neck, waited for Diana's count on the drums, and came in right on beat like she was supposed to. She caught a grin from Sabrina out of the side of her eye and knew she had gotten it right this time. She reached somewhere deep inside her and pulled out her reserve energy, pushing through the vocals, catching the harmony with the other three women. She had to admit, they sounded tight. If nothing else, Deacon and Sabrina's fights made sure they sounded better than ever.

"Okay, ladies, let's call it a night," Sabrina said finally, turning off her keyboard.

"Thank God," Diana murmured, dropping her drumsticks on the floor and pulling herself up off the stool. "My arms were about to give out."

"I know I've been killing you ladies," Sabrina said after swallowing a gulp of water. "But you all sound awesome."

"Well, after all that, we better," Kya said, working over a wad of gum. JJ grimaced as she watched the woman chew. That gum had spent as long in Kya's mouth as they had all spent in rehearsal.

"Get out of here," Sabrina said, shooing them through the doors with a grin. "Go enjoy what's left of your night. Except for you, JJ. You look terrible. You need to take something..."

"Or get some... thing," Kya said with a laugh.

JJ ignored Kya's comment. She had gotten used to the crass remarks that floated around among the Deacon Hill team. She was a far cry from Granville Church and the life that she lived around it. She was in the real world now. She had figured that out not long after she joined the band, when she realized the true nature of Sabrina and Deacon's relationship. No one seemed to mind that they were involved with each other, and only Sabrina seemed to mind that Deacon was often also involved with several other women at the same time. It's not like she didn't know these things went on. But when you went on tour with people, pretty much living with them from day to day for weeks, everything was more in-your-face.

"The only thing I'm going to enjoy right now is a long soak in that tub in my hotel room," Diana said as she stepped out the door behind Sabrina and Kya.

"I hear that," JJ said, glad to feel the cool night air on her face as she stepped outside. "Maybe that will do me some good."

Diana and JJ waved to Sabrina and Kya as they went off in different directions.

"Wanna split a cab with me back to the hotel?" JJ asked.

"Here's one now," Diana said as one stopped in front of them. Both women slipped inside and JJ closed her eyes for a moment as the car slid away.

"Girl, you really do look terrible," she heard Diana say.

"I feel terrible," JJ said, barely having enough energy to respond. Her head pounded and her brow was damp with sweat, despite the coolness of the evening. "Thank God we're off tomorrow night. I am not sure I'll be able to make it out of bed."

"You better get as much rest as you can," Diana said. "No one can afford to be sick right now. We're barely halfway through the tour with four more weeks to go."

"I know, I know," JJ mumbled. "I think I just need to rest. We've been having some crazy forty-eight-hour days lately."

"Don't I know it," Diana said. "I haven't spoken to my son for days. I know my baby misses me."

JJ had seen a picture of Diana's three-year-old son. He was a darling. JJ couldn't imagine leaving her child like that to go on tour. But she never said that to Diana. She knew the woman already felt enough guilt about being away from her child so many days out of the year.

They didn't talk anymore on the ride to the Marriott Hotel. In fact, the last thing JJ remembered was saying bye to Diana before slipping into her hotel room. She was barely able to kick off her shoes and drop her bags at the door before falling onto the couch. She closed her eyes and wrapped her arms around a thick cushion. Maybe she would make it to the bed later.

She didn't know how long she had been sleeping when the phone woke her. She reached blindly for it, every ring adding an edge to her headache. She finally managed to grab the receiver from where she had knocked it on the floor.

"Hello?" she moaned.

"Uh, Judith Isaacs, please?"

JJ let out a deep sigh. "Simon, it's me."

"Wow, you sound awful."

She buried her face in the cushion to block out the light. "Thanks. It's only worse than it sounds."

"That bad, huh?"

"Yeah," JJ mumbled. "I just need some rest though, and I'll be fine."

"What are your symptoms?"

She smiled despite her discomfort. "You gonna diagnose me over the phone, Doctor?"

"Humor me."

She took a deep breath. "Pounding headache, aching joints, nausea, disturbed sleep, chills and cold sweats. Did I mention headache?"

"Hmm," Simon murmured. "Sounds like you might be dehydrated. Or on the verge of the flu, or suffering from withdrawal. Or having morning sickness."

"That specific, huh?" JJ asked.

He chuckled. JJ liked the sound of his laugh. Something about it was comforting, making her miss Toronto, miss home. How long had it been since she had talked to her sisters? Even her talk with Sheree that morning had been more like a two-minute check-in on the drive over to the rehearsal studios. She would have to do better than that.

"How is Sheree?" she asked, unwilling to end their easy banter but knowing that it was the reason for his call.

"She's doing well," he said, his voice deep and soothing to her ears. "We did an ultrasound this afternoon and the baby's growth is progressing nicely. There seems to be no further separation of the placenta and her levels are stable. If she continues this way over the next six weeks, then she should have a healthy delivery."

"Hmm," JJ said, letting his words settle in. "Is there anything you're worried about?"

She heard him pause at her question.

"Simon," she probed. "Just tell me what it is."

"Right now, I'm more worried about you than I am Sheree."

He said the words quickly, as if trying to do it before he lost his nerve. Her heart sped up suddenly, and she wondered if that was just the effect of the energy drinks she had been imbibing all day, or something else.

"I'm..." She was going to say fine, but even she knew better than to try and pull that off. "I'll be better with some sleep."

"You sure about that?" he asked gently.

"No," JJ said, too tired to fake optimism. "But I hope for the best. Thankfully I'm off all of tomorrow. No rehearsal during the day, no performance at night. I think I'll probably spend the whole day in my hotel room. Probably in bed."

"Sheree's worried about you," he said. "She can tell you're not okay."

"Tell her not to worry," JJ said. "I've got it—"

JJ dropped the phone and rushed to the bathroom, as a sudden tightening in her stomach sent a tide she hadn't expected rushing to her throat. She made it to the toilet just in time to expel the contents of her stomach.

What in the world was happening to her? She hadn't been this sick in ages. It was like her whole body was fighting against itself. She sat on the floor, resting her back against the door, waiting until she mustered up enough energy to move back to the couch, or better yet, the bed. She had just closed her eyes when she heard her cell phone ring. She contemplated letting it go to voice mail but didn't want to chance someone coming to her room and finding her on the floor in the bathroom like this.

Crawling back to the main area, she dug her cell phone out of her purse near the door.

"Hello?"

"What happened? Are you okay?"

It was Simon.

"I'm fine. My stomach just raised an objection."

"Maybe you should call a doctor..."

She let out a single laugh at the irony of the situation. "I'm talking to a doctor."

She heard him sigh on the other end, in what sounded like frustration.

"Judith."

Warmth flooded through her when he said her name. "Say it again," she murmured.

"What?"

"My name. Say it again." She didn't know where her brain was. Maybe she had left it in the bathroom with the contents of her stomach. But right now, all she wanted to know was if she would get that feeling again if he repeated her name.

"Judith—"

Yup. There it was.

"—you need to see a doctor," he finished calmly.

Gripping a side table, she pulled herself up to her feet, then waited to see if she would be able to stay upright. When she was sure she could, she made her way back to the couch and replaced the hotel phone on the console. Then, holding on along the way, she shuffled over to the bed.

"Simon, I'll be fine," she said, with more conviction than she'd thought she could muster. "Thanks for updating me on Sheree."

"Judith, listen..."

Wow, that never got old.

She smiled. "Goodnight, Simon."

Then before he could protest further, she ended the call and fell into bed.

Chapter 18

Boom-boom-boom.

JJ wasn't sure if she was sleeping or awake.

She opened her eyes to the light of the sun reflecting off the wall.

Boom-boom-boom.

She stretched and sat up. Her headache had downsized to a dull ache behind her eyes, a big improvement from the night before. But she felt dazed and somewhat disoriented. Like she wasn't sure what was real and what was not. She yawned and tried putting one foot on the floor. A little wobbly, but she would manage.

Boom-boom-boom.

By the time the pounding stopped, she had made it to the door. When she pulled it open, her heart stopped.

"Simon!"

There he was, standing in the door of her hotel room in all six foot five of his glorious mixed-heritage beauty. His broad frame, which JJ was sure was zero percent fat and 100 percent bone and muscle, filled her doorway. His intense, greenish-gold eyes stared down at her from under thick brows and long lashes. His locks, pulled back, framed his strong face.

This couldn't be happening. He couldn't actually be here,

standing in her doorway, looking unbelievably gorgeous and like a gift from heaven. She must be delirious and this must be a hallucination. A very good hallucination. And as if confirming it, JJ suddenly felt light-headed. She closed her eyes as she felt the room begin to spin.

"Easy, don't pass out on me now." Simon's voice was close to her ear as his hand grasped her upper arm, holding her steady. She in turn wrapped her arm around his for more support before opening her eyes.

"Hey," she said again, her words coming slower than normal.

"Hey." His eyes searched her face in concern. "Can I come in?"

She nodded and he stepped carefully inside, dropped a bag on the floor, then closed the door behind him, all while holding her upright. Then he turned his eyes on her again. More concern.

"I'm okay," JJ said slowly, loosening her grip on his arm while trying to focus her eyes on him so the room would stop spinning. "Really, I'm fine."

He watched her cautiously as she let go of him completely.

"You're sure?"

"M-hmm." She smiled and took a step back from him. Then her legs gave out.

This time he caught her with both hands and led her over to the couch, where he sat down next to her. She closed her eyes and laid her head back. She could feel his eyes on her, but she didn't look. She couldn't deal with the room spinning anymore.

"Simon," she began, her words heavy on her tongue. "What are you doing here?"

"You needed a doctor." His voice rumbled gently through her. "And I had a feeling you weren't going to call one. Was I right?"

She smiled.

"That's what I thought," he said knowingly.

She felt him get up from beside her and she opened her eyes slowly. She saw him digging through the contents of his bag by the door. When he found what he was looking for, he straightened and brought the bag and the item over to the couch. He sat down beside her again.

He touched her face gently and turned it away from him. "Have you eaten this morning?" he asked, putting something in her ear.

"I don't know," JJ murmured. "What time is it?"

He seemed to pause for a moment. " Around nine a.m."

"Then no."

He took out a stethoscope and placed it in his ears before gently turning her to the side so she was facing away from him. She felt the flat surface press against her back.

"When was the last time you ate?"

JJ shrugged. "Yesterday. Lunchtime. Maybe."

He was quiet for a moment as he listened to her heartbeat and breathing. Then he turned her back around so she could rest against the back of the couch.

"Did you throw up again last night?" he asked, his brows furrowed.

JJ nodded.

He placed his hand against her forehead and she let her heavy eyelids fall closed, his cool fingers a comfort to her hot, clammy skin.

She heard him let out a deep breath.

"Judith, I'm going to ask you something, and I need you to tell me the truth."

"Okay." She would tell him anything when he called her Judith.

"Have you been taking anything? Any medication, drugs?"

JJ's eyes snapped open and she pushed his hand away from her face.

"No," she protested, sitting up. But it was too fast. The room began to spin again and she fell back against the couch.

She took a couple deep gulps of air to settle her racing heart.

"I'm not stupid, Simon. I don't do drugs," she said, winded.

"Okay, okay," he said gently. He had taken her hand and was rubbing his thumb against the back of it. It was having a relaxing effect on her.

"Maybe not drugs, but supplements. Any kind of pills?"

Oh no. JJ groaned and covered her face with her hands.

"Where are they?" he asked.

"My purse, by the door."

She felt the couch shift as he got up. She heard rustling, then silence. Then he was sitting beside her again.

"Judith, look at me."

She dropped her hands and pulled herself up slowly, turning slightly so she was facing him.

"You know what these are?"

"Caffeine pills."

"How long have you been taking these?" His brows were drawn so tightly together that they almost met.

She sighed. "Not long. Two weeks, maybe. It was just so I could get through the shows. I haven't taken any for a couple days."

He held up her empty energy drink can.

"Have you been drinking these?"

She nodded.

"Have you ever had both of them together?"

JJ shifted her eyes away. She couldn't bear the look on his face. It was a mix of concern, frustration, and some other things she couldn't read but were too much for her to handle.

He sighed. Then slipped a hand behind her neck, pulling her to him. She rested her head willingly against his chest and closed her eyes, preferring the firm strength of his torso to the plush softness of the Marriott sofa.

"Dear God." He mumbled the words in her hair. "Do you know what could have happened to you?"

"Very bad things?" she murmured.

She felt his chest vibrate with his grunt.

"No more caffeine pills."

"Okay."

"And no more energy drinks."

That was going to be a hard one. "Simon..."

"No more," he said. "I don't care if you have three shows in a row and no sleep in between. No more energy drinks. Promise me, Judith."

Well, when he said her name like that...

"Okay," she said.

"Good."

"Are you going to have to save my life again?" she asked, against his chest.

"Luckily it didn't get that far this time," he said. He gently eased her away from him, retrieved something from his bag, then moved over to the tiny counter area that held a kettle and coffeemaker. She watched his back as he mixed something. Then he returned to the couch and handed her a half-full glass.

"Sorry I don't have a straw," he said, holding the almost clear liquid to her lips.

She drank the slightly sweet beverage slowly, allowing her stomach to get used to the presence of the substance. It took a while, but she finally got to the end of it. Then he pulled her back to him, letting her rest against his chest again. Her eyelids were almost closed when his voice interrupted their descent.

"I think you should be good to lie down again," he said. "What's it going to be, couch or bed?"

She closed her eyes. "Bed, please."

Slipping an arm around her waist, he helped her to her feet, then supported her all the way to her king-size hotel bed. The sheets were still rumpled from where she had just gotten up and the room was a mess, with her clothes from the night before in a pile on the floor. Her mother would be ashamed that she let someone see her place looking like this. But then her mother probably wouldn't approve of her entertaining her sister-in-law's doctor in only pajama shorts and a tank top.

Leaving those thoughts for when her head felt more like her own, JJ crawled back into bed and fell back onto the pillows. When he was sure she was settled, he turned to leave the room.

"Simon."

He stopped and turned to look at her, and an unexpected wave of affection hit her.

"Will you be here when I wake up?" she asked.

He smiled. "As long as you wake up before my ten o'clock flight."

"Okay," JJ said, sliding down into a sleeping position.

She closed her eyes with an image of Simon standing by the door, his beautiful, intense eyes watching her as she drifted off to sleep. Not a bad image to make dreams about.

Chapter 19

By the evening, JJ felt significantly better than she had at the start of the day when Simon first showed up. Half of it had to do with sleep. It had been months since she had slept as much as she had in the past twenty-four hours, and her body was grateful. But she was convinced that the other half of it had everything to do with Simon. She had asked him if he would be there when she woke up. But he had done her one better and woke her up every few hours with a glass of some awful concoction that she was surprised her stomach was able to hold down. He refused to tell her what was in it, but whatever it was, it managed to eliminate her dizziness by midday and provide her with enough energy for a game of Scrabble by midafternoon. Maybe it had nothing to do with the medicine at all. Maybe it was just the house call. Something about being with Simon made her feel better, feel calmer, more relaxed. Life with Simon felt different—in a good way.

By the time evening rolled around, she was itching to be outdoors. Simon didn't need much convincing. A leisurely walk a couple blocks away from the hotel found them at a restaurant with a patio and several vegetarian options.

After dinner she had insisted on going to the airport with him despite his protests. He eventually caved, and so here they were, riding a cab to JFK International Airport together. She was sitting next to him in the backseat, her right arm touching his left, his left knee brushing against her right. She had gotten used to those small contacts during the day. His firm grip on her arm as he helped her out of bed earlier that day. His hand on the small of her back as he opened doors for her that evening. His fingers grasping hers now, as he helped her out of the cab at JFK. She held on to his hand a little longer than she needed to, and he let her. She didn't want him to go, because when he left, it would mean that her twenty-four-hour vacation would be over and she would have to go back to life as it had become.

They walked inside in silence, his single bag slung over his shoulder. The drop-off area was busy, as it always was at JFK. Travelers and airport security moved around them at a brisk pace. He had to go. His flight would leave in a little over an hour. It was time to say good-bye.

"Well, this is it," he said, turning to look at her.

She nodded. "Thank you, again. I still can't believe you came all the way here for me."

She reached up and wrapped her arms around him tightly. He seemed surprised, as it took a couple moments before he returned her emotional embrace.

"You'll be fine," he said, patting her back awkwardly. "Just keep yourself hydrated, get some rest, and keep your promise."

He held her back from him so he could look at her. "If you start throwing up again though, straight to a doctor. Okay?"

She smiled. "Okay."

He looked at her a long moment before dropping his arms from her shoulders and stepping back. She hoped he didn't say good-bye. She couldn't bear to say good-bye to him.

"I'll see you, Judith."

She watched him step back, then turn and walk toward the check-in point. She suddenly remembered the moment she had watched him walk away from her outside the hotel in Paris. They had been separated by EMS workers and she had lost sight of him. The next time she caught a glimpse of him, he was walking toward a car and she was being pulled down into another. It would be four-and-a-half years before she would see him again. How long would it be this time?

He glanced back at her and seemed to freeze when he caught the look on her face. In a single movement, he turned and was walking back to her.

"What's wrong?" he asked, his brows drawn together in a way that had become familiar to JJ over the past twelve hours. Too familiar, in a way that nothing in her life had been familiar in the past few months. She should have been happy about that. This was what she had wanted, right? The dream of celebrity, the chance to sing onstage in front of millions of people, the chance to have a career that was real, the chance to matter. So what was this niggling feeling of restlessness she couldn't escape?

Grabbing her hand, he pulled her over to a cluster of attached chairs. He eased her down into one before taking another beside her.

"Judith, what's going on?"

JJ waved her hand lightly. "You have to go, Simon. You're gonna miss your flight."

"I've got an hour," he said. "Talk to me. Are you feeling sick again?"

JJ shook her head. "No. I'm fine."

"If you were fine you would look me in the eye and say that."

She turned to look at him, and the neutral expression she had tried to frame her face with crumpled at the sight of the concern on his. She sighed and sank back into the chair. She stared out at the swarm of people around her. Everyone moving with purpose. Everyone going somewhere. She wished she felt as sure as they looked.

"Have you ever felt... like something was missing?" she asked finally, her eyes still taking in the scene around her. "Like there should be... more?"

Simon was silent for a long moment. Then he gently squeezed her hand, which he was still holding.

"Is that how you feel?" he asked.

JJ rubbed her hands across her face as she tried to understand how she was feeling.

"I don't know," she said. "I finally have what I want. This dream that for a long time I wouldn't even dare to dream, singing onstage, traveling the country doing what I love, it's finally happening. I'm in front of thousands of people almost every night. I sing with Deacon Hill—*the* Deacon Hill, top ten R & B recording artist in North America. People recognize me on the street. Some girl even asked me for my autograph once. I stay in five-star hotels, wear designer clothes, get paid a ridiculous amount of money, which I barely have to use because so much is already paid for. I never thought this could happen to me. But it did."

She turned to Simon. "So why do I feel like... like..."

"Like what?" he asked gently.

"Like there should be something else. Like there should be more?"

A look of understanding flitted through Simon's eyes. Then he sat back, quiet. JJ rested her head against the back of the chair and closed her eyes. She couldn't pinpoint exactly why, but she knew that she was unsettled. She had gotten her dream, but it felt like it wasn't enough.

"That day in the elevator," Simon said suddenly. "Do you remember where you were going before we got stuck?"

JJ opened her eyes and glanced over at him. "I was on my way to the airport."

He smiled. "You wanted to go to the Rue de Rivoli because you heard that they had tons of little shops that sold inexpensive souvenirs."

"Oh yes! That's right," JJ said as the memory came back to her.

He shook his head, the smile still on his lips. "You were stuck in an elevator, barely over a panic attack, and all you were worried about was that you wouldn't have time to get something extra for each of your sisters and for the teenager you were teaching guitar. I think you said her name was... Tiffany?"

"Stephanie," JJ corrected. "Stephanie Corwack."

JJ hadn't seen Stephanie since last Christmas. She had taught the young woman how to play guitar for several years, but their friendship had stretched beyond the music. Stephanie, who was the only child of a single father, had adopted JJ as her big sister in many different ways, and it had been an emotional parting when Stephanie had left for college two years earlier. Long phone calls and lengthy e-mails had become the basis of their friendship since then, but over the past year JJ's contact with Stephanie had dwindled significantly. In fact, Stephanie had sent JJ an e-mail several weeks ago that she had yet to look at, much less respond to.

JJ closed her eyes again.

"You know, a while ago you talked about a lot of things," Simon began again, his voice taking on a gentle, lazy quality. "But I didn't hear you mention your sisters, or your family, or your spirituality."

"I haven't spoken to my sister Sydney in almost two weeks," JJ said. She shook her head. "Usually, we can't go a couple of days without talking to each other. But ever since we had that fight..."

JJ let the rest of the sentence drift off. She still remembered the argument over Rayshawn more than a month ago. They had both offered some sort of semi-apology. But the air wasn't anywhere near clear. Even though they had tried to connect since, their interactions had been strained at best.

"You know, the girl in the elevator?" Simon mused. "Family was all she talked about. And faith. Those were the most important things in her life."

The very things that were in flux in her life now.

"Maybe it's that shift that has you feeling lost," Simon said quietly. "Maybe you haven't quite adjusted to that change in priorities yet."

He was right. In many ways she was still transitioning. And figuring out how to balance all those old priorities with her new life was proving to be a great challenge.

But maybe it was all a phase—just an adjustment period. It was her first time on tour and maybe this was how people felt when everything was so new. After it was all over, she would be back in Toronto and there would be time to reconnect with her family. Then it would be easier to nurture her spiritual life the way she used to.

"You know what? You're right," JJ said, sitting forward. "It's just the adjustment, just the tour. It's the first time I have been on something like this, something so intense. It's taken a lot to get used to. Even my body is out of whack, which is probably why I got sick in the first place." She took a deep breath. "I'll be fine. I'll get through the tour, and when I get back to Toronto, everything will be okay. My family is not used to this. But we just need time. We'll adapt. We always do."

JJ kept nodding her head, as if by doing so she could convince herself that her words were true. Simon looked at her and she thought she saw something akin to sympathy in his eyes.

The call for his flight came across the airport intercom and JJ stood up.

"Even though I don't want you to, you have to go," she said with a sad smile.

He stood, his eyes still searching her face. Then he shocked her by leaning down and pressing a kiss against her cheek.

"I hope you find what you're looking for," he murmured close to her ear.

She wanted to respond, but her brain was mush. All she could think about was the feel of his lips against her cheek, the warmth of his breath on her ear, the contrast of his coarse stubble against her soft skin.

Then before she could recover, he was gone. Slicing through the crowd and disappearing, leaving his kiss on her cheek and his words in her brain.

JJ sat down on the chair she had just vacated. If she hadn't been confused before, she definitely was now.

Chapter 20

It was way too early in the morning.

This is what JJ knew for sure as she took the stairs down to the lobby early the next Saturday morning. Everyone else was sleeping. The show they had played the night before at Philadelphia's Mann Center had been completely sold-out. JJ had heard that people who had missed the New York show had driven in for this one. The rumor was that scalpers were selling last-minute tickets on the street for sometimes more than twice their value. Their second show later that night promised to be just as packed, and if JJ knew what was good for her, she would have stayed tucked into her sheets and not gotten up until an hour before their four p.m. sound check. But for some reason here she was, ten fifteen in the morning, stepping through the glass doors of her hotel, oversized sunglasses on, light jacket thrown over a simple blue summer dress, clutching a piece of paper with an address hastily scribbled on it.

It wasn't hard to find a cab. The second driver she asked actually knew the address, and so JJ sat back for the ride. In twenty minutes she was in Chestnut Hill, a neighborhood in the northwestern part of the city that didn't seem like it belonged in fast-paced Philadelphia at all. Furthermore, the beautiful European-style stone structure that the driver stopped in front of looked from the outside to be more like a cathedral than the kind of church she was used to. Nonetheless, the gathering of people just outside the front steps told her it was exactly what she was looking for.

JJ paid the driver and murmured her thank-you before stepping out of the vehicle onto the sidewalk. Usually she didn't much enjoy being in churches where she knew no one. She enjoyed the fellowship of her spiritual family and craved the freedom that came from being with people who shared her beliefs. But today she was just content to be somewhere where God might be also.

The restlessness hadn't gone away. She wasn't adjusting like she thought she would. Instead, she was feeling more and more unsettled as the days went by. She had needed to escape, and in the past the quiet inside a church building had served as her haven. Maybe here, today, she could find that tranquility again.

"Welcome to Chestnut Hill Community Church!"

JJ smiled, but not nearly as brightly as the greeter, a large woman old enough to be her mother. She took the offered hand and was shocked when the woman pulled her into a gentle hug that was, surprisingly, not as intrusive as she thought it might be.

"Glad you could make it," the woman said when she let go.

There is was. That serene atmosphere. "Thank you," JJ murmured.

The woman nodded, then turned to the person behind JJ and offered a similarly genuine greeting. JJ chuckled to herself and slipped inside the sanctuary.

The church was narrow and welcoming with its two aisles of padded pews and well-worn carpeted floors. She sighed and felt her muscles relax as she sank into the deep cushions of her seat. Light piano trickled through the sanctuary, bringing the buzz of voices and movement down to a hum. JJ closed her eyes and let the music flow over her, let the chords imprint on her heart, let them stir up further the feeling of longing and nostalgia that was gently swirling inside her.

JJ missed this. The opportunity to sing without rules or expectations. The freedom and the openness to be who she was in a place where she would not be judged. The serenity she experienced when she was able to leave the world behind. She used to be able to experience that on her own, in her own time with God. But that had seemed so difficult of late.

JJ didn't want it to be over, but when the minister finished the message, she knew it was time to go. Slipping out of her pew, she made her way down a side aisle, hoping to beat the crowd out the door and avoid any awkward visitor moments. But the voice with the microphone stopped her.

JJ turned around slowly from the back of the church and stared. She watched as the woman's honey-colored fingers moved skillfully over the acoustic guitar as she sang the song, "Open My Eyes," a song JJ had loved to play when she first learned guitar. When Christ's love had first become real in her heart. It seemed like such a long time ago, but that song brought back the memories. The feeling of nostalgia was almost overwhelming, like a throbbing ache without the pain. And now, she couldn't just walk away without knowing if it was the singer or just the song.

She waited in the back row until the crowd had mostly dispersed, then she walked through the remaining stragglers to the front. The woman's blond-streaked auburn hair hung in straight long layers over her slim shoulders as she secured her guitar in the case. When she finally stood, she came face-to-face with JJ.

"Hi!" she said, offering a bright smile. "Are you a visitor?"

JJ nodded. "I am."

"I thought I saw you somewhere near the middle," the woman continued, offering a hand to go with her smile. "I'm—"

"Cymmone Slater," JJ finished. "I know who you are."

"And you're part of Deacon Hill's new female band," Cymmone said with a knowing smile. "I knew there was something familiar about you when I saw you in the congregation."

JJ's eyebrows shot up. "How did you..."

"The posters," Cymmone said. "They're everywhere. Plus you guys were on the front page of a tabloid in the supermarket, and the line at the cashier was kind of long, so..."

JJ laughed. "Wow, this is new for me. But I bet you must be used to it by now."

The woman gave a little laugh. "Not so much. I still get surprised when people recognize me. Especially after so long."

"Three years is not that long," JJ said. "Especially when you're an *American Icon* winner."

Cymmone shrugged. "I guess."

JJ noticed a faraway look in the woman's eyes, followed by a grimace that she quickly shook off.

"Anyway, that was a long time ago," Cymmone said, her smile returning quickly.

It was also clearly a time she wasn't eager to talk about. JJ could only imagine why.

"I just came up here to see if it was really you," JJ said before the awkward moment could get any more awkward. "And to say I really enjoyed your song. I didn't even know you were a Christian."

"A lot of people don't," Cymmone said. "For a while, I forgot myself."

Second awkward moment. JJ wasn't sure what to say to that, and so she said good-bye instead and headed back toward the exit.

"Hey, wait!"

She turned around to find Cymmone walking toward her.

"Would you like to stay for lunch? We have lots of food and everyone here is friendly. I promise not to bring up your singing if you promise not to bring up mine."

JJ smiled in spite of herself. No matter where she went, there were some things about church life that never changed.

"Thanks, but I can't," JJ said. "I have to get back to my hotel and prepare for the show later. I was just about to call a cab to take me back to the Crowne Plaza."

"No need," Cymmone said, already pulling keys out of her purse. "I'll give you a ride."

"You don't have to—"

"I know. But I want to," Cymmone said. "I'll get my car. Meet me out front."

Before JJ could protest, Cymmone had disappeared through a side door and out to where JJ guessed her car was parked on the side of the road. JJ walked out to the front of the church, wondering if there was any way out. She hadn't seen any taxis on her way in, and even if she called one right now, Cymmone would get there before it did. She didn't really know this woman—well, that wasn't entirely true. All of North America, and many beyond, knew Cymmone Slater. She was a winner of *American Icon,* the annual talent show scouting singers from across the USA. She had sung to the world on live television for thirteen weeks, beating out several others for the top spot, which included a recording contract with Dynamite Music Group (DMG) and an opening spot on a DMG major artists' tour. But the contest had just been the beginning. She had blown up the music scene, recording duets with several major artists, doing commercials for Pepsi and MAC Cosmetics and dating celebrities right, left, and center, from NFL players to actors. And then, just as fast as she had risen to pop culture's forefront, she had fallen off the radar. Disappeared.

JJ was still scouring her mind for the last time she had seen anything in the media about Cymmone, when a white Ford Expedition pulled up to the curb. One of the heavily tinted windows rolled down.

"Come on, let's go!"

JJ sighed. The day had been strange enough. Why not?

"Excuse the toys and snacks," Cymmone said, tossing a stuffed animal into the back, where JJ caught sight of a car seat. "This is the mommy-mobile."

"You have children?" JJ asked, pulling the front passenger door closed behind her and slipping on her seat belt.

"Three little ones," Cymmone said, beaming. "Two boys and a darling baby girl."

JJ shook her head. "Wow. Is that why you dropped off the music scene?"

Cymmone sighed and JJ caught the grimace again. "Yes and no."

It was obvious to JJ that this wasn't the easiest or the most pleasant conversation for Cymmone. Maybe she should just leave this alone.

"So you sing for Deacon Hill?" Cymmone asked.

Guess Cymmone had decided to leave it alone also.

JJ settled back for the ride. "Yeah," she said. "It's fairly recent though. Before that, I wasn't much more than your local small-event singer. Girl-with-a-dream kind of thing."

"So this is your big break," Cymmone said.

JJ looked out the window. "You could say so."

Silence hung between them for a spare moment before Cymmone broke it.

"So I'm just gonna tell you this because I have a feeling I know where you are, and because I know that God didn't accidentally put you in my mother's church the one morning I happened to be there too." Cymmone sighed. "You asked me why I dropped off the music scene. I tell most people it was because of my family, and that's the truth. But it was mostly because of my husband. I dreamed of being in this business since I was a little girl. I ate, slept, and breathed music growing up. I sung in every choir in church and at school. I started going to auditions when I was eighteen, and I qualified for *American Icon* when I was twenty-four, the last year I would have been eligible. I knew I could sing. People had been telling me all my life. But I was still shocked when I stood on that stage and America voted me the winner. And then everything got crazy. Things started moving so fast. They moved me out of Atlanta to LA. Set me up with producers, songwriters, managers, vocal coaches, image consultants, the whole celebrity machine. I loved it. It was exactly what I wanted. Until I realized that it was changing me. I was singing songs I didn't believe in, wearing clothes that a year earlier I wouldn't be caught dead in, and going places where I would never have gone on my own. And the worst part was, I was totally okay with it because everyone around me was doing it, and because I had no compass to direct me. No one to pull me back to center—to help me check myself."

"What about your family?" JJ asked.

"What about them?" Cymmone asked dryly, glancing at JJ. "I was on the road all the time. There were times I would be living out of hotels for months, going weeks without even talking to my family. And my spiritual life? Well, that was nonexistent. There's no time for church when you're spending ten hours a day rehearsing and the other ten traveling or in meetings. No time for devotions. No time for reflections on who you are becoming."

Cymmone let out a deep breath. "And then I met Brady."

JJ noticed the smile on her face when she talked about the man JJ suspected was her husband.

"He got into my life and refused to go," she continued, the smile still steady on her lips. "He would call me almost every day, even if it was just to say hey; send things that reminded me of home to my various hotels to keep me from getting too homesick. There were times when he would drive for hours, or fly across the country just to spend an hour with me."

"After we got married he told me he knew God had made us for each other from the first moment he met me. Can you believe that?"

"I don't know," JJ teased. "Sounds a little creepy to me."

Cymmone laughed. "Yeah, I told him that too. But the thing is, he never pushed me. Never forced me to settle down. Never asked me to change my life for him. He was just there, accepting me and all my baggage with his love, and his compassion, and his faith. That man had a faith that never gave up. And he used to pray me out of some situations. I think that was what made me realize what was missing. I was going from day to day, stage to stage, performance to performance, giving my everything every time, but I was empty. And it was only when I saw Brady that I realized what was missing—my connection with my first love, my God."

"So is that why you quit?"

Cymmone rolled her eyes. "I didn't quit. I just prioritized, which meant scaling back on the music side of things. It's not that I don't love singing—I do. But I couldn't give my everything to my career and give my life to God at the same time. I tried, JJ, I promise you I tried. But this industry..." She shook her head. "It's all or nothing if you want to be at the top. And I could have given my all, but I would have lost myself. Maybe there are people who can do it. Maybe you're one of those people who can put everything out there, be in the middle of it every day without compromising who you are, without losing that connection. But I couldn't. And when Brady asked me to marry him, I knew I couldn't be with him and continue the way things were. Not because he would ask me to change—he never did. But because I couldn't love him the way he deserved to be loved and continue the way I was going. I wasn't even loving my family the way I should. I had to make a change."

JJ nodded, understanding what Cymmone was saying but not sure that she could make the same decision. After all, she didn't have a Brady in her life, giving her another option. And even if she did, singing was who she was. She couldn't give that up for a man. She shouldn't have to.

"Do you regret giving up so much?" JJ asked after a long moment. They were back in the center of Philadelphia again. They would be at the hotel soon.

Cymmone was thoughtful. "I'm not going to lie and say I don't miss being onstage as much. I do. But I don't regret my choice. I prayed about it, Brady prayed for me about it, my family prayed for me about it, and when it was time to make that decision, I was sure. And after I decided, I just felt at peace with all of it." Cymmone bit her lip. "This business is great, JJ. And if you're singing with Deacon Hill it must mean you have an awesome voice, and if God has allowed you to get to this point it must be for a reason. Just don't lose yourself."

JJ turned toward the window again, wondering how she would even be able to tell.

"After all, 'what shall it profit a man if he shall gain the whole world and lose his own soul?' "

The verse from Mark 8:36 weighed heavily on JJ. Was she losing her soul? That sounded so extreme. But she hadn't changed that much. Had she?

The SUV stopped and JJ realized they were in front of the hotel. She turned to Cymmone. "Thank you."

Before she could open the door, the woman stretched across and pulled her into a loose embrace. JJ couldn't remember the last time she had been hugged this often in one day.

"Take care, JJ," Cymmone said as JJ slipped out of the vehicle. "And call me if you need to talk."

JJ took the card the woman pressed into her palm and closed the door of the vehicle. She waved as Cymmone drove away, then turned and headed into the hotel. It was almost one o'clock. In an hour she would have to start getting ready. She wouldn't mind hearing a familiar voice before then. She pulled out her cell phone and pressed speed dial four as she headed for the stairs. It rang only once.

"Well, it's about time you called."

JJ smiled. "Hey, Sheree. I missed you too."

And suddenly she didn't feel as homesick anymore.

Chapter 21

JJ ended up at the Mann Center an hour earlier than call time. Most of the setup from the night before was still out and in place, and so there was little reason for the crew to come in early. Going directly to the dressing rooms, she dropped off her bags and headed back out with her guitar. She hadn't stepped far out the door when the sound of Beethoven's *Moonlight Sonata* caught her ear. As she followed the music down the hallway, the chords became more defined and the melody clearer.

His back was to her, and she stepped quietly into the room, careful not to disturb him as he played. She also knew that piece on piano—a result of her early teenage years spent in weekly piano classes—but she couldn't have played it as smoothly as Deacon. As he gracefully played through the complicated composition, JJ watched in awe. His form was precise, his fingers confident in their accuracy, his body leaning into the music with every run and transition. When he struck the final note at the sonata's strong and vibrant end, JJ's hands came together in spontaneous applause.

"I had no idea you could play like that," JJ said from the doorway.

Deacon turned halfway around on the piano stool, an embarrassed smile on his face. "I had no idea I had an audience."

"You're classically trained?" JJ asked.

He nodded. "Been playing piano since I was eight. I think my mom always knew I would be a musician; she just thought it would be in the classical, not R & B genre."

"They're both art," JJ said.

"Not the way she tells it," Deacon said with a grin. He nodded to the seats nearby. "Come sit. Tell me about your musical background. I'm guessing you spent a few years on a piano stool as well."

"Oh yes," JJ said, accepting his invitation and pulling herself up on a high stool with a low back. "Started when I was ten. Two hours every week with Mrs. Elliot. They were the best and worst days of my life."

Deacon laughed. "Does no one have purely positive piano-teacher stories?"

"I've yet to hear one," JJ said, pulling her guitar into her lap. "Mrs. Elliot did her best, and I did learn, but I think my true love has always been guitar. My dad taught me to play when I was thirteen. After that, you couldn't get the thing out of my hands."

"Alright, let me see what you got," Deacon said, getting up.

"Noooo," JJ said, holding out a hand to stop him. "I would never pollute your ears with my piano playing. It's pedestrian at best and rusty today because I haven't touched a piano in months."

"It can't be that bad," Deacon said, tilting his head to the side.

JJ pursed her lips. "Trust me, it is."

"So how can I be assured of this classical background of which you speak?" he asked, his brow crinkling in mock suspicion.

JJ laughed. "Guess you'll just have to take it on faith."

Deacon shook his head. "I can't believe I never knew this about you before. Do you write a lot of your own stuff?"

JJ idly plucked a melody on the guitar. "I used to, but not as much now. There isn't much time when you're on tour with a major pop star."

He smiled. "True. But don't get too caught up in all this," he said, waving a hand around. "At the end of the day, it's really about the music. That's what got us all here in the first place, right?"

"Right," JJ said. "It's easy to forget though."

"True," Deacon said, turning back to the piano. "So let's try harder not to. Follow me."

He started playing again, slowly at first and then more confidently. JJ smiled when she realized what he was playing. "His Eye Is on the Sparrow." A song her mother used to sing in church a lot when JJ was younger. Did Deacon have church roots to add to his classical background?

Instead of asking questions, JJ did what the man said and began to accompany him on the guitar. When he got to the second verse, he let JJ take the lead and switched to the accompaniment. He smoothly transitioned into another gospel song JJ knew, and she couldn't help but sing softly along as she played. Deacon's voice joined with hers, and soon they were singing in two-part harmony. It had been a while since she had played and sung like this. The last time she could remember had been with her brother, Dean, a couple weeks before she left for the tour. She had found him messing around on the piano in their mother's basement. She didn't know how it had started, but it had ended with them playing and singing together, everything from Mahalia Jackson to Stevie Wonder. It was one of the most genuine moments she had had with her brother since he had returned from the hospital after the car accident. It almost made her cry to think about it.

At the end of the second song, Deacon transitioned again into something else. When JJ realized what it was, she stopped playing.

"What's wrong, Miss Isaacs?" Deacon asked with a smile as he continued playing. "Don't recognize your own song?"

She did recognize it. It was her song from the audition. The song that had convinced Deacon to have her in his band. He was playing it. Perfectly.

He stopped when he realized she hadn't joined him.

"You're playing 'I'm Yours,' " JJ said, her voice barely above a whisper. "You're playing my song."

He nodded. "It's a great song."

"But..." She shook her head, confused. "How?"

He looked away. "I couldn't get that song out of my head. I listened to the tape from that audition over and over until I knew it so well I could play it myself."

He turned back toward JJ. "Will you play it with me?"

Deacon Hill was asking her if he could play her song. The song she and her brother had written in their mother's basement years ago. The song that she had written to keep her strong after her father died. He wanted to play that song with her. What could she say?

Nothing.

She just nodded and repositioned her guitar.

He let her take the lead this time, and accompanied her on the piano instead. Then he began to sing. He sang JJ's song. Every word from memory, like he had written it himself. JJ could barely breathe, barely continue playing. Tears filled her eyes, ran down her cheeks, and dripped onto the smooth, glossy wood of her guitar. She had never experienced this feeling before—this validation of who she was. She spent her days practicing other people's music, singing other people's lyrics. But no one else had ever sung one of her songs. She had never heard her music through someone else's experience. But today, she did. It was overwhelming.

When they came to the end, she couldn't even look at Deacon. Her face was wet, and the sleeves of her shirt did nothing to help.

Deacon didn't say anything, just allowed her to collect herself. Then when she did, he shattered her again.

"I want to do your song. Tonight. At the show."

JJ couldn't speak. She searched his face to see if he was joking. But he was not.

"If it's okay with you, that is," Deacon said tentatively. "And if you think I have it down. I want to sing it. And I want you to play it. We'll bring out the piano. I'll play the accompaniment and sing. But it will just be you and me. No band, no backing track, no synthesizer."

"But... but there's no time. We didn't rehearse. What will the others think?"

"We'll run through at sound check," Deacon said simply. "And the others will think what I tell them to think. This is my show and I'll do what I want. The only person who has a say right now is you. If you say no, then..."

"Yes," JJ said, nodding, fresh tears rolling down her cheeks. "Yes. You can sing my song. I'll play. I'll do it."

JJ couldn't believe this was happening. And she probably wouldn't believe it was happening until they played it that evening onstage in front of thousands. That is, if she could play it. She was so nervous now, her hands shook so much that she didn't think she would be able to play the chords.

"Easy," Deacon said with a chuckle. He must have seen her hands shaking because he got up, walked over, and gently held her hands over the guitar. "You'll be fine, JJ. This is your debut. It's natural to feel nervous. But you'll be fine. I promise."

JJ closed her eyes and began praying silently for serenity. When she realized what she was doing, she stopped and her eyes snapped open. She hadn't done that in a long time. Though there was no evidence Deacon was a practicing Christian, he made the group prayer a part of their pre-show huddle every night. JJ went through her routine prayers and awkward conversations with her estranged Savior during her spare moments in her room, but it had been a while since she had prayed like this. Reflectively. Submissively. Coming to God like it was the only thing she could do, like he was the only thing she needed, like she wanted to be lost in him. And she did. In a way she hadn't wanted to be in a long time. Maybe it was the song. Maybe it was the memories of the service that morning. Maybe it was her utter confusion about her present. Whatever it was, it had caused her to surrender to him. Maybe not forever, but for the rest of this moment. And before she could talk herself out of it again, she closed her eyes and finished her petition. She had wandered far away from the home of his arms, but if he would take her back there now, even for a moment, she would go willingly.

She ran through the song again with Deacon, a new confidence and peace filling her as she did. She didn't know how things would go later, onstage, but she was letting go of any anxiety.

She continued to enjoy that wave of confidence, right up until the pre-show briefing.

"Alright, everyone, I just have a few adjustments for the night," Deacon announced before they broke to get dressed. Kate, Andrew, and a few guys from the sound crew joined them onstage, and everyone else stopped moving to pay attention.

"So we're still going to open with "Satisfied," like we do every time. But after the dancers do their piece, we're going to start the second set with something new," Deacon said. "Backstage is going to bring out a piano and I'll start with a new song I'm trying out. No accompaniment. Just me and the piano. And JJ on guitar."

JJ felt as though every eye turned her way. She looked down at Deacon's feet and tried not to fidget.

"After that, the rest of the band will come in and we'll continue the second set as planned."

"Is this the way we'll be doing it for the rest of the tour?" Sabrina snapped. JJ flinched at the ice in her tone and kept her eyes at Deacon's shoes.

"We're just trying it out," Deacon said easily, not engaging her at the same level. "We'll see how it goes, how the crowd responds, and take it from there."

Murmurs went up from the group, and Kate stepped closer to Deacon and mumbled something to him. From the half roll of Deacon's eyes, JJ suspected it was not an affirmation of the change.

"Look, guys," Deacon said, his tone sharpening as he interrupted the hushed voices. "We're just trying something new. We've done the show the same for the past five cities. What's wrong with mixing it up?"

"Why fix it if it ain't broke?" Kya mumbled through her snaps of gum.

"Because it's my show and I can do whatever the hell I want," Deacon snapped. His words were in response to Kya, but his eyes swept everyone on the stage. "Now, if you have any more concerns to raise about this, we can discuss it after the show. Otherwise, let's get moving. We have two hours to curtain." Then without another word, Deacon strode from the stage.

Sabrina glared at JJ as she turned to follow. "Don't mess up," she threw behind her. Except instead of *mess* she used another four-letter word that JJ had not often encountered, previous to the tour.

"Don't let them get to you," Diana said, looping her arm through JJ's and pulling her toward the dressing room. "They're just jealous. We all know that you're not the kind of girl who's going to be singing backup forever. Just go out there and do your best. If Deacon thinks you got this, then you go get it."

JJ tried to remember that, through the questioning looks she got all evening. More than once she found herself closing her eyes and drifting back to that place of submission she had found earlier in the rehearsal room with Deacon.

By the time the two opening acts had finished their set and JJ was in place behind the curtain, she was ready to go. No matter how confused she was during the day, how many doubts and fears kept her awake at night, it all melted away when she stood in this spot onstage. Standing in the darkness behind the curtain, she could feel the crowd only feet away. Their energy hummed through her like electricity. Her fingers tingled, her muscles were relaxed and ready. Her guitar felt as light as a feather, and it would do what she wanted it to for the next few hours. She was born to be onstage, and she knew it.

Like every night on tour, the minutes melted away. She didn't even have time to be nervous because before she knew it, Deacon was sitting behind the piano and she was standing in the shadows stage left.

"How you doing, Philly?"

The crowd cheered in response to Deacon's question.

"Alright," he said with a laugh. "Well, in the spirit of brotherly love, I wanted to do something special for you tonight. I want to bring you a new song about love. This is a song we've never done before. And to help me, I'm going to invite JJ Isaacs, our lead guitarist, to give me a hand. JJ?"

JJ was surprised at the crowd's cheers as she stepped into the spotlight slightly behind Deacon. She took a deep breath, realizing this was the closest she had come to performing solo before a major crowd. He nodded at her and she let out the breath she was holding. Then she closed her eyes and began playing "I'm Yours." She heard Deacon start on the accompaniment, and then his voice came in smoothly on the first verse. Everything slipped away and it was just her, him, and the music. The performance was seamless and so intuitive that when he nodded to her, she knew to take the backup harmony for the chorus, even though they hadn't rehearsed it.

When they finally got to the end of the song, and he played the last note, there was a pause of silence like she had never heard before at any of their shows. And then the crowd came in cheering and screaming. The applause seemed almost endless. Deacon nodded at JJ and smiled. She returned the nod before slipping back to her place backstage.

The rest of the show seemed to whiz by as they moved from one song to another. The crowd never seemed to tire and was still screaming for more after two encores. Even after the lights went down out front and everyone was backstage, she was still buzzing with the show's energy.

"Great job out there, JJ!"

"Thanks," JJ called back to a guy carrying a huge speaker on his shoulder. She didn't even know who he was, but since she had stepped off the stage after their last set, she had been getting lots of congratulations from people she had barely said two words to before. Everyone seemed to be extra happy tonight, especially Deacon, who had nothing but praise for everyone during their post-show debrief. He had since disappeared into his dressing room with Sabrina and slapped a DO NOT DISTURB sign on the door.

"You rocked the house, girl!" Diana screamed, throwing her arms around JJ. "I'm so proud of you."

JJ laughed, Diana's excitement contagious. "Thanks. But, girl, I was so nervous. When he called my name I thought I was gonna throw up."

"Well, you didn't show it," Diana said, pursing her lips. "You looked like a regular out there."

"Yeah, like a regular climber." JJ almost fell into Diana as Kya pushed past them to her own area.

Diana rolled her eyes. "Forget her. She's just mad it wasn't her." Diana looked over her shoulder at the tall woman reapplying lipstick in the mirror. "It can't always be about you, Kya."

"Whatever," Kya said. "At least it sometimes is. It ain't never about you, Die-ana."

Diana hissed before turning back to JJ. "Anyway, you know you gotta come out with us tonight. We're gonna celebrate."

JJ shook her head. "I don't know. I was gonna check in with my sisters, then crash. I never even got to tell them that Deacon was doing my song tonight."

The truth was that almost immediately after her performance, she'd had this overwhelming desire to talk to Sydney. Her sisters had been the first people she had thought of after she stepped off the stage. Well, actually they had been the second. The first person had surprised her, and for a moment she had wondered if her doctor friend had been thinking about her too.

"Oh, come on, JJ," Diana said, eyes wide. "You have to come out with us, even just for dinner. You know everyone's gonna want to celebrate after the amazing show we had, and you were definitely a part of what made this show amazing."

"Everyone was amazing," JJ said, sweeping her cosmetics

into their case and zipping it shut. "I think that's the best crowd we've had since LA."

"I know," Diana said, pulling the pins out of her hair and letting her medium-length tresses fall loose. "I am looking forward to going to Atlanta tomorrow, but I am so glad we get that week off after. Touring is kicking my butt."

"Don't I know it," JJ said, zipping her outfit into her garment bag before lifting the whole thing off the hook. "That's why I gotta check out of these nights out every now and then. I don't know how the rest of you keep up."

"Just barely," Diana said with a laugh.

"Anyway, girl, I'll catch you in the morning," JJ said, gathering her things and heading through the door. "Remember, the tour bus leaves at one p.m. tomorrow. Don't party too hard tonight. You too, Kya."

"Girl, please, this body is too fine to be inside," Kya said.

Diana rolled her eyes. "Bye, JJ."

JJ adjusted the shoulder straps of her travel bag as she walked through the backstage area to the exit, waving to the crew along the way. She pushed open the door to the outside and cool air swept over her flushed skin. Contentment settled in her stomach and she could feel it in the smile on her face. This had been a good night. Scratch that. This had been a great night.

She couldn't wait to tell Sydney and Lissandra how amazingly the night had gone. She was really starting to miss them. She quickened her pace as she headed to the bank of taxis waiting to take them back to the hotel.

"Is that my singing sensation, JJ Isaacs?"

JJ turned around at the sound of Deacon's voice. He had just exited the back doors followed by a couple guys from the crew, and Sabrina tucked contentedly under one of his arms.

JJ paused and grinned. "Yeah, it's me. Off to celebrate?"

"Heck, yeah!" Deacon said with enthusiasm. "We're heading to G, on Seventeenth Street. You're joining us, right?"

"Actually, I was thinking of heading—"

"Oh no," Deacon said. "Nobody's heading home tonight.

Everybody's partying. We've already ordered food, reserved a VIP spot. This is gonna be a serious all-nighter."

"But, Deacon..."

"Gentlemen," Deacon said, nodding to the guys with him, "I think our lady here needs some help getting to the car."

Sabrina let out a laugh and JJ watched suspiciously as Deacon's bodyguards, Miles and Cyrus, began heading her way. She started to back away.

"Miles, Cyrus, don't..." She might as well have saved her breath. Before she knew what was happening, she had been heaved fireman-style over Miles's shoulder.

She shrieked and pounded on her captor's back to get him to put her down, but she was sure her protests barely registered over the laughter of the others.

"Just go with it," Sabrina said between giggles as JJ found herself carried across the parking lot. She didn't even realize that Diana and the rest of the singers and crew had come out of the building until she found herself deposited in the back of an SUV beside a laughing Kya.

"Sorry, little lady," Miles said after shutting the door to close her in. "Just following boss's orders."

JJ wanted to be mad at Miles but couldn't bring herself to it after seeing the sheepish look on his face. To his credit, at least he had been gentle with her.

"Guess you're partying with us after all," Kya commented as the SUV pulled off. "God knows your little straight-and-narrow butt needs to have some fun."

Chapter 22

JJ had never been to G Lounge before, but she had heard that it was one of the more upscale spots in Philadelphia—the kind of place where you might spot a celebrity if you were there at the right time. When she got inside she could see why: modern clean interiors, cool neon lighting, and a general atmosphere of sleekness. If there was a lineup outside, JJ never saw it as they went through a private entrance and straight to the VIP lounge, which was situated in what looked like a vault. They hadn't sat down a moment before cocktail waitresses with trays of appetizers began to serve them.

"I didn't know places like this served food," JJ said, nibbling on a miniature stuffed dumpling. The flavors were amazing for such a tiny portion of food. Sydney would love this.

"They don't," Diana said. "But when you roll like Deacon, well, you can get whatever you want."

"Where is Deacon, anyway?" JJ asked. "I thought he and Sabrina would be right behind us."

"They'll be here," Kya said with a laugh. "After they finish their post-show celebration."

Kate and Andrew, whom JJ rarely saw, joined the group after a while. They seemed in equally good spirits.

"Kate! Haven't seen you at one of these in ages," one of the longtime crew members mentioned. "I didn't know you socialized with us commoners."

Kate laughed. "Well, sometimes you have to make an appearance with the people." She turned toward JJ, her eyebrow raised. "JJ! How's it going? Adjusting to life on the road?"

"After six tour stops, I better be," JJ said with a laugh. "It's been amazing though."

"I saw your performance with Deacon tonight," Kate said, her eyes twinkling. "Great job out there. Looks like we might have to keep you around."

Before JJ could respond, Kate's attention was pulled away by Andrew.

"You hear that, girl?" Diana whispered. "The end of this tour might not mean the end of your work with Deacon Hill. Isn't that exciting?"

"It's only exciting when you have it on paper with a signature," Kya said, sipping on a martini. "People talk a lot of junk at these things. In the morning when the alcohol clears, they don't remember much of it."

The scowl on Kya's face was all the warning JJ needed to not get her hopes up. Besides, with everything going on in her life right now, she didn't mind delaying thinking about the future for bit.

The food and the alcohol kept coming without fail. JJ tried to enjoy the night and ignore the parts that always made her uncomfortable when she was out with the team. Like Kya making out with one of the crew members in a back corner, or a few of the others rolling up dollar bills to do lines off the table. She shook her head, amazed that such brilliant, artistic people could ruin their brains with cocaine. Heck, she was amazed that people still did cocaine. Didn't all that go out in the seventies?

She tried to think about how normal it had all become to her. The first time she saw Andrew snort the white stuff, she had run out of the room. She had heard about that kind of thing growing up, but had never been around people who did it, much less seen people do it firsthand. Now it was such a regular affair that she just turned the other way. But whenever the coke came out, she knew that it was her time to go. She was about to whisper her departure to Diana when Deacon and Sabrina finally arrived. They nearly fell over someone's legs as they stumbled into the VIP area, but no one seemed to mind. JJ could tell that wherever they had been, they had started their own party because they were both clearly wasted.

"JJ! You're here!"

JJ tried not to gag from the smell of alcohol on Sabrina's breath as she leaned over to hug JJ. "Hey, Sabrina," she said, gently pushing the woman away.

Sabrina didn't mind but stumbled farther into the vault, wedging herself between two of the stagehands. JJ's eyes widened as she watched Sabrina brazenly flirt with both men, even kissing one of them. She glanced over at Deacon and, sure enough, the furrowing of his brows let her know he had caught everything.

JJ stood up to go to Sabrina, but Diana grabbed her arm and shook her head.

"Don't get involved," she said. "They do this every time we go out. It's Sabrina's way of getting back at Deacon. Trust me, they'll both be over it tomorrow. You pick a side and it might never be forgotten."

"So everyone just lets them do this?" JJ asked, looking back and forth between Sabrina and Deacon.

Diana nodded. "Everyone knows to stay out of it."

JJ shook her head. More and more she was beginning to wonder if she could ever really fit into this life. As she watched Deacon do shots with Cyrus, she wondered if she wanted to.

"I'm gonna go to the bathroom," JJ said. She excused herself to the washroom, where a cool splash of water in her face revived her senses enough for her to know she needed to leave immediately. She dried her face with a paper towel and headed back to the table to say her good-byes.

Before she even got close to their section, she could hear their voices. She knew it was Deacon and Sabrina. She had heard them argue before. By the time she had pushed through the crowd to the VIP lounge, they were both gone.

"What happened?" JJ asked. "I heard them screaming."

Kya, who was now sitting up front with her male companion, rolled her eyes. "They got into it again and Sabrina took the limo and left."

"So where's Deacon?" JJ asked. Kya shrugged and her make-out partner looked just as clueless.

"He stormed out of the club," Diana said, taking a skewer of grilled chicken from a tray on the table.

"Drunk?" JJ asked. "Did anyone go after him?"

No one seemed to be paying attention to JJ, and those who were didn't seem concerned.

"Don't think so," Cyrus said, glancing at Kya and Diana for confirmation. Diana shook her head.

"So you all are just sitting here while Deacon walks around drunk in Philadelphia," JJ said. She met their indifference with disgust. Then she grabbed her purse and headed to the exit.

"This always happens," Cyrus called after her. "He just needs time to cool off, then he'll be back."

She heard Diana call out that he would be fine, but she didn't stop. Outside the club, the night was cool and busy. It was almost two a.m., but people were still milling around up and down the sidewalk. JJ didn't know which way to turn.

"Lord help me," she breathed absently. She turned and walked in the direction of the most lights. Most of the places she saw were closed, save a few bars.

"Deacon!" She called his name a few times, but there was no answer. People looked at her inquisitively, but no one stopped to question her. She kept walking, keeping her eyes peeled for a tall black man with low-cropped hair, a black leather jacket, and spotless men's Jimmy Choos. When she had almost given up hope, she saw a figure staggering slowly ahead. He paused awkwardly then took a few more uncertain steps.

"Deacon!" He didn't respond. But when she grabbed him and turned him around, she breathed a sigh of relief.

"Deacon, geez, I've been looking for you!"

He stared at her through glazed, reddened eyes.

"The limo," he slurred. "I wasssss looking forrrr the limo."

JJ grimaced as his hot, alcohol-tainted breath hit her full force. He looked a hot mess, not like the superstar on posters plastering the city or even like the man who had performed for a crowd of thousands just hours earlier.

"It's gone," JJ said gently. "Sabrina took the limo."

"Sabrina." His eyes grew dark. "She . . . she . . ."

"It's okay," JJ said, realizing he was struggling with his words. "Why don't we get you sobered up a little and then you can tell me the rest?"

Deacon nodded. "Okay."

JJ stumbled a little as he threw a heavy hand over her shoulder. She squeezed her eyes shut for a moment. What now? She could go back to the club, but she didn't think she could carry the majority of Deacon's weight that far.

She looked around for somewhere open. Across the street, a restaurant. It looked empty and someone was sweeping out front. But maybe she would have some luck. She half dragged Deacon across the road, listening to him mumble about Sabrina and losing the limo.

When she got to the restaurant, there was a couple sitting inside at a table and a man at the counter. She stumbled in and settled Deacon in the nearest chair, glad to have his solid 210 pounds off her shoulders.

"Ma'am, we're about to close."

She looked up at the waiter and gave him her best pleading look. "I know," she said. "But I just need a cup of coffee for my friend. Just to sober him up a little while our transportation comes."

The waiter pursed his lips.

"Just ten minutes and a cup of coffee," JJ pleaded. "That's all I need and I'll be out of here."

The waiter sighed. "He's gonna need black."

JJ breathed a sigh of relief. "Yes. Thank you."

Once he was gone, she turned back to Deacon and found

him with his head on the table, snoring. She sighed. Maybe that was best, for now anyway.

Pulling out her cell phone, she called Miles. He hadn't been at the club, so she assumed he had been the one to take Sabrina back to the hotel. Chances are he would be sober enough to come get them. Cyrus, the other half of Deacon's detail, had been knocking back shots the last time she saw him, and as such, was not a preferred driver of transportation.

JJ was sure the phone rang about a dozen times with no answer. She would have thought she had the wrong number, except it was programmed into her phone and she had used it just the day before.

"Speak to me."

"Miles, this is JJ. Where are you?"

"Back at the hotel," Miles said, his voice low and hushed. "Look, this isn't really a good time..."

"Yeah, for me either," JJ said. "I'm sitting across from a passed-out Deacon. We're in a restaurant near the club and they're about to throw us out. I need you to come get him."

JJ wouldn't normally have taken that tone with Miles, but as Deacon's employee, he should have been the one carting a drunk Deacon around, not JJ.

"Whoa, Deacon's with you? Why isn't he at G with Cyrus? He was supposed to keep an eye on him while I took Sabrina back."

"Look, we can talk about who did what later. Right now, I need you to come pick him up."

She heard Miles curse on the other end. "JJ, I can't. I got Sabrina, and if she knew I was leaving to pick up Deacon..."

JJ couldn't believe what she was hearing. Miles wouldn't leave because it would upset Sabrina? Was something going on between Miles and Sabrina? JJ shuddered, deciding immediately that she didn't even want to know. This tour group was more twisted than she had imagined.

"Miles, I don't know what's going on between you and Sabrina, and I don't want to. But at the end of the day Deacon is your boss, and if that's the case, then shouldn't he be your first priority?"

There was a pause on the other end.

"Not everything is the way it seems, JJ," he said finally, his voice dropping even lower.

A chill ran through JJ as Miles's words sank in. Now that was a cryptic message if she had ever heard one.

"Look, I won't be able to leave, but I'm gonna have someone come get you. Message me your location."

"Okay," JJ said, still too stunned from Miles's previous statement to offer much more.

"Just sit tight. Someone will be there," he said. "Oh, and JJ?"

"Yeah?"

"Good looking-out for Deacon," he said. "Lots of people would have said it wasn't their business and left him out there. And maybe it would have worked out and he would be fine. But I'm glad you didn't let that happen."

"Thanks for taking care of this for me," JJ said. "I'll let you know when we make it to the hotel."

By the time JJ ended the call and messaged Miles the address to the restaurant, the waiter was back with a tall cup of steaming black coffee and a glass of water. JJ managed to revive Deacon and have him take small sips from the coffee until it cooled enough for him to drink more. The couple who had been occupying a table when JJ came in had left, and JJ could feel the waiter's eyes on her, wondering when she would do the same.

"Don't worry," Deacon slurred, almost face down in the coffee cup. "We'll leave them a big tip."

It was the first fairly coherent sentence Deacon had put together since she found him, and it gave her hope. Just as the waiter was about to approach her again, a black SUV with tinted windows pulled up out front. JJ recognized it as the one Miles had driven Deacon around in earlier that day.

"Time to go," she said, getting up and digging in her purse for enough to cover the half-finished coffee and the waiter's time. Before she could, however, Deacon pulled out five twenties and dropped them on the table.

"Let's go," he said, nodding to the door.

Despite the apparent return of his sobriety, he still needed

JJ's help to get him out the door and to the car. With the driver's help she got him inside, where he almost immediately passed out again.

"Man, he is totally smashed," the driver said after buckling him in.

"Yup," JJ said, getting in the backseat beside Deacon. She'd had enough experiences with Lissandra to know that she needed to monitor Deacon so he didn't end up choking on his vomit. That would definitely void everything else she had done thus far to find him and make sure he ended up in his hotel room instead of face down in a gutter.

JJ let out a breath she didn't know she had been holding as the vehicle pulled away from the curb. She closed her eyes and wondered how her amazing night had turned into this. This man who had been a career icon, an open door to her future, a mentor even, was now lying drunk beside her, drooling down one cheek, without a friend in the world to help him. What would America think if they saw this? She shook her head. *Indeed, all that glitters is not gold.*

They took a back entrance to the hotel. JJ had to fight her anxiety and accompany Deacon up the private elevator to his suite. Miles's friend, the driver, who remained unnamed, seemed to know exactly where he was going. JJ began to wonder what they would do when they got to Deacon's room, but her worry was unfounded. Before they could even knock, the door to the suite opened and Miles was standing on the other side.

"We'll take it from here, JJ," Miles said. "You've already done more than anyone could ask."

JJ shrugged. "Just wanted to make sure he was okay."

Miles nodded and helped Deacon inside. "It's appreciated."

JJ nodded. She glanced at them one more time before turning and heading back to the elevator, the only access off the floor. It was only when she was back in her own room that the exhaustion of the night hit her full force. As she changed out of her clothes into sleepwear, the questions that she had been probing all night floated to the surface again. What had Miles meant about things not being what they seemed? What was the hold Sabrina seemed to have over all of them? What was with everyone's indifference? But the biggest one was the question she had for herself: Was this what her life would be like in this industry? Is this what fame looked like? And if so, was she willing to accept that?

JJ was still pondering that question as she closed her eyes, but instead of answers, all she got was unsettled, troubled sleep.

Chapter 23

"He did *what?*"

"He sang my song onstage," JJ said, grinning even as she relayed the story to her sister. "He played it too, kinda Stevie Wonder style. I did backup on the guitar and harmony on the vocals for a few spots."

"Wow, JJ, that's amazing," Sydney said, her excitement palpable across the distance. "I can't believe this. Deacon Hill sang your song! Dang, I wish I had been there. I would have screamed through the whole thing."

JJ laughed, enjoying her sister's enthusiasm as she sat poolside enjoying an early breakfast. Despite the exhaustion from the night before, she hadn't been able to sleep past seven. And with nothing else to do until it was time to head out on the road with the tour team, she had changed into a swimsuit and come down to the hotel pool to do a few laps and have breakfast. The bright sunshine lighting up the clear sky had energized her and motivated her to catch up with her calls while enjoying the last of her meal. Sydney had been first on her list.

"That must have been the best night of the tour so far," Sydney said.

"Yeah, it was," JJ said.

JJ bit her tongue and decided to hold back the less pleasant details of the night. Although they hadn't spoken for almost two weeks, as soon as Sydney answered JJ's call it had been like nothing had ever happened between them. She had been nothing but happy to hear from JJ. They were having such a good conversation thus far, JJ didn't want to do anything or bring up any subjects that might spoil it.

"Anyway, how are things with you?" JJ asked, plowing ahead. "You pick a date for the wedding yet?"

JJ knew she had hit a subject of interest to Sydney when her sister immediately started gabbing about all the preparations she and Hayden had started making for the wedding.

"We are thinking six months or so from now," Sydney said. "You know, give Sheree time to settle in with the baby and be recovered enough to go out. Hayden wants her to be a part of the wedding. He wants her to feel a part of our new family."

"And you?" JJ asked. "How do you feel about that?"

Sydney paused. "I think it would be good. Sheree seems a lot different from before. I visited her a few times in the hospital and I can tell that she's really trying. There's a lot of water under the bridge between us, but we both love Hayden, so we have to try and make it work."

"She's not a bad person," JJ said. "I think she's just not used to having people care about her. I don't know the details, she hasn't told me much, but I think things were pretty unstable for her growing up, and she had to look out for herself. Having your guard up like that can make you hurt others when you're only trying to protect yourself."

"Speaking of hurting others, you will never guess who came to visit Sheree," Sydney said.

"Dean?"

She heard Sydney gasp. "Yes! How did you guess?"

JJ smiled. "I had a feeling. He wants to know about that baby. As much as he's hurting over what Sheree did, he doesn't want to miss out on the chance to be a part of that kid's life—you know, like how Dad did after the divorce? We almost never saw him, remember?"

"Yeah, I remember," Sydney said. "That actually makes sense."

"He just needed time to get over the initial pain of seeing her again," JJ said. "He'll come around, as long as we don't push him."

"Listen to you, all deep and perceptive," Sydney said. "This is the JJ that I remember. I miss you, girl."

JJ sighed. "Yeah. I miss me too."

The sisters chatted a few minutes more about work and family goings-on. It was the best conversation JJ had had with her sister in months. Maybe what they needed was some space to be able to appreciate each other more.

In the middle of a story about Lissandra's latest adventure, a call came in on the other line. When JJ saw who it was she switched over to put her new caller on hold.

"I gotta go, Syd," JJ said, when she switched back over to her sister.

"The Deacon Hill machine ready to suck you back in, eh?"

JJ paused. "Uh, no."

"Who then?" Sydney asked.

Another pause. "It's Simon."

"Simon?"

"Dr. Massri."

"Oh, so he's Simon now?" Sydney asked, her voice laced with amusement.

"Syd, don't even go there."

"So you're ready to kick me, your flesh and blood, off the phone so you can talk to Simon."

"I've been talking to you for over an hour!"

"So is this a regular thing for you now?" Sydney asked, her curiosity piqued. "Is this like your daily call from Simon?"

JJ rolled her eyes at the way her sister kept saying his name. "No, he just calls me to keep me updated on how Sheree is doing."

"He doesn't call me!"

"Sydney!"

But it was too late, her sister was already dying with laughter on the other end.

"He's still there. I have to go," JJ said.

Sydney could barely contain her laughter. "Tell Simon I said hello!"

JJ let out a breath as she clicked over.

"Hey, Simon," JJ said. After hearing Sydney do it so many times, she had to stop herself from saying his name in the same tone as her sister.

"Hey, yourself," he said, a smile in his voice. "How are you?"

JJ grinned. "Good. Great, actually."

Especially now that she was talking to him, she thought.

"You sound great," Simon said. "Definitely not as stressed as you did two days ago."

That had been Friday evening between rehearsals and sound check. After a hectic week of traveling and suffering Sabrina's mood swings, JJ had been more than a little on edge.

"Yeah, I just got done talking to my sister. It was the best conversation we've had in ages. On top of that, we had a great show last night," she said, settling back into her chair. "Deacon sang one of my songs."

Why had she told him that? She hadn't planned to. It just sort of slipped out.

"One of your songs?" Simon asked, pleasant surprise tipping into his voice. "You mean something you wrote yourself?"

"Yes," JJ said with a laugh. "The song from my audition, actually. He said he loved it and wanted to sing it on the show. We had been jamming out—singing hymns, of all things—when he just started playing my song and told me he wanted to do it. We barely had time to rehearse. But the performance was amazing."

"That's incredible," Simon said.

"I know," JJ responded, enjoying the way enthusiasm was slipping through his normally calm demeanor.

"Judith Isaacs, look at you," he said with admiration. "Guess you've adjusted, not feeling as lost as before."

JJ let out a sigh. "For those moments on the stage, yes. But everything else is so insane. Sometimes I wonder if I am cut out for this life."

"What do you mean?" Simon asked. She could almost see his brows furrowing in concern.

Instead of filtering like she had with her sister, she told Simon everything, from the coke snorting at the club to Deacon storming out drunk, to her odd conversation with Miles on the phone. After all, he had already seen her at her worst, hopped up on caffeine pills and energy drinks. There was little left to hide from him.

"Sometimes I feel like I've stepped into this alternate universe," she said. "All this crazy stuff is going on around me and no one seems to care. To everyone else it seems okay."

Simon was silent on the other end, as if giving JJ space to think through everything she had just shared with him.

"You think you could live with that?" he asked after a few moments, voicing the exact same question she had been asking herself the night before.

"I don't know." JJ closed her eyes and rested her head back. "Guess my confusion is back."

She heard him pause on the other end. "Have you been praying about it?"

"I have, actually," JJ said.

"And?"

"And I still don't know," she said in defeat. "A lot of things have happened to make me think, make me question. But the truth is, I just don't know, Simon."

"You will," he said. "In time, you will."

There was a pause on the line and JJ remembered their last moments together in the airport. Since then, the calls had started going not just from Simon to JJ but just as often from JJ to Simon. Furthermore, neither of them had bothered to pretend that the calls were just about Sheree anymore. There were times when they spoke and Sheree wasn't mentioned at all. But as to what they were doing with their new friendship and the unspoken tension that crackled between them—there had been no talk about that.

"When will I see you again?" Simon asked suddenly.

"We get a weeklong break after Atlanta," JJ said without hesitating. "I should be back in a little over a week."

"Good," he said.

"Good?" JJ asked.

She heard him chuckle. "Yes, good."

"Why good?" she ventured hopefully.

"Because I need to see how my patient is doing, whether she's been following doctor's orders," he said.

JJ bit her lip. "Oh. Is that all?"

"Well, Judith, that's a lot," he said, his already deep voice dropping an octave. "It might require a long drive out of town, or a dinner or two."

JJ smiled. "Is that so? Is this some new kind of medical service, Doctor?"

He laughed. "More like experimental. As in, it's never been used before now."

"Sounds interesting," JJ mused.

"Think it's something you might try out?" Simon asked.

Before JJ could answer, a newspaper fell right on top of her plate, jostling her coffee cup. She looked up to see Sabrina standing over her, wearing oversized sunglasses and a scowl.

"Uh, let me call you back." JJ ended the call with Simon without waiting for his response.

"Something wrong?" she asked, looking up at her unwelcome guest.

"I don't know," Sabrina snapped. "Who were you just talking to?"

JJ's brow crinkled. "My sister-in-law's doctor?"

"Smiling like that?" Sabrina folded her arms. "Sure you were."

"Okay, Sabrina," JJ said, trying to stave off the annoyance that came from having newspaper in your eggs. "You want to tell me what's going on, or am I going to have to guess?"

"Maybe you should," Sabrina said. "I am sure your guesses would be better than mine. For one, could you guess why there's a picture of you hugged up on Deacon in the *Enquirer*?"

Before JJ could respond, Sabrina reached down and flipped

open the tabloid to the second page, where there was indeed a picture of her and Deacon together.

JJ groaned. "Sabrina, this is not what it looks like. This was from last night after Deacon left G Lounge drunk. I was just helping him into the vehicle that took him back to the hotel."

"And took you too, right?" Sabrina asked accusingly.

"Yes, but—"

"And did you help him to his room too?" Sabrina asked. "And help him out of his clothes and into bed?"

JJ's eyes widened. "You can't think…"

From the look on Sabrina's face and the way her pale skin was turning red, that was exactly what she was thinking.

"Sabrina, nothing happened with me and Deacon," JJ said. "I never even went into his hotel room. I helped him to the door and that was it!"

"You expect me to believe that, with a picture like this?" she said, waving the newspaper in JJ's face. "Nothing is going on with you and Deacon? So why all of a sudden is he giving you solos onstage and hanging out with you one-on-one?"

So that's what this was about. JJ was starting to get the full picture. She pushed back her chair and stood up so she was face-to-face with Sabrina. At this level she could see something beyond the anger in the woman's eyes: fear.

"Nothing's going on with me and Deacon," JJ said calmly. "Sure, he sang the song from my audition onstage last night, but I had nothing to do with making that happen. And everything else? Like I said, it was just an odd night. If you don't believe me, ask him yourself."

JJ could almost see Sabrina deliberate as she wavered between believing and not believing. Finally she slammed the paper on the table and stepped right into JJ's space.

"I'm watching you, JJ Isaacs."

Then before JJ could respond, she stormed away from the table and through the doors that led back to the hotel. JJ felt the eyes of those in the pool and on the patio watching her, but she ignored them, sinking back into the chair she had just vacated. She looked down at the crumpled paper in front of her. There it was, the photo of her and Deacon in the *Enquirer.* And seeing the photo of Deacon with his arm draped across her shoulder, her hand on his chest, she could understand how people might make assumptions. When had they even been photographed anyway? At that time of the morning, who would have known they were there? Had the waiter at the almost closed restaurant tipped someone off? Or had it been a random passerby with a camera phone?

She was about to crumple the paper and toss it when another shot caught her eye. She grabbed the paper and held it closer to make sure she was seeing right. She felt heat rush to her face when she did. On the next page was the picture of a well-known hip-hop artist in a strip club receiving a lap dance from a very scantily clad woman. Next to it was a smaller photo of said celebrity's wife. But that was not the image that had her seeing red. It was who was sitting beside the hip-hop artist, receiving a lap dance of his own. Rayshawn, her manager slash boyfriend, who was very much on his way to becoming her ex-boyfriend. JJ crushed the paper and tossed it into the garbage by the door as she headed inside to her room. This was exactly why she didn't read tabloids.

Chapter 24

Five days and twenty hours.

JJ stuffed clothes into her suitcase at lightning speed, mentally counting the days until she would be away from all the Deacon Hill craziness and back in Toronto with people who didn't think their nose was an intake spot for chemicals and their bodies a rental spot for visitors. She needed a break. From the hotels, from the stages, from the rehearsals, even from singing. Just some time when she could wake up in her own bed, eat dinner at her kitchen counter, and just be normal. Just be JJ, little sister to Sydney and Lissandra, big sister to Zelia, Dean, and Josephine, daughter to Jackie, sister-in-law to Sheree, and aunt to what would soon be the most beautiful boy or girl in the world. She couldn't wait.

And then there was Simon.

Simon, whom she found herself thinking about at the most unexpected times. Like in the morning when she woke up, before she got out of bed. Or on the tour bus late at night, when everyone else was asleep and all she could do was stare out the window at the white lines on the highway. Simon, who wanted to see her when she got home. Simon, who had saved her life once. Maybe twice. Simon, whom she felt like she had known for a lifetime but was still very much a mystery. Simon, who she knew was praying for her, even if he had never said it.

JJ shook her head and chided herself for slowing her pace as she thought about the man who had come back into her life. Why hadn't she met him a year ago, instead of in the middle of all the whirlwind changes in her life? And by the time she was back in Toronto again, more permanently, he would be back on a plane, on his way somewhere out of her life. Timing. Their timing had always sucked.

JJ sat on the suitcase to zip it shut, just as her hotel phone rang.

"JJ, this is Miles. We're on our way to pick you up in thirty minutes. Meet us at entrance D."

"Thirty minutes!" JJ said, suddenly feeling frantic. "I thought the tour bus wasn't due to leave for another hour and a half!"

"You're not going with the tour bus," Miles said. "Thirty minutes."

He hung up before she could ask any more questions, and though JJ wanted to deconstruct his statement further, there was a lot she would need to do to be ready in half an hour.

She managed to take care of it all and was taking the stairs down to the main floor when her cell phone rang. From the caller ID she knew it was Miles. He was probably already waiting for her, so instead of answering, JJ shoved the phone into the purse resting on top of her luggage and wheeled her suitcase through the wide corridors of the hotel's main floor. When she got to the secluded exit, Miles was standing at the door chatting on his cell phone and looking impatient.

"We're late."

JJ barely managed to grab her purse before he lifted her suitcase and carried it out the door. He placed it in the trunk of his signature black, heavily tinted SUV before opening the back passenger door for her. JJ's mouth fell open.

"Deacon!"

"JJ, let's go," Miles said. "We don't have all day."

The car door had barely closed behind her before she turned to Deacon. He was wearing a dark dress shirt with the sleeves rolled up and dark glasses that hid his eyes completely.

"What are you doing here?" JJ asked.

A smile curved his lips, but it seemed tired. "Getting ready to head to Atlanta, of course," he said. "What else?"

"You're right," JJ said. "The better question is, what am I doing here?"

"Enjoying my courtesy," Deacon said sincerely. "After what you did for me last night, there was no way I was going to let you sit on a bus for twelve hours. You're flying first class with me to Atlanta."

JJ's mouth fell open.

Deacon chuckled. "It's okay. I'll give you a few moments to take it in."

JJ wanted to protest, wanted to tell him it was unnecessary. But she had come to understand certain things about Deacon, one of them being that if he set his mind to something he was going to do it. Besides, she was already in the car on the way to the airport, and the truth was, she hadn't been looking forward to that twelve-hour bus ride either.

"Thank you," JJ said finally. "You know this is totally unnecessary though. I would have gone looking for anyone."

"You know, I actually believe you," Deacon said with a smile.

"How are you feeling today, anyway?" JJ asked, regarding him with concern. "You were pretty banged up last night. Those sunglasses trying to keep out something other than the sun?"

Deacon turned away and looked out the passenger window.

"I'm alright," he said quietly. "Better than this morning, that's for sure. I woke up with a hangover so bad I could barely see straight." He shook his head. "I don't think I'll ever get that drunk again."

JJ pursed her lips. "I suspect you've said that before."

He turned to look at her, seemingly surprised at her response. Then his face relaxed into a smile.

"Yeah, I have," he said sheepishly. "Guess I forget how bad it can get."

"Or things get so bad you want to forget," JJ offered.

He gave her that surprised look again. "Are you always like this?" he asked. "Always so shrink-like?"

JJ laughed. "On my good days. Comes from being the middle child in a crazy family with lots of kids."

"Lots of issues?" Deacon asked.

"Yup," JJ said. "And I had to learn to see them fast, so I wouldn't end up taking everything personally."

Deacon nodded. "Makes sense."

"Speaking of issues," JJ began, looking down, "I'm not trying to cause any trouble between you and Sabrina. I don't know that she would agree with this extension of courtesy."

"You let me worry about Sabrina and that silly picture in the paper," Deacon said, turning to look ahead even as his face hardened. "She should know by now that that junk don't mean anything. But that's her, always flying off the handle over things that aren't important."

JJ shifted uncomfortably. As much as she was glad for the opportunity to improve her relationship with her boss, she wasn't trying to become his relationship counselor either. She had enough problems of her own to handle. Plus, Sabrina had warned her off, and in order to have a peaceful life, JJ wanted to heed the warning and stay out of the Deacon-Sabrina drama.

"What you did last night, that was important," Deacon said, turning to look at her. "A lot of them pocket-watchers that I roll with act like they have my back, but when it comes down to it, a lot of them leave me hanging. I'm just glad someone like you was there."

JJ shrugged. "Like I said, it's not a big deal. I would have done it for anyone."

"If you say so, JJ Isaacs," Deacon said with a smile. He shook his head. "You really are a newbie to this industry. Can't wait to see what you will be like five years from now, after the business does its work on you. All I'll say is, be careful. People are never what they seem, and they'll take advantage of your kindness."

As they rode to the airport, Deacon told JJ what it had been like for him his first few years in the industry, how he had been stuck in the background writing for and producing other artists. It took more than five years before he got his big break.

"You would never believe some of the songs I've written," Deacon said with a laugh. "Hits with someone else's name on them. I don't mind though—it's part of the business."

"Really?" JJ asked. "But how can you see people getting famous off of your songs, see crowds weeping over your lyrics, and not feel some resentment?"

"Because that's how it is," Deacon said with a shrug. "That's the cycle. I sing lots of songs that I didn't write. And when they become hits, you think anyone goes back to read the CD jacket cover to see who wrote it?"

"I do," JJ said.

"That's because you're a musician, a writer," Deacon said. "But even the singers who work with me don't care. Nobody cares. But they should. That's why, before I made it, I promised I would never sing someone else's music without giving them their due credit. That's why you don't have to worry. You'll get credit for your song and paid for every time we sing it. And we will be singing it from now on."

JJ's eyes widened. "You're going to do the song again in Atlanta?"

"Definitely," Deacon said with a nod. "And Kate's even considering working it into the rest of the tour. We'll talk about that after the break. But for sure, this week we gotta rehearse for your song."

JJ couldn't stop grinning. They were going to sing her song! Again! In Atlanta! Maybe on the rest of the tour! She wanted to jump up and down and start cheering, but there wasn't enough space in the vehicle, so she just settled for smiling all the way to the airport.

She was still smiling when they drove right into the airport and onto the tarmac. The SUV stopped a few feet from a small passenger plane. The doors to the vehicle opened and the wind rushed in, startling JJ with its force. She managed to climb out of the van and follow Miles and Deacon to the steps of the plane. It was only when she got up to the top of the steps behind them and Sabrina stepped in front of the entrance that JJ's smile faded.

She could no longer see Deacon and Miles, who had disappeared inside the plane, but she suspected that was part of Sabrina's plan. With the wind howling around them, she could barely hear, either. But she didn't miss Sabrina's words as she leaned close to JJ's ear.

"You didn't think I would let you spend two hours alone with him, did you?" she hissed for JJ's ears only. "If you think you can sneak in here and use him as your ladder to the top, you better think again."

JJ sighed. "I never thought that."

She could tell from Sabrina's eyes that the woman didn't believe her. But instead of responding, Sabrina turned around and headed deeper into the plane. JJ sighed and followed slowly, suddenly wishing that she had opted for the twelve-hour bus ride instead. Private jets were so overrated.

Chapter 25

"In twenty-four hours I'll be home!"

Simon's deep laughter rumbled through the phone line. "Someone's excited."

"You have no idea." JJ balanced the phone between her ear and shoulder so she could use her hands to stuff clothes into the suitcase open on her bed. She knew it was only a week and in eight days she would be back on the road for the last three stops of the tour in Miami, Chicago and Toronto. But she was choosing not to think about that. She was going to focus on her one week of freedom

"Now that we've done the Atlanta shows, all I can think about is my one week free of hotel beds and restaurant food and sound checks, and Sabrina's scowl. If we didn't have that press event tomorrow afternoon, I would be on a plane to Toronto tonight."

"Don't worry, you'll be here soon enough," Simon said with an unhurried ease that JJ had come to appreciate.

"How's Sheree doing?" JJ asked, looking for the left shoe of the pumps she had worn onstage earlier that night.

"She's great," Simon said. "Very occupied with her fan club."

JJ let out a laugh. "What?"

"Your sister-in-law is something else," Simon said. "She's got all the nurses under her spell. I promise you, Judith, every time I go in to see her there are at least two of them in there. Did she tell you she did Janice's hair in prep for her wedding?"

"Better," JJ said with a grin. "She sent me pictures she took with her iPhone."

Simon groaned. "Can you believe she did all that from her hospital bed?"

"You let them have curling irons and hot combs in her room?"

"As if I could stop them," Simon said. "They even got the chief nursing officer on their side."

JJ laughed. "I think you were out-womaned."

"You better believe it."

JJ smiled, enjoying her phone time with Simon. She had gotten used to his calls, so much so that on the days she didn't speak to him, she longed to hear his voice; needed to hear his voice. He had become her calm in the midst of the Deacon Hill chaos and a nice way to forget about her private embarrassment over Rayshawn. It had been almost five days, and she had yet to confront him about the strip-club debacle. He had been conveniently unavailable to take her calls. JJ knew that was intentional. But she refused to think about him anymore. She needed her upcoming vacation too much to let him ruin it.

"What time does your flight get in?" Simon asked.

"Around six-ish," she said, moving to the bathroom to begin packing her cosmetics and toiletries. "I should clear customs by seven."

"Then I'll be there at around six thirty, just in case you get in early."

JJ wasn't sure when it had been decided that he would pick her up at the airport. She had mentioned to him in passing that Sydney and Lissandra were catering an event that night. He had mentioned that he happened to be off that evening. She didn't quite remember if she had asked or he had offered, but somehow they had ended up with this arrangement.

"Do you mind if we stop at the hospital?" JJ asked. "I can't wait to see Sheree and see the new ultrasound pictures of our little bugaboo." She sighed. "I can't believe he'll be born in just a month!"

"He?" Simon echoed.

JJ stopped packing. "It's not a he? It's a she?"

Simon laughed.

"What do you know, Simon Massri!"

"I'm not talking," he said mischievously.

"You know, don't you!" JJ accused. "You know if it's a girl or a boy!"

"Of course, I know. I'm her doctor."

"Then you have to tell me," JJ whined. "Pleeeese... I promise I won't say anything."

"Ha! No way. You and your sisters can't keep any secrets!"

"That is not true!"

"Really," Simon said. "So I guess it was okay for me to know that you used to Google my name after you got back from Paris."

JJ screamed. "Ahh! Who told you that!"

Simon laughed. "One of your sisters. I think her name was Zelia?"

JJ closed her eyes as images of ways to kill her sister flipped through her brain. Zelia. One day her inability to keep a secret was really going to cost her her life.

"How did she even know? The only person who knew that was Sydney, and Sydney didn't even know that you were the guy, unless... Sheree!"

JJ listened to Simon die of laughter on the other end of the line.

"See what I mean?" he said, his British accent thicker at the end of his hearty laughter. "And you want me to tell you the baby's sex? Sheree would be trying to kill me in the morning."

He chuckled again. "The lot of you are like a bad spy network."

JJ smiled and stood to get back to her packing. "You do have a point. But trust me, Zelia is the worst. You would never believe the secrets that girl has let out. If we want to do anything, or keep anything from Mom, we have to make sure she doesn't know it."

"Yeah, there's one like that in every family. In ours, it's my mother. God bless her heart, she couldn't keep a secret to save her life," Simon said. "When my brother was going to propose to his girlfriend, he couldn't figure out her ring size, so he asked my mother for help. Instead of just trying on one of Darla's rings to get an idea of the size, Mum gets Darla to try on all these rings and then gives some convoluted excuse that she's buying rings for all the women in the family for Christmas and needs to get them made in July so they would be ready in time. Of course, Darla doesn't say a thing, and she acted surprised when Andrew proposed a month later. But later on, she admitted that my mother's ring fiasco let her in on the whole thing."

JJ giggled. "Your poor mom. Not a dishonest bone in her whole body."

"Yeah," Simon said. "You would love her. You should meet her one day."

"It seems only fair," JJ said. "You've met my whole family, and we haven't even gone out on a single date."

"Haven't we?" Simon asked, amused. "I thought that was what we were doing when we went to the reserve."

"That was more like a kidnapping," JJ said.

"And dinner in New York?"

"An apology for making me gag over your healing concoctions."

"Or your winnings from hustling me into drinking it with you," Simon added.

A knock on her hotel door pulled JJ from the bathroom.

"I did not hustle you."

"Oh yes, you did."

She opened the door and froze.

"Simon, there's someone here. I have to go."

"Is everything okay?" he asked, his voice immediately turning serious.

"Uh, I'm not sure yet."

"Call me later—no matter what time."

Since Simon's tone didn't offer much room for discussion, JJ agreed before ending the call. Then she gave her full attention to the surprise standing at her front door.

"It's almost midnight. What are you doing here?" JJ asked, checking the hallway to see that no one else was witnessing their exchange.

"I'll explain in the car," Deacon said, sticking his hands in his pockets nervously. "Right now, I need you to get your coat and come with me. I need you to drive me somewhere."

Chapter 26

Apprehension twisted inside JJ, but the look on Deacon's face told her that he had come to her because he had no one else. So she grabbed her coat and her purse and followed him out the door of her suite. Deacon headed to the elevator, but JJ turned toward the door to the stairs.

"Where are you going?" Deacon asked, confused.

"I don't do elevators," JJ said, her hand on the door to the stairwell.

"We're going up to the rooftop parking," Deacon said. "I don't have time to take the stairs."

"Then you don't have time for me," JJ said. "I don't do elevators."

Deacon's face wrinkled in confusion. "This some kind of phobia?"

"Something like that."

He sighed. "Alright. Let's go."

Neither of them spoke as they took the stairs up to the rooftop parking. Deacon's hand on her back kept her close as they moved quickly through the sparsely lit parking area to the dark Navigator that Miles used to transport Deacon around while they were in Atlanta. This led to JJ's first question.

"Where's Miles?" JJ asked.

"Keeping an eye on Sabrina," Deacon responded. He pressed a button on the key and the car chirped before the doors unlocked. Opening the driver's door, he ushered JJ in before closing the door and coming around to settle himself on the passenger side.

JJ closed her eyes and said a quick prayer before backing out of their spot and following the arrows toward the garage exit. Deacon typed in their destination on the GPS, and JJ waited until they were a few blocks away from the hotel before she opened her mouth again.

"Okay, so you want to tell me what's going on?" JJ asked.

"Not really," Deacon said. "But I suppose I owe you an explanation."

She looked over at him. He was wearing the same dark expression that he'd had since she opened her hotel-room door almost fifteen minutes earlier. She was starting to get used to Deacon's severe mood swings, but this one she had never seen before. He was wearing shades, even though the night was dark, and weariness, like a heavy wet blanket, rested on his person.

"I need to go see someone," he said. "But no one can know about it. Not Kate, not Miles. No one."

"Not even Sabrina?"

"Especially not Sabrina."

"But won't they know you went somewhere, since you're not out partying with everyone else as usual?" JJ asked.

"Maybe, but they know Miles is my transportation, so they'll just think I took someone back to my hotel room. There's a DO NOT DISTURB on the door to support that."

JJ blinked. "So you would rather Sabrina think you are cheating on her than have her know where you're going?"

He turned to look at JJ. "I would rather lose Sabrina, and everything that comes with her, than let anyone know where I'm going. That's how serious it is."

JJ's head was spinning with questions. Where was she taking him? What was so important that he had to hide it from the people closest to him? And what did he mean about everything that came with Sabrina? More and more she felt she was missing some critical information connected to her bandmate.

It took Deacon's yelling her name for her to realize that she had missed the turn that the GPS ordered. She had to make a U-turn to get back on track.

"Just take it easy," Deacon said, glancing wearily from JJ to the rearview mirror. "I don't need us getting stopped by the police. That's why I asked you to drive me, anyway."

"What, you can't drive yourself?"

"My license was suspended. DUI a couple months back. That's why Miles drives me everywhere. And that's why I couldn't take the chance of driving myself. Sure, it's late and I might not get caught, but if I did, it would be in the news everywhere and that would ruin everything."

"Look, Deacon, I'm not feeling real comfortable with this," JJ said, beginning to slow down. Maybe there was time for her to back out. "If this is something illegal..."

"It's not," Deacon said, touching JJ's hand on the steering wheel. "It's just something that no one can know about. After what you did back in Philly, I know I can trust you."

"Deacon, you don't know me," JJ said. "You don't know that I won't sell your secret to the tabloid willing to pay the highest price."

"I do know," Deacon said. "And when we get where we're going, you'll see why."

They were both quiet the rest of the ride, as the city faded behind them, making way for the Atlanta suburbs. A little more than an hour later, JJ pulled up to a massive metal gate and the GPS announced that they had reached their destination.

Deacon pulled out his cell phone and dialed a number from memory.

"I'm here."

The gates creaked slightly as they swung open on their own, and JJ followed the long driveway under a canopy of trees until a huge, three-story mansion came into sight. She began to have flashbacks of the night she first auditioned for Deacon. She wondered if tonight was going to be a similar life-changing experience.

JJ stopped the SUV in front of the walkway that led to the main entrance. The front doors opened, silhouetting a tiny female figure.

"Let's go, we don't have a lot of time." Deacon jumped out of the vehicle and JJ followed suit, having to jog a little to catch up with him before he disappeared inside the house.

As JJ entered, the house seemed as large as Deacon's but felt different—more homey. The front doors led into a wide passageway that opened up into a living area. Even through the muted lighting JJ could see the plush, overstuffed couches with colorful throws tossed over them. A few stuffed animals were scattered about, and a stack of colorful DVDs sat on the floor below the large flat-screen television.

"How is he?" Deacon asked the older woman who had met them at the door, as he cut through the living room toward the stairs.

"Still weak, but better now than he was a few days ago," the woman said. She touched Deacon's arm. "Ever since you called, he's been asking for you."

JJ saw the pain in Deacon's features and her mind raced. Who was this person who Deacon needed to secretly see? His father? A brother? The woman leading their way up the stairs could easily be Deacon's mother, but he wasn't relating to her as if she was a parent. Then before she could question further, the door to a bedroom opened and JJ saw.

She let out a gasp. Even with his flushed, caramel-colored skin and shock of tightly coiled brownish-black hair, the resemblance between the little boy and Deacon was obvious. No one had to tell her. This was Deacon's son.

"Uncle D!"

"Xavier!"

The little boy's face broke into a wide grin and his eyes lit up when he saw Deacon. Sinking down onto the side of the bed, Deacon pulled the little boy into his arms and held him close. JJ was almost sure she heard something like a sniffle, but she couldn't be sure because Deacon's back was to her.

"How are you, little man?" Deacon asked when he finally let the boy go.

"I'm okay," Xavier said. "Grandma says I'm getting better."

"What are you doing up so late?" Deacon chided. "It's way past your bedtime."

"Mommy said you were coming tonight, and I wanted to wait up until you came," Xavier said. "Plus I've been sleeping all day. Mommy wouldn't even let me play video games. All I could do was read books."

Xavier made a face to let them know how he felt about that, and Deacon chuckled. JJ had to cover her mouth to hide her own laughter.

"Is that so?" Deacon said with smile.

"Yes," Xavier said, nodding. "Ask Grandma. Isn't it true, Grandma?"

The older woman chuckled and nodded. "It is."

"Okay, Xavier, it's time for bed," a voice called. From her position just outside the door, JJ couldn't see who, but knew that tone well enough to know it could only come from a mother.

"But Mo-mmmy..."

"No buts! You wanted to wait up see your uncle and now you've seen him. I'm taking your temperature and then you're going back to sleep."

Something pricked at the back of JJ's mind, but she couldn't quite reach it. She moved away from the door to give Deacon and his "family" a few private moments together. Looking over the banister, she got a full view of the living room. She noted the piano in the corner, which she had missed during her earlier observations. Somehow it made sense that Deacon would be involved with another musician. Isn't that the way it went in this business?

"See you in the morning, little man."

"Good night, Xavier."

"Good night, Mommy. Good night, Uncle."

JJ turned around just as the door to Xavier's bedroom closed. Then she got the second shock of the night. She gasped.

"Now you see why I knew I could trust you," Deacon said as he caught her shocked expression. "JJ, Xavier is my son."

He glanced at the familiar woman who was at his side, watching JJ. "This is Cymmone. She's Xavier's mother."

Chapter 27

"So let me see if I understand this: Xavier is Deacon's son, but Xavier thinks Brady is his father?" JJ asked.

It was the following morning and she was sitting at the kitchen counter having breakfast with Cymmone. She had spent the night in Cymmone's guest room while Deacon had slept on a cot in Xavier's room. During the night, Xavier's fever broke and he had woken up with more energy than the day before. Through the patio doors, JJ could see him playing out back with Deacon.

"Yes," Cymmone said. "When I stepped back from the spotlight, I was already pregnant with Xavier. Brady knew about it, but he also knew that I loved him and that there would never be anything between me and Deacon. In spite of my pregnancy, he still wanted to marry me. So I said yes."

"But why let Xavier think Brady is his dad?"

Cymmone sighed. "That was all Deacon's idea. He didn't want Xavier growing up in the spotlight, being constantly photographed and followed around. He wanted him to live an ordinary life, the way Deacon had, growing up. He knew that if people knew Xavier was his son, that would never happen."

"And Brady was okay with that?" JJ knew she was asking very personal questions, but she couldn't stop herself.

"Not at first, but Deacon insisted, and after a while, we all just agreed." Cymmone looked toward the patio. "Sometimes I wonder, though, if that was the right decision."

JJ followed Cymmone's gaze to where Deacon and Xavier were horsing around. She watched Xavier squeal as Deacon picked him up and spun him around a little. JJ had never seen Deacon look so happy—not even when he was onstage.

"He loves that little boy," JJ said absently.

"And Xavier adores him too," Cymmone said. "Sometimes I wonder if somewhere deep inside he already knows the truth."

JJ was struggling. She tried to understand what Cymmone, Deacon, and Brady must have been going through, the circumstances that had caused them to make the decision they made. But having grown up most of her life in a situation where her parents didn't live together, she had a perspective that maybe was unfamiliar to Deacon and Cymmone. And despite the challenges her family situation may have caused, she would never have wanted her parents to lie to her about any of it.

"You can't think there's any way this could end well," JJ said. "Xavier is going to figure out the truth one day, and if it's not from you or Deacon or Brady, he's going to end up resenting one or all of you for it. And even if you break it to him later on, how devastated and angry is he going to be about having grown up being told a lie?"

Cymmone's eyes were glassy when she turned to look at JJ again.

"I think about that every day. Believe me, I do," she said, her quiet voice shaking. "But it's complicated. Brady loves Xavier like his own. He was there when he was born. He could never think of him as anything but his son. And maybe if Deacon was a deadbeat dad, this would be easier. But he's not. He loves Xavier too. Anytime Xavier needs Deacon, he's there. Why do you think I was in Philly the same time as the tour? Xavier wanted to see Deacon, and that was the only way to do it without drawing too much attention. You remember a year ago, Deacon canceled the last three shows of his tour?"

"Yeah," JJ said. "I remember fans were upset, until they were offered free tickets to a show later in the year. News said it was because Deacon was injured during a rehearsal."

Cymmone shook her head. "Xavier swallowed a pen cap and it got stuck in his throat. We had to rush him to emergency. Deacon was there before Xavier was even admitted."

"Pilgrimage to Africa right before this tour?" Cymmone offered.

JJ's mouth fell open. "No way..."

Cymmone nodded with a smile. "Camping with Xavier, Brady, and my brother."

"But there were pictures!"

"From when he went there earlier this year."

JJ sat back in her chair and looked outside again at Deacon with a new appreciation. "Wow."

"Yeah. I know this doesn't make sense to you, JJ, and you probably think we're wrong for doing this, but we don't see any other way," Cymmone said, getting up from her stool and taking her mug over to the kettle. "It's not just about keeping Xavier out of the spotlight, it's also about raising him in a way that is pleasing to God. Deacon would make a great dad, but the way he lives would be a lousy example of the kind of man Xavier should be. I want Xavier to grow up in the knowledge and wisdom of Christ. I want him to have a personal relationship with Christ—to see him as his all in all. How could God want him to grow up in an environment where that would be impossible?"

"So you're saying God wants you to lie to your son instead," JJ said.

Cymmone's mug slipped through her fingers and tipped over on the counter, creating a soppy mess of green tea that spread across the surface and began to drip onto the floor.

JJ jumped up and dashed over to grab the nearest kitchen towel and began sopping up the mess. Then she realized Cymmone was standing by the counter, her hands shaking. JJ abandoned the towel and pulled the woman into her arms.

"I'm sorry," JJ muttered. "I didn't mean to hurt your feelings like that. Sometimes I just say the first thing that comes to my mind without filtering."

She led Cymmone back to their seats, and Cymmone slipped onto the stool once more, burying her face in her hands. Tiny sobs shook her body.

"Brady's not here," she said, her words muffled by her hands.

JJ had noticed. As she lay in Cymmone's guest bed the night before, trying to fall asleep, she had wondered about it, thought it odd that a man would choose to be away from his home while his child was sick and his wife in distress—especially a man who was as good as Cymmone had told her Brady was. In the light of the morning, with Cymmone's explanations, it didn't seem so strange anymore.

"He took the baby and our other son to his dad's place for the night. He won't say it"—Cymmone sniffled—"but he can't be around Xavier and Deacon. It's hard for him to watch them together, watch Deacon in our home, maintain this lie."

"Have you talked to him about this?" JJ asked. "About how you think he feels?"

Cymmone shook her head. "It's too hard. This thing is like a boulder in the middle of our marriage. But it's too late to change it now. We have to do this to protect Xavier. We have no choice."

JJ sighed and slipped onto her own stool. "You know, Cymmone, I think that's the biggest lie the devil tells all of us: We have no choice. I know I certainly bought that one long enough." JJ shook her head. "But the truth is, we always have a choice. We can choose to trust God or to do things our way. We can wait for his direction or we can start walking on our own. It's the devil that makes us think that we lose when we wait on God—that we don't have a choice. But with God nothing is impossible. We think there is only one way to make things go right, but he has a thousand ways to work out our situation that we haven't even thought of yet. But when we sacrifice doing what we know we should, to try and protect what we have, it just hurts us in the end."

Cymmone nodded. "You're right. I guess I am just afraid of losing what I have, and I don't know how to trust God to work things out for me. It's hard, girl."

"Don't I know," JJ said. "It's hard to let go of what we think we have in our hands for what we don't know. But based on what I'm seeing, holding on to what you thought you had, this deception about your son you've created to keep the peace, it's only been causing you more problems. Doesn't it kind of make sense to try it God's way?"

Cymmone smiled and wiped the moistness from her eyes. "It does."

"What's all this crying about up in here?"

Deacon stomped through the patio doors, a giggling Xavier wedged under his arm like a sack of potatoes. JJ giggled and Cymmone couldn't help but smile also.

"Just some girl talk," Cymmone said. "What you doin' with my baby?"

"Your baby?" He turned to one side as if to look around, swinging Xavier along with him. "What baby?"

He swung to the other side. Xavier shrieked, delirious with mirth.

"You mean this one?" Deacon asked, swinging the little boy into an upright position.

"Yes, that one," Cymmone said. "You put that boy down before he throws up all his breakfast."

Deacon tickled Xavier, who erupted in more laughter, then set the little boy down. Xavier collapsed on the floor, breathing heavily but grinning.

"Xavier, go get the stuff you made for your uncle. He's gonna be getting ready to leave soon."

"But he just got here," Xavier whined.

"Yeah, it's cool," Deacon said, leaning back against the kitchen counter across from Cymmone and JJ. "I got time."

"JJ told me about the press event you guys have in a couple hours," Cymmone said. "You don't have time. I'm surprised your cell isn't already ringing off the hook."

"I turned it off."

"Deacon!"

"Look, I came to see my . . ." He stopped and glanced over at Xavier, who was watching them intently. "My nephew. I don't need any distractions. And I can cancel the event—"

"No, you can't."

"It's my tour."

"And this is my house and I'll kick you out if I want to."

JJ looked away from the two of them as they stared each other down. It had become intense quickly. She could only imagine what it had been like when the two of them dated.

"Look," Cymmone said, breaking first. "I know you were worried about Xavier, but he's fine now, so let's not make this a big deal. You being missing like this will just draw more attention than it needs to. Just come by later this week during your break. Okay?"

Deacon frowned, and for a moment he looked younger than the three-year-old on the floor.

"Okay, fine, I'll go." He looked over at Xavier. "I'll be back tomorrow to check on you though, alright?"

An hour later, after they said their good-byes and Cymmone promised to think about what JJ had said, Deacon and JJ were on the road again. Almost as soon as they slid through the high metal gates, Deacon had slid back into his sour mood. JJ could tell he was upset about leaving his son. For Deacon, a few hours with Xavier weren't nearly enough.

"You miss spending time with him, don't you?" JJ said about halfway down the drive.

"I'm sure Cymmone filled you in about why things are the way they are," Deacon deadpanned, his gaze fixed on the road ahead. "This is what's best for Xavier."

"How about what's best for you?" JJ asked.

"What could be better for me?" Deacon asked dryly. "I get to live the celebrity life, sing for millions, make more money than I can spend, travel the world with no attachments. What more could a thirty-two-year-old single man ask for?"

The life he described sounded anything but good coming

from Deacon's mouth. It might be what many thought they wanted, but it didn't seem to be satisfying him.

"I guess it goes without saying, but you can't tell anyone about any of this."

"I know," JJ said.

"Sabrina's gonna ask you."

"I won't say anything."

"She's gonna piece it together," Deacon warned. "She's probably already gone to your room and figured out you weren't there all night. She'll check with everyone else, and before we step into that event she'll know that you were with me. And she'll think a lot of things. I don't care what you tell her, but..."

"She won't hear about this from me," JJ said. "I promise."

Deacon sighed and rubbed a hand over his face.

"She can make things really hard for you."

JJ rolled her eyes. "I can handle Sabrina."

A couple hours later, when she stepped into the rooftop photo shoot and press event for Deacon Hill and She-La, JJ had to admit that she was less sure than she had felt in the car with Deacon. JJ could feel the eyes on her. Everyone's eyes. Even though she had come on her own and Deacon hadn't even made an appearance yet, it felt like everyone knew what had happened the night before and was talking about it. When Diana yanked her into a corner, her fears were confirmed.

"Tell me it's not true," she whispered as they stood near a corner of the Skyline Terrace of the Peachtree Club. "You were not out all night with Deacon."

JJ closed her eyes, wishing that Diana had started with something other than a direct question. "You're my friend, Diana, and you know I would if I could, but I can't talk about this."

Diana's eyes widened and she swore softly. "You were with him! JJ, what were you thinking?"

JJ rubbed her palms together nervously, scanning the rest of the event as she did. Almost everyone was here, including the entire band, Kate, Andrew, and Deacon Hill's press team. Atlanta's top radio station, V-103, was already set up with the DJ spinning hits and broadcasting live for the special-format show. If everything went according to plan, Deacon Hill and She-La would take over Atlanta, their pictures on bus shelters, their faces all over the local magazines and blogs, their hits on everyone's Top 40 list. That is, if Deacon ever showed up. He was usually fashionably late to events, but this was bordering on rude.

"What time is this whole thing supposed to wrap up, anyway?" JJ asked, sidestepping Diana's question. "I have to be at the airport by three."

"Hmm," Diana said, pursing her lips. "Act like you don't hear me. But you better not try that when Sabrina backs you into a corner, and you know she's coming."

"She's gotta catch me first," JJ muttered.

She had kept a constant eye out for the red hair and freckles as soon as she'd arrived. That was the only way she could successfully avoid Sabrina. So far it was working. From where she was standing, she could see Sabrina in the corner with the hair-and-makeup crew. She had been there for a while now, giving JJ a much appreciated moment to relax.

Sabrina had just gotten up from her chair when Deacon breezed through the doors between Miles and Cyrus.

"Sorry I'm late," he said with a wide grin. "But I'm here, and I'm ready to party."

The energy at the event immediately shifted to match the vibe Deacon brought in with him. JJ shook her head, amazed at how he seemed to be able to switch moods with the press of a button. It made her a little sad. It must be something to live most of your life putting on an act for everyone else.

"Alright, everyone, let's huddle," Kate said, waving her ever-present clipboard. "Listen up. Deacon's going to start off with the host for V-103 while the band sets up. We'll do the signature track to open. Ryan Lue and his guys are going to shoot throughout the performance and do shots after. Then Deacon will do the full interview. We'll record the sound bites for V-103, take some candid shots, and then everyone can get drunk and go home."

"Sounds like a plan," Deacon said.

"Alright, let's move and make use of this great sunlight."

JJ and Diana headed for the makeshift stage area. JJ had barely taken two steps when a shoulder slammed into hers from behind, causing her to stumble to the side. As she struggled to catch her footing, she caught the swing of bright red hair.

Diana grabbed JJ's arm and helped steady her. "Told you she was coming."

JJ let out a deep breath. Two more hours. Just two more hours and she would be on a plane, on her way home. She could survive two hours. Or so she thought until she opened her guitar case and found her guitar's B string cut. She cried out as if the cut had been to her own flesh.

"Who did this?" She jumped up angrily and looked around. There was no mistaking the fact that the string had been cut. It had been fine the night before when JJ put it away after the show. She always checked her guitar before and after every show. The instruments were stored with the rest of the band equipment, so only someone from the band would have had access to it.

"Who cut my string?" JJ asked more loudly. She knew she was getting hysterical, but this guitar was special. It had been given to her by Dean, and had her initials carved into the body. She could have gotten a new one at some point, but on this guitar she felt closest to home. No one should have touched her instrument.

Her eyes swung around the band, past Diana, Kya, the guys setting up the amps. None of them would look at her. They hadn't done it, but they all knew who had. Her eyes landed on Sabrina. The smug look on the woman's face said it all.

For a moment JJ lost herself. Dropping the case of her guitar, she stormed through the electrical cords and mike stands, straight for Sabrina. The woman's eyes widened a little. JJ's own eyes narrowed. Sabrina had no idea who she was dealing with. JJ might appear sweet on the surface, but she was an Isaacs woman at heart, and people who knew what that meant knew to watch out.

JJ stepped right around the keyboard and into Sabrina's face, nose to nose with her, so close she could see every freckle on her pointy nose. So close Sabrina could see the fire blazing in JJ's eyes.

"Don't you ever touch my guitar again," JJ hissed. "Or I promise you, strings won't be the only things broken on this tour."

Sabrina blinked rapidly and drew a shaky breath. In that moment JJ knew that Sabrina was more steam than engine. She talked a big talk, but when it came down to it, she was nothing but a little loudmouthed girl pretending to be bad.

"Leave my man alone, and we won't have a problem," Sabrina growled back.

"You having trouble with your man, you take it up with him," JJ said. "Leave me out of it."

"I would, if I could get a moment with him," Sabrina said, her eyebrows furrowing angrily. "Every time I turn around you're with him, which means that you're my problem. See, I'm not like everyone else around here. I know D—every single chocolate inch of him. So I know he's not sleeping with you. But something else is going on with the two of you, and I want to know what it is."

A chill swept through JJ. Deacon didn't give his girlfriend enough credit. She was better at piecing things together than they thought.

"Ahh, there it is," Sabrina said, her lips twisting into a sick smile. "You really should work on that, honey. Your eyes give away everything."

JJ already knew that. "Nothing's going on, Sabrina."

"And you're also a terrible liar," Sabrina added. Her face hardened. "What's Deacon hiding?"

JJ pressed her lips shut. She wasn't saying another word to Sabrina. She stepped back and turned to walk away, but Sabrina grabbed her arm roughly.

"I'm not finished with you..."

"Ladies!"

Both women turned to look at Kate, who was leveling eyes of steel at them.

"Everything going okay?"

Coming from Kate it wasn't really a question, more like a demand to make everything okay so that the event they had spent thousands of dollars putting together went off without a hitch.

JJ yanked her arm out of Sabrina's grip and walked back over to her guitar.

"Everything's fine," she said, unzipping the inside pocket of the case to look for a new string. She was done fooling with Sabrina. The woman could shoot her nasty glances and try her cheap tricks all evening. JJ was going to fix her guitar, play this event, smile for the camera, and get out of Dodge as soon as she could muster.

She glared at Deacon as he posed with the DJ and grinned at the camera. Him and his secrets. She wasn't even involved, but it was causing her nothing but trouble. It almost made her wish she could rewind to that night at the club and take Cyrus's advice to leave Deacon alone. It seemed the old saying was holding true: No good deed goes unpunished.

Chapter 28

Simon stood back from the crowd at gate eight, waiting. He watched people exit the passageway onto an elevated balcony and look out into the sea of people below for that familiar face. He watched their faces break into smiles, their bodies propel into motion as they moved to meet their companions at the bottom of the ramp. More smiles, many warm embraces, occasionally a few tears.

It made him think of all his airport visits. The ones where he was on the arriving end. Where he was doing the traveling. Sometimes there was someone there to meet him. But mostly there wasn't. Lately he had been noticing the smiling, expectant faces more. And more and more, deep in the back of his mind, in a place he didn't dare explore, he had started to wonder what it would be like to have a familiar face waiting for him. Someone who would smile when he stepped onto that narrow balcony and come to meet him at the other end of the ramp.

He knew there was a reason that he was having those thoughts as he stood at gate eight, waiting for JJ, but he didn't dare explore that either. He shifted his weight from one foot to the other, fingered his car keys in his pocket, popped a piece of gum in his mouth, and tried to remember when he had become this impatient.

He saw the hair first. Thick, larger-than-life spirals with reddish highlights framed her face and cascaded down to her shoulders. Wearing a T-shirt and jeans and a blazer, she looked incredibly sophisticated yet casual. He couldn't see her eyes through the oversized glasses, but the faint frown tipping her pouty lips let him know that she wasn't completely happy. He smiled as he watched her glance around like the others did, looking for that familiar face that should be waiting. Looking for him. And when she saw him, he knew because the frown disappeared and slowly a huge smile took its place. It was the most beautiful thing Simon had seen in a long time.

Even with a guitar case on her back, pulling a suitcase in each hand, she managed to cut through the crowd and be down the ramp before he got to it.

"Hey," he said as they got closer to each other. She dropped her bags and guitar and threw her arms around him. Simon stumbled back a bit, thrown off balance by the unexpected affection.

"Hey, yourself." He heard the words against his chest where her face was pressed. He felt the weakness in her limbs and he couldn't help but pull her a little closer.

"Tired?" he asked when they finally let go of each other.

"You have no idea," she breathed. "But I'm so glad to be home."

Before he thought about it, he reached down and gently removed her glasses, sliding them up into her hair like he had seen her do once. He caught the questioning look in her eyes.

"I wanted to see you," he said with a shrug.

She looked at him through her large hazel eyes for a long moment.

"You're an interesting man, Simon Massri."

He lifted an eyebrow. "Is that good or bad?"

He was treated to her smile again. "It's good," she said, adjusting her purse on her shoulder. "Very good."

"You mind if we continue this in the car?" he asked, grabbing her travel bags. "I'm not the biggest fan of airports."

JJ nodded. "After the last few weeks, neither am I."

Toronto Pearson International Airport was nothing short of a chore to get out of, but they made it through the maze of floors and parking lots in good time. As soon as they got in the car and started driving, JJ put her arm on the console between their seats and rested her hand on top of his, curving her fingers into the space between his forefinger and thumb. Simon didn't want to move, didn't want to breathe, just wanted to keep driving, past the airport, past the hospital, past everything for as long as the gas in his tank would allow him, as long as he could keep the feel of her soft, warm skin on his.

But he couldn't. And he hated himself for it.

It took him three exits to get past his selfishness.

He sighed. "Judith..."

"I know."

He looked over at her, her head back against the headrest, her eyes closed, and hated himself a little more.

"I know," she said again. "But can we talk about it tomorrow? Right now, can I just hold your hand and we not overthink it?"

Instead of answering, he opened his palm and threaded her fingers in his.

"You still want to go to the hospital tonight?" he asked. "Sheree will still be there tomorrow, you know."

"I know, smarty-pants," she said, amusement in her voice. "But I promised her I would see her tonight, and I will, if only for a few minutes. Just let me catch a nap on the way and I'll be good."

"Didn't sleep on the plane?"

"Too wound up."

"We'll talk about that later."

He watched her smile at his response before settling deeper into the passenger seat and turning her head to the side, into a more comfortable position. He relaxed his hold in case she wanted her hand back. She curled her fingers around his a little more without moving or opening her eyes.

The city flew by as they headed east on the 401, then down the Don Valley Parkway toward the city center. They caught the tail end of the peak-hour traffic, and though they hit some snags it was a fairly smooth commute. They made a fifteen-minute stop at the hospital, then they were on the highway again.

Seeing Sheree seemed to wake JJ up, and she chattered all the way home, interspersing her musings with directions. It was almost eight thirty when Simon pulled up to the older North Toronto dwelling. Two cars were parked in the driveway, and Simon figured that her sisters were already home.

She tried to help him with her luggage, but he wouldn't let her, sending her to unlock the door instead.

"Woman, did you pack your whole life into these suitcases?" Simon asked as he backed into the front door.

"Not her whole life. She still has a bunch of junk left upstairs."

Simon turned to find two of JJ's sisters standing behind him.

"Hi, Dr. Massri. We met before. I'm JJ's sister Sydney," the slimmer of the two said, offering her hand. "This is Lissandra."

The other woman, smiling, offered a nod.

"Hello, yes, nice to see you again," Simon said, letting go of Sydney's hand. "I'm just going to go ahead and—"

"Leave?" Sydney asked, her eyebrows raised. "No, you can't. You have to stay and eat. JJ already started in the kitchen."

Simon's eyes widened. "Started? When? She just got here..."

"It's what we do," Sydney said, grabbing his arm and propelling him forward as Lissandra closed the front door.

Before he knew what was happening, he was sitting at the kitchen counter with a glassful of some mango-ginger concoction that JJ said would be the best thing he ever tasted. On the other side of the counter, JJ was cutting up vegetables and other items while Sydney rolled out dough. Lissandra was at the blender making more drinks.

They had pitas and an assortment of dips for their late evening supper. Conversation floated among the three women, and they drew Simon into the mix as if he were a regular participant at their kitchen-counter sessions. He had thought that they might interrogate him. After all, he was the Elevator Guy and he knew they knew all about him, thanks to their family network. But there was no probing, no overt or underhanded questions about what was going on between him and JJ. Maybe a secret look exchanged among them, or a sly comment dropped by Lissandra every now and then, but nothing else. Their greatest interest in him seemed to be his opinion on why men cared so little about the complexities of planning a wedding. This came primarily from Sydney, who, he learned, was engaged to be married to some former professional basketball player whose name sounded only vaguely familiar. He laughed as they ribbed each other, he tasted everything they put in front of him, and tried to stay focused on their conversation, though his eyes wanted to focus only on JJ. By the number of times his gaze locked with hers, however, he suspected it went both ways.

When he looked up and realized it was after ten, he was shocked. He stood up from the stool and the movement drew three pairs of eyes.

"You're leaving?" JJ asked.

"It's getting late," Simon said, bringing his plate to the sink. "My mum always said you should leave before you're asked to, or you won't be asked back again."

He turned to look at JJ. "And since I hope to be asked back, I reckon I better get out of here."

"You've got nothing to worry about there," Lissandra said with a smile. "You'll definitely be asked back. Right, JJ?"

JJ rolled her eyes and ignored her sister. "You don't have to go just yet."

"You promised me you would get some rest."

"When did I do that?" JJ asked, even as she stifled a yawn. "I don't remember anything like that."

Simon chuckled. "Sure you don't."

"JJ, why don't you see Simon to his car while we clean up in here?" Sydney suggested. "With our porch light out, he might not be able to find his way to the sidewalk."

"Yeah," Lissandra said dryly. "Especially with all those bright streetlights out there."

JJ pushed a chuckling Simon toward the door.

"Your sisters are a trip," he said as they walked leisurely down the front steps.

"Yeah, a long, difficult trip sometimes," JJ said wryly. "They sure took a shine to you though."

"Excellent. That should buy me some goodwill for the future."

The night was quiet with only the sounds of crickets and the occasional car in the distance. JJ seemed to be taking her time walking to the car, and Simon didn't mind much. It was interesting how he had spent most of the evening by this woman's side, and yet it still didn't feel like enough.

"Work tomorrow?" JJ asked. They had reached the Jeep. But instead of waiting for him to open the door, she rested her back against the side of the vehicle unhurriedly. He leaned back beside her.

"I'm going to the reserve tomorrow, and then I'm off for the rest of the week."

JJ turned to look at him, her eyebrows raised. "For the rest of the week?"

"For the rest of the week."

She smiled and tilted her head up to the sky. "Can I come with you?"

The grin that hijacked his mouth was so wide it hurt. "If you want."

"I want."

He sighed. "Judith, Judith, Judith."

She jumped up suddenly and turned to look at him. The moonlight illuminated her eyes and made him see things there that couldn't possibly be. Feelings that couldn't possibly exist, given how little time they had spent with each other.

Then all of a sudden he was looking at her lips. Wide, full

lips that told him almost as much about what she was feeling at any given moment as her eyes did. Lips that caught his attention every time she spoke, every time she laughed. Lips that were now slightly parted…

He hadn't realized he had stepped forward until he felt the pressure of her palm against his chest and saw her head tilt toward him, her eyes turn hazy, her lids slide halfway closed. The night was warm, humid, but it was the electricity that crackled between them that pricked his skin, singed his senses. This woman. This woman could easily be the end of him.

He stepped back until he felt the solid frame of the Jeep beneath his shoulder blades once more.

"I'll pick you up around nine in the morning," he said, barely able to choke the words through his constricted throat. "If that's not too early."

She stared at him for a long moment. Her eyes like hot coals of fire, burning through him. Then she took a step back and looked down, breaking their gaze.

"Nine's fine," she said. "I'll be ready."

Simon nodded. But neither of them moved. Simon would have given a month's wages to know what she was thinking. He knew what he'd been thinking—thinking of doing—only a few moments earlier. But with JJ he could never be totally sure. The embrace at the airport, the hand on his in the car, the looks across the kitchen counter. Was he reading more into things than he should? Sure, they had spent hours talking to each other over the past few weeks, but what did that really mean? Was he just some friend for her to lean on during the whirlwind of her life, or was it something more?

He shook his head. This was way too much thinking for one night. And so he reached out and pulled her closer, folding her into his arms.

"Good night, Judith," he murmured into her curls. "I'll see you in the morning."

He felt her arms slip around his torso and squeeze for a moment before they both let go.

"Good night, Simon."

Before he could do something more dangerous, he opened the driver's door and got in. Starting the engine, he nodded for her to go inside before he left. When he finally saw the front door close, he turned the vehicle around and headed down the road, away from JJ's house. Before he even hit the end of the block, he was counting the hours until he would be back again.

Chapter 29

Even though she was tired when Simon left the night before, JJ found herself up and wide awake a few minutes after seven the following morning. Outside it was drizzling, the perfect weather for sleeping in. She turned over and burrowed deeper into the covers, but sleep wouldn't find her. With a sigh she gave up, reconciling herself to the fact that there would be no more sleeping that morning.

She stared up at the play of light on her ceiling and tried to remember the last time she had been awake in her own bed at seven a.m. How long had it been—weeks? Months, maybe? Since her music career had tripled its demands on her life, she had barely gotten a full night's rest. And when she did sleep, she often clung to those precious moments tightly, knowing that it might be a while before she had them again.

But there had been a time, recent enough for her to remember, when her early mornings were spent on her knees, or poring through the Word. It seemed like her life had become a lot more chaotic and confusing since the absence of seven a.m. appointments with her Father.

Pulling the covers aside, she slipped out of bed and into the padded slippers near the door. Then she headed to the living room and plopped down on the couch. Her sister's Bible lay open on the coffee table where JJ had seen it the night before. It was open to Luke 15. JJ glanced over the verses, remembering its contents as she did. This was the chapter of lost things. Lost sheep, lost coins, lost people. It was the same chapter the minister had preached from the last time she was in church—the first time she had met Cymmone.

"Okay, I get it," JJ said out loud. She was losing herself. She had suspected it for a while now. It clawed at the edges of her mind every time she had a spare moment to wonder. She was like the lost sheep in verses four to ten: far away from the pack, lost, and very aware that she was lost. But as much as she tried, she couldn't seem to find her way back to where she was before.

"Good morning, early bird. Thought you would be asleep until 8:59."

JJ craned her head to see her sister coming down the stairs.

"I think I would need more than a minute to get ready," she said dryly.

"Okay, fine," Sydney said, sinking onto the couch beside JJ. "But two hours?"

"What is this, an interrogation?" JJ asked, miffed.

"No, just miss my time with my baby sister," Sydney said, throwing an arm around JJ and squeezing her until JJ squealed for mercy. They were both laughing when Sydney finally let go.

"Remember when we used to do this all the time?" Sydney asked, settling back onto the sofa.

"Do what?"

"Wake up early like this, talk, read that book on your lap that I suspect you haven't looked at in a long time."

JJ looked down at the Bible then back up at Sydney. "Isn't it a bit early for you to be this judgmental?"

"You left your Bible here when you went on tour," Sydney said. "The one that has all your marks and highlights in it."

"Maybe I got a new one!"

"Did you?" Sydney challenged.

JJ sighed. "No."

"I'm not judging you, JJ. Sorry if it felt that way."

"No, it's not you," JJ said. "It's me. *I'm* judging me. Feeling a little bit like a lost sheep."

"You just got back," Sydney said. "Give yourself some time."

"I don't mean like that," JJ said. "And not just today. For a while now. Even while I was on tour." JJ let out a long breath. "It's like I've turned into someone else, and I can't find my way back to who I was before."

"Hmmm."

JJ looked across at Sydney. Her sister's eyes were closed and her head rested against the back of the sofa.

"That's it?" JJ asked. "No I-told-you-so?"

Sydney shook her head. "The way I figure, all of us are lost in some kind of way. You're the lost sheep, lost and knowing you're lost but not able to find your way back. Lissandra's like the lost coin, lost with absolutely no idea that she's not where she's supposed to be. And me, I guess I'm the prodigal son, still trying to find my way back home."

JJ bit her lip. "I never thought about it like that, but I guess you're right."

"The one thing we have in common, though, is that God is out to find all of us, whether or not we know we're lost and whether or not we can find our way back," Sydney said. "He never stops looking for us; never stops trying to get us to let go of what we think is our security and come home; never stops watching the road, hoping for a glimpse of us somewhere in the distance."

"When did you get so smart?" JJ asked.

"Right after I nearly ruined my life last year with the Sheree madness."

They both fell into a comfortable silence.

"What's the deal with you and Simon?" Sydney asked.

JJ chuckled. "It took you long enough. I'm surprised that you waited almost a whole twelve hours to ask."

"Well," Sydney said, "after your little speech about being a grown woman, I didn't want you to feel like I was plowing through your business."

"Sorry about that."

"We already did the apology thing," Sydney said. "We both said some harsh words, but that doesn't mean some of it wasn't true. Now back to Simon. What's going on there?"

"I don't know," JJ said. "We're friends. I guess."

Sydney turned to look at her sister with a frown. "Okay. What does *that* mean?"

"It means we talk a lot on the phone, but he doesn't want to kiss me."

Sydney let out a laugh. "Explain, please!"

JJ covered her eyes. "I don't know. Last night at the car, there was a moment where I thought it was going to happen, and then..."

"And then what?" Sydney probed.

"And then he backed away from me like I had rabies or something."

Sydney put an arm around her sister. "Awww, J, maybe he was feeling unsure of himself."

JJ cocked an eyebrow. "Have you seen this man? Why would anyone as gorgeous as he is, as accomplished as he is, ever feel unsure of himself?"

"I don't know. That tends to happen when you have eyes for a celebrity singer who spends all day with handsome and powerful men like Deacon Hill," Sydney said.

"First of all, I am not a celebrity singer, I am just the backup. Secondly, Simon knows nothing is going on between me and Deacon," JJ argued.

"Yes, he might know that in his head, but he's still a man," Sydney said. "And he has to feel sure that you are interested before he will risk rejection at that level."

"You know what, maybe this is all for the best anyway," JJ said. "Look at me. I'm a mess. I don't need to be messing with Simon and messing him up too. I feel so out of place most of the time, whereas he is so in place all the time."

"Maybe that's why you're so drawn to him," Sydney mused.

JJ sighed. "I've been thinking about that, the confidence he has in his faith, in who he is, in his purpose in life. He is so sure of himself, Syd, but not in an obnoxious kind of way. It's enviable. And if that's the reason I can't stop thinking about him, then maybe I shouldn't be with him. It wouldn't be fair for me to use him like that."

"Why would you be using him?" Sydney asked, her surprise clear from her tone. "Maybe there are things that you could learn from him, and things that he could learn from you. After all, a couple should complement each other. That's the way God planned it."

"Please," JJ said. "There is nothing he could learn from me right now. I'm like the waffling palm to his sturdy oak."

"Well, I'll let you in on a secret," Sydney said. "Your waffling palm is built to stand the storm. It may sway from side to side, bending and almost touching the ground. But the roots will stay firm, and its flexible strength means that it can take the pressures without breaking. Why do you think the Bible says the righteous man will flourish like a palm tree?"

JJ bit her lip as she thought about her sister's words.

"I know you feel like you're struggling now, baby sister," Sydney said, laying her head on JJ's shoulder. "But remember, we went through the tough times in our family together. Mom and Dad's divorce, their fighting, being caught in the middle, stepdads one and two. Of all us Isaacs kids, you've been the most resilient. You're our palm tree. You bend but you don't fall down. You always end up coming back up straight. I know this time will be no different. You'll find your way to where you're supposed to be."

"Stop," JJ said, sniffling. "It's too early for me to start crying."

JJ was still thinking about her sister's words an hour later as she ran a wide-toothed comb through her wet hair. She still had half an hour before Simon would show up, but she was practically ready. When the doorbell rang, however, she ran downstairs.

"Is that him already?" Sydney called from her bedroom

"I don't know..."

JJ pulled opened the door. Her jaw hit the floor when she saw the visitor.

"Hey, JJ."

"Rayshawn!"

Chapter 30

The morning had become too exciting for her liking. Instead of getting ready to meet Simon, JJ found herself standing on her front steps dealing with Rayshawn. She scowled. Boy, did he have a way of turning up at the worst times.

"What are you doing here?" JJ asked. She folded her arms and tried to appear unfazed by his presence. In gray denim pants and a Ralph Lauren polo, he looked surprisingly fresh and alert for eight thirty in the morning. A number of feelings bubbled to the surface as she looked at him. Annoyance, resentment, a little bit of anger, and an unwelcome stirring in her lower stomach that she refused to acknowledge.

"You're mad at me," he began. "I get it—"

"Mad?" JJ asked, her eyebrows jumping to her hairline. "No, mad was two months ago when I didn't hear from you after I got signed with Deacon Hill. Mad was two weeks after that when I called you almost every day and I got no answer. Mad was a month ago when I was so sick I couldn't move and someone else had to come take care of me. Mad was before I saw you enjoying a lap dance from a stripper on the second page of the *Enquirer.* I was mad then. I am way past mad now."

"Look, JJ, I'm sorry. I'm a jerk. I accept that," he said, reaching out for her hands. "But there were reasons..."

"Reasons?" She pulled her hands out of his reach. "What reasons? What reason can explain why the stripper at some nasty club has seen you more recently than I have?"

He squeezed his eyes shut and pinched the bridge of his nose. "Look, JJ, I know how things look," he said finally. "But I would never do anything to hurt you. That club thing...I didn't even plan it. I was there with my boy, he was friends with the owner, and before we knew what was happening, the strippers were there and someone was snapping a picture. I promise you nothing happened. And believe it or not, it was for you. Everything I do is about you, JJ."

JJ let out a harsh laugh. "You have got to be kidding."

He rubbed his hands over his face. "Babe, I'm serious. Why else would I be standing on your front steps at eight thirty in the morning? You know I hate mornings."

"Maybe you were hoping for an early morning booty call," JJ spat.

"Babe, no offense, but if that was all I wanted I would go somewhere else—"

"Unbelievable." JJ turned around to shut the door in his face, but he grabbed her arm.

"Not because I don't want you," he continued, "but because I respect you enough to know how important that is to you. I don't want you to feel pressured to be someone you're not. When you are with me, I want you to be sure of who you are."

JJ stopped short. Was it just a coincidence that Rayshawn had brought up the very same thing she had just been talking with Sydney about only moments earlier? It made her wonder, was she really herself when she was with Rayshawn? That was what she had told her sister. But was it really true? Musically, she was—mostly anyway. But that was just one part of her. What about the other parts? The sister, the daughter, the believer, the mentor. Could she be all of those things with Rayshawn, or did she feel like she had to hide some of those parts away when she was with him?

JJ stared at Rayshawn for a long moment. She saw the passion for life in his eyes. The same passion that had drawn her to him that night at Lost and Found, where she first met him.

"Why are you here, Rayshawn?" she asked. There was no sweetness in her tone, but the edge was gone also.

"I need to talk to you," he said.

"Now is not a good time," JJ said, more than a little glad that she was occupied. "I have plans later this morning."

"It won't take long," he said. "I promise."

"Rayshawn, I'm expecting a friend to pick me up around nine."

He took her hand. "This is important. I really need to talk to you. It's about your future. Our future."

JJ watched him, wondering where all the feelings she had thought she had for him had gone. Right now she felt nothing. She pulled her hands out of his grasp.

"Wow, you're really mad at me this time," he said, raising an eyebrow. "Is this like, pick-the-movie-for-the-night mad?"

"You're gonna have to try harder than that," JJ said, folding her arms.

"Pink-tulips-and-chocolate-almonds mad?"

"Keep going."

"Takeout-from-Banjara's-including-mango-lassi-plus-a-foot-massage mad?"

JJ snorted. "The ice is cracking."

Rayshawn rubbed a hand across his chin thoughtfully. "Babe, I don't know. We're climbing really high up on the apology scale here."

JJ looked over at him for a long moment. "Isn't it kinda sad, though, that we have such a well-developed scale? We haven't even been going out a year yet."

Rayshawn frowned and shot a glance at her. "What are you saying?"

JJ sighed. They did need to talk. Their relationship was about to undergo another serious transition.

"You're right, Rayshawn," she said, taking a deep breath. "We do need to talk. But I can't now. Can you maybe call me later?"

Rayshawn searched her eyes. "JJ..."

JJ heard a car pull up at the end of the driveway around the time she heard the front door open. She glanced back as her sister came to the front door. She needed to get Rayshawn out of here.

"Rayshawn, please," she said, touching his arm. "Later, okay?"

He sighed and nodded. "Okay, later."

Then before she could react, he leaned in and kissed her. JJ jerked away but it was too late. She turned around and there was Simon coming up the driveway. Sydney's eyes widened as she looked back and forth between JJ and Simon. But Simon was unreadable. His thick eyebrows were furrowed and his locks pulled back from his face as he stared at her, then Rayshawn, then her again.

"Who's that?" Rayshawn asked, slipping a hand around JJ's waist. "Your sister's boyfriend?"

JJ opened and closed her mouth, not quite sure how to answer the question. Who was Simon to her? He had graduated from the title of her sister-in-law's doctor. To some extent he had even moved beyond being just Elevator Guy. But what he was to her now, she still wasn't sure.

Turns out, she didn't need to be sure. Not right then anyway.

"I'm Simon." He stepped forward and stretched his hand out. "And you are?"

"Rayshawn."

The men shook hands only inches away from where JJ stood, hoping that the ground would open and swallow her.

"Nice to meet you," Simon said.

Rayshawn nodded. "Likewise."

"Anyway, looks like it's not such a good time. I'm gonna head out," Simon said, fishing his keys out of his pocket. "Sydney, Judith."

He nodded at Sydney but barely glanced at JJ before heading over to his Jeep. JJ looked over at Sydney, who was shooting daggers at her with her eyes and jerking her head indiscreetly toward Simon when she was sure only JJ was looking.

"Wait," JJ said, stepping out of Rayshawn's grip and heading toward the Jeep. "I'm still coming."

"Whoa," Rayshawn said, reaching for her again. "Still coming where? Where you going with him?"

"I told you I had an appointment this morning," JJ said, pulling free of his hold.

His fingers grasped at her forearm once more. "JJ!"

"Rayshawn, stop." She yanked away again, glaring at him. "I can't do this with you now. I have to go."

She hurried down the walkway and across the street to where Simon was standing at the door to the Jeep, watching the scene unfold. His brows had now formed a single unit and his hand tightened in a fist around his keys.

Rayshawn's eyes grew dark. "Is this what you wanted to talk to me about? Your friend here?" His hands clenched as he stormed across the street. "Why wait? Let's talk about it now."

Before JJ could respond, she found herself looking at Simon's back. He had stepped between her and Rayshawn and she could barely see past him. He didn't say anything, but his presence was enough to stop Rayshawn in his tracks. The men squared off with each other for a moment. Then Rayshawn swore under his breath and stormed back to his car. JJ, Simon, and Sydney watched as Rayshawn got in, slammed the door shut, and then peeled off, tires screeching, away from her home. JJ knew Rayshawn had a temper. She'd seen hints of it a few times. But this was the first time she had ever felt afraid of him.

Simon turned around and reached for the driver's door of the Jeep. "You shouldn't be with that guy," he said quietly without looking at her.

"I'm not," JJ said, her eyes following him.

"Whatever you say." He got into the vehicle and closed the door.

"I'm still coming," JJ said.

Simon sighed and stared ahead through the windscreen. "I don't think that's such a good idea."

"Are you saying I can't come?" JJ clarified.

"No, but—"

"Then I'm coming."

Before he could say another word, JJ walked around to the passenger side, got in, and buckled her seat belt.

"We're already late," JJ said when he hadn't moved. "Let's go."

Simon shook his head. Then without saying a word, he started the engine and pulled the car out onto the road. As they drove away, JJ caught the smug smile on Sydney's face. She was glad her sister approved of her actions, because JJ had every intention of making sure there was no confusion in Simon's mind about how she felt. The next step toward doing that was providing an explanation for what just happened.

"Rayshawn is a guy I dated for a while," JJ began once they hit the highway.

"You don't have to explain."

"I know, but I want to," JJ said. "So just hear me out."

JJ watched a weary look settle on Simon's features. But he nodded, giving her the go-ahead to say what she needed to.

"Rayshawn was the one who opened the door to professional-level performing for me," JJ said. "He found me singing in a little lounge downtown and offered me the chance to do more. He got me my first gig with Jayla Grey and then this one with Deacon Hill. It was a crazy time in my life, with lots of changes, many of which my family didn't adjust well to. For a time, Rayshawn felt like the only one supporting me, and with both of us spending so much time together, with everything being so intense, we started having feelings for each other."

JJ glanced over at Simon, but his eyes were focused on the road and his face was blank. The only sign that he heard a word she said was the tension in his jaw, and his power grip on the steering wheel. She might as well get it all out while she could.

"For a while things seemed to be going fine. But then..." JJ shook her head. "Have you ever been in something that you know is wrong, but you spend all your energy trying to prove to others that it's right, and you almost convince yourself that it is?"

Simon rubbed a hand over his face and sighed. "Yes."

"Well, it was like that. And once I went on tour, it kind of all fell apart. I saw who the real Rayshawn was and realized he wasn't someone I could be with," JJ said.

JJ raked her hands through her hair. "I think I decided weeks ago that it was over, but it was easier to ignore it while I was on tour and we never saw or even spoke to each other. Plus it's complicated. He's still my manager and I'm still under contract with him. Then he shows up this morning, and before I can say what I need to, you show up. And you saw what happened after that."

She turned to Simon. "Believe me, there's nothing between me and Rayshawn. Nothing but business."

He didn't say anything. Didn't look at her. Just kept his eyes on the road.

"Simon, come on, I just poured out my life to you. Say something. Anything. Tell me what you're thinking."

He snorted. "You don't want to know what I'm thinking."

"I do," JJ said. "Even if you think it will hurt, tell me."

He looked over at her for the first time since she had gotten into the car, and his eyes pierced her with the depth of their intensity.

"I think it's like you said at the airport in New York," he said finally. "You're a bit lost. And I think you're still trying to figure out what you want and what you're willing to give up in order to have it. And until you make that decision, I don't think you can be really sure of anything."

His words stung. But she had asked what he was thinking, and he certainly had told her. JJ sat back in her seat, not quite sure what to say. She knew she was drifting. Only hours earlier she had said as much to Sydney. But she thought she had made a decision when she stepped back from Rayshawn. Except she hadn't really stepped back from Rayshawn, she had just kind of let things happen without dealing with it. Furthermore, could she really have a business relationship with Rayshawn and keep it just business, after everything they had been through?

She sighed loudly.

Simon glanced over at her and grimaced. "You sure you still want to go to the reserve today?"

JJ nodded. She might as well. Thinking about her own life was exhausting. What better way to take a break than to focus on someone else's? Working on the reserve was exactly what she needed; that is, if she could survive this new, silent Simon. Since he had given his assessment of her, he had barely said a word. JJ checked the time. If this trip was like the last, they had at least an hour and a half before they got to the airstrip. She let out another sigh. It was going to be a long drive.

Silent Simon lived on for the rest of the day. Thank God for Nigel, or JJ was sure she would have lost her mind. Though 75 percent of what came out of Nigel's mouth was fluff, it was fluff that filled the space left by what was not coming out of Simon's mouth.

The reserve was exactly like it had been the last time JJ was there, and there was a feeling of welcome familiarity, even in the despair of it all. Here at least, she knew she could be useful. And when Marianne greeted her with a huge smile and an equally huge embrace, JJ was glad she had bullied her way into Simon's Jeep earlier that day.

It was almost six when they broke for the evening, but the sun was high in the sky. JJ smiled and raised her face up to the sun. She absolutely loved this mid-August time of year. Loved the humidity that clogged her pores, the occasionally scorching heat that licked at her bare calves and arms, the cool summer breeze that broke the intensity just when it was about to become too much. She strolled down the street, away from the clinic toward the truck that would take them back to the airstrip. She found Nigel and a fat-bellied young boy sitting on the edge of the open truck bed, eating multicolored Popsicles.

"Hey! Where'd you get that?" JJ asked.

Nigel slurped drops of liquid that ran down the side of his Popsicle. "I have special friends."

He slapped five with the boy sitting beside him.

"You his Popsicle friend?" JJ asked, raising an eyebrow at the boy.

The boy licked his own fast-disappearing treat. "Maybe."

"What's a girl gotta do to get one of those?" she asked, pointing at Nigel's frozen treat.

"Got fifty cents?" the boy asked.

"If you can find me one of the double ones, I'll give you a dollar."

The boy popped off the back of the truck and disappeared between two houses, flip-flops slapping against the dusty ground.

"So you and Massri are fighting, eh?" Nigel asked.

JJ took the seat the boy vacated. "What makes you say that?"

"Please," Nigel said. "The silence between the two of you is deafening. What did you do?"

JJ's eyes popped open. "Why does it have to be me?"

"'Cause Mr. Straight and Narrow is so cautious when it comes to stuff like this that he would never do anything," Nigel said. "Especially when it comes to you."

"What's that supposed to mean?"

"Look, I like you, Elevator Girl, so let me give you a clue," Nigel said, resting his free arm against the side of the truck. "Simon is head over heels for you."

JJ shook her head. "You must have me confused with someone else."

"If anyone's confused here, it's you," Nigel said. "I've known Simon forever. He's only been like this with one other woman, and he almost married her."

JJ's eyes widened. Simon had almost married? The idea surprised her. Although the more she thought about it, the more she knew it shouldn't have. That was the kind of guy Simon was. He was an all-or-nothing kind of guy. Just like he gave everything he had to his work and his patients, she knew that whatever woman he was with, he would give everything to her. It would never be a casual relationship. It would be all or nothing—he couldn't do anything in-between.

"Why didn't he?" JJ asked. "What happened?"

"With Elena?" Nigel asked, biting a chunk out of the flavored ice. "I'll let him tell you the details when he's ready. But let's just say, when it came down to the wire and she had to make a choice, she didn't choose well."

The boy returned with JJ's Popsicle, eliminating the opportunity for her to question Nigel further. By the time they finished slurping their summer treats, Simon had returned to the truck after his last case and was ready to go.

JJ watched Simon's profile from the backseat, more curious than ever about all that had gone on in his past. What kind of woman would Simon Massri love enough to marry? Who was Elena? And why in the world would she not choose Simon?

A plane ride and another two hours in the Jeep, and JJ was standing on her curb. As she watched Simon disappear down the road, she realized she now had more questions than she'd had when he had picked her up early that morning.

She had just climbed her front steps when a silver Escalade pulled up. She walked back down to the street as the window rolled down.

JJ rested a hand on her hip. "Were you following us, Nigel?"

"Absolutely," Nigel said. "How else could I invite you to dinner at my penthouse condo?"

"Are you hitting on me?"

"Sorry, no," Nigel said. "I'm not dating black women right now."

"Of course," JJ said, knowing that with Nigel there was no point getting offended. "So what's this dinner thing about then?"

"I'm having a few friends over tomorrow evening," he said with a grin. "Would love it if you could join us."

"When did we become friends?"

"When I realized that my best friend's going to stay miserable if we don't get you back on his good side."

JJ sighed and looked off in the direction where Simon's Jeep had driven. "You might be talking about the impossible there."

"Aren't you a Christian? Don't you folks say all things are possible with Christ?"

"When did you ever go to church?"

"Every weekend until I turned sixteen," Nigel said. "My parents were Catholic."

"Ahhh."

"So, can I tell my housekeeper to buy more steaks?"

"I don't eat red meat."

"Come on, JJ," Nigel said, getting impatient.

"I don't know..."

"I'll tell you the rest of the Elena story."

JJ perked up. "Okay, fine. But if it gets more awkward with Simon, I'm leaving."

"Sure, sure," Nigel said. "You have sisters, right?"

"Yes," JJ said cautiously.

"Bring them with you." He reeled off the address to his home, which happened to be a condo building JJ knew very well because she had seen it on a celebrity homes show.

"See you tomorrow at six!" Nigel said. Then, before JJ could protest, he was peeling off down the street.

She sighed. One of these days her neighbors were going to complain because of all her speeding visitors.

Chapter 31

"You're being a jerk. And I should know because all my ex-girlfriends seem to think I have the corner on that market."

Simon scowled at Nigel and went back to grilling veggies at the barbecue pit set up on one side of Nigel's rooftop entertainment space. He hadn't really wanted to come to Nigel's little dinner shindig. He had been to his friend's similar get-togethers in the past, and on every occasion, without fail, they had descended into drunken revelry as soon as the food was gone and the drinks came out. Simon wasn't in the mood to navigate that kind of crowd that night, but his friend had insisted, pulling the we-don't-hang-out-like-we-used-to card that he used whenever he wanted to get Simon to do something. Nigel knew Simon felt guilty for neglecting their friendship, and he used it to his advantage. Simon hadn't figured out why Nigel had been so insistent, until the terrace doors to the roof had slid open and JJ and two of her sisters walked out. He could have strangled his friend.

"I'm not being a jerk," Simon growled. "But if I was, it would be your fault."

"How is it my fault?"

Simon glared at Nigel.

"Look, just because you don't want to talk to Elevator Girl—"

"Her name is Judith."

"—doesn't mean I can't be friends with her." Nigel took a swig of his drink. "In fact, her sister's kinda cute. I might have to ask them all over again. Soon."

"And you wonder why we don't hang out as much anymore."

Nigel leaned back against the railing. "You're just mad 'cause she's having more fun than you." He chuckled. "Look at her."

Simon had done nothing but look at her all night. No matter how he wanted to ignore her, he couldn't. Even now, though he wanted to defy Nigel's suggestion, his eyes drifted over to the other side of the deck, where she was chatting and laughing with a couple whom Simon had seen before at Nigel's events. Nigel was right. She was enjoying herself. Definitely not experiencing any of the discomfort Simon was writhing in.

Simon grunted and went back to the grill.

"I get it, Massri," Nigel said. "You're pissed off that she was involved with some other guy."

"*Is* involved," Simon corrected.

"Was, is, it doesn't matter," Nigel said. "She's fair game as long as there's no ring in the picture."

"It's not that simple."

Nigel slapped his hand against the rail. "It is that simple. I don't know why everything has to be so complicated for you. It doesn't matter who homeboy is, you have home-court advantage. You have the whole romantic elevator backstory going on. Women love that crap, live for it. It's the stuff chick flicks are made of. If I were you, I would be milking that all the way to glory."

"She's not interested."

"Of course not," Nigel said. "That's why she's wasting a night of her one-week vacation standing on my roof chatting with people she's never met before, just so she can be close to you. Because she's not interested."

Simon frowned thoughtfully and glanced away from the grill over to JJ again. Nigel did have a point. But what was he supposed to do, when he wasn't sure what was going on in JJ's head? She claimed nothing was going on with her and Rayshawn, but that didn't match up to the picture he had seen the day before. Furthermore, why had she never mentioned him before? She volunteered information about everything else in her life, everything that happened on tour, things Simon suspected she didn't even tell her sisters. But this one thing she had kept back. Why?

"You need to quit sulking over this grill and go handle your business," Nigel said. "Get over there and talk to her, tell her you can't stop thinking about her, ask her out on a real date. Get in the game, Massri."

Simon raised an eyebrow at his friend. "Is that what your game looks like? No wonder you can't keep a woman."

"You got jokes. That gives me hope." Nigel took another swig of his drink before pushing himself off the rail. "My work here is done. Now to find that other Isaacs woman."

"One of them is engaged," Simon warned as his friend began to walk away.

Nigel grinned. "I know. I saw that ring from a mile away. It's the other one I'm interested in. Wish me luck!"

"Good luck." Simon shook his head. From what he had already seen of Lissandra, Nigel would need it.

Simon moved the cooked eggplant, zucchini, celery, and carrots to the warming rack and put away the tongs. He did a quick survey of the deck and found her at the food table. He took a deep breath. *Might as well.*

"There's fish on the grill if you can wait a few minutes," he said as he dug through the cooler for a bottle of water. She had been squinting at the grilled chicken suspiciously, and he knew that she would prefer another meat alternative.

She turned to look at him, surprised. "He speaks! And full sentences too."

Simon tipped his head to the side and walked over to her. "Guess I deserve that."

"Enjoying your friend's dinner party?" JJ asked, bypassing the meat and loading her plate with broccoli and cauliflower instead.

"Not really."

She poured a dollop of dip on the plate. "I could tell."

"Didn't expect to see you," he said, stopping near her.

JJ smiled. "I think that was part of Nigel's plan."

He had missed that. Her smile, the way her eyes crinkled at the side when she did, and the slight dimple in her cheek. He also missed their easy banter, their long talks, the way she looked into his eyes without looking away.

"What happened, Judith?" he asked quietly, even as he searched her face for answers. "I thought we were going somewhere."

Her smiled faded. "I thought so too."

"Then why didn't you tell me about Rayshawn?" Simon asked, squinting at her. "You never mentioned him. Not even once. Why?"

JJ looked away, but not before Simon caught the regret that framed her features.

"I don't know." She raked a hand through her hair. "That's a lie. I do know."

She picked up her plate and walked away from the food table, and he followed her to a portion of the terrace where only a four-foot ledge separated them from everything below. He watched her play with her broccoli and look everywhere except at him.

"Judith, talk to me."

She looked away at the Toronto city skyline.

"After how tense things were at first at the hospital, I guess I never thought anything was possible with us," JJ began. "But then, when you came to see me in New York, it was like...I thought maybe...it felt like there was a possibility that there could be something."

She placed her plate on the ledge and pressed her hands against the concrete. "I didn't say anything about Rayshawn because I knew that if I did, you would back off immediately, and I didn't want that. I didn't even know what was going on with Rayshawn. We hadn't spoken for weeks, and before that, it was bad. And you, Simon...you were like...like a breath of fresh air. I didn't want to lose that."

She covered her face with her hands. "Geez, when I'm with you, it's like I have no filter..."

Simon smiled and gently eased her hands away from her face. "It's okay. I kind of like it."

"Sure you do," JJ said. "You get to know everything I'm thinking and I'm the one who ends up wondering if I'm the only one... feeling things."

He tugged at her wrists, pulling her closer to him.

"Judith."

She looked up at him, her eyes wide-open windows to the vulnerability in her heart. He felt a crushing sensation in his chest. Yes, this woman was definitely going to be the end of him. Slipping his hands around her neck, he slid his fingers into her warm, soft curls and pulled her even closer. He watched her eyes slide closed, her glossed lips part, and her breathing grow shallow.

Then he did the thing he had wanted to do since the moment she had turned around in that hospital room and jump-started his heart. He kissed her. Slowly at first, savoring that first contact, boxing up the memory of the sweet fullness of her lips so he could revisit it in the future. But then her arms slipped around him, her fingers tightened around his shirt and pulled him closer, and the urgency in her touch gave him the freedom to probe her lips further, kissing her deeper, losing his fingers in the glorious thickness of her hair until a tingling somewhere far, far away in the back of his mind reminded him where they were.

He pulled away from her lips but not from her embrace. It took her a moment to catch her breath and open her eyes, and when she did, the look she gave him nearly knocked him over.

A whistle and a wolf call drew his attention to the eyes whose attention they'd attracted. The gleeful look on Lissandra's and Nigel's faces told him the source of the whistle and the wolf call. Across the terrace, smiles and chuckles greeted them.

"Oh God." JJ hid her face in his chest, and he laughed, running a hand over her hair.

"I can't believe you did that," she mumbled into his chest.

"Excuse me? *We* did that," Simon corrected in amusement. "You were just as much involved as I was."

JJ lifted her head from his chest and grinned. "I was, wasn't I?"

"You definitely were."

They gazed at each other a long moment, and Simon instinctively knew what would happen next if they kept staring at each other like that.

"How about we go chat with your sister and my friend, so we keep out of trouble?"

"Why?" JJ asked, slipping her hand into his as they headed across the terrace. "Trouble isn't so bad."

He chuckled. "You do have a point there."

"See why you should come to my parties, ladies?" Nigel said as Simon and JJ joined their group. "I always provide the best entertainment."

"I'll say," Lissandra agreed.

"I can't lie," Sydney said, winking at JJ. "I'm pretty impressed, Nigel."

"Is he always like this?" JJ asked Simon. "Taking the credit for everything?"

"Yes," Simon said without hesitation. "For as long as I've known him."

Simon entertained them with a Nigel story from their undergraduate years, and when Nigel attempted to outdo him with a Simon story from their medical school days, the women seemed to enjoy it just as much. But what Simon enjoyed most was the feel of JJ by his side. Even as the conversation continued within the group, a more personal conversation seemed to pass between Simon and JJ with each squeeze of their enjoined hands, every nudge of their shoulders, every private exchange of glances. Simon could get used to this, get used to being with her all the time. It was only Tuesday, but the fact that she would be gone again on Sunday was already bothering him.

When she stifled her third yawn, Simon knew it was time to call it a night. He lowered his mouth to her ear. "Looks like it's someone's bedtime," he murmured.

"Whose? Yours?" JJ murmured back. "I hear as people get older, they need more sleep."

He chuckled at her jab at their age difference. "I'm not the one yawning after every syllable. This is what happens when young girls try to play grown-up."

JJ slapped his arm chidingly. "You'll pay for that comment, mister. Let's hope you can keep up with this young girl tomorrow morning."

He raised an eyebrow, intrigued. "What's tomorrow morning?"

She grinned mischievously. "Pick me up at six a.m. and you'll find out."

Then she tipped up and planted a kiss on his lips that extinguished any further inquiries. Moments later, as she and her sisters exited the terrace, Simon was still staring after her.

"See?" Nigel said, placing a soda in Simon's hand and slapping him on the back. "Things are always more fun when you're hanging with me."

Simon chuckled and took a sip of his soda. For once he had to agree with his friend. Hanging out with him tonight might just be the best thing he'd decided to do in a long time.

Chapter 32

"Okay, I'm here and I brought gifts!" JJ announced as she breezed into Sheree's hospital room around midday the next day.

Sheree clapped her hands excitedly. "Ooh, let's see!"

"I've got a copy of the latest *Essence* magazine and also, against my better judgment, the newest *Enquirer* magazine," JJ said, pulling both out of her black canvas shopping bag and laying them on the bed.

"Don't hate," Sheree said, grabbing the *Enquirer* magazine first. "This is where I saw that infamous picture with you and Mr. Hill."

JJ grimaced and kept digging in the canvas bag. "I also have a bar of Cadbury dark chocolate, approved by your doctor; Essie nail polish in Beach Bum Blu, as requested; socks; new headphones; and the *Soul Food* season one DVD, which, by the way, was the hardest thing to find on this list!"

"Thank you, my-baby's-favorite-auntie! You're the best," Sheree said, blowing kisses at JJ. "Now bring your butt over here and come try out my new bed."

JJ squinted as she examined Sheree's sleeper more carefully. "Wait, you got a bigger bed?"

"Yup," Sheree said with a grin as she scooted over, making space for JJ beside her. "They brought it in yesterday."

"Wow," JJ said, settling in beside Sheree. "This is nice. My whole butt can actually fit on it this time."

"Yeah," Sheree said. "And I still got tons of space. Awesome, eh?"

"Okay, spill," JJ said with a smile. "Who hooked you up? Nurses stole a bed from the VIP wing for you? I hear you're in with them like that."

"Nope," Sheree said, shaking her head. "Dean got it done."

JJ's eyebrows went up. "Dean!"

"Yup," Sheree said with a smile. "And he didn't even tell me. I went to have some tests done, came back, and it was here. No one would tell me where it came from. But you know me, I started doing some digging and I found out he arranged it. I don't know how, but I know it's him."

JJ squinted at Sheree for a long moment. "Okay, so I feel like I'm missing out here," she said. "I know that he's been visiting and you guys have been spending time together, but are you two...?"

"No," Sheree said, shaking her head. "Too much has happened for us to just get back together without some serious third-party intervention. But we're both committed to this kid having the best parents in the world, and for that to happen, we have to at least have a decent relationship with each other. That's what we're working on."

JJ smiled. "Is that the rehearsed speech you're giving everyone?"

Sheree sighed. "Yes."

JJ laughed. "I knew it!"

"I can't lie," Sheree said. "I love that man something terrible. Always did, though it might seem hard to believe, given what I did. But if I could take it all back, I would. I would do anything for another chance to make it right with Dean."

"I don't know," JJ said. "I don't want to get your hopes up, but it looks like he might be opening the door to that."

"Yeah, but what if it's just all this baby stuff?" Sheree asked, worry lining her forehead. "You know how people get at the prospect of a child. And then the baby comes...or doesn't, given my state..."

"Stop," JJ said, sitting up suddenly. "Don't let me ever hear you say anything like that again."

"I'm sorry. I can't help it. I'm just so afraid that something will go wrong with the baby." Sheree brushed at the tears that trickled down her cheeks. "I don't deserve something so precious, and I love this baby so much already. If I lose it...I feel like I have to prepare for the worst or I might not survive it if it happens."

JJ wrapped her arms around Sheree, who laid her head on JJ's shoulder, sobbing.

"It's okay," JJ said. "Nothing is going to happen. This baby is going to be born completely healthy. We have to believe that God is going to see us through this."

JJ knew she needed to stay strong for Sheree, but her own worry was not far from the surface, and as Sheree buried her pain in JJ's shoulder, JJ began to cry herself. Wow, they were a mess.

"What's going on? Did something happen?"

"Oh my God, is the baby okay?"

Sydney and Lissandra rushed into the room, looking equally disturbed at the sight of the two women on the bed, crying.

"No, no, nothing's wrong," JJ said, wiping her eyes and pulling herself together first. "Sheree was just worried about the baby, that's all."

Sydney and Lissandra turned their eyes to Sheree, who had lifted her head from JJ's shoulder and was wiping her cheeks with a tissue.

"The baby's going to be fine, Sheree," Sydney said, slipping into a chair at Sheree's bedside and taking her hand. "We just have to keep praying and keep believing. In fact, let's do that now."

Sydney grasped Sheree's hand and reached for Lissandra's. Lissandra rolled her eyes but took Sydney's and then JJ's hand, even as JJ put her arm around Sheree's shoulders.

"Dear God, our father, our creator, and the designer of every human being on this earth, we bring to you this baby and its mother. We know that nothing is too hard for you and so we pray that even now you reach down and touch them. Bring healing and health to their bodies. May this baby be born healthy and strong, and may everyone know from this that nothing is impossible with you."

Sydney squeezed Sheree's hand and the woman took up where Sydney left off.

"Dear God. I know we haven't been that close, but thank you for showing yourself to me through these women, this family that has accepted me even though I have done them so much wrong. Thank you for your love, which is greater than anything I could understand. I know my life has been a mess, but it's not this child's fault."

Sheree begin to sniffle again, and JJ rubbed her shoulder.

"Please do not punish my baby for all that I've done wrong. Please let my child be born healthy and strong and grow in fullness, and I promise I will do all that I can to help him to know you and love you. Give him to me, Lord, and I will give him back to you."

"Dear Daddy," JJ began, tears springing to her eyes. "Thank you for sticking it out with me even when I wandered away from you. Thank you for loving me through these people, even through Sheree, though she doesn't know it. Thank you for this grace you've given to all of us. We are here because of this child. This child who is a gift from you to us in so many ways. This child you have used, through sickness and health, to bring our family closer to each other and closer to you. And if that is the reason that you have allowed this to happen, Lord, then help us not to miss the lesson. But, Lord, I pray now that you put your hand of healing here and bring our sister Sheree to full term with this baby. May this child be born without difficulty in full and complete health. And may he be yours completely."

There was a pause as they waited to see if Lissandra would say anything. JJ knew her sister was rarely the praying type, but they always gave her a chance just in case she surprised them. This time she did.

"And, God, help us to forgive each other, so we can love this child and teach this child how to love. We're trusting you. Don't let us down. Amen."

"Amen," the other women echoed.

The stillness of the moment wrapped around each woman, and none of them said anything for a few minutes.

"Don't worry," Lissandra said finally, settling into a chair beside JJ and propping her feet up on the foot of the bed. "The Isaacs family's got strong genes. That boy's gonna be a fighter."

"Boy?" JJ asked, perking up. "Is there something I need to know?"

"Only that Lissandra's sure that it's a boy," Sydney said, rolling her eyes.

"I know these things," Lissandra said smugly. "When Mom was pregnant with Josephine, I said it was going to be a girl, and it was."

"Mom already had four girls," Sydney said dryly. "That wasn't a guess. That was a reasonable deduction."

"And," Lissandra continued, ignoring Sydney, "when our neighbor was pregnant four years ago, I said it was going to be a girl, and it was."

"Maybe you just prefer girls," JJ said. "It doesn't seem like you ever predict boys."

"Until now," Lissandra said, raising a finger. "Trust me. It's a boy. Sheree, you can go ahead and pick out boys' names."

"Actually, me and Dean agreed on Dominique," Sheree said. "It means 'belonging to God.' It's good for a boy or a girl, so either way it works."

"Dominique Isaacs," JJ said. "I like it."

"Dominique Royce Isaacs, if it's a boy," Sydney said. "All the men in our family have the middle name Royce."

Sheree sighed. "I wish my family had traditions like that."

"They do," Lissandra said dryly. "She just said all the men in our family have the middle name Royce. That's your family too, now. Regardless of what happens with you and Dean, you and Dominique are stuck with us."

Sheree smiled. "Thanks, Lissandra. I think that's the nicest thing you've ever said to me."

"M-hmm," Lissandra said. "And if you give us back our money, we could get along even better..."

"Lissandra!" JJ and Sydney said at the same time.

"What? I'm just saying..."

"Anyway," Sydney said, moving the conversation along, "I'm surprised you're here, JJ. Thought after last night you'd be with Simon."

"Whoa, what happened last night?" Sheree asked, looking back and forth between JJ and Sydney.

"Go ahead and tell her," Lissandra said. "Tell her how you were making out with Dr. Massri on the roof last night."

"I was not making out with him," JJ protested. "It was one kiss!"

"Two, actually," Sydney corrected.

"And I'm sure there was some action going on this morning, since you disappeared with him at the crack of dawn," Lissandra said.

"He kissed you!" Sheree squealed, slapping JJ with the magazine repeatedly. "How could you not tell me he kissed you! That should have been the first thing out of your mouth when you came in here! And where did you go with him this morning?"

"We went swimming at Centennial Pool in the West End," JJ protested. "It wasn't a big deal."

"M-hmm, that's why you can't get that grin off your face," Sheree said.

"Girl, please, she's been grinning like a cat with a canary since last night," Lissandra said. "That man's done turned her into a dang fool."

"Shut up, Lissandra," JJ said with a laugh.

"You know it's true."

"This is awesome," Sheree said, clapping her hands together. "And to think, you might never have run into him if I hadn't moved into your house and fainted that fateful day in May. You know you better make a toast to me at your wedding."

"Whoa! You guys need to slow that train all the way down," JJ said. "We haven't even gone on a real date yet!"

"And when will that be?" Sydney asked dryly. "Tonight? Or better yet, the moment you leave here? In fact, I bet he's waiting for you in the parking lot."

"Ya'll are trifling," JJ said. "Every last one of you."

Just then JJ's phone rang. Sheree snatched it out of JJ's hands and tossed it to Lissandra.

"Guess who's calling?" Lissandra held the phone out so they could see the screen. "Dr. Massri himself."

"Give me that," JJ said, reaching for the phone. Lissandra tossed it to Sydney, who answered the call.

"Hello, Dr. Massri. How are you?" she asked.

JJ rolled her eyes and leaned back in the bed beside a laughing Sheree, knowing it was no use trying to get the phone from her sister.

"Judith?" Sydney repeated, looking over at JJ. "Oh yes, she's right here."

Sydney held the phone over to her sister. "It's for you, Judith."

JJ grabbed the instrument and put it to her ear to the laughs of her sisters.

"Hey, Simon."

He chuckled. "Your sisters giving you a hard time?"

"Yes," JJ said. "Sheree included."

"You still want me to come and get you?" he asked.

"Yup. In an hour, maybe?" JJ said.

"Make it two," Sheree said. "You're gonna do my nails and watch *Soul Food* with me."

JJ sighed. "Sheree says two."

He chuckled again. "Okay, that's fine. See you in a couple."

"Bye."

"Bye."

"Bye, Simon!" the other three women chorused. JJ could hear his laughter as she ended the call.

"You all are terrible," JJ said, getting up off the bed. "I'm going to use the washroom."

"Great. By the time you come back, Lissandra should be done setting up this DVD," Sheree said, handing the case to Lissandra.

"Season one?" JJ heard her sister say as she headed to the bathroom off Sheree's room. "Season three was the best."

She paused and looked back at the three of them, Lissandra trying to figure out how to work the DVD player attached to the TV, Sydney and Sheree hunched over the magazine. It reminded her of how it was when all her sisters used to have their girls-nights-in. It reminded her of family. Sheree was part of their family now. Instinctively JJ knew that whatever happened with the baby and with Sheree's marriage to Dean, the woman would always be a part of them, for better or for worse. In many ways, Sheree had been lost in the life she had been living before, hurting people to get what she wanted. But God had brought her to them and taught them all something in the process.

Sydney was right. No matter how lost they all were, they had one thing in common. God was waiting to bring them all home.

Chapter 33

"Okay, so where are we going now?" JJ asked as Simon took the Jeep on the ramp to the 404 north.

"To dinner," Simon said, resting his free hand on the armrest between them.

"Isn't it a bit early?" JJ asked. "It's barely four. Plus I'd like to go to dinner in something more dressed up than shorts and a peasant top."

"We won't be eating right away. And as for what you're wearing…" JJ watched his eyes run the length of her form, then his mouth tilted into a smile. "You look fine to me."

"Keep your eyes on the road, mister," she said, even though a smile was pulling at her own lips.

"I'll try, but you don't make it easy."

The easy banter flowed between them as they headed north of the city and slightly east. When JJ saw signs for Uxbridge, she began to suspect what was going on.

"You're taking me to your home, aren't you?" JJ said, sitting up suddenly.

He glanced over at her slyly. "Maybe."

"Wow, I get to see the home of Dr. Simon Massri. I'm intrigued," JJ said, rubbing her palms together.

He chuckled. "Well, you showed me yours, so I guess I should show you mine."

His place wasn't huge, but it was wide. The bungalow-style house sat comfortably among the shelter of tall black-cherry trees, which JJ knew had to be older than both of them. Wide steps led up to a wraparound porch, anchored at the corners by stacked stone pillars. Two huge windows balanced a wooden, screened door that led to the inside. She couldn't wait to see what was beyond those doors. What she had already seen gave her a peek at another side of Simon.

"This is beautiful," she breathed as she walked ahead of him to the front door.

"Thanks," Simon said.

She had caught him watching her first reactions to his place and suspected that what she thought about it would be important to him. He had nothing to worry about. She was liking what she saw.

When he opened the front door and she stepped inside, she decided she loved it. The house had a chalet feel to it. The floor was made of lighter stained wood, and the same wood was used to panel the walls from the floor almost halfway to the ceiling. The ceiling itself was constructed of exposed wooden beams from which hung the lighting fixtures.

Standing in the living room, she could turn in a full circle and see almost the whole house. Large, but still managing to pull off a cozy feel. Cabin-like, but completely livable. When she finished her 360-degree examination, she was face-to-face with Simon.

"Well?" he asked. "What do you think?"

JJ couldn't really tell him what she thought—that she loved the house so much that she was ready to kick off her shoes and spend the rest of her vacation curled up on the soft couch that faced the huge picture windows and glass doors.

"I love it," JJ said, beaming. "It's nothing like I imagined a doctor's house to be. But it's exactly who you are."

She sighed and glanced around again. "All it needs is a vegetable garden around the back to be complete."

He smiled and took her hand. "Come with me, Miss Isaacs."

JJ let him lead her through the dining room to the screened-in deck, and out the doors that led to the backyard. When JJ stepped outside, she felt like she had stepped into another world. Whereas the front of the yard was shadowed by trees, the backyard opened up into a large grassy field, with enough open space for JJ to run free and turn cartwheels.

Her toes itched for it, and so she slipped out of her shoes and took off skipping through the grass. Memories of her early teen years, of summers spent at her grandmother's home in rural Ontario, came back to her.

"Having fun, Pippi Longstocking?" Simon called as he walked toward her.

She grinned. "You have no idea."

"Good." He grinned. "But if we want to eat, we have work to do."

He nodded toward the only structure within sight behind the house, a box-shaped, shiny gray building. When they got close enough, she realized that the structure was not gray, but made of glass. And when Simon opened the doors and let her inside, she realized exactly what it was.

"You have a greenhouse?" JJ squeaked.

Simon nodded. "This way I can grow the vegetables I want, throughout the year."

She shook her head. "Simon Massri, you never stop surprising me."

He slipped an arm around her. "Good." He planted a kiss in her hair. "I like to keep it interesting."

"You certainly do that," JJ said, leaning against him. "So is this where we're going to pick our dinner?"

"That's right," he said. "This is what we're going to need."

He began to name ingredients, some JJ was familiar with and others she would need help finding. With the basket he had found for her, she wandered through the rows of plants, picking out the vegetables they needed while he adjusted the temperature and checked hydration.

JJ couldn't believe how big the greenhouse was and how many varieties of fruits, vegetables, herbs, and beans Simon had going. She wondered when he found time to take care of them, and who did it when he was away.

"Judith." Simon put his hand on her shoulder and turned her around. "Taste this."

She opened her mouth and took a bite of the small tomato he held out to her. It was sweet. Sweeter than any tomato she had tasted in a long time. And fresh in a way that she couldn't describe.

"Oh, this is good," JJ said, pulling his wrist close so she could take another bite. "You grew these?"

"From seeds," Simon said proudly. "Could you ever go back to supermarket tomatoes after these?"

"Are you kidding me?" JJ asked. "I haven't had supermarket tomatoes in years. Sydney would kill me. But these taste even better than the ones we get from the market."

"No pesticides, and organic fertilizer," Simon said. "Did you get everything on our list?"

JJ grimaced. "Except the mushrooms. They look kinda scary."

Simon chuckled and pulled JJ back over to the area where clusters of mushrooms were growing.

"There's nothing to be scared of," he said, pulling a knife from his pocket and stooping down.

"I don't know," JJ said, peering over his shoulder. "They look like the stuff that used to grow on the rotting wood near the back of my grandma's yard."

"Those you shouldn't eat. But these," Simon said, cutting off a few near the base, "will taste great."

"I'll take your word for it, hon," JJ said, holding the basket out for him to drop them in. Produce in hand, they made the trek back to the house and into the kitchen. JJ grabbed a seat on a stool by the counter, content to watch Simon work until he needed her. But before she could settle in too comfortably, he set her to work washing and cutting up vegetables.

"How do you find time to tend all those plants?" JJ asked. "In fact, before you answer all that, when did you even buy this house, seeing that you are almost never in one place."

"I got this place the same time my parents moved here," Simon said. "My mom insisted that I have somewhere of my own where I could leave all my stuff, instead of storing it in boxes at their house."

JJ laughed. "Like permanent storage space?"

"Yeah, something like that," Simon said, pulling pasta from the fridge. "Since my parents seem to have decided that they want to settle and retire here, this seemed like the place to do it. This way at least I have a place near them, so if anything happens, they're not out in the cold."

"Sounds like you're protective of them."

Simon shrugged. "Someone has to be."

"So back to the when-do-you-find-time-for-the-garden thing."

"Everyone has a hobby, Judith," he said, reaching around her for a pot. "This is mine. It relaxes me, so I make time for it. And when I am away, my cousin stays here and takes care of the place and the garden for me."

JJ nodded. She glanced at him out of the corner of her eye, then went back to slicing the mushrooms.

"Don't you ever get tired of the constant traveling?" she asked without looking at him. "I mean, do you ever plan to, I guess, settle down?"

There was silence behind her, and for a while she wondered if he had heard her question.

"I don't know," he said after a long moment. "Sure, I get tired of it sometimes. I could live the rest of my life without eating another restaurant meal, and if I could find a way to travel without sitting in airports for hours, I'd do it. But I like what I do. I like the people I get to help. And I've never had a reason to 'settle down,' as you put it."

He stopped moving and JJ turned away from the cutting board to look at him.

"Honestly," he said, "this is my house, but right now that's all it is—a house. If I ended up in South Sudan and felt like it was where I wanted to spend the rest of my life, I would give this up in a heartbeat. I guess I'm just waiting on something to make somewhere feel like home—somewhere that I really want to come back to."

JJ turned around and began slicing again. "Who's Elena?"

She heard something fall behind her, but she didn't dare turn around. She could feel Simon's eyes burning holes into her back, but she would rather feel them than see them, so she kept chopping.

"What did Nigel tell you?"

"Nothing," JJ said. "Except that she was very important to you."

"She was," Simon said.

She heard cupboards open and knew he had gone back to what he was doing. So he wasn't going to tell her. That was fine. The truth was, she probably shouldn't have brought it up in the first place. If their relationship had been as serious as Nigel had suggested, she should have waited for Simon to broach the topic. But she couldn't not ask—not after everything Simon had said about not having a reason to settle down or a place that felt like home.

"We were engaged."

JJ turned around to look at him, surprised that after the lengthy pause he had chosen to continue. Instead of looking at her, he was placing another pot on the stove. He tipped in some olive oil then scraped in some cloves of garlic.

"I met her while I was in Ecuador," he continued. "She was an Oxfam ambassador working in a community near where I was stationed. I was supposed to be there for only six months, but after we started spending time together, well, it stretched out into a year. She extended her term with her project also, so our commitment to each other was mutual. Or so I thought."

"What happened?" JJ asked. She had abandoned her mushrooms completely to hear the story.

"Onions?"

She handed him the plate with chopped onions.

"I asked her to marry me," Simon said. "She said yes. My parents were back in London at the time, so I took her there and she met the whole family. They loved her. My mom especially, 'cause they shared the same background. Then we went to Ireland and met her family. That went great too. Everything seemed to be going great. Mushrooms?"

JJ handed him the plate of mushrooms. He glanced at the plate and raised an eyebrow at her.

"Bigger chunks, more flavor," JJ explained.

He smiled and shook his head before scraping them into the sizzling pot. The delicious aroma of the garlic filled JJ's senses and triggered her hunger center.

"How soon till dinner?" JJ asked, eyeing the pot longingly.

"Soon," he said.

"Okay." JJ pulled out a knife and a long loaf of thick, crusty bread. "I'll make the garlic bread. Tell me the rest of this story."

He nodded. "I had to go back to Ecuador to finish up, and she was supposed to join me. She was a week late, and when she finally got there, things were off. After weeks of probing, she finally told me that there was someone else her parents had intended for her to marry, and that they were pressuring her. I was floored. I hadn't suspected anything like that when I met her parents, and she had never mentioned this other guy before.

"From there, things just kept going downhill. She would tell me nothing had changed, she still wanted to get married, but then she kept stalling on the wedding plans, trying to push the date. When she finally called it off, I wasn't surprised. It hurt. But I'd had a feeling."

"I'm sorry, Simon," JJ said as she watched him check the pasta, grate cheese, and do anything to keep from looking at her.

"Yeah," Simon said. "She got married a couple months after that. I saw her brother not long after, and he told me."

JJ grimaced as she laid the bread on a baking tray. "Yeah. That must have been hard."

"It just made me more skeptical, you know?" Simon said. "People can tell you they love you, tell you they want to be with you, but sometimes the words and what's real are not the same. How can you really know that people mean what they say?"

"I guess that's what love is about," JJ said, slipping the tray into the oven. "It's taking that risk. Nigel told me you hardly date anymore. Is that why?"

"When did you and Nigel have all these conversations?" Simon asked, throwing a questioning look at her. "Should I be jealous?"

"Not even a little," JJ said, wiping the crumbs from the countertop. "I just wanted to know who you are, and sometimes I felt like I couldn't crack the surface."

Simon added tomatoes to the pot. "I guess I do hold back a bit. That's what makes me bad in dating situations. Plus there's the whole celibacy thing, and the whole traveling thing. They don't exactly make me the ideal boyfriend for most women."

JJ pulled glasses and plates out of a cupboard before heading to the dining table.

"Good thing I'm not most women then."

They ended up eating outside. They agreed that warm days in Toronto were too good to waste indoors, so they took Simon's pasta with tomato-mushroom sauce, garlic bread, and salad out to a wooden picnic table sitting in a shaded section of his backyard.

JJ tried to hold back from stuffing herself, but she couldn't. They had done an excellent job on dinner. Okay, so maybe most of the credit went to Simon. JJ knew homemade pasta sauce was better than anything off the shelf, but she was convinced that the fresh-off-the-vine ingredients brought the level up to heavenly.

For dessert, they took a bowl of strawberries—also from Simon's garden, but allowed to chill—down to the very bottom of the yard, where large stones lined a shallow creek. JJ shook her head as she settled on the ground beside Simon.

"You have a river in your backyard. Seriously?"

He laughed. "It's nowhere near a river. More like a stream. And it's dry most of the time. The rain a couple days ago is the only reason why we're seeing anything now."

"Still, a football field–sized backyard, a greenhouse, and a stream behind your log cabin home are pretty impressive," JJ said. "I can't believe you have all this going on. I never would have guessed."

"Now you know something about me that very few people know," he said, lazily leaning back on his palms. "Now you have to tell me something about you to even the score."

"I think you know all the major points. My family, my seamstress career, my new singing career. That's pretty much everything," she said.

Simon didn't seem convinced. "Nah, there's got to be more. Something about yourself that no one could guess, or find out on the Internet. Something unexpected."

JJ bit her lip thoughtfully for a moment, then smiled. "Okay. Here's something."

He turned a little to get a better view of her face.

"I almost stayed in France."

Simon's eyebrows rose. "As in, for another year?"

"As in, indefinitely," JJ said, loving the surprised reaction she'd garnered. "I loved every moment of the year I spent in Europe. I don't think I was really ever homesick. When I was halfway through, the woman running the company I had my internship with offered me a job. So for the last half of my time in France, I worked for her. It was enough to live on. I looked at apartments in Paris, even houses in the countryside. I started getting the documents together for a work permit. I was ready to start my life there."

"So what changed your mind?" Simon asked.

"My dad had his first stroke," JJ said simply. She looked off into the expanse of field before her but barely saw any of it. "My whole family seemed to fall apart. Mom went a bit crazy, Sydney had to take over the business, and she and Lissandra were pretty much swamped trying to handle that and take care of Dad. Josephine was still a teenager, Dean was still in school, and Zelia was in school and between majors. It was just chaos. I had to come home. My family needed me."

Simon nodded. "Do you ever regret not staying?" he asked after a moment.

"No," JJ said. "Coming back was the right thing to do. But I sometimes wonder how things would have turned out had I stayed. Life would have been so much different." She sighed. "It's funny how one thing can change your whole life."

"Like a sudden stroke," Simon said.

"Or a broken elevator," JJ replied.

Simon looked over at her, and as their eyes locked she felt herself falling into him again. He seemed to hold her in place as he traced a finger down her nose, across her bottom lip, under her chin. Then he used the same finger to pull her closer. JJ melted into him as his lips met hers. His kisses kindled a fire in her that started in her toes and spread through her whole body. What had she been doing before she met this man? Before she kissed this man? No man she had ever been with had made her feel the way Simon did. It was like he looked at her and saw her thoughts; he touched her and touched her soul; he kissed her and singed her senses.

When they finally separated, she rested her forehead against his, unable to bear the feeling of distance from him.

"Simon," she whispered, her eyes still closed.

"Judith?"

She sighed at the effect of her name on his lips. "What happens now?"

"What do you mean?" he asked.

She pulled back and opened her eyes, waiting for him to do the same. When he finally did, she saw that he knew exactly what she was referring to.

"In less than four weeks, Sheree will have the baby and you'll be on a plane to Malawi," she said.

"And in less than four days, you'll be on a plane back to the tour," Simon said. He rubbed a hand over his face. "We always seem to have the worst timing."

They sat in silence, staring at the water. JJ knew she couldn't keep doing this if there was no future for her and Simon. She was already in too deep, and the more time she spent with him, the more she felt like he was ruining the possibility of her having a relationship with anyone else. He was the man she had dreamed about years ago, come to life. How could she ever get over that?

"What will happen at the end of your tour?" Simon asked, still looking at the water.

"I don't know," JJ said. "But Kate, Deacon's manager, told me to start looking for a place in LA. Plus Deacon talked about recording my song that he did on tour, so I would have to be there for that too. Honestly, Simon, I really don't know."

"What do you want to happen?" Simon asked.

"I want to not lose you again," JJ said.

He looked over at her, surprised.

JJ shrugged. "We might as well be honest with each other from the start."

"Well, if we're being honest," Simon began, "then I'll tell you, I want to see where this could go. It's insane how much I think about you, Judith, how much I care about you, and we haven't even spent that much time getting to know each other. I know that has to mean something, and I would never forgive myself if I didn't at least make a decent go of it with you... that's if you want to."

JJ smiled. "I want to."

He grinned. "Okay, then."

"Okay."

JJ's eyes fell to his mouth. He leaned forward to kiss her, but just before they made contact, JJ jumped back.

"What about our schedules?" she asked worriedly. "When would we see each other?"

"We're seeing each other plenty right now," Simon said, zooming in on her lips.

"Yeah, but after next week, it's another three weeks until I'm back in Toronto," JJ said. "And then almost right after, you're gone and who knows if you'll be back soon after..."

"I'll be back," Simon said, cupping her cheek.

"But when?" JJ asked. "How are we going to get to know each other? We barely had time to talk while I was on the road."

"Talking is overrated."

"Simon!" JJ slapped his arm to get him to focus. "This is serious."

He sat back and gave up on his pursuit of her mouth. "I know this is serious," he said, taking her hand. "But, Judith, I met you five years ago in a hotel in France. We never exchanged contact information, never even knew each other's last names, but we managed to run into each other here, in a hospital in Toronto. Don't you think God might have had something to do with that?"

JJ's eyes widened.

Simon smiled. "Yes, I have been thinking that, too," he said, answering her unspoken statement. He kissed her fingers.

"Judith, angel, we both know we want to be with each other. We'll do the best we can to make that happen, but at the same time, we both have to do the things that God has put in our hearts to do: your music, my medicine. At the end of the day, if you and I together is God's design, our efforts will be successful and it will all fall into place. But if it is not, no matter how we plan, it will never work."

JJ took a deep breath, acknowledging the magnitude of Simon's statement.

"So what are you saying?" she asked, wanting him to clarify it.

"I'm saying, let's just enjoy the time we have with each other now and promise to make time for each other when things get crazy again," Simon said. He leaned in toward her. "I flew out to see you once, remember?" he asked, tucking a curl behind her ear. "I have no problem doing that again..."

He kissed her nose. "And again..."

He kissed her cheek. "...and again."

He kissed her other cheek.

"Okay, okay, I get it." JJ grabbed his face and pulled him closer, finally affording him the kiss he had long sought.

Simon was right. One day at a time was all they could do, along with placing the whole thing before God. This would be new to her, praying about her and Simon. But it was worth a shot. After all the mistakes she had made so far in the relationship department, she could use a little help.

Chapter 34

"JJ! Phone!"

JJ burrowed a little deeper into the pillows, languishing in the pleasure of not having anywhere to be for several hours. She had been out all night with Simon. But it had been completely PG as they sat on the hood of his Jeep at a lookout point near his home, waiting for some constellation that could only be seen after midnight on a few nights during the summer. JJ had thought the whole thing was a hoax to get her to stay out with him, and she had told him so. But when he pointed out the cluster of stars at around one a.m., JJ realized that Simon was the real deal—a man who was clearly interested in being with her, but could be with her at one o'clock in the morning without trying to get into her pants. He would never understand how his appeal rating had skyrocketed with just that one thing.

She closed her eyes and tried to picture his face, the angle of his jaw, the curve of his lips when he smiled. The feel of his lips when he...

"JJ, I think it's someone from the tour," Sydney said, sticking her head through JJ's bedroom door and tossing her the cordless. "Where is your cell phone?"

JJ shrugged and took the call off hold. "JJ Isaacs speaking."

"JJ, this is Andrew."

"Hi, Andrew," JJ said with a smile as she rolled over onto her back. "How is it going? Enjoying your week off?"

Andrew harrumphed. "It's more on than off. There's so much happening here, which is actually why I'm calling."

JJ's chest tightened. "Oh?"

"Yeah," Andrew said. "Have you checked your e-mail this morning?"

"Uh, no," JJ said, sitting up and glancing around the room for her cell phone. "Did you send me something?"

"My assistant should have e-mailed you your electronic ticket," Andrew said. "I know I told your manager anytime tomorrow would be fine, but turns out we need you here in the morning."

The tightness turned into a heavy weight. "Wait, you spoke to Rayshawn? You need me back tomorrow? Why?"

"The extension of the tour," Andrew said with a touch of impatience. "We need you to sign the new contracts and submit the original music for the new song so we can get our production people working on it. Plus we want to firm up some dates for recording. Didn't your manager tell you all this?"

No. Rayshawn had not told her anything. In fact she had not spoken to him since the Monday morning when he had peeled away from her front curb. How could he make all these arrangements without telling her? She dug through her purse for her iPhone.

"Why didn't you call me directly?" JJ asked, bypassing Andrew's question.

"We did," Andrew said. "My assistant was trying to get you on the phone all afternoon yesterday."

JJ pulled out the phone and sighed. The battery was dead. Just like it had been yesterday afternoon while she was with Simon. She had been so sleepy when Simon dropped her off, she had forgotten to plug it in.

"When we couldn't get in touch, we called Rayshawn and set everything up." She heard Andrew sigh on the other end. "Is this going to be a problem?"

JJ bit her lip. Of course this was going to be a problem! She was supposed to have a whole weekend more at home with her family, with Simon. Her vacation wasn't supposed to be over so soon! But what kind of professional would she sound like if she said that to Andrew?

She took a deep breath. "I actually hadn't planned to be back until Sunday..."

"We know," Andrew said. "That's why we are covering the cost of the earlier ticket."

She heard a voice in the background and Andrew put her on hold. As she waited, JJ tried to think of all the ways she could get out of this tour extension and salvage the last remaining days of her time off. When Andrew came back on the line, she thought she had something.

"Look, Andrew, I know you need me back but—"

"JJ, I have to go," Andrew said distractedly. "I'm just about to step into a meeting. Just check your e-mail and make sure you have the ticket. If not, call my office and they will take care of everything."

"But, Andrew, I can't come back tomorrow!" JJ protested. "Andrew? Andrew?"

He was gone.

She fell back on the bed and closed her eyes. This was turning into a terrible day.

"Trouble at work?" Sydney asked, stopping at JJ's bedroom door as she buttoned up her blouse.

JJ flopped an arm over her eyes. "They want me back in LA tomorrow."

"I thought you were here till Sunday!"

"I'm supposed to be," JJ whined. "But they extended the tour, and they need me to sign contracts for the use of my song, and Rayshawn agreed to all of this without even telling me!"

"Rayshawn?"

"Yes, Rayshawn," JJ growled. "My ex-boyfriend, current manager Rayshawn. Ugh, I could kill him!"

Sydney shook her head. "You know why he's doing this, right?"

JJ groaned. "Yes."

"You need to find new management," Sydney said, rolling up the long sleeves of her shirt. "That man is going to have you over a barrel soon, if you don't."

"I need to find a lawyer first, to get me out of that contract," JJ said, getting up. "But first I need to check my e-mail."

"Good luck," Sydney called as she disappeared down the hallway.

JJ crawled across the bed to the travel bag in which her laptop was still resting—probably uncharged. She was hanging off the side of the bed when Sydney stuck her head back in the room.

"Hey, wait. Did you say the tour was extended?" Sydney asked.

"Uh-huh."

"But that means you won't be here for—"

"Sheree's delivery? Yeah, I thought about that," JJ said. It was actually the first thing that had come to her mind when she heard about the extension. When the tour was first announced, she had worried about how close the end of the tour was to Sheree's due date. If she went into labor early, JJ might not be there. But now, with the additional tour dates, it was almost certain that she'd miss the birth.

"Oh, JJ, she really is counting on you," Sydney said, worry creeping into her voice. "I mean, Dean is more involved than before, but you're the one who's had the best relationship with her through this whole thing—"

"I know," JJ said, cutting her sister off. "Trust me, I know."

JJ sighed and flopped down on the bed, suddenly tired. In less than ten minutes, her day had gone from awesome to awful. Last night, she had been looking forward to her weekend. This morning, the thought of it brought her a headache.

Sydney leaned against the doorway. "You're not looking forward to going back, are you?"

JJ didn't have the energy to fake it. "No, not exactly."

Sydney bit her lip. "JJ, when the thing you love to do starts feeling like a burden and brings you anxiety, you should ask yourself if the way you're doing it is the right way. You love singing. The fact that you're dreading going back to a job that allows you to make a living doing what you love is something you should seriously think about."

A couple minutes later, as JJ scanned through Andrew's e-mail on her computer, the weight that had been sitting on her chest since she spoke to Andrew seemed to double. They had extended the tour to six more locations: Boston, Memphis, New Orleans, Houston, Denver, and then back to LA to end the tour. Furthermore, the tour extension stops were scheduled merely a day apart, as opposed to the more relaxed two-stops-a-week schedule that the previous section of the tour had run on. This meant they would play in Boston on Saturday and Sunday nights and then play in Memphis Tuesday and Wednesday. Friday and Saturday they would be in New Orleans. All six additional stops were crammed into two-and-a-half weeks.

Five-and-a-half more weeks of living on a tour bus and occasionally in hotels. Five-and-a-half more weeks of keeping Deacon's secrets. Five-and-a-half more weeks of being antagonized by Sabrina, of avoiding drugs and alcohol, of not seeing her family, of not seeing Simon. Five-and-a-half more weeks. Could she do that? She wasn't sure. Sydney's words came back to her. When had she stopped loving, and started dreading, her job? Was it when Sabrina cut her guitar string? Was it when she was out that night looking for Deacon? Or was it when she was lying sick on a hotel bathroom floor in New York? When had this lifestyle lost the glitter that it once had? When had it become a burden?

She needed to talk to someone. She needed someone to help her make this decision. To tell her that this was her dream and that she shouldn't let the tough moments overshadow the good ones. Someone to tell her that her voice was a gift from God and she had to use it. Someone to tell her that he would be there for her no matter what she decided, that he would come for her whenever she needed him.

But her someone was probably sleeping in, like she had planned to. And the truth was, she needed to make this decision on her own, with a clear head. For herself. For her future. Sure, her career wasn't comfortable right now, but she had to start at the bottom and keep climbing until she got to a point where she could go it on her own, set her own rules, and make things the way she wanted them to be.

She closed her eyes and leaned back against the bed's headboard.

"God, I don't know what to do. You opened this door for me, allowed me to have a chance in this industry. But I've gone through so much hell so far. Now I have to make this decision: keep my promise to Sheree, or keep this commitment to my job. I want to do both, but I can't. And then there's Simon. I don't know how we could ever work if we're never in the same place. And I want to be where he is, but I want my career too. I don't know what to do. Help me."

She kept her eyes closed and waited. Waited for a light to shine above her head. Waited for the perfect solution to pop into her mind. Waited for something. Anything that would tell her what to do. But it was silent except for the faint sound of her sister in the bathroom down the hall.

She opened her eyes and slunk out of bed. Maybe the answer would come at some point, but in the meantime she had some people to see, and she was pretty sure none of them would like what she had to say.

Chapter 35

Rayshawn had perfected the art of disappearing. JJ had called all three of his cell phones, his office phone, and his home numbers without success. When she ended up at the Franklin and Forbes offices, his secretary could give her no help other than to let her know he would be out of town until the following week. Frustration bubbled through JJ as she exited the main lobby doors of the downtown Toronto high-rise where the office was housed. Rayshawn was avoiding her, but she would find him eventually, and when she did, he would get more than a piece of her mind.

In the meantime, however, she had less than twenty-four hours, and a lot to do. Her next stop—at the hospital to see Sheree—was successful, if success was measured by delivering her message to her sister-in-law. If success depended on a positive response to that message, then she sat at a total fail.

"What do you mean, you won't be here for the delivery!"

JJ glanced at Sheree's heart monitor, worried that it might spike suddenly, but so far it was holding steady.

"They extended the tour," JJ said, slipping into a chair next to Sheree's bed. "I just found out a few hours ago."

"But how can they just do that?" Sheree moaned. "Didn't you sign a contract or something?"

JJ sighed. "I did. That's why they're calling me back early. I have to be in LA tomorrow morning to go over the changes."

Sheree ran a hand over her face and JJ saw that the woman's forehead was damp with perspiration. She had noticed that Sheree didn't looked as relaxed as usual when she came in. There were bags under her eyes, and she lacked her usual energy and zeal. The pregnancy was getting to her. Probably the bed rest too. It couldn't be easy, stuck on your back for most of the day, barely getting any sunshine, looking at the same four walls. Plus her stomach looked like it was about to pop. The woman kept shifting, trying to find a comfortable position.

"Are you okay?" JJ asked, helping Sheree adjust a pillow behind her head.

"No, I'm not okay," Sheree grumbled. "I feel like an obese Oompa Loompa, and my butt feels numb half the day. Plus my tits are leaking like old balloons. Yesterday, Dean came in and I had two huge wet spots on my chest."

JJ covered her mouth to stifle a giggle, but it slipped out anyway.

"You're laughing at me!"

"I'm sorry," JJ said, trying to hold back the laughter. "It's just you...I can just picture you with Dean, and your hospital gown... What did he say?"

Sheree rolled her eyes. "Nothing. He just kept looking at my chest, which I can understand, 'cause these babies have increased in size since the last time he got a close look. But then he asked me if I was okay and pointed to my chest, and I nearly died."

JJ's voice shook as she asked, "Did you have to explain that it was normal?"

Sheree let out a chuckle. "Yeah, after he came back from dashing out of the room. You should have heard the excuse he made up. The poor man couldn't deal."

JJ snorted and Sheree let out a giggle. Before long they were both laughing.

"Aww, my brother," JJ said when they finally settled down. "He's not used to this stuff at all."

"Don't I know it," Sheree said. "But after we talked about it, he was cool. Even asked me what other strange things I had to deal with. We had a good little chat."

"I'm sorry, Sheree," JJ said, touching her sister-in-law's hand. "I can't imagine how crazy your body must be now."

"Trust me. You can't." She sighed. "I can't wait to get this munchkin out of my belly. It's time."

"Three more weeks," JJ said with a sigh. "And then it's D-day. We're almost there."

"I thought you were going to be with me to the end, JJ," Sheree said. The sadness that slipped into her voice was worse than the anger she'd expressed when JJ announced she would not be around for the delivery.

"I'm glad that Dean is here," Sheree continued. "And he promised to be here for the delivery. But it's you who has been here for me through all of it. Not even my crazy mama has shown her face, and she knows I'm pregnant." Sheree grabbed JJ's hand and held it tightly. "You've been like family to me. I can't imagine you not being here for this."

"God knows I feel terrible, Sheree," JJ said. She sighed. "I wish I could somehow be here, but based on the draft schedule they sent me it doesn't seem possible."

Sheree nodded. "I understand."

"Let's not count it out yet, okay?" JJ said. "Maybe things will change between now and when I go back. I just wanted to give you a heads-up, just in case."

"Heads up on what?"

JJ looked up to find her third and final appointment standing at the door.

"Dr. Massri!" Sheree exclaimed. "They told me you were off today. Should have known you would be with JJ. So I guess you're mourning with me too?"

"Sheree—" JJ began, trying to cut her off. But it was too late.

"Mourning what?" Simon asked, stepping into the room. His intense, multicolored eyes looked more green than gold as he glanced between JJ and Sheree. He was dressed ultra-casual in khaki shorts and a short-sleeved plaid shirt, with his dreads only half pulled back. But the look was ultra-sexy to JJ, and all she wanted to do was slip into his arms and forget her problems for the rest of the day. But she had a feeling that after Simon heard her news, in his arms was the last place she would be welcomed.

"The tour extension," Sheree said. She looked back and forth between JJ's guilty expression and Simon's surprised one. "Oh . . . you didn't know."

She turned a sheepish expression on JJ. "Sorry."

But JJ was busy watching the look on Simon's face. Apologies and questions were reflected in their eyes before either of them said a word.

"You had lunch yet?" Simon finally asked.

JJ shook her head.

"Give me a few minutes and we'll go." He turned toward Sheree. "Just thought I would stop by and see how my favorite patient's doing."

"Great!" Sheree said, the sarcasm dripping from her voice. "Just feeling like a whale in a sauna, even with the AC cranked all the way up. Nothing a little delivery won't solve."

Simon smiled as he checked her charts, then the machines by her bedside. "Everything looks okay, so that's good."

"Thanks for checking in," Sheree said with a smile. "I'm fine, really. I just can't wait to have this baby."

"Soon enough," Simon said. "Anything I can get for you in the meantime? I may not have power like Janice, but I can pull a few strings here and there."

Sheree chuckled. "I'm fine. Just take your girlfriend here out, and make sure she enjoys the rest of her time in Toronto."

Simon glanced over at JJ, who was still sitting quietly next to Sheree. He cracked a smile that made JJ let out the breath she had been holding.

"I think I can manage that," he said finally.

After they both said their good-byes, JJ and Simon slipped out of the hospital room into the hallway.

"Your car or mine?" JJ asked.

Simon took her hand gently, threading their fingers together. "Neither. Let's walk for a bit."

The day was turning out to be hot and humid, but JJ didn't

mind as they walked down University Avenue in the heart of downtown Toronto. She knew Simon didn't mind it either. He loved the warm weather—probably more than she did. He didn't say anything, just ran his thumb gently against hers. She leaned closer to him, occasionally resting her head against his shoulder. She felt in place, just like she always did with Simon. Like she was exactly where she needed to be, and she didn't need anything else.

They found a tiny Vietnamese restaurant that was so narrow there was only room for a single row of tables. They opted for the back patio, where they sat next to each other and deliberated over whether it was too hot for curry. When their order of rice-paper rolls and banana-blossom salad arrived, the real conversation began.

"Andrew called me this morning and told me they are extending the tour," JJ began, deciding to go straight to the heart of the matter. "They already bought me a ticket. I fly back tomorrow morning."

"So you already agreed?" Simon asked, pausing from his meal to look up at her.

JJ sighed. "I didn't have a chance to disagree. The agreement was already drawn up, and apparently when they couldn't reach me, they reached Rayshawn and he gave them the okay..."

"Rayshawn?" Simon asked, his left eyebrow rocketing up to his hairline. "I thought you told me you were done with that guy."

"Personally, yes," JJ said, hating that she had to talk about Rayshawn with Simon again. "But professionally he's still my manager, and I'm still under contract."

"So you're telling me that this man is still going to be in your life?"

JJ sighed again and put down her chopsticks. "Yes. Until my contract is over."

"And how long is that?"

"Six months."

Simon pushed his plate away and took a long gulp of water. When he put his glass down, he still wouldn't look at JJ. The blank expression that she remembered from the first time they had discussed Rayshawn slipped onto his features.

"Simon." She touched his arm. "I didn't ask for this. I don't want it. But this is my job."

He rubbed his chin, even as his jaw tensed. "How long is the extension?"

"Three more weeks."

He turned to look at her. "So that's what Sheree was talking about. You won't be here for her delivery."

"It doesn't look that way. Not unless the birth of her baby fits perfectly into the week we are scheduled to perform in Toronto."

"She was really counting on you, JJ," Simon said.

JJ ran her hands through her hair. "I know. I feel like the worst aunt in the world." She bit her lip. "At least I know you will be there for her."

She reached over and slipped her hand under his dreads to the nape of his neck. "I am so glad you said yes when I asked you to stay. For more reasons than one."

He smiled. "Trying to butter me up, Miss Isaacs?"

She smiled back. "Is it working?"

He reached for one of the rolls. "Lucky for you, you don't have to try very hard."

She leaned over and kissed him on the cheek. "I am really, really getting used to having you around, Simon Massri. You sure you don't want to come on tour with me? You can be my personal bodyguard."

"The way things are going, you might need one soon." He nodded toward the doors, where two young women were trying to be discreet as they stared at JJ and whispered.

"They're just jealous 'cause I have a hot boyfriend," JJ teased. She chuckled as she saw a tinge of pinkness color Simon's fairer skin.

"Eat," he said, handing her the chopsticks she had discarded. "That should keep both of us out of trouble for a while."

She grinned but took his advice. How had she ended up with

this man? He was definitely worth the wait. So gorgeous, so amazingly kind, and so unbelievably understanding. Other guys would have thrown a fit. Other guys would have made demands. But Simon was giving her so much room to breathe that she almost wanted to beg him to tie her down.

"Speaking of being around, they offered me a position here in the University Health Network," he said, dishing some of the salad onto his plate.

JJ's eyes brightened. "As in a permanent job?"

"More like a long-term contract," Simon said. "It would be after I get back from Malawi, of course, but it would have me in Toronto for a longer time after that."

"Would something like that even interest you though?" JJ asked. "I know how much you love to travel."

He swallowed his bite of salad. "I haven't said yes. But I'm thinking about it."

JJ dropped her chopsticks again and twisted in her chair till she was facing him.

"You're thinking of staying here?"

He shrugged. "Why not?"

Something was happening in JJ's chest. It was like someone had placed a balloon there and was slowly filling it with air. Filling it and filling it until she couldn't hold anymore. She also couldn't breathe or speak. All she could do was launch herself at Simon, wrapping her arms around him and burying her face in his neck. She didn't care who was looking or what people might think. They didn't understand what was going on, what this man was considering for her. Tears she didn't expect or understand began to leak from her eyes, and she began to tremble.

"Hey, hey," he said, holding her gently. "I hope those tears mean you're glad."

JJ nodded, still unable to speak.

"Was that a yes?"

JJ pulled back so he could see her face.

"Yes," she said. She pressed her forehead against his before kissing him softly. "Absolutely yes."

Chapter 36

By the time her plane touched down at LAX in Los Angeles, all the serenity that JJ had acquired from her last few hours with Simon had dissipated. She was nothing but a ball of nerves. Her sister's words came back to her in full force. She really shouldn't dread coming back to work. Especially when work was doing the one thing she loved most in the world. Something was definitely not right with this picture.

As she walked through the airport, pushing her luggage on a cart and looking for the signs for a taxi stand, another sign caught her eye. One with her name on it. One with Miles holding it. She hurried over to him.

"Miles! What are you doing here?" She hugged the bulky security guard, more out of surprise than real enthusiasm.

"I'm here to take you to the hotel," Miles said with a smile. "What else?"

"Special treatment?" JJ asked. "This is new. Did everyone get a raise or something?"

Miles chuckled and took the cart from her hands, leading her out the doors to the pickup area where his signature black SUV was parked. This one, however, had California plates, so she knew it wasn't the one he'd had in Atlanta or New York.

He opened the back passenger door for her and her mouth fell open.

"Deacon?"

"Shhh," he said, glancing behind her to make sure no one noticed them. "Will you get in and stop alerting the whole airport that I'm here?"

She slipped into the vehicle and closed the door as Miles loaded her luggage into the back.

"Okay, now I am officially worried," JJ said. "Is everything okay?"

"Everything's fine," Deacon said. But his eyes were hidden behind his usual dark glasses, so she couldn't verify.

"Then why are you picking me up?" JJ asked. "Are you going to be needing my help again?"

"No," Deacon said. He waited until Miles was in the vehicle and they had pulled away into the traffic leaving the airport. "I'm actually here to do you a favor."

JJ's curiosity was officially piqued. She settled back in her seat, turning questioning eyes on Deacon.

"I'm listening."

"Good," Deacon said. "Because I am about to tell you something completely confidential. No one knows but me, Miles, my lawyer, and one other person. You can't tell anyone else."

Great. More secrets. JJ took a deep breath. "Deacon, I don't know..."

"I'm leaving Sound City."

JJ snapped forward. "You're leaving the label? What...how... but you...what?"

"I'm serious," Deacon said, his face hardening. "I'm done with Hugh Kelly and his money-making machine. This tour extension? They just sprang it on me. I didn't ask for it, didn't agree with it. And it's been like this for the last couple years. I feel like I have no control over my own life, and I can't live like this anymore. I'm out."

"Deacon," JJ began. "Clearly you're upset about everything. But no one just leaves their label. Those contracts are tighter than a celebrity prenup."

"This isn't a spur-of-the-moment thing, JJ," Deacon said. "My lawyers have been working on this for over a year, trying to find a way out for me. I have eighteen months left in this prison, and so even if I leave them I won't be able to perform until that time runs out. And since any new material I would want to put out would come under their purview, I probably won't be recording either."

"That's terrible, Deacon," JJ said. "You live for performing. Are you really ready to give all that up for a year and a half? What will you do?"

"Focus on what's important, and who's important in my life," Deacon said, looking at JJ purposefully. "Deal with a lot of my responsibilities that I've had to neglect because of this life I've chosen."

JJ nodded, understanding exactly what he was saying. He wanted to be more involved in his son's life. He was making this decision for Xavier as much as he was for himself. Clearly a lot had happened in less than a week.

"Anyway, the reason I'm telling you all this is because it changes what I can do for you at the end of this tour," Deacon continued. "You have amazing talent, and if things were going better, I would make sure you were a part of my team. But now I can't do any of that. As it stands, at the end of the tour, She-La will be disbanded and you will be back on your own."

JJ sighed and eased back into her seat once more. She had been thinking about what would happen with the band after the tour. She had heard about artists like Prince helping their band members develop careers of their own. It wasn't unheard of in the industry, and at the very least she had hoped that her time with Deacon Hill would give her the exposure and the connections she needed to further her music career. But now it seemed like there would not be as much of that as she thought.

"Look, I have friends," Deacon said, leaning toward her. "I can look into a few things for you. But honestly, once this firestorm with the label starts, I'll probably be in industry quarantine. Fighting with your label is bad for business, and no one really wants to be associated with that."

"Yeah, I know," JJ said. "I've heard."

"It sucks, but this is the only way I know to get my life back."

"Thanks for giving me a heads-up," JJ said. "Does Sabrina know about this?"

Deacon snorted. "She'll know the same time her daddy finds out. Then she'll have to find some other man to manipulate."

JJ frowned. "What are you talking about? Who is her dad?"

Deacon looked at her as if she had asked who was the current president.

"Hugh Kelly. Didn't you know that?" Deacon asked, surprised. "Why else do you think she has so much pull?"

The pieces began to click together in JJ's mind like a puzzle. Sabrina's father owned Deacon's label. That's why he kept warning JJ about Sabrina. That's what Miles had meant the night she called him to pick up her and Deacon. And that's why no one was willing to get in the middle whenever there was a fight between Deacon and Sabrina. Just one word from Sabrina and any of them could be gone in an instant. No one was willing to take that chance. No one except JJ, because JJ was the only one who hadn't known.

"So you're dating the daughter of the label's owner?" JJ asked. "Is that why she's in the band? Did she even have to audition?"

She heard Miles chuckle from the driver's seat and Deacon grinned.

"You're really going to have to stay more informed if you want to survive in this industry."

Moments later they pulled up in front of JJ's hotel. JJ lingered in the backseat as Miles got out to retrieve her luggage.

"I hope everything works out with you and your son," JJ said quietly. "You both need each other."

Deacon nodded. "Thanks."

JJ opened the door.

"Remember, no one else," Deacon said as she stepped out.

JJ nodded. "You have my word."

She waved to Miles and trudged wearily into the hotel lobby. She barely registered what the clerk said as she checked in, but just knew that her bags would be sent up to her room. She was more than happy to take the stairs to her fifth-floor room. It would give her time to process everything that Deacon had just told her. First the tour extension, now Deacon leaving the label. The past two days had been crazy. But when she slipped the key card in and opened her hotel room door, she knew that the madness had just begun.

Chapter 37

JJ grabbed the nearest object and threw it as a surge of energy powered through her.

"You sneaky, conniving bastard..." The vase near the hotel door missed its target and went crashing into the wall behind. "I have been calling you for the past two days and you didn't even have the decency to pick up the phone and answer?"

"Wait, I can explain..." Rayshawn ducked as JJ's structured Coach purse came at his head.

"You can explain how you went behind my back?" Her left wedged sandal went first. "Made decisions for me without consulting me? All because you were mad at me?"

Her right wedged sandal followed swiftly after, striking him in the shoulder. He groaned and rubbed the injured spot.

"No, JJ, it's not because of that," Rayshawn said, backing away. "Can you stop throwing things and just listen? Please?"

JJ did want to stop throwing things, but only so she could put her hands around Rayshawn's neck. She was so angry at him, and she suspected it was not just because of what he did with her contract but also because of all the other things he had done to hurt her. Things she had ignored or allowed him to brush aside. And with everything that had happened so far, she was too tired and too frustrated to have any more patience with him.

She closed the hotel room door with a slam.

"You have sixty seconds," she said, folding her arms. "Start talking."

"We only have a verbal agreement with the label for the tour extension," Rayshawn said. "Nothing is in writing, therefore nothing is binding. That's the point of this morning's meeting—for you to sign."

"That's my point, Rayshawn," JJ snapped. "You didn't give me a chance to agree or not. I never got to decide if I wanted to continue with this tour or not."

"That's fine," Rayshawn said. "'Cause you're not signing on anyway."

JJ's eyes narrowed. "I don't understand."

"If you'd have a seat," Rayshawn said, motioning to an armchair in the sitting area, "I could explain."

JJ glared at him for a long moment, gaining a tiny bit of satisfaction from the way he twitched under her fierce look. When she felt he had suffered enough, she sat down on the nearest couch and waited.

He took a breath and chose the armchair opposite her.

"I told you, JJ, everything I do, I do for you," Rayshawn began. "You know I care about you, but it's not just that. I know that you are talented. I know you're going to make it big. I believe it. And when I saw how they responded to you at the audition for Deacon and got the reports on how things are going on the tour, I knew we had to take advantage of that."

"The label has you and all the other singers for She-La on a tour contract, which means that when the tour expires, so does their relationship with you. I did a little checking and realized that Kya and Diana aren't signed to any agency. In the past couple weeks we signed them with us. They are now under Franklin and Forbes management."

"So basically you now manage almost all the members of

She-La," JJ said, beginning to catch the drift of where he was going.

"Exactly," Rayshawn said, his eyes lighting up. "With everyone in one place, we can negotiate with you as She-La, versus individual members. Do you know how much more power that gives us? Especially now that they want to extend the tour and have to sign all of you on for the additional shows?"

"Yeah, I get it," JJ said. "Now you can strong-arm Sound City for more money."

Rayshawn shook his head. "You're still thinking too small, JJ. This is way past money. We're talking about your future here. She-La is making a name for itself with Deacon Hill. We don't want that to end with the tour. With all of you under the same management, we can negotiate for a development contract. We're talking about two, three years of label money and resources dedicated to making She-La the next Destiny's Child."

The anger began to slide away as JJ started to understand the full picture.

"This is your future, JJ." Rayshawn was now sitting at the edge of his seat, fully animated. "You told me you were tired of feeling like a pawn in everyone else's game. Well, this is the chance to make it your game."

It was tempting. So tempting that she almost forgot that she was angry with Rayshawn. Almost.

"You're forgetting one thing," she pointed out dryly. "You don't have Sabrina. And since her daddy owns the label, she'll never sign with you."

"True," Rayshawn said. "But the label is trying to extend this tour and finalize this agreement within three weeks. It's much easier to get one person to play ball than find three new band members. The numbers work in our favor. Besides, we're offering Sound City first dibs on giving us the development contract. If they agree, Sabrina gets to stay a part of the band."

"And if they don't?"

"Torrina plays keyboard, and her contract with Jayla Grey is up at the end of the summer," Rayshawn said with a shrug. "We'll dye her hair red and paint on some freckles."

JJ almost laughed until the she realized that Rayshawn wasn't joking.

"You can't be serious," she said. "You think you can just replace Sabrina with Torrina and no one will notice?"

"I do," Rayshawn said. "And even if they do notice, no one will care. Think about it. Does anyone even remember who the original third and fourth members of Destiny's Child are? No. They only remember Beyoncé, the headliner. You're the headliner, JJ. You could be the next Bey. And all this drama around you and Deacon in the tabloids? That only boosts your stock."

JJ couldn't believe what she was hearing. This was another of those reality-check moments where she was reminded that only about 10 percent of the music industry had anything at all to do with music. The rest was promotion, image, and fabrication.

"I can't listen to this anymore." She got up and headed to the hotel refrigerator. She needed some juice, water, anything liquid and cold to snap her out of the craziness that was happening.

"I know this is a lot to take in," Rayshawn said. "But you have some time to absorb it all. Like I said, no one's signing anything this morning. In fact, I'll be going with you to meet with Andrew. Kya and Diana are gonna meet us there. We'll request the modified contract then."

JJ took a sip of the water in her hand and turned to look at Rayshawn. "You're really confident this will work, aren't you?"

"Completely." Rayshawn leaned back, his hands locked behind his head. "They say yes? We have a developmental contract for two years. They say no? We have two other labels waiting to sign us on. This is a win-win for all of us."

"And just out of curiosity," JJ asked, her eyes narrowed, "who would be managing She-La?"

He grinned. "Who do you think?"

Two more years being managed by Rayshawn? She took another long gulp of water.

"Anyway, there will be lots of time to talk about this in the next couple days," Rayshawn said. "Right now we need to get over to Sound City."

JJ finished her water, her brain too numb to think anymore.

"Let's go then," she said, walking over to the corner to retrieve her shoes. "Might as well get this over with."

Rayshawn raised an eyebrow as his eyes ran the length of her ripped jeans and tank top. "Uh, not that you don't look great, but aren't you changing?"

"Why get dressed up?" JJ asked as she retrieved her purse and its contents from the floor. "With the mess you're about to start over there, why risk getting my good clothes dirty?"

Rayshawn smirked but got up and headed to the door. "I guess you do have a point there."

JJ closed her eyes and whispered a quick prayer.

Lord, help me. I have no idea what I've gotten into.

Chapter 38

JJ had never heard grown men shout the way they did at Sound City.

It began with the frown that slid onto the label's lawyer's face almost as soon as all four of them walked into the narrow conference room. Andrew, Kate, and the lawyer had expected only two.

"What's going on?" the lawyer asked. "I thought we were just meeting with JJ Isaacs this morning."

"There's been a slight change," Rayshawn said, sliding his chair closer to the table.

Kate and Andrew exchanged a look that suggested they suspected what was about to go down.

Kate clasped her palms together. "Care to expand?"

"As you know, these three artists previously negotiated their contracts with Sound City individually," Rayshawn began. "However, since they all are now under the management of Franklin and Forbes, we would like to negotiate their tour extension as a group."

That's when the shouting started.

Andrew stood up, his face red. "You slimy son-of-a..."

Kate placed a hand on Andrew's arm. "These are not the terms under which this meeting was coordinated." Her tone was clipped and her blue eyes icy.

"True," Rayshawn said. "But there are now new terms. And I think all of us agree that there needs to be some renegotiation. We want a new contract. Not just for a few more weeks, but for at least twenty-four months, with terms related to the development of this group of women as a single commercial offering."

"You mean you want a contract with She-La," Kate clarified.

"I'm not standing for this bull," Andrew raged, slapping the table. "George, get Hugh and Tony down here."

The lawyer slipped away from the table to the phone in the corner as Andrew continued to grow more irate.

"You don't walk into our label and set terms. This is our label! We make sure you have work!"

JJ never knew Andrew could get so angry. She had seen the man get gruff on tour, but this was beyond anything she had ever experienced. Rayshawn, however, didn't seem the least bit ruffled. He was almost as cool as Kate, who said nothing but frosted them with her glare.

It wasn't long before the door opened and in walked Hugh Kelly. He was a wiry man with a permanent frown who looked like he'd had a hard life before he finally made it in the music business. In the car on the way over, JJ had done the research she should have done months ago, so she knew that the man who entered behind him, the one built like an NFL linebacker, was Tony Kelly. He was Hugh's only son and Sabrina's brother. He ran Sound City with his father.

"What's going on?" Hugh asked, his voice raspy as if overused.

"This little punk wants to give us terms for our artists," Andrew snapped. "He wants to renegotiate as the band. Trying to get his filthy hands in the pot." He glared at Rayshawn again. "You think you know what it takes to make it in this business, you good-for-nothing piece of crap? You were just born yesterday. You think you can come in here and interrupt our plans while we're trying to make something happen with this tour?"

"I'm just trying to get the best for my clients."

"Your clients? You don't know the first thing about getting the best for your clients," Andrew spat. "And you!" He raked his angry glare over Kya, Diana, and JJ. "You hussies were nothing before we gave you a stage."

"Hey, watch your language with my clients!"

"Yeah," Kya snapped, getting up. "Who do you think you're talking to like that, old man?"

"I'll talk to you however I want, you gold digger..."

JJ sank lower in her chair as they shouted across the table at each other. So this was what it was like to enter the twilight zone.

"Alright, alright," Hugh said, sitting down and pulling a cigar from his jacket pocket. "Calm down, Andrew, you're about to give yourself a stroke."

JJ watched Hugh. There was no way. He wasn't going to light that cigar in the room, was he?

"So you think you can write the rules, do you?" Hugh asked as he held the flame from a gold-plated lighter to the end of the cigar.

JJ watched in a mix of shock and awe as he puffed on the brown roll of tobacco before exhaling white smoke into the room. She was wrong. She wasn't in the twilight zone. She was in some weird 1980s mob film. Any minute now, Tony in his tight black shirt was going to jump Rayshawn and hold his face down to the floor until he signed the version of the contract that Sound City wanted.

"No, Mr. Kelly," Rayshawn said. "I just want to discuss some new terms with the label and see what we both can agree on."

Hugh nodded. "And the rest of you are okay with him negotiating for you?" he asked, motioning his smoking cigar toward Kya, Diana, and JJ.

The other two women nodded as JJ massaged her scalp.

Hugh took another big puff and sat back. "Okay, let's hear what you got."

Andrew cursed and dropped back into his chair. Kate pursed her lips but opened her notebook. Kya looked pleased and Diana looked less frightened. JJ felt sick.

Deciding she'd had enough cigar smoke for one day, JJ stood. "If you'll excuse me."

She didn't wait for a response and heard no objection when she stood up and left the room. What had started as a tingling in the back of her neck that morning had turned into a full-on headache. This crazy day had taken everything she had, and all she wanted to do was close her eyes and forget that she had ever heard of Sound City, Deacon Hill, and even Rayshawn.

A text message to Rayshawn was the only notice she provided that she was leaving before she asked the receptionist to get her a taxi. A scroll through Yelp found her a hotel where Rayshawn would not have access to her room and where no one would be able to find her until rehearsal for the next show began in two days. She couldn't leave LA yet, but she needed to escape. She needed space to think, to process. She had some big decisions to make, and this time she wouldn't let anyone make them for her.

Chapter 39

"Hey, angel, how is LA?"

JJ sank back onto the queen-size hotel bed, her whole body relaxing with just the sound of his voice.

"Baby, you would never believe the day I just had." JJ reeled off the events of the day to Simon, from Deacon's news when he picked her up at the airport, to Rayshawn's presence in her hotel room, to the events of the meeting with Andrew and the label.

"Can you believe they are actually negotiating with Rayshawn on this, all the while not knowing that Deacon is planning to leave the label in a matter of weeks?" JJ sighed. "Simon, this is crazy."

"It is," Simon said. "But at least you won't have to deal with it. You told Rayshawn no, right?"

JJ was silent.

"Judith, you told Rayshawn you wouldn't sign on with him, right?"

"Simon, it's not that simple," JJ said wearily. "This is my career. And with Deacon leaving the label, there's nowhere for me to go after this tour is over."

"There is always somewhere for you to go, Judith. You're talented and everyone knows that. You'll be singing for the rest of your life," Simon said. "But we talked about this Rayshawn thing. You told me six months."

"That was before I knew about Deacon leaving and about Rayshawn signing She-La on a development contract."

"So you're okay to sign on to work with this guy for two more years?" Simon asked. "After the way he's treated you? Look how he's manipulating your life now. You don't think he'll continue to do that?"

"I won't let him," JJ responded.

"That's easy to say, Judith," Simon said. "But I've seen what this business has done to you, how it has drained you physically, emotionally, and spiritually. How it has caused you to neglect the things in your life that are most important to you. How it has put you in places where you are uncomfortable. How it has changed you. And you can say whatever you want about me not knowing you well enough to know you have changed, but we both know you have. And I'm not saying all the change was bad. I'm not even saying that this business is all bad. But I'm saying the direction that Rayshawn has been pushing you has not been good."

"I'm a big girl, Simon, and I run my life. Not Rayshawn," JJ said, an edge slipping into her voice. "I can take care of myself, and I can handle Rayshawn."

"It's not about you being able to handle him," Simon said. "Maybe you can do that professionally. But this man also has feelings for you. You think it's easy to just switch that off and go back to being strictly professional after your history with each other?"

"Is that what you're worried about?" JJ asked. "Simon, nothing is ever going to happen with me and Rayshawn. That is so over."

"How can it be over when you're still working with him? When he'll still be a part of our lives?"

"Our lives?"

"Yes, our lives, Judith," Simon said. "Don't you get it? This is what we're doing, integrating our lives together. That's what you do in a relationship. And we can't work if Rayshawn is in the middle. You've got to see that."

"So being in a relationship with you means I have to sacrifice my career?" JJ asked. "How can you ask me to give up this opportunity?"

"How can you be so ready to jump into this opportunity without giving it some serious thought?" Simon asked. "Seriously, Judith, have you even prayed about this? What about all that talk about feeling lost? Is this the path that you think is going to make you feel at peace with your life?"

"Now who's trying to manipulate who?"

As soon as the words were out of her mouth, JJ knew they were the wrong ones. She had been angry at Simon for pointing out her failure to seek divine guidance. Everything with the contract changes had happened so fast, she hadn't had time to think about it. To pray about it. Simon was right about her not thinking it through well enough. He was right about everything. And JJ had bitten his head off for it.

She sighed. "Simon, I'm sorry. I shouldn't have said that."

Silence fell between them on the line. JJ wasn't sure what to say. Wasn't this what she had worried about from the beginning? That their career choices would get in the middle of whatever was happening between them? And now here it was. She couldn't understand why he was against her extending her contract, and he couldn't understand why she didn't see why. She knew they were at an impasse.

"No, you're right," he said slowly after a long moment. "Maybe I have been trying to manipulate you. I do wish you were here more, and I guess that is part of why I wish you wouldn't sign the extension."

His words sounded good, but JJ couldn't help the ominous feeling that began to build in the pit of her stomach.

He sighed. "If you feel that this is your opportunity to get where you want to be, then you should take it. I don't want you to be with me and always wonder if you missed out on the career you could have had."

Coldness sliced through JJ with Simon's words. "What are you saying?"

"I'm saying that I want you to have your dreams," he said gently. "Do what you have to do, Judith."

She blinked back the tears that were filling her eyes. "And what about us?"

Another pause, then a rustle on the other end. "I don't know. Maybe we'll run into each other in an airport someday."

JJ could barely breathe. Huge, silent tears rolled down her cheeks as panic gripped her chest. "So this is what it's coming down to," she said, trying hard to keep her voice steady.

"Maybe we were wrong," he said. "We thought that seeing each other again after so long meant something. But maybe we were just trying to make something out of what was only a coincidence."

"You and I both know that's not true," JJ said. "What I feel for you is more than just the result of a coincidence. And I know the feeling is mutual."

"I'm not sure what I know anymore," he said.

JJ sniffled. "Can we at least talk about this?"

He sighed. "Maybe some other night. Right now...I've got to go."

"Simon, wait—"

"Take care, Judith."

The click on the other end of the line was final. Like the clasping of a latch, or the clicking of a lock on a door. Maybe the door to Simon's heart.

What had she just given up?

Chapter 40

JJ woke up Monday morning in Miami with a pounding headache. After spending the weekend in LA, she had flown into Miami on Sunday night to meet up with the team for the next stop on the original tour. They still had to play Miami, Chicago and Toronto before the tour extension would kick-in and she needed to psych herself up at least for the last three stops to which she was already contractually obligated. But she still couldn't get past what had happened over the weekend with Simon.

Despite the brief length of their relationship, she had gone through all the stages of grief in mourning it. She had been in denial until several calls to him on Saturday and Sunday had proved fruitless. Simon always answered her calls, and even when he couldn't he usually called her back within the hour. But in the past two days, she had heard nothing from him except his voice mail recording. Anger had come soon after. How dare he ask her to change her career for him? How dare he not be reasonable? What about all he had said about making their relationship work? By the time she got to the bargaining stage, she realized that she needed to do what he had accused her of not doing: talk to God about the decisions laid out before her.

JJ pulled her knees up to her chest in the middle of the hotel bed and rested her head on her knees.

"God, I really don't know what to do here," she whispered. "I love singing. I love this feeling of performing onstage. I love the opportunities it gives me to meet people, to show others like me that you can come from somewhere simple and make it big. But I know that this life is full of ugly things. I hate being around the drugs and the drinking and the promiscuity. I hate not being able to be there for my family. I hate that it's already caused me to lose Simon. But if I give this up, what am I supposed to do? I'll have no job, no money, no plan. What will I possibly gain?"

Her confusion continued to drag her down as she walked into rehearsal a few hours later. She soon realized, however, that she wasn't the only one struggling.

"Look who decided to show up!" Sabrina's voice echoed across the empty room from where she lay on the edge of the stage in a leopard-print romper. "How nice of you to grace us with your presence."

JJ rolled her eyes. "Whatever, Sabrina. I'm half an hour early."

"Yeah, well, we were here long before that," Sabrina snapped as she sat up. "But I guess since your manager hustled the label, you think you can do whatever you want to."

JJ sighed. She knew word would get around, but she never thought anyone would bring it up during work time. She had overestimated the level of professionalism of the team—particularly Sabrina's.

"Sabrina, the guys have barely finished setting up the instruments, and Kya and Diana aren't even here yet, so chill out."

JJ walked past Sabrina onto the stage and grabbed her guitar, plugging it into the system herself instead of waiting for the one guy working to set it up for her. And why was one guy working? There were usually at least three sound hands that worked with them for rehearsals and for shows.

"Hey, Joe," JJ said. "Where are the other two guys you usually work with?"

"Fired."

"Fired!" JJ echoed. "When? Why?"

"Just this morning," Joe answered. JJ noted that the usually friendly man didn't look up but kept his eyes on the sound board. "Management said they couldn't afford to have three guys doing that job anymore."

"Hmm," Sabrina said as she seated herself behind her keyboard. "Must be the cost of all those new contracts."

JJ didn't know whether what Sabrina said was true or if she was just trying to guilt JJ. But if the latter was the goal, it was working. JJ wasn't sure she even wanted all these changes herself, but she felt responsible for them and for the trouble they seemed to be causing everyone. How she wished this all wasn't happening.

"Really sorry to hear about that, Joe," JJ offered.

He nodded but still wouldn't look at her.

"Hello, everyone!"

JJ turned around just in time to see Kya breeze into the room, a big smile on her face. Diana came in right behind her, without as much fanfare but with just as big a smile. JJ narrowed her eyes as she watched both women. She could only imagine who they had spent their morning with. Maybe with Rayshawn, signing more contracts. A package had been waiting for her when she arrived at the location for rehearsals. She hadn't yet opened it, but she already had an idea what it was. If Diana and Kya had indeed already signed, then it meant they were waiting on her to make everything final. Well, they could go ahead and wait a little longer. JJ wasn't in the mood to sign anything.

Sabrina scowled at all of them. "Now that we're all here, maybe we can get started."

JJ sighed and picked up her guitar. It was going to be a fun rehearsal.

Sabrina tortured them with her brutal rehearsal regimen for the next two and a half hours. JJ sang until her throat felt like it was about to go hoarse and played until her fingers felt like the tips had been rubbed raw. If Sabrina wanted to establish who was in charge, she had made her point very clear.

JJ was sure they would have continued in like manner if Deacon had not interrupted so he could get JJ to rehearse with him. Sabrina scowled and pretended to be annoyed, but everyone knew there was nothing she could really do, and so JJ shook her head, grabbed her guitar, and followed Deacon into his own rehearsal space.

"Thank you," JJ breathed as she dropped onto a stool in the smaller room.

Deacon grinned. "Sabrina going a little psycho on you?"

"You have no idea."

Deacon chuckled and settled down onto the piano stool. "Don't worry about her. She's just marking her territory." He looked up at her, his eyebrows drawing together to reflect the concern in his eyes. "I bet she's giving you a hard time about the new contracts too."

JJ took a deep breath, ready to defend herself. "Honestly, Deacon, I had nothing to do with that. That was my manager and his bosses. I knew nothing."

"I know," Deacon said, raising his palm to let her know she could relax. "I know. It's just part of the business. Everyone who's been around long enough knows that. Even Andrew, who's walking around barking at everyone, knows this is just the way things are." Deacon snorted. "He's probably pissed he didn't think of the whole thing first. But I guess he didn't know you guys would be so popular."

"If he only knew how soon all of it is going to end," JJ said dryly.

Deacon shot her a knowing look. "You haven't—"

"No," JJ said, shaking her head. "I gave you my word. I won't."

Deacon nodded. "Good. 'Cause I suspect the label wouldn't be signing this new contract with your boy if they knew what was coming up soon."

"So you're going for certain," JJ said. "Are you even gonna do the tour extension?"

Deacon shrugged. "Not sure yet. Depends on what my lawyers say. But if I do, those will be my last shows with Sound City. Probably my last shows for a long while."

JJ shook her head. "Ticket holders for this tour have no idea how lucky they are, do they?"

"Nope," Deacon said, running his fingers over the keys. "It's a shame that the fans are the ones who will have to suffer. That's why I want to make these last shows the best possible."

And JJ could see he meant every word as they went through the rehearsal. He was more meticulous than she had ever seen him, going over every detail until their duet sounded perfect.

"Hey," he said, stopping suddenly. "Let's try something. Let's switch instruments. You play the lead and sing it. I'll play the guitar."

JJ's eyes popped open as he reached for her guitar.

"Deacon, no!" she protested. "I told you, my piano playing is terrible."

"Yeah, I heard that," Deacon said as he removed the strap of her Fender from around her shoulders. "But do it anyway."

Once Deacon had placed her guitar over his shoulders and began testing out the strings, JJ knew there was no point arguing. With a sigh she sat down in front of the piano and put her hands on the keys.

It was a gently used instrument. The padding under the keys seemed to be worn down well enough that there was little resistance when she pressed down. That was good. It had been a while since she had played. At least she knew she wouldn't have to lean into the keys to get a good, solid sound.

"I'm gonna need some time to warm up," JJ said. "It's been a while."

"Do what you gotta do," Deacon said distractedly as he played around with her guitar. She suspected that it had been a while for him also.

She picked through the chorus until her fingers remembered

the progression, then played through the whole song, humming as she did. When she finally felt confident, she started from the beginning. She didn't try to play it the way Deacon did. There was no way she could do that. Instead, she played it the way she remembered and sang it the way she remembered. Deacon picked up the accompaniment on the guitar, coming in a bit cautiously at first, but finding his confidence around the second verse.

The difference was baffling. With JJ singing and playing the lead and Deacon accompanying and picking up the harmony, it sounded like a totally different song. It felt like it too.

"That was interesting," Deacon said with a small smile.

"It was," JJ said.

"I like it," Deacon said, standing up as he removed her guitar. "Let's play it that way tonight—you playing the lead on piano, me singing and playing guitar."

JJ's brows furrowed. "Deacon...are you sure? I mean, my playing..."

"Is fine," Deacon said. "It's not bad, it's just different. And I like something different. Besides, I don't know when I will be on tour again, so I'm going to enjoy it as much as I can."

JJ sighed as she realized that the same went for her. The way things were going, who knew if she would ever be onstage again after this. She might as well enjoy the experience.

"Okay," she said with a cautious smile. "Let's do it."

Chapter 41

"Mum, where are you?"

"I'm in here!"

Simon shook his head and pulled the front door to his parents' condo closed behind him. He could explain to his mother why "I'm in here" didn't necessarily bring him any closer to finding her, but after thirty-three years he wasn't sure what good it would do.

Slipping off his shoes at the door, he padded through the terra-cotta tiled hallway to the lower-level living area. The room was immaculate, as always, with every plant looking lush and green and every cushion in place. A home décor magazine, a dozen paint swatches, and a thick, leather-bound day planner lay on the polished wood coffee table, but his mother was nowhere to be found.

He continued on through the dining room, past the heavy glass dining table for six, and grabbed a banana from the bowl on the kitchen counter before heading up the carpeted stairs. He found his mother in her favorite place, a smaller upstairs sitting area that held his father's large flat-screen television and his mother's brown suede couch. A cream-colored carpet that only people without children would consider buying lay beneath another low, polished wood coffee table.

"Hey, Mum." Simon leaned down and kissed his mother's cheek before settling on the couch beside her.

"Love, come look at this," Fiona Massri said, patting her son's hand as she turned up the volume on the television. "That Mountain fellow is coming to town."

Simon looked at the screen and grimaced. "Hill, Mum. His name is Deacon Hill."

"Hill, Mountain, I can never remember," Fiona said with a wave of her hand. "Your cousin nearly yapped my ear off this morning. She wants to come here and stay with us so she can go to this concert."

"Who, Melanie?" Simon asked, raising an eyebrow. "She's thirteen. Uncle Fredrick's letting his thirteen-year-old daughter come all the way to Toronto to go to a Deacon Hill concert? What is he—"

"Shhh," Fiona said, tapping him, "they're talking about his show in Chicago."

Simon didn't want to be shushed. He also didn't want to see anything about Deacon Hill. But as he watched his mother's green eyes focus with fascination on the TV screen, he knew that he had no choice.

The screen panned over a packed concert venue with lots of screaming fans.

> "... Hill played to a sold-out audience last night at Chicago's Allstate Arena. But that's not all. Toronto music lovers will be glad to know that our city is getting a bit of the spotlight on this tour through homegrown talent JJ Isaacs, who sings a duet with Deacon during the show. *ET Canada* got a chance to chat with Isaacs last night and is here to bring you the exclusive."

The image switched, and suddenly Simon was looking at JJ as the host of the show held a microphone in her face. Her skin glistened under the camera lights and her eyes were bright and shining. Her hair, which his fingers could almost feel, was doing that tight curly thing it did sometimes when it was really humid and she was outside for long. The sight of her was like a dagger to his heart.

> "Deacon Hill's new band, She-La, has been an unexpected high point for this tour, and you, JJ, have been a breakout star. How does it feel playing for thousands with Deacon Hill?"
>
> JJ smiled. "Honestly, it's a feeling I can't explain. Last week we played Miami, tonight Chicago. It's been crazy travelling all over North America. If someone had told me a year ago that I would be doing this now, I would have laughed at them. But Deacon gave us all this great opportunity to be in this rocking girl band. And two of us from the band are from Toronto, so all I can say is Go Canada! I hope we're making you proud."
>
> "You definitely are. And will we be seeing you all in Toronto?"
>
> "Absolutely," JJ said with a grin. "We can't wait to play for all our family and friends less than a week from now in our home city. I know that's going to be amazing—"

Simon stood up from the couch. "I can't watch this."

Without waiting for a response from his mother, he left the room and walked down the hallway to the second-level washroom. He splashed some water on his face, but it couldn't wash away the ache in his chest or the image of JJ imprinted on his brain. It had been nine days since he had last held her in his arms, eight since he had spoken to her, two since he had heard her voice on his voice mail. It felt like eternity. But it would have felt worse if they had allowed it to drag on to the inevitable end—to the part where she decided there was no space in her life for him.

"Okay, you can come back now," Fiona called. "She's gone."

Simon sighed and wiped his face with a paper towel before trudging slowly back into the room with his mother. The TV was off and she was picking at strawberries on a plate on the table. He leaned against the doorway until she patted the couch beside her.

"Still haven't spoken to her, have you, love?"

Simon shrugged as he sat back on the couch beside his mother. "What's the point? You see where she is, what her life is like."

"What does that have to do with how you feel about each other?" Fiona asked.

"Mum, it's not just about feelings," Simon said, feeling exasperated. "It's hard to form a relationship with someone when you never see each other."

"Who said that relationships were supposed to be easy?" Fiona asked. "So both your lives are transient and complicated. If you both are willing to try, then shouldn't you make a go of it?"

"That's easy for you to say," Simon grumbled.

Fiona reached over and clapped him on the back of his head.

"Oww!" Simon groaned, more out of shock than actual pain. "What was that about?"

"To jog your apparently short memory," Fiona said, her Irish accent becoming more pronounced with her stirring emotions. "You seem to have forgotten how little I saw your father when you were younger. I spent months alone with you while he was away on assignments. Before you were five years old, I doubt we ever spent more than five solid months together."

"But that was different," Simon said. "You were already married, you had a child, you were committed to each other."

"Ha!" Fiona responded. "It was worse before we got married! Why do you think I got pregnant so fast? So I could guilt him into spending more time with me."

Simon grimaced. "Oh, Mum."

"Stop," Fiona said with a laugh. She placed her hand on his arm. "I stuck it out because I knew who your father was from the beginning. He loved me. I was sure of that. But he needed to be out there. He needed to feel like his life had a purpose and he was fulfilling it. It's not that he didn't want to be with me, it was just that he didn't know how to be who he was—to be the man I fell in love with—without being available to help others where he could."

She squeezed his arm. "You get that from him."

Simon sighed. "I was willing to stay here for her."

Fiona smiled. "For now."

He looked at his mother questioningly.

"You couldn't stay in one place if you tried, Simon Massri," she said, touching his cheek. "At least not now, while you're young and you have that driving force in your heart that makes you feel like you have to save the world. You would have stayed for a few months, a year even. But then you would be itching to be somewhere else."

"I don't know about that," he said stubbornly.

"I do," Fiona said. "And since I've known you before you knew yourself, you should trust my judgment."

Simon cracked a smile.

"It's not a bad thing," Fiona said, leaning her head on her son's shoulder. "It's just who you are. But I'm guessing that's not the reason you're here sulking over Judith."

"I'm not sulking."

Fiona snorted. "Tell your forehead that. You have so many lines there, I could hang the wash."

Simon began to get up, but Fiona grabbed his arm and pulled him back down. He glanced back, surprised at how easily she was able to overpower him.

"What happened with you and her?" Fiona asked.

Simon let out a long, harried breath.

"Her former boyfriend happens to be her current manager," Simon said, frowning at the wall in front of him. "And this guy is a piece of work, Mum. Got a temper like an Irish drinker and he manipulates her life for his benefit. But she can't even see this. She can't see how toxic he is, how being around him and his lifestyle changes her, and not in a good way. And now she's planning to sign a contract extension with him."

"Ahh," Fiona said. "Now it becomes clear."

"Yes," Simon replied with a nod. "You see now why this is so hard?"

"I do," Fiona said.

"Thank you," Simon said, sitting back with a sigh of relief. At least someone understood.

"You think she's going to be Elena all over again."

"What?" Simon jumped up. "No. It's not that at all. It's just that I am so different from him, as long as we're together we're going to disagree over him..."

"Then she'll eventually choose him over you."

"No, it will just be harder for us to work," Simon said defiantly. "This has nothing to do with Elena."

"Okay," Fiona said, holding her hands up in surrender. She reached for him, and he resumed his position in the couch. Nonetheless, threads of tension continued to run through him. He knew his mother, and she never gave up that easily.

"You said she was planning to extend her contract?" Fiona asked.

"Yes," Simon responded. "Another two years."

"Hmm," Fiona said thoughtfully. "So she hasn't actually done it yet—she's still thinking about it?"

Simon paused. "Uh, yes."

"So you didn't actually give her a chance to make that decision. You assumed she would, and so you ended your relationship with her based on that assumption."

Simon frowned. He knew his mother wasn't finished.

"Mum, it's what would have happened anyway," he said.

"That must be interesting," Fiona said.

"What?"

"Being God and knowing everything."

Simon rolled his eyes. He had walked right into that one. But his mother was right. He had jumped the gun with JJ. He hadn't given her a chance to make a choice. "Okay, so I made an assumption," Simon admitted.

"Yes, you did," Fiona said. "Furthermore, so what if she chose to re-sign with her ex-boyfriend manager? Don't you think she's smart enough to handle this guy on her own? After all, she was doing it before you came along."

"But, Mum." Simon sighed. "He sucks the light out of her. When she's with him, in that life, she's so... lost. I just... I hate to see her like that."

"So you just give up on her?" Fiona asked. "Quit without trying? Leave before she does, so you don't get hurt?"

Simon rubbed his hands over his face. Coming over to see his mother might not have been his best decision of the day. He had been quite comfortable wallowing in his position of self-righteousness before he spoke to her. Darn her years of wisdom and her knowledge of him.

"There are two things you need to realize, love," Fiona said gently. "Firstly, every woman is not Elena McCullough. If you treat every one of them like they are, then you'll always be alone. Are you going to give one woman that much power over your life?"

Simon pursed his lips but said nothing.

"Secondly," Fiona continued, "Judith Isaacs is her own person. You have to let her make her own decisions. But if you're serious about being with her, you can't pull away every time you disagree on one of those decisions. Her choosing differently from what you would want for her—even when you think what you want is what's best—doesn't mean that she doesn't care about you. It doesn't mean that your relationship is over. It just means that you have to show her patience and compassion and care for her while she is being her own person. Just like she's gonna care for you while you're being your own stubborn person."

"What if I'm holding her back?" Simon asked.

"What if you're keeping her grounded?" Fiona replied. "Those are things you can't know unless you stick it out."

Simon put his head back against the headrest and closed his eyes. He wished God would give him clear-cut directions on Judith. If there was ever a time in his life when he needed a voice-of-God-from-a-burning-bush experience, it would be now.

Fiona chuckled and squeezed his arm. "This one has really got you, hasn't she? I have never seen you turned inside out over any woman like you have been over this Judith. Not even Elena."

Simon turned to look at his mother, surprised. She nodded in affirmation of her statement.

"Have you prayed about this, my God-fearing son?" she asked. "I don't quite understand your intensity when it comes to your faith, but I admire how devoted you are to God. How dependent you are on his perceived guidance. Don't you think he cares as much as you do about what Judith's life is like when she is in this industry? Don't you think you should ask for his direction?"

Simon squeezed the bridge of his nose. Truth was, he was afraid to pray about Judith. He was afraid his prayers would end up with him begging God to bring her back to him. Just like he had prayed with Elena. But they hadn't worked that time, and he wasn't sure he could bear it if they didn't work this time either.

"You once told me that prayer wasn't so much about asking for what you want but about drawing closer to God until you want what he wants for you," Fiona said as if hearing his thoughts. "Maybe that's what you should be aiming for."

Simon put his arm around his mother's shoulders. "I thought you ignored me when I talked about my faith."

Fiona smiled. "I never ignore you, love. I just don't respond to everything right away."

She squeezed her son as tightly as her slender arms would allow. "I love you, Simon," she said. "I just want to see you happy."

"I know, Mum," he said, hugging her back. "I know."

His mother was happiest when she was with his father, and Simon knew she wanted that same happiness for Simon. After Elena, he had started to accept the idea that maybe his happiness was to be found somewhere else, in what he could do for others, in the places where he could be God's hands and feet for those who needed it most. But Judith had shown him that there could be more. And for a while he thought he could have both. Something in his heart, a voice that he tried to listen to, also told him he could have both.

The problem was, he had no idea how.

Chapter 42

One more show and she would be back in Toronto.

That was all JJ could think about as she tested her mikes and earpiece. After two concerts in Chicago, she was exhausted. Everyone was. But they had one more performance—the KISS 103.5 live event. They were the surprise artists in the lineup. So *surprise* that they had to do a chunk of their sound check onstage, behind a curtain, just ten minutes before their performance. JJ didn't care though. The quicker they got through this, the quicker she could be on a plane home.

"We want to thank everyone for coming out this afternoon," JJ heard the host begin from the other side of the curtain. "Don't you think we've had a great show so far?"

The screams of the crowd showed their response in the affirmative.

"Great! But the best is yet to come. We have a surprise guest for you this evening. You have seen them all over the news, heard their jams on every station, including KISS 103.5, and a few of you may have caught them in concert just last night at the Allstate Arena. Ladies and gentlemen, coming to you live, right here at the KISS 103.5 Summer Sizzle, help me welcome Deacon Hill and She-La!"

Everything was still behind the curtain as JJ waited with Kya, Sabrina and Diana for Deacon's cue.

"'I got everything you need to keep you satisfied.'"

The curtains opened and Deacon's voice came across the speakers in smooth a cappella as he sang the first line of "Satisfied," the song that headlined the tour. The crowd's screams went up a notch as he entered from the back of the venue, wading through the masses of people toward the stage. JJ barely heard Diana signal the timing on her drumsticks above the roar of the crowd, but they had played that song so many times over the past two and a half months that she really didn't need to. Diana and Sabrina together on percussion and keyboards, with Kya and JJ slipping in on guitar moments later. The whole thing was so seamless they never even needed to look at each other. JJ was sure the music for "Satisfied" had been somehow imprinted into her fingers. She would be ninety-eight, with arthritis and Alzheimer's, and still be able to play every note perfectly.

Deacon was in his element, moving easily between songs, with She-La so familiar with his performance that they were able to follow him with backup vocals on every track. The four songs they played flew by quickly, and JJ had almost pulled the amp out of her guitar in preparation for their exit when Deacon went impromptu.

"You all having a good time?" Deacon asked.

The crowd screamed in response.

"Chicago, are you having a good time?"

The screams were louder.

"Alright," Deacon said, waving a hand to quiet them down. "I have a special treat for you. Something we've never done since the start of the tour. There is a young woman who has been with us from the start of this *Satisfied* tour. She has an amazing voice, amazing talent. One day, you are going to see this girl on your Top Forty countdown, and when you do, I want you to remember that you heard her here first."

Deacon turned around and winked at JJ. Her heart fell straight through her stomach to her feet.

"Ladies and gentlemen, singing the song she composed, "I'm Yours," introducing JJ Isaacs!"

The crowd cheered, but JJ barely heard. She was too busy recovering from the shock of what Deacon had just done. She was going to kill him. Slowly, with something nice and dull. But before she could figure out how, he was pulling her from her spot behind him to the front of the stage.

"Deacon, no, I can't!" she hissed.

"You don't have a choice," Deacon said with a grin. "Just play the lead on the guitar and sing it. I got you."

JJ stared out into the audience and a feeling of nausea swept over her. She couldn't do this. Doing a duet with Deacon Hill was one thing. But she couldn't sing a solo for these people. She had never sung on her own in front of a crowd like this before. She was going to throw up.

A sound from behind caught her attention. She looked back and saw Deacon standing behind Sabrina's keyboard, ready to go. He gave her a nod and began to play.

JJ closed her eyes and let her hands fall to her guitar. Isn't this what she wanted? Wasn't her ultimate goal to be a solo artist? She might as well see if she could hack it. The first few notes on the guitar came in shaky, but she quickly found confidence in the melody. And when she opened her mouth to sing the song, she almost couldn't believe what she heard coming back to her. Was that her? JJ Isaacs? When had she learned how to sing like that?

But she soon forgot about that also and got lost in the song. Around the second verse she found the courage to open her eyes and look at the crowd. They weren't idling about waiting for the next performance like she thought they would be. They were actually watching her, listening to her. Behind her she heard Diana come in, adding percussion. Then Kya slipped in with guitar backup. Guess they had heard the song enough times that they figured out how to accompany it. But the fact that they chose to do it for her humbled her completely.

When it was all done, when she had sung the last note, the crowd screamed their appreciation. JJ couldn't believe it. Couldn't believe all that was for her.

She grinned. "Thank you," she mumbled before shrinking back into the band and retreating to the backstage area. She floated through the narrow space in a haze, barely hearing the "Congratulations" and "Nice work" that came her way. It was only when she was face-to-face with a grinning Deacon that the fog cleared.

"Well, well, look who's a solo artist!"

JJ shoved him hard in the chest, causing him to stumble back into a temporary wall. Out of nowhere, Miles and Cyrus appeared.

"Whoa, easy boys," Deacon said, placing a restraining hand on each man before they could haul JJ into the air. "I got this."

"How could you do that to me?" JJ shouted. "You totally blindsided me out there!"

"That was the point," Deacon said. "If I had told you you were going to do the solo, would you have said yes?"

"Of course not," JJ snapped.

"Exactly," Deacon replied, straightening his sunglasses.

"But I didn't even get to rehearse!"

"We rehearsed this yesterday, and the day before."

"But that was just impromptu, to see how it would sound," JJ protested.

Deacon chuckled. "JJ, I'm an international performer on a major US tour. I don't have time to do impromptu for no reason. Don't worry, you were great."

"I was not," JJ said, folding her arms. "I felt terrified."

"But it also felt amazing, didn't it," Deacon said knowingly.

JJ opened her mouth to argue but realized she couldn't. It *had* been amazing—one of the best feelings she'd had in a long time. Now she knew why artists were willing to do anything to stay in the spotlight. That feeling of performing live? It was positively euphoric.

"That's what I thought," Deacon said when she still hadn't

responded. He grinned and squeezed her shoulder. "It's only the beginning."

Still speechless, JJ watched him head off down the passageway. It had been a crazy evening, and all she wanted to do was talk to the one person who always calmed her down. But he was the one person she couldn't reach. As she sat in the back of the taxi on her way to the hotel, she dug through her bag for her cell phone. Her heart leaped in her chest when she saw the little envelope icon at the top left-hand corner of the screen. She dialed into her voice mail.

"Hey, JJ, it's me. Heard you had a great show this weekend and blew up on a solo tonight. This is just the beginning. Once the tour is over, we can get started recording tracks with you and She-La. You gotta get back to me with that contract first, though. I messengered a copy to your hotel, just in case something happened to the one I sent over a few weeks ago. Call me when you sign it. Peace."

JJ deleted Rayshawn's message without hesitation. She laid her head back against the console and sighed. So the message hadn't been from Simon. That was disappointing. But after almost two weeks without contact, what did she expect? She knew he was avoiding her. But that didn't stop her from missing him something terrible.

With her stomach in knots, she dialed the numbers she knew by heart before pressing the green call button. She was painfully aware of the thump of her heartbeat and the knot in her throat. It rang four times, then she heard his voice.

"Hi, you've reached Simon. I can't talk now. Leave me a message, or better yet call me back later. Not a fan of voice mail." *Beep.*

"Simon, it's me. Call me."

She didn't need to say more. It had been the same message when she called two days earlier. She was still waiting for him to call her back.

Chapter 43

She was still waiting for his call when she got to the hotel. So much so that the driver had to tell her twice that she had arrived at her destination. She handed him a couple bills, not sure if she had given too much or too little and overall too distracted to care. She ignored Rayshawn's package at the front desk. She took the stairs up to her fourth-floor room. She opened the door and slipped out of her shoes. But she didn't cry until she was lying in the middle of the bed. How could she have so much joy and so much misery all at once? Her body buzzed from being onstage, singing solo. But her heart broke from having no one to celebrate with.

She didn't know how long she lay with her wet face in the pillow before she finally heard her phone ring. She picked up.

"Hey, girl! Saw your solo performance tonight! It's already up on the KISS 103.5 website as one of the clips from the show. You were amazing!"

JJ didn't want to hear anything more about a solo. She didn't want to talk anymore about a solo. She just wanted to fall asleep with the hope that the ache in her heart would be avoidable for the next few hours. She felt like she had lost her best friend, and she couldn't deal. But for Cymmone she would muster a polite thank-you before she ended the call.

JJ yanked some tissues from the box by the bedside and blew her nose. "Thanks," she mumbled.

"Oh God, girl, what's wrong?" Cymmone exclaimed.

JJ thought about how much it would take to explain everything to Cymmone and she started crying again.

"Oh no, I see this is an emergency. What hotel are you staying in?" Cymmone asked.

Through her sobs, JJ managed to communicate the name of the hotel and her room number. She thought she heard Cymmone say she would be right over, but that didn't make sense, so when the line went dead, she just put her face back into her pillow.

She was still in the same position when someone knocked on the door. With her tears subsided to whimpers, she clutched her pillow and stumbled over to the door. She pulled it open when a glance through the peephole confirmed Cymmone to be on the other side.

"Sweet Jesus," Cymmone murmured, her eyes widening. "How long have you been crying?"

JJ shrugged before looking down at Cymmone's hands. "You brought your baby? What are you doing here, Cymmone?"

Cymmone swept into the hotel room, baby carrier in one hand, Louis Vuitton purse in the other.

"I've been in town for meetings all weekend. Talking with a label about doing a contemporary Christian thing," Cymmone said, setting the carrier down on the carpeted floor in the living area.

JJ saw that the adorable baby wrapped inside was sleeping. For a moment her negative mood slipped.

"Ooh, she's so gorgeous," she cooed with a raspy voice. "What a sweetheart."

"I know," Cymmone said with a smile as she took off her light coat, revealing pajamas. "You know the best part? She's a much better sleeper than Xavier was. This kid will sleep through a storm. That's why I wasn't worried about bringing her with me on this trip, or over here tonight. You know I was already in bed, girl?"

"Oh, I'm so sorry," JJ said, her face crumpling. "If I knew you were planning to come over..."

"From the way you sounded on the phone, you didn't know a darn thing," Cymmone said, plopping down on the couch. "And I need to know all about that. But first you're going to wash that makeup off and get in the shower. No bath. Shower. Showers make everything less terrible."

"Cymmone—"

"Did I just give you instructions?" Cymmone said, switching to her mommy voice. "You better get moving, ma'am."

JJ rolled her eyes but went to do as she was told. Cymmone was right. After the shower she felt a lot better. When she returned to the living room, she found chicken wings with dip, potato wedges, and root beer spread out across the living room coffee table. Cymmone was simultaneously scrolling through the pay-per-view listings and talking to the hotel staff about alternate options.

"Cymmone! Who's eating all this food?" JJ asked, even as she grabbed a chicken wing from the tray. She took a bite. "Mmmm, honey garlic."

Cymmone grinned at the look of indulgence on JJ's face before covering the mouthpiece with her hand. "Been a long time since you had those, right?"

"M-hmm," JJ mumbled as she slipped onto the couch beside Cymmone and reached for another.

"Yeah, I know," Cymmone said. "I so do not miss those crazy performer diets. No one should have to live like that."

JJ would have responded, but she was too busy licking the honey-garlic sauce off her fingers. Her stomach had not been this happy for a while. She was glad Cymmone was in town. She was even happier when a knock on the door provided her with something she hadn't seen since she left Toronto and which she hadn't eaten for much longer.

"Poutine!"

JJ nearly hugged the red-vested woman who rolled the room-service tray into the room, and when she popped a cheese- and gravy-covered French fry into her mouth, it felt like home.

"My room service bill is going to be a mint," JJ said as she happily selected another French fry.

Cymmone waved her hand as she hung up the phone. "The label will cover it." She folded her legs up under her as she turned to JJ. "So our movie will be ready in a few," she said as she stole one of JJ's French fries. "In the meantime, you want to tell me why your eyes look like they've been stung by bees?"

JJ sighed. "Simon."

Cymmone raised her eyebrows. "Ooh, it's a guy!"

"Not just any guy," JJ said. She reached for her cell phone and scrolled through until she found a picture. She handed Cymmone the phone. "This guy."

"Hello, mama!" Cymmone said with a grin. "He is definitely a man worth crying over. What happened?"

JJ explained everything from the beginning, starting with how they first met several years earlier, to seeing him in the hospital again earlier that year, to him coming to see her on tour, to their week together in Toronto on her break. By the time she was done, she was crying again.

"We can't get past this thing with the new contract," JJ said, sniffling. "He thinks it's a bad idea."

"So he doesn't want you pursuing this career?" Cymmone asked, surprised. "That doesn't sound like the man you described."

"No, that's not it," JJ said. "He thinks I can sing anywhere. He just doesn't want me signing again with my manager. He doesn't like the guy, thinks he's manipulating me. And in a way, he's right. I know Rayshawn hasn't been the most honest with me—"

"Whoa, Rayshawn who?" Cymmone asked, stopping JJ with a hand on her arm. "Rayshawn Forbes?"

"Yeah," JJ said with a nod. "You know him?"

Cymmone snorted. "I've heard of him. And trust me, your boyfriend's giving you good advice to stay away from him."

JJ's eyes widened. "What have you heard?"

Cymmone grimaced. "Let's just say he's very good at his job but very bad at keeping clients. A lot of his formers have become stars, so if that's what you want, I guess that's the way to go. But he's done a lot of shady stuff. Plus he has a reputation of sleeping with his clients—" When Cymmone caught the look on JJ's face, she stopped short. "Oh, JJ..."

The guilt from her moment of weakness with Rayshawn came back like a flood. Just thinking about it now made JJ cringe. How could she have thought she felt anything serious for him? Those days felt like so long ago now.

JJ shook her head. "It's okay. It was just one time...a slip. I would appreciate if..."

Cymmone did a zipping motion across her mouth. "My lips are sealed."

JJ sighed and pulled a foot up into the chair, propping her chin against her knee. "I feel like I've made a mess of everything, Cymmone," JJ began. "I keep feeling like I'm losing myself in this business. But every time I try to get my footing, I end up falling further."

"I know that feeling," Cymmone said. "Trust me, I was there. The thing is, hon, you have to know what your boundaries are."

"What do you mean?" JJ asked.

"You have to know where you draw the line. What you will do and you won't do," Cymmone explained. "How many days out of the year are you willing to be away from home? What can your agent sign for you and what do you have to give first approval for? Who will you share the stage with and who won't you? What is a deal breaker for you? Nudity? Swearing? Misogyny? What could your label, your agent, your tour manager ask you for and you would say no? What would make you leave your label?"

JJ ran a hand through her hair. "I don't know. I never thought of that. I'm not a solo artist so..."

Cymmone shook her head. "Doesn't matter. See, that's what happens to a lot of people. They never think about it until they are asked to do it, and if you don't know your answer until you are asked, then it is a lot easier for you to be persuaded to do things that you thought you would never do. That's what happened to me."

JJ bit her lip. This was why it was so hard to make this decision now. Because she hadn't set up her boundaries. In many ways she had forgotten her standards, the ones tied up with her relationship with God, the ones that made her JJ Isaacs. That was why she was feeling so lost.

"When you're a child of God, that whole process becomes so much more important," Cymmone continued. "It's both harder and easier too."

"Harder because your boundaries are so much higher..." JJ began.

"But easier because they're already laid out for you in his Word and because the Holy Spirit has already written them on your heart," Cymmone said. "That discomfort you're feeling? It's not pressure from Simon. It's the feeling of your career pushing against your boundaries. But it's a good thing, because it's God's way of protecting you."

JJ closed her eyes. "So what does this all mean? Do I just give this all up?"

Cymmone grabbed her bottle of root beer and took a sip. "I can't tell you what to do, hon. You have to make this choice on your own," she said. "But just know this: If God opened this door for you, he can open another. And with that voice you have, I am almost sure there will be more than a few doors flying open for you. But even if they don't, you have to decide what is more important to you—having everything in this world you ever wanted, or having the peace of knowing that you already have everything you need."

JJ grabbed another chicken wing and took a bite.

"Thanks, Cymmone," she said after swallowing. "Way to make things a lot more difficult."

Cymmone laughed. "Don't worry. You'll make the right decision. The girl who convinced Deacon and me to stop lying to our son definitely has God guiding her."

JJ raised her eyebrows. "So you both decided together?"

"Why do you think he's leaving the label?" Cymmone asked. She smiled at JJ's surprised look. "Yes, he told me he was leaving. We all talked about it together. Me, Deacon, and Brady. It was about time the three of us sat down and had an honest conversation."

JJ nodded. "I'm glad. For all of you. Hopefully things will be better with you and Brady too."

Cymmone wiggled her eyebrows. "They already are!"

JJ smiled, but after a moment it faded.

"Don't worry, JJ," Cymmone said with a knowing smile. "He'll come back. He loves you. He'll come back."

"I don't know if he loves me," JJ said. "We barely know each other. But I really hope you're right."

"Alright!" Cymmone said, waving her hand in the air. "Enough of this borderline depressing talk, time for some pigging out. When someone else is paying for your hotel room, you better take advantage!"

As Cymmone tried to figure out how to start the movie, JJ couldn't help but stare at her. She was so grateful that God had brought this woman into her life. She reached over and put her arms around a surprised Cymmone.

"Thank you."

Cymmone hugged her back. "No problem. I wish I'd had someone to be there for me when I was where you are. Just promise me you'll pass the favor on."

JJ whispered a prayer. She needed God to see her through this situation. To help her make the right decision. To get her back to the place where her world felt in place, whatever that looked like.

God, if you get me through this, I promise I'll pay it forward.

And she meant it.

Chapter 44

"Twenty minutes to showtime, people. Deacon wants everyone in the huddle in five."

The backstage announcement sent JJ rushing to the bathroom, where she lost her tea and crackers to the porcelain bowl. The week between the Chicago show and Toronto had flown by, and the performance that had seemed so far away was now here. In twenty minutes she would be onstage in her home city. In forty she would be singing her song to an audience packed with people. But this time, she would be the lead.

She felt her stomach muscles clench again.

She almost wished Deacon hadn't given her prior warning this time. The waiting was worse than the shock of being called on last minute.

JJ sat on the closed toilet seat and shut her eyes tightly.

"Dear God, I don't know if I can do this," JJ whispered. "Was this really what I asked for? I'm scared. Help me through this. Give me something."

She sat there a moment longer, until her stomach began to relax and her pulse began to slow a fraction. She was practicing taking deep breaths when a knock came on the door to the stall.

"You'll be fine, JJ."

Diana's voice was soft and reassuring on the other side of the door.

"That voice of yours is a gift. Whenever you open your mouth to sing, no matter what you're feeling and regardless of what Sabrina tells you, it always comes out amazing. And that's all you have to do tonight, open your mouth and sing."

Open her mouth and sing. It wasn't so hard. JJ knew she could manage that.

She got up and opened the door to the bathroom stall. "Thanks, Diana," she said, giving the made-up woman a look of appreciation.

Diana smiled and winked. "No problem. We Toronto girls have to look out for each other."

JJ smiled and felt herself relax a little more.

"Come on," Diana said, nodding toward the door. "Everyone's meeting for the huddle. And by the way, you got a call while you were out."

JJ took her cell phone from Diana. It wasn't a call. It was a text message. JJ stopped walking when she realized who it was from. Simon.

Hey, Judith. Heard things have been going well on the tour. I'm glad. Looks like staying on has been the best decision. I'm sorry if I made you feel guilty for choosing it. Have a great show tonight. I know you'll be amazing.

JJ reread the text message at least ten times as she stood frozen in the washroom doorway. What did this mean? Was he saying that he was wrong to end things or was he saying that ending things had been the best thing for her? Was this an olive branch or another good-bye? Somehow, instead of making things clearer, his message had only made it more confusing. She wanted to text him back immediately, call him right away. But she was already beyond late for the huddle.

Thanks. Talk soon?

That was all she was able to manage in the walk from the washroom to the backstage hallway. Then she was being pulled into the circle and swallowed into the Deacon Hill pre-show ritual of affirmations and prayer.

Everything seemed to move in a whirlwind after that. Before she knew it, they were onstage performing the opening number. Then Deacon was on. And before she could blink, the first set was over and she was standing in the middle of the stage, after a hasty outfit change, with her guitar in her hand and the lights in her face. She was grateful for the lights. As much as they had her sweating in places she never knew she could, they also prevented her from seeing exactly how many people were out there watching her. She knew the crowd was huge. She had heard that the show was sold out weeks prior. And even though she couldn't see them, she could definitely hear them. They were already cheering. They had heard her performance at the Chicago event. They had seen the video on YouTube, which at her last check had 120,065 hits. They had heard the interviews she had done on Toronto radio and TV all week. They had seen the pictures of her and Deacon, which had somehow resurfaced during the most recent hype. They knew her—or thought they did. And that scared her, because that meant they had expectations.

And then there was the fact that she was in her hometown, playing for her hometown. For her friends, her family, her colleagues, her classmates from college, high school, even elementary school. The people from her church. Everyone who really knew her. It was enough to make her freeze up completely. She would have thrown up, but there was nothing else in her stomach.

I know you'll be amazing.

Would she? It was time to find out. She took a deep breath, closed her eyes, and remembered the reason she had written the song in the first place. A sense of peace flowed over her.

"'I'm yours, whenever you want me, however you need me, I'm yours, always and completely.'"

Every sound seemed to stop as she sang the chorus of the song a cappella. It was a bold move. Nothing but her voice to start. No music to disguise any nervous tremors or any unexpected cracks in her vocals. No. If she was going to do this, it was going to be all or nothing. She was either going to soar like a fighter plane or go crashing down in a ball of flames.

The voice that left her body didn't even sound like her own. But it *felt* like hers. And when it was time, her fingers came in with the guitar accompaniment with the confidence of someone who had played before thousands for years, instead of only a few months. Somewhere in the back of her mind, she heard Deacon come in on the piano. He joined her for the harmony when she got to the chorus the second time, and stayed with her throughout. Deacon. He might be a mess personally, but professionally he was the consummate artist. She could depend on him to hold his own, add his flair without upstaging, and roll with her unrehearsed changes to the arrangement. She really enjoyed singing with him.

It would have been easy to get carried away with the music. To close her eyes and get lost in the song. But she had been onstage long enough to know that focus and discipline were almost more important than musical talent, and so she stayed present through the whole performance. At the end, when she called the audience into the performance with her, they came right in, singing the lines of the chorus with her. She looked over at Deacon, surprised, but he just nodded and they kept singing.

When the final chords faded into the audience's screams, JJ could barely believe it was all over. She felt like an inflated parachute that had come to rest gently on the ground. It was over.

It was over! She had done it. She laughed, couldn't stop laughing, even as Deacon pulled her into a hug.

"Great job," he whispered before heading downstage. JJ waved at the crowd—her crowd—before following.

The rest of the show was like a blur. She didn't remember if she played, but she must have, because her fingers were tired after the second encore. She didn't remember if she spoke to anyone, but she remembered the flash of camera bulbs and the smiles of the reporters backstage. She didn't even remember putting her guitar away, but there it was, sitting in the case at her feet in her dressing room. There was movement around her, people changing, people still trying to talk to her, but she couldn't focus, couldn't breathe. She had to leave.

Getting up suddenly, she stumbled out of the dressing room, down the hallway and out the back doors. The cool air rushed up to greet her, and she sucked in huge gulps, filling her aching lungs. Then before she could settle her rapidly beating heart, the tears came. Huge gasping sobs racked her body as she crouched down in the parking lot, overwhelmed by emotions. She was here. Here where she never, ever imagined she could be. Six months ago, barely anyone knew her. Now her picture was in magazines. A year ago, she had never sung outside the walls of her church. Today, she was pouring her heart out at the Molson Canadian Amphitheatre, on the same stage where artists like Bryan Adams and Justin Timberlake had performed. She—Judith Jamie Isaacs—a twenty-six-year-old, middle-class black woman from Toronto with nothing for herself except a loving family and a dream. And a God who made all things possible. She couldn't believe any of this was happening. And the more she thought about it, the more the tears flowed. So she just sat down on the ground and let them. She couldn't stop them if she tried.

She wasn't sure how long she sat out there. But it was the shouting of her name that finally brought her back to reality.

"JJ! JJ, where are you?"

She stood up and looked around. It was Diana.

"I'm here!"

"Girl, you have to stop leaving your phone everywhere," Diana said, walking across the parking lot toward her. "That thing has been ringing nonstop. Somebody is definitely trying to reach you."

JJ glanced at the screen. Six missed calls in the last hour! She scrolled through. One was from an unrecognized number, two were from Sydney, one from Lissandra, and two from Simon!

She dialed him back first, but it went straight to voice mail. Same for Sydney and Lissandra. Her sisters were probably stuck in traffic somewhere, trying to get out of downtown Toronto after the concert. Someone had left her a voice mail, however. She dialed in to her mailbox.

"This message is for Judith Isaacs. This is Nurse Simpson calling from the High Risk Pregnancy Unit at Mount Sinai Hospital. You were listed as an emergency contact for a Mrs. Sheree Isaacs. We need you to contact the clinic immediately on an urgent matter related to her care."

JJ felt her heart still in her chest.

Sheree and Dominique.

She rushed back toward the building as she dialed through to the next message. It was from Sydney. Her sister's words sucked the breath out of JJ's body.

"JJ, something's wrong with Sheree and the baby. She's unconscious and the hospital is saying they might have to rush her into surgery. Get over here as soon as you can."

JJ didn't need that last prompt. She rushed through the door, almost slamming into Miles in the process.

"Whoa, watch out now..."

"Miles!" JJ grabbed the man by the front of his shirt, ignoring the surprised look on his face. "I need you to take me to Mount Sinai Hospital now. It's an emergency!"

Chapter 45

She was gone.

JJ felt her stomach seize in panic as she burst into the hospital room and found it completely empty, the sheets stripped from the bed, the side table stripped of the magazines, flowers, makeup, and illegal snacks that had sat there for the past several weeks. It was all gone. Everything was gone. The room was completely sterile.

JJ began crying.

She held on to the door frame for support as the strength drained from her body. Where was Sheree? She couldn't be...

"JJ! What are you doing down here?"

JJ spun around at the sound of Janice's voice. She couldn't speak, couldn't put together a coherent sentence. Couldn't even manage one word.

"Everyone's down the hall," Janice continued, barely pausing. "Sheree's stable, but she's still unconscious."

Sheree was unconscious. That meant that she was alive!

Relief showered over JJ, and with renewed energy she hurried to catch up with Janice just before they turned the corner at the end of the hall.

They had moved Sheree to a new room. It was clearly smaller, given the difficulty her family was having fitting into the space.

But from the machinery she saw connected to the walls and hanging overhead, it was better equipped to deal with serious medical issues.

"JJ! Oh God, thank God you got here!"

Sydney swallowed JJ into a hug the moment she stepped through the doors behind Janice, but JJ barely noticed her. Her eyes were glued to Sheree, who lay on the narrow bed under a mass of lines and wires. There was tubing running from Sheree's swollen face to a ventilator, more tubing where an IV connected to her arm, and attached to her chest were soft pads that connected to a monitor. And that was just the stuff that she recognized. There were other wires and machines beeping around her bedside that JJ had no clue about.

The echo of the beeps sounded loud in JJ's ears. Dean, Sydney, Lissandra, Zelia, and her mother were all crowded around Sheree's bed. But the solemn mood silenced all of them. Apart from her mother, who had her eyes closed as she held Sheree's hand and whispered silently, no one said anything.

JJ clung to her sister in weakness as the distress of the moment temporarily weighed her down. She had just spoken to her friend the day before, and now she was lying in a hospital bed looking like she was barely clinging to life. How had things changed so suddenly?

"What happened?"

"She went into hypovolemic shock due to blood loss," a voice said from behind her.

JJ turned around to see that Simon had entered the room. Her heart stopped at the sight of him. She had missed him so much that seeing him now made it hard to breathe. But the look on his face alarmed her. His brows were knotted so tightly they almost touched, and that worried JJ more than the picture of an incapacitated Sheree. If Simon had told her Sheree was fine, she would have believed him. But the deeply concerned expression on his face chilled the blood in her veins.

"How did that happen?" JJ almost demanded. "I thought you all were monitoring her bleeding. That's why she's been here."

"So far, her bleeding had been observable," Simon explained, distancing her with his doctor-to-family tone. "But we discovered that she has also been bleeding internally, and it has been collecting in her uterus. The hemorrhaging is what resulted in her slipping into shock."

JJ gasped.

"Fortunately, we were able to catch it almost immediately and we've started her on a transfusion," he reassured them. "Despite what it looks like, she is improving."

"So why is she still unconscious?" JJ pressed.

"It's her body's way of protecting her while she recovers," Simon said patiently. "We were only able to get consent for the transfusion a couple hours ago, so she's only had that long to begin to recover."

JJ ran a hand through her hair. "That's why you were calling me, to get consent."

Simon nodded. "Yes."

JJ closed her eyes. "I'm sorry. I was tied up at the show for the last four hours."

"Don't worry, I signed off on it," Dean said. "When they couldn't reach you, they called me."

"And what about blood for her?" JJ asked. "Do you need me to donate?"

After the first incident at the hospital, they had made sure to find out who, if any, of them could be a blood donor match for Sheree in the event of an emergency. The doctors had told them that in some cases of complicated pregnancies, women lost a lot of blood during the delivery process and needed transfusions. That was when they had found out that JJ and Sheree shared the same blood type.

"Your sister actually did that earlier," Simon said, nodding across the room.

JJ followed his gaze to where Lissandra sat on the other side, and JJ noticed for the first time the bandage on her sister's arm.

Lissandra shrugged. "We have the same blood type, remember? It was no big deal."

JJ nodded. "Yes, of course."

She looked around at the people in the room. It felt like her family had taken care of everything. She was glad Dean was there, fulfilling the supportive role he should have been in from the beginning, as the baby's father. It was clear from everything that had happened over the past few hours that her family had indeed put the past behind them and were treating Sheree like she was one of their own. At least JJ knew that whatever happened, there would be someone there for Sheree if she couldn't be. In fact, from the looks of things, she wasn't needed as much as she used to be.

"Okay, everyone, your ten minutes is up," Simon said. "Sheree needs her rest if she's going to recover, and hospital policy says I have to kick you all out of the room."

JJ looked around, surprised, as everyone stood up to leave.

"But I just got here," she squeaked. She looked up at Simon hopefully, but he was writing on the chart.

"Sorry," he mumbled without looking at her. "She's critical, and I've already bent the rules, allowing everyone in here at once."

Lissandra and Zelia slipped through the door with their mother while Dean squeezed Sheree's hand and Sydney planted a kiss on the unresponsive woman's cheek. JJ stood at the foot of the bed, not wanting to go but not knowing what she would do if she stayed either. She reached out and squeezed Sheree's toe, one of the few parts of her body not connected to wires. Her toes were painted in Beach Bum Blu, the same nail polish JJ had brought to her weeks before. It seemed so long ago since she had laughed and smiled with her friend, talked about baby names, prayed with her for the safety of her child. And now here they both were, unable to communicate with each other.

"I'm sorry I wasn't here," JJ whispered. "I wish—"

"Judith."

Simon's firm voice from the door interrupted whatever else she had planned to say. She stepped back from the bed and gave Sheree one last look before leaving the room.

In the hallway she turned to look for Simon but only caught

the back of his white coat as he headed down the corridor. She sighed. Guess that bridge was completely burnt and the ashes washed away.

She refocused her attention on her family, who were preparing to leave.

"Good show tonight." Lissandra threw the comment behind her as she headed down the hall toward the elevators, her phone attached to her ear. "Next time hopefully we can catch the whole thing."

"We had to leave early, obviously, because of everything," Sydney explained. "But we caught the first part of your solo. You were great, hon. Congratulations."

"Thanks," JJ said as she accepted her sister's embrace.

"Yes," Jackie echoed with a soft smile as she slipped on a light summer jacket. "You were good. I'm glad I finally got to see it."

JJ smiled as her mother kissed her cheek.

"Thanks for coming, Mom. I really appreciate it," JJ said. "Thanks, all of you."

"Alright, we're going to head out," Sydney said, looking around. "Dean, you still staying?"

JJ glanced over at her brother, who had settled into a chair in the waiting area near where they were all standing.

"Yup," he said with a nod. "I'll let you know if anything changes."

"Okay," Sydney said with a nod. "Mom, I'll walk you down. Zelia went to bring the car around. JJ, we'll see you."

JJ watched as her mother and sister headed in the same direction Lissandra had gone. An odd sensation began to fill her. She sat down in the chair next to Dean.

"Looks like you all have everything under control."

Dean looked up from his cell phone. From the look on his face, she knew he was only using it to distract himself.

Dean let out a sigh. "Yeah. It's too bad something like this had to happen before we all stepped up the way we should have."

JJ shrugged. "Everyone's been doing the best they can under the circumstances."

"But we should have been doing more," Dean said. "I should have been doing more. I should never have let Sheree go through all this on her own. And you, JJ, you should never have had to take all this on. You have your own life to live. You didn't need to be burdened with all this..."

JJ shook her head vigorously. "No, Dean. Don't think that. It's not a burden. It never was. Sheree has been like another sister to me."

"But I am her husband, and I should have been here." Dean frowned. "I'm going to be here. From now on. You don't have to carry this anymore, JJ. I've got this."

JJ sat back, confused and not sure what to say. She felt like she had just lost something, but she couldn't quite put her finger on what it was. In fact, it felt like somehow, in the past couple hours, she had been... replaced? She had missed a moment to be there for Sheree. She was glad her family had been there to fill the gap. But now it felt like she wasn't really needed anymore.

Dean slung an arm around JJ's shoulders. "You had a great night tonight. You should be out celebrating."

He kissed her cheek before easing her to her feet. "Don't worry about Sheree. She will be fine. You get out of here. Go have yourself a good time."

JJ found herself walking down the hallway toward the exit, alone. She was leaving. But she had nowhere to go. Dean had told her to celebrate, have a good time. But how could she? When the woman who had become closer to her than she had ever imagined was lying in the hospital in critical condition? When the man who had snuck his way into her heart wouldn't even look at her? When her family seemed to have no need for her? How could she celebrate when all she felt was depressed and alone?

Chapter 46

The Molson Canadian Amphitheatre was almost empty. It had taken over an hour for the crowds to clear, for the media and VIPs to leave the backstage area, and for all the autographs to be signed. JJ had been a part of all of it. Who knew people would want her autograph?

She looked out into the dimly lit space, remembering the thousands of people who had filled the amphitheater a short time earlier. Before this week, the last time she had been here was a year ago. She had been in the audience and someone else had been performing. She never thought she would be the one onstage. And yet she was. She had sung for thousands. People had called her name. Her face had been on the screen. It was everything she had dreamed about. But it had lasted for only a few moments, and then it was over.

She swung her legs back and forth as she sat on the edge of the stage, enjoying the quiet moment. This could be her life. This could be her future. She had to admit, it wasn't half bad.

"Can't believe it, can you? That just moments ago this place was filled, and all those eyes were on you."

JJ felt Deacon sit down beside her and she looked over at him.

"Do you ever get used to it?" she asked.

He shook his head. "Not really. Maybe I haven't been doing

it long enough. I will get into the performance and forget about the audience for a while. But then I will have a moment during the show when I look out there and see all those people and realize that they are there for me. They came for me. It's unbelievable."

JJ nodded. "It is."

"Think you could do this for the rest of your life?" he asked.

JJ snorted. "Only a handful of people do this for the rest of their life."

Deacon tilted his head to the side. "True. But a lot of people do it for a long, long time. And it can be a good life."

"But you're planning to give it all up," JJ said, looking at him again.

He smiled. "It's a good life, but it's not everything. There's more to life than this."

His words startled JJ. There was more to life than this. She knew that. That was the doubt sitting in the pit of her stomach, the knowledge that this wasn't it. That all the stages in the world couldn't fill her with the wholeness that came from having those things that were most important: her family, her loved ones, her faith.

"It's easy to forget, you know?" JJ said after a moment. "I lost myself for a while because I forgot that. Lost my faith, my relationship with God that used to keep me grounded."

Deacon nodded. "This business gives you a lot of opportunities, but you also lose out on a lot. You get the fame, the money, the freedom to do what you love. But in a way, you lose your freedom too. You lose the chance to love without limits. You lose the chance to find love that's real. You lose the chance to know who you really are. And that can take a toll on a person."

JJ bit her lip. "You think you can have it all? Freedom and fame?"

Deacon squinted into the darkness thoughtfully. "I used to think I could."

As they sat in silence, JJ realized that even though Deacon was a millionaire pop star, underneath all the expensive clothes and cars, under the Gucci sunglasses and the celebrity lifestyle, he was just an ordinary guy trying to find happiness and live a life that was worthwhile. The surprising thing was that it was probably harder for him than most.

"Did you love Cymmone?" JJ asked after a long moment.

Deacon smiled but kept looking out into the darkness. "I think I did. But I loved my career more. Things turned out better this way."

"For you?"

Deacon stood up. "For her."

JJ watched him as he walked back across the stage. "See you in Boston, JJ."

"Bus is leaving in fifteen minutes!"

JJ recognized Diana's voice from backstage and sighed. Since they had come back from the break, the schedule had them leaving the city at night, after the performance, instead of the following morning. JJ suspected that Andrew had something to do with that. Probably didn't want to pay for an extra night at the hotel. Kya thought it was because he was miserable and wanted everyone to be miserable too, by eliminating the one night they would have off to celebrate.

Either way, it didn't matter. Within the hour they would be on a bus on the way to Boston. The ten-hour bus ride would put them in Boston just in time for hotel check-in. After a quick nap, they would be in rehearsal and prepping for the next concert in a day and a half.

With one last look out into the empty amphitheater, she got up and turned to go. She only got two steps.

"You should really stop sneaking up on people like that," JJ said.

"It's not intentional," Rayshawn said, hands in his pocket. "I thought you would hear me. Looked like you were off somewhere."

JJ shrugged. "Just thinking."

"About the great show you had tonight?" he asked, taking a step closer. "You were awesome, by the way."

JJ smiled. "Thanks. Guess you saw it?"

He nodded. "That I did. Have to keep an eye on my best client."

A silence fell between them as they considered each other. JJ took in Rayshawn for the first time in a long while: his dark pants, white V-neck shirt, gray sweater with the sleeves pushed up to expose his muscular forearms. He was something to look at, that's for sure. And for a long time JJ had enjoyed looking at him. Got a tingle up her spine when his eyes were on her. But in that moment, as she looked at him, the man she had given too much of herself to, she felt nothing.

He misunderstood her gaze. JJ knew it when he closed the distance between them and took her hands in his. When he spoke, his voice was deep and thick with something that wasn't love but that she had mistaken for love at some point along the way.

"JJ..."

"Where's the contract?" she asked.

His face twisted in confusion. "What?"

She pulled her hands out of his. "Where's the contract, Rayshawn? Isn't that what you came here for?"

Something she couldn't read flitted through his eyes.

"Come on, JJ," he said. "I came to see you perform."

JJ stepped closer and slipped her arms under his sweater, encircling him. But before he could return the embrace, she stepped back and held up the rolled-up, letter-size brown envelope she had pulled out of his back pocket.

"This is it, right?"

The look that came next she could definitely read. Guilt.

"Okay, JJ," he said flatly. "I came hoping you would sign the contract too. Only because I know the next couple days are going to be crazy and you won't have time to think about it."

He earnestly clasped his hands together in front of him. "JJ, this is an amazing opportunity. I have negotiated hundreds of contracts, and trust me, this is one of the best. They're giving you three years. Full label resources. Two albums and tours guaranteed. And you get to retain the rights to the songs that you write. Do you realize how amazing that is? They're giving you the world on a silver platter."

What shall it profit a man, if he shall gain the whole world...

"You can't lose with this."

...and lose his own soul.

"I figured you would need a little time after the tour," Rayshawn continued. "You know, to see your family, spend some time at home. So we worked in a three-week break between the end of this tour and the start of the work on the contract. But after that, it will be full throttle. We got a place for you in LA where you can stay until you find something permanent. It's a great little apartment that our artists in transition use, fully furnished, of course. But once you get your advance from the contract, plus the money you made on the tour, plus the signing rights for Deacon Hill to use your song..."

Rayshawn was talking a mile a minute now. JJ watched his lips move, but his voice was fading away somewhere into the background. She looked down at the contract. She was holding the beginning of the rest of her life in her hands. All she had to do was sign. She thought of Sheree, about how Dean was back in her life for good, about how Sydney, Lissandra, and the rest of the family had accepted her as their own. She wouldn't have to worry about Sheree anymore. She had made peace with Jackie over her involvement in the music business. And as far as Simon was concerned...well, there were some things she would just have to allow time to solve. But the truth was, her life in Toronto was tied up neatly.

She took a deep breath. "Okay."

Rayshawn stopped midsentence, his brown eyes widening in surprise. "Okay?"

"Okay," JJ said with a nod.

Rayshawn grinned and punched the air. "Yes!"

He grabbed her and spun her around. JJ squealed in surprise. "Put me down!"

Rayshawn laughed and set her back down on the stage. "I'm sorry, I'm sorry, but, JJ, you just made the best decision of your life."

He dug into his pocket. "Let me get you a pen..."

JJ watched him as he searched frantically for the writing instrument. Watched the man she was essentially committing the next three years of her life to.

"JJ, everyone's on the bus waiting on you." Diana's impatient voice cut into JJ's thoughts. "We have to go."

"Okay, okay," JJ said. It was going to be like this from now on. People demanding her attention. Pushing her from one place to the other. Always on the move, never a moment to spare. This was what it took to be a star.

She grabbed the pen from Rayshawn, hurriedly signed in the three spots marked with an *x*, then shoved the document back into the envelope and into Rayshawn's hands.

"I'll scan you a copy," Rayshawn called after her as she stepped away.

JJ hurried through the backstage area, barely catching up with Diana as they made their way to the bus waiting outside the arena. When they got there, the driver was loading the last bags into the luggage area. JJ paused and looked around at the dark night sky. She was at the heart of the city. Her city. She could see the CN Tower lit up against the city skyline. This was her Toronto. It would always be. But for now, it was time to spread her wings.

Climbing into the bus, she took her seat near the window and slid it open, sucking in the cool evening air. She put her fingers to her lips and blew a kiss into the night sky.

"Good-bye, Toronto."

Chapter 47

"It's time, isn't it? This baby is coming now, isn't it?"

Simon sat down on the stool next to Sheree's bed. This was a new bed, in a new room. She had been moved again the day before, when her contractions started. They knew then that any change, from a spike in her heart rate to the movement of the child, might trigger delivery, and that the process would be quick and possibly complicated. But one thing was certain: Sheree would have to have a cesarean section.

"The baby is coming soon," Simon said, careful to keep his voice relaxed. He wanted to keep Sheree as calm as possible, especially since he was about to give her news she didn't want to hear.

"How soon?" Dean asked. He was sitting on the other side of Sheree's bed. Simon was impressed with how present the man had been over the past few weeks. He didn't know the whole story with Dean and Sheree, but from the bits and pieces he had been told by Judith and overheard during family conversations in Sheree's hospital room, he knew that their relationship was probably as complicated as her pregnancy. Whatever was unsaid between them, however, was not keeping Dean from supporting the mother of his child. He had been there every day for the past few days, asking questions, getting Sheree anything she needed, showing her something that lingered in the space between loyalty and love.

"That's actually what I'm here to talk to you both about," Simon said, turning his gaze to Sheree. "Both your and the baby's heart rates are good, your pressure is stable, and you are doing much better than you were earlier in the week. This is a good window for you to deliver."

"So you want to induce?" Sheree asked.

Simon paused. "Because of the extent of the separation of the placenta from the uterine wall, the safest option for you and the baby right now is a C-section."

Tears pooled in Sheree's eyes almost immediately, and although Simon kept his face relaxed, he felt like a hand had tightened around his heart. He had spent so much time with Sheree and her family in the past few weeks that he had formed an emotional bond with her, and he hated seeing her upset. But he knew this would be best for her.

Simon watched Dean take her hand and her fingers tighten around his.

"But you mentioned that you were trying to avoid that," Dean said.

Simon nodded. "And before last weekend, it might have been possible. But with the level of blood loss you experienced, Sheree, we believe that the separation may now be severe. This is the best way to ensure that both you and baby come out of this with the best health possible."

Sheree nodded, swiping at tears that rolled down her cheeks. "Okay. If you say this is the safest way, I believe you. When can we do it?"

"We booked tentatively for you early tomorrow, but if you think you could manage it, we would like to try for this evening. I have contacted the anesthesiologist and the surgical team, and they can be available."

Simon avoided mentioning his other worry, that Sheree was showing preliminary indicators of declining kidney function. If unchecked, that could lead to a new set of health problems that would make delivery even more complicated and dangerous if delayed much longer.

"I can have everything ready for you to sign off on in a couple minutes, and then the nurse will prep you for the surgery," Simon explained. "We're going to have to move you to an operating room, but that's just down the hall. If there's anyone you want to call, you should do so now."

"JJ," Sheree said, turning to Dean. "I want to talk to her."

Dean glanced up at Simon at the mention of his sister's name. Simon met his gaze blankly. He knew less about where JJ was and what she was doing than the rest of them. And as he prepared to take Sheree's and her baby's lives in his hands, he couldn't afford to be thinking about JJ even a little.

"She's gone," Dean said, dropping his eyes back to Sheree. "You know that. She got on the bus to Boston two days ago."

"I know," Sheree said, the tears rolling down her cheeks. "But I need her. Can you try to call her again? Please? I just need to talk to her..."

Simon knew he didn't need to be here for this. He stood up. "I'll just be outside."

He pushed through the hospital door and strode down the hall, trying to push the thoughts from his mind. This was one of the times he wished he was better at separating himself from his patients. Nigel was excellent at that, at compartmentalizing everything. That's what made him great with MSF. They could send him into situations that went completely against his morals, that challenged every fiber of his being, and he would go in and do his best work. Simon? Simon's emotions were a little less flexible. They were like a river constantly running through him, which he sometimes found difficult to dam up.

"Nurse Thompson, can you call Dr. Brighton and let him know the surgery is a go for this evening?" Simon said, stopping at the nurses' station. "And can you call the anesthesiologist and let him know he can come down in about forty-five minutes? You should be done prepping Mrs. Isaacs by then, right?"

"Should be," Janice said. "Shouldn't take long." She gave

Simon a sympathetic look. "So you finally broke it to her about the C-section."

Simon nodded. "I really hoped we could have done a natural birth. She's young, and it's her first child."

"Who's going to be born alive and at full term, thanks to you," Janice said reassuringly. "Don't beat yourself up. You've been great for her. She's lucky to have you. All of them are."

Simon chose to ignore the last comment. "I'm gonna go put together the consent forms. I'll see you down there in a bit."

Tension slipped into Simon's shoulders as he walked into the doctors' lounge. He had known for a few days that this might be necessary, but he still didn't like it. There were so many risks with a C-section. Potential injuries to the bladder or bowel, higher risk of infection, longer recovery time. He would do his best, but there were so many things that could happen.

Glad that the room was empty, he sank onto the couch, put his head back, and closed his eyes. This was his God time. He didn't know if he would have time for it again before the surgery, so he had to get it in now. He needed it. Needed the peace that came from just those few moments with the God who was in control of everything. Simon already knew that he wasn't doing this surgery; the one who knows the intricacies of every human being was doing it. He was just using Simon's hands.

In the stillness of the room, he remembered all the times that God had used his hands to do so much more with so much less. So many times he had delivered babies with nothing more than clean towels and hot water. Times when he had correctly diagnosed conditions just like Sheree's, without ultrasounds or extensive blood tests. That voice of quiet assurance had guided him in those moments, and it would guide him now.

Peace flowed quietly over Simon in waves so gentle they rocked him into a calm state only shades away from sleep. When he finally opened his eyes and stood up, the tension was gone. His limbs were relaxed, his body and mind refreshed.

By the time he got back to Sheree's room, it was full. All of JJ's sisters were there, even one he had never met before but recognized from JJ's descriptions. JJ's mother was clasping

Sheree's hands and saying something quietly to her. On Sheree's other side sat a very tall gentleman who Simon had never seen before but whose resemblance to Sheree declared him to be her brother. Sydney's hands on his shoulders confirmed that he was also the fiancé that Simon had been told about over JJ's kitchen counter. The whole family was here.

"Whoa, looks like we have a full house," Simon said, barely able to get into the room.

"Hey, Dr. Massri," Sydney said. "We know we can't stay, but we just wanted Sheree to know we're all here for her."

Sydney's fiancé stood and Simon had to look up a bit.

"I'm Sheree's brother Hayden," he said, stretching his hand out to Simon. "I hear you've been taking great care of her. Thank you so much."

Simon nodded. "God's been taking care of her. So has this amazing family that you're marrying into."

Hayden smiled and exchanged a look with Sydney. "I know."

With the forms signed and everyone kicked out of the room, the anesthesiologist arrived to give Sheree a spinal block to numb the lower part of her body for the surgery. Once she was all prepped, it was time. Simon opted to walk with her as they wheeled her into the operating theater. Dean was nearby, dressed in scrubs, looking more nervous than Sheree.

"You guys are doing great," Simon reassured them. "The whole thing should take an hour, and then your baby will be here."

However, as they began the process of transporting her from the room, Simon could see the panic start.

"Wait." Sheree's breathing was accelerated as she gripped the sides of the gurney. She shook her head. "I can't."

"Yes, you can," Dean said, leaning down. "You're almost there."

"No, I can't..." She was crying now. Simon slipped his fingers around her wrist, checking her pulse. He glanced up at Nurse Thompson and shook his head. It was racing slightly. This was not good.

"Sheree," he began in the calmest tone he could muster,

"I'm gonna need you to try and relax. Try taking a deep breath..."

She was still sobbing. Dean looked up at him helplessly. Simon took a deep breath of his own. This was not what he wanted to be happening right now.

Just then the door to the room flew open.

"I'm here, I'm here. Has she had the baby yet?"

Simon felt like someone had knocked the wind out of him as Judith burst into the room. Her cheeks were flushed, as if she had been running, but her eyes were bright as they swept the room, pausing a moment on him but ultimately settling on Sheree, whose face broke into a huge grin.

"JJ!"

Sheree reached out and grabbed the woman's arm like a lifeline. JJ managed to embrace her sister-in-law without pulling out any of the cords attached to her. They both were crying.

"Thank God you're here!"

"I couldn't miss this. I'm so sorry I wasn't here before, hon."

"It's okay, you're here now," Sheree said between sniffles.

"Oh, I can't believe you're having the baby!"

"I know! Oh God, I'm going to be a mother!"

"I know!"

Simon cleared his throat, hating to interrupt the two but knowing that there was an operating room full of professionals, prepped and waiting to perform the surgery.

"We have to go," he said gently to Sheree.

JJ untangled herself from Sheree. "I'll be right outside, honey."

"No!" Sheree gripped JJ's arm so tightly Simon could see her fingers pressed into the woman's flesh. "You have to come with me."

"Sheree, I can't," JJ said, glancing between Simon and her sister-in-law. "You already have Dean."

"No, I need you too," Sheree insisted, her voice bordering on hysterical. "Dr. Massri, please, please let her come in with me. I can't do this without her."

"Please, Doctor," Dean added. "JJ's been here through all of this. I know Sheree would feel more relaxed during surgery if she was there."

Simon took another deep breath then glanced toward the clock. They were already a few minutes late. He looked over at Nurse Thompson. She shrugged, silently telling him it was up to him, but he could see the slight smile that played at the corner of her lips.

"Alright," he said with a sigh. "But you need to be in scrubs. And we can't wait more than five minutes for you."

JJ's face broke into a smile that nearly did Simon in.

"Thank you." She jumped up and rushed back through the doors.

"Go to—"

"I know!" he heard her reply from the hallway. His eyebrows lifted in surprise.

"She volunteered here all through college," Nurse Thompson explained. "She probably knows more about where everything is than you do."

Simon sighed and nodded toward the door. As they wheeled Sheree out of the room and down to the OR, he said a silent prayer for Sheree, for the baby, and for himself. They were all going to need God if they planned to make it through the next hour.

Chapter 48

He was beautiful.

Dominique Royce Isaacs was the most gorgeous thing JJ had ever seen, and as she gazed at him through the glass at the hospital nursery, tears sprang to her eyes. How could she have even considered missing this, the birth of her first nephew?

"God, you are truly awesome. Thank you for bringing me here in time for this," she whispered.

"Thank you for coming back for this. Sheree got through this so much easier because of you."

JJ smiled at her brother's comment but kept her eyes on Dominique.

"I think Sheree was the one who got me through everything. Dominique too," JJ said. "Look at him. It really puts everything into perspective, doesn't it?"

Dean chuckled. "That it does."

She looked over at her brother as he gazed at his son. "Congratulations, Daddy."

His grin spread wider. "Thank you."

They stared at the little bundle of happiness, fogging up the glass with their coos and smiles until their mother came down and eased them aside to make space for herself.

"Look at my little grandson," Jackie cooed. "He looks just like his grandma."

"What?" Lissandra said, squeezing between JJ and her mother. "He does not. He clearly looks like me. Do you see those eyelashes?"

"You all have got to be joking," Hayden said, coming up behind them. "You know he's got those Windsor genes, strong and mighty. Look at those shoulders."

"Aww, baby, you're seeing things again," Sydney said, slipping an arm around his waist. "I told you, you need to go get your eyes checked."

They all laughed, and a warmth that JJ hadn't experienced in a long time spread through her. She had missed her family, more than she realized.

"Quit hogging the window, JJ." JJ's younger sister Zelia wiggled her tiny frame in front of JJ, effectively stealing her spot at the now crowded window. "Isn't it enough that you got to be in the room for the delivery? You think you can just win favorite aunt like that? You're gonna have to fight me for it."

JJ laughed but willingly surrendered the spot to Zelia, who promptly put her arm around her brother in a hug. JJ sighed. Zelia was right. She had spent a significant amount of time ogling Dominique. It was time to go back and see how the new mother was doing.

By the time she got to Sheree's room, the woman was stirring.

"JJ, how is my sweetheart?"

JJ smiled. "So perfectly beautiful and so beautifully perfect. Can you believe Lissandra was right about it being a boy?"

"I can, actually," Sheree said with a weak smile. "You know your sister is a know-it-all."

JJ laughed. "You're right."

She slipped into the chair near Sheree's bedside. "How are you feeling?"

"Tired and sore, even though I've been sleeping for so many hours. But Dr. Massri said it will be like that for a while. He said everything looks fine though. They're keeping me under observation for a few more days, then I should be able to go home."

"We'll have to switch your bedroom to the one downstairs," JJ said. "That way you have everything on one level."

Sheree bit her lip, and JJ raised an eyebrow.

"Okay, spit it out," JJ said.

"Dean wants me to move in with him at your mom's guesthouse," Sheree said.

JJ opened her mouth to respond, but when she saw how closely Sheree was watching her, she pressed her lips together. After a long moment, she spoke. "What do you think?"

Sheree sighed and put her head back. "I think he's caught up in the moment and wants to think he can be super dad. He doesn't realize how difficult things will be while I'm recovering."

JJ let out a sigh. Thank God Sheree was thinking the same way she was. There was no way Dean would be able to take care of Sheree on his own. But he wouldn't understand if anyone other than Sheree told him that.

"I want to stay with you, with Sydney, even Lissandra," Sheree said. "I like having all of you around all the time. I feel safer. You think your sisters will mind having a baby around?"

"Ha! I think they'll love it," JJ said. "You should see the way they're staring at that poor fellow in the nursery. They are going to spoil him rotten."

Sheree smiled. "What about you? Will you be around to spoil him rotten?"

JJ smiled. "As much as I can be."

"That's what I like to hear!"

"Speaking of being around, where is that doctor of yours?" JJ asked. "I haven't seen him since he left the OR yesterday. And that was almost twenty-four hours ago."

Sheree's smile faded. "He didn't tell you?"

JJ felt coldness slice through her. "Didn't tell me what?"

Sheree shifted uncomfortably. "That he is leaving. He passed my care on to Dr. Brighton. The baby is born and healthy, and I'm stable, so his work with me is mostly done. Whatever specialist care is still needed can be handled by Dr. Brighton."

JJ stood up. "He's gone?"

"As far as I know," Sheree said with concern. "Today was his last day. In fact, he came by to say good-bye right before you got here."

JJ ran her fingers through her hair, shreds of panic ripping through her.

"He's gone. Again." Her breathing was starting to disintegrate into short gasps. "I'm never going to see him again."

"What are you talking about?" Sheree said. "You know where he lives. Didn't you say you went to his house? Just go talk to him. Fix this thing between the two of you."

JJ shook her head. "No . . . you don't understand. He's leaving. He has a job in Malawi waiting for him . . ."

"Oh no," Sheree said, her eyes widening

But JJ was already grabbing her purse and heading toward the door. "I gotta go."

Chapter 49

She rushed down the hallway toward the stairs, holding on tight to the railing as she flew down the steps. Thank goodness she was wearing running shoes, or she would have fallen on her face a hundred times over.

How could he just leave without saying good-bye? Was he that done with her? How could their feelings for each other just dry up like that?

They couldn't. She refused to believe they could. She had to talk to him. She wasn't going to let him walk away again without a fight. She just had to find him first.

Her memory was firing on all cylinders and she found her car without a problem, swinging it out of the hospital parking lot so fast she almost hit a black Lamborghini coming out from a side lot. She heard brakes screech and smelled burning tires, but felt no impact. Thank God. She did not need to add a car accident to this day.

The door to the luxury sports car flew open and the driver jumped out.

"Are you crazy? What the hell are you doing! This is a four-hundred-thousand-dollar car!"

JJ couldn't have been happier to see the angry face glaring at her windscreen.

"Nigel!"

She jumped out and raced over to him, grabbing him by the shoulders. "Where is he?"

"JJ?" Nigel echoed, confused. "What are you doing here? Where is who?"

"Simon!" she almost shouted. "Where is Simon?"

Nigel's face fell and his eyes filled with sympathy. "Oh, JJ. I'm sorry. He's going to—"

"Malawi," JJ finished, nodding frantically. "I already know. But I need to know where he is right now, at this minute."

Nigel ran a hand through his hair. "I don't know—his house? Maybe on the way to the airport..."

She perked up and her hands tightened around his arms. "He was going home first?"

Hope sprang into her heart.

"Maybe," Nigel said. "I'm not sure. He just worked a twenty-hour shift with that delivery, so I assume he would go home, grab a shower or something before he left..."

"Thank you!" JJ said as she raced back to her car. "You know what time his flight is?"

Nigel shrugged. "Not sure. Just know it was an overnighter. He wanted to be out of here...uh...quick."

JJ saw the embarrassment on Nigel's face as he realized exactly what he had let slip. But JJ didn't care. She released the parking break and began to maneuver around Nigel's car.

"He'll have to go through me first," she threw back as she peeled out of the parking area.

Highways became her friend as she sped north on the Don Valley Parkway toward the 404 expressway. The DVP was a pain in the behind for anyone trying to get out of Toronto in a hurry. But since it was after seven p.m., she had managed to avoid the rush hour. Nonetheless, JJ felt like she wasn't moving fast enough. Every minute she was on the highway was another minute when Simon could be slipping out of her reach.

How could she have been so stupid? How could she not have seen it all along? She had everything she needed right here. The people who loved her, a city that would nurture her as she grew her career, and a man who was willing to put down roots for her. Yet she was willing to give that up for the chance at a fast life that would probably take more from her than it would give. It had taken seeing her nephew come into the world, seeing the miracle of creation, for her to realize it. There had been more meaning in that moment than there had been in her whole year. And she wanted more of those moments. But she wanted them with Simon.

It felt like forever, but she finally pulled into the driveway of Simon's Uxbridge home. Forgetting the keys in the ignition, she stumbled out of the car and breathed a sigh of relief at the sight of his Jeep in the open garage. She ran up the steps and banged on the front door.

No answer.

She knocked again, this time for longer and with more intensity.

The door flew open.

"Did you forget somethi . . . Oh. Hello."

JJ stared into huge brown eyes that were not Simon's.

"Who are you?"

The woman at the door cocked her head to the side, the dark, spongy dreads in her high ponytail brushing her bare shoulders. Her full lips stretched wide, framing her cool coffee features into a smile that filled her whole face.

"You must be Judith," she said. Carved wooden bangles jingled happily as she stretched out her slim, unmanicured hand to JJ. "I'm Rashida, Simon's cousin."

JJ took the woman's hand absently. "How'd you know I was . . . never mind. Where is he? Where's Simon?"

The same look that she had seen on Nigel's face less than an hour earlier was replicated in Rashida's eyes.

"I'm sorry," she said. "You just missed him. He came back, got his stuff, then left for the airport."

JJ raked both hands through her hair as nausea crept through her. She had missed him. Probably passed him on the highway. Maybe even on the road into Uxbridge.

"I would call him, but he left his cell phone here," Rashida said. "I won't hear from him until he lands early tomorrow morning. I'm sorry..."

So he was gone. Completely gone. Catching him at home had been her last-ditch effort, but it had proved fruitless. Finding him at the airport would be near impossible. She didn't even know his flight time or gate number. And even if she somehow figured it out, by the time she rushed across the city to Pearson International, he would have passed through check-in and into the restricted area of the airport where she would have no access to him.

It was time to accept the truth. It was over.

She thought she mumbled thanks before she trudged down the steps to her car, but she couldn't be sure. She was just so overwhelmed. She pulled the car out of the driveway under the sympathetic eye of Rashida and headed down the road, back toward the highway. But when she got to the end of Simon's road, she had to pull over, her eyes so blurred with tears that she couldn't see.

She was a mess. She knew that. But there was nothing she could do about it. She rested her head against the steering wheel, too weak to do anything else. She was so tired. Tired of being disappointed. Tired of realizing too late what was really important. Tired of chasing something that seemed constantly unreachable. If only she had wasted less time mired in the land of uncertainty. If only she had walked away from Franklin and Forbes, and Rayshawn, and Sound City, the first time she saw the flashing red lights of her heart, instead of waiting until everything was burning down around her.

"God, I'm sorry for waiting so long to come back to you," she whispered. "Thank you for waiting for me anyway. I don't know what tomorrow will bring, but this time I'm going to wait for you to bring it to me."

She put her head back against the seat and lifted her eyes to where a full moon filled the night sky. It was so clear and beautiful in the absence of all the smog and streetlights and distractions of the city. She could see why Simon loved it here. In a place like this she could meet God, have the quiet time with him that she needed to refresh her soul. She closed her eyes and let the rays of soft white light wash over her. The tears stopped. Her breathing leveled out. The queasiness in her stomach settled. It was going to be okay.

Chapter 50

It took a few more minutes before she felt strong enough to start the ignition again and pull off the curb into the road. This time she made it to the highway. She considered going back to the hospital, but she knew she was still too fragile to deal with anyone else for the rest of the night. So when the exit for her home came in sight, she gladly took it. The one good thing about the night was that, with the excitement of Dominique's birth, everyone would be at the hospital and she would have the house to herself.

The night was cool and welcoming as she got out of her parked car, and so instead of going straight inside, she sat on the curb near the street. JJ smiled to herself. Jackie would have a fit if she saw her now. She hated when her girls sat on the ground outside. She would scold JJ, Sydney, and Lissandra from the front door when the three of them used to sit on the curb as teenagers and watch the boys from the block play street hockey during the summer. During those days, their only concern was escaping the wrath of their mother, and so they would be sure to sit a few feet away from the driveway, behind the rosebushes, so their mother couldn't see them from the front window.

Simon would love a story like that. He had had so few of those normal moments of childhood that he always loved hearing about all of hers. She closed her eyes. She could almost feel him next to her, catch the slight, fresh smell of citrus that she often enjoyed when she was around him. She sighed and opened her eyes. She had it bad.

"Bet your mom would have a fit if she saw you sitting on the ground like that."

The sound of his voice doubled her heartbeat and set off a quiet symphony inside JJ that grew louder and louder with every stir of emotion. She trembled, hoping that her senses weren't playing some cruel trick on her. But she was too scared to turn around to check. If she was just imagining him there...

She felt the air shift next to her.

"Judith."

Her name on his lips was the combination to open the lock-box of her emotions. She couldn't stop her body from turning toward him, her eyes from devouring every feature of his beautiful face, lit by the moonlight. The music grew louder.

"I thought you left."

He reached over and with gentle fingers wiped a renegade tear from her cheek.

"I thought you left," he echoed softly.

"I did," JJ said, leaning into his hand. "I got all the way to Boston before I realized that it wasn't what I wanted."

"And what do you want?" he asked, peering into her eyes with his soulful ones.

JJ closed her eyes for a moment, realizing suddenly what song she was hearing. It was her song, "I'm Yours." The one that she had sung for millions but had never sung honestly until this moment.

"I want to be where God wants me to be," she said, committing to the words anew as she sat on her curb with Simon. "I want to do what he wants me to do. I want to be his completely."

It was so liberating to say those words out loud. She let out a breath that she felt like she had been holding forever. A breath that freed her to let go of her need to have a picture-perfect future; a breath that left her room to breathe in all the uncertainty and all the unimaginable possibilities God had in store for her.

"What about your career?" he asked with concern. "The tour extension, the new contract?"

JJ shrugged. "I signed Rayshawn's name instead of my own. If I'm going to be God's completely, I have to choose him first. And with the life that contract was offering me, I couldn't do that."

He nodded. "I'm glad to hear that."

She reached over and rested her hand on his arm. "Your turn."

She watched his jaw flex as he wrestled with what to say.

"I got all the way to the airport. But I couldn't go."

"No?"

"No." He shook his head. "I wanted to. I really did." He paused to look at her. "But there was something I wanted more."

JJ smiled as the music in her heart began to swell. "What did you want more, Simon Massri?"

His eyes roamed over her face for what felt like forever.

"You."

JJ felt like someone had taken ten-pound weights off her shoulders, allowing her to fly free. Simon Massri wanted her! He had changed his plans again, for her! This time there was no way that she would let him get away.

She threw her arms around his neck, holding him tightly to her.

"I'm sorry for walking away like that." His voice was intense with remorse as he spoke the words near her ear. His hands touched her hesitantly, as if afraid, as if unworthy. "I should have stuck around. I never should have made you feel like you had to choose."

"It's okay," she whispered against his neck. "I get it. Believe me, I do. I'm just glad you came back. Thank you for waiting for me."

JJ felt the rush of warm air as he let out a breath. His arms encircled her now, cocooning her in the warmth of his affection.

"I waited five years," he murmured back. "What's a few more days?"

JJ pulled back to stare at him, amazed at how deep into her heart this man had crawled. She rested her forehead against his. "I am never letting you go, ever again."

He grinned as his eyes fell to her mouth. "I'm going to hold you to that."

And then he ended the conversation with his lips on hers. JJ surrendered herself to his kisses, deciding in that moment that Simon Massri was the last and only man she wanted to kiss for the rest of her life. He was the man she had been waiting for, the man God had been holding for her. The wait had been long and painful in some parts. She had stumbled into heartbreak and misery in her impatience. But God had not given up on her. Despite her wavering faithfulness, he had blessed her. And everything she had gone through, all the waiting she had done, was worth it for what—and who—was waiting at the end.

A horn blared and car lights illuminated the curb, where JJ sat with Simon's arms around her. With one last kiss, Simon reluctantly pulled away.

"I think we have company, angel."

JJ looked up, instantly recognizing her sister's car, even before Lissandra's voice came loudly through the driver's window.

"So this is where you ran off to without even saying goodbye," Lissandra teased. "To go make out with your boyfriend on the curb. If Mom saw you, she would light your ba'hind with licks!"

Simon turned to JJ, confusion all over his face. "What's licks?"

JJ laughed out loud before kissing him on the cheek. "Oh, honey, you are so cute when you're confused."

He scratched his chin. "Sometimes I don't understand everything your sister says."

"Sometimes neither do I," JJ said, running her fingers over his smooth dreads. "But we got lots of time to try and figure it out."

A slow smile spread his lips as he gently wrapped one of her curls around his finger. "Lots and lots of time."

The touch of his hand jumpstarted her heart into a new rhythm. The music was back. But this time it was a different song. One she had never sung before. A duet. But her partner, the one God had picked for her, the one holding her in his arms at that moment, was exactly on pitch with her. And she could already tell that together, they would be hitting all the right notes.

A READING GROUP GUIDE

HITTING THE RIGHT NOTE

Rhonda Bowen

About This Guide

The questions that follow
are included to enhance your group's
reading of this book.

Discussion Questions

1. How do you feel about JJ's response to her sister Sydney's engagement news? Do you think she should have been happier?

2. What were your first impressions of JJ's relationship with Rayshawn? Do you think it's okay to hide your romantic relationships from your family sometimes? Are there ever good reasons to hide a relationship?

3. Do you think Sydney was justified in being upset with JJ about her relationship with Rayshawn? Is it really any of Sydney's business who her sister dates?

4. Do you think Simon should have brought up his past connection to JJ during their first meeting at the hospital? Why do you think he waited to say something? Why did she?

5. What do you think about the almost instant attraction between Simon and JJ? Do you think it's possible to have feelings for someone after meeting them only once? Do you think Simon and JJ's feelings are real, or were they just magnified because of the circumstances under which they first met?

6. Do you think Sheree has really become a better person, or is this just an act until the baby is born?

7. Do you think JJ's relationship with Rayshawn could have worked, despite the differences in their spiritual beliefs? Why or why not?

8. Was JJ's break into the entertainment industry based only on talent and hard work, as Rayshawn suggested, or did God provide that opportunity for her? Do you think God has a part in the opportunities we receive in life? If yes, how big a part?

9. How hard do you think the entertainment industry really is on a person's faith? Is it possible to be super successful in the business but also hold on to Christian values?

10. Do you think Xavier's parents were justified in lying to him about who his father was? Is it ever okay to keep that kind of information from a child?

11. Should JJ have told Simon about Rayshawn? When would have been the best time for her to tell him?

12. Do you think JJ made the right choice in the end, in regards to her contract? Did she really have to choose? Couldn't she have had it all—the contract, her faith, her family, and Simon?

13. Do you think JJ and Simon have a real chance, or is it impractical for them to try and have a relationship, given the nature of both their jobs?

Don't miss Rhonda Bowen's

Get You Good

On sale now at your local bookstore!

Chapter 1

Sydney was never big on sports.

It wasn't that she was athletically challenged. It was just that chasing a ball around a court, or watching other people do it, had never really been high on her list of favorite things.

However, as she stood at the center of the Carlu Round Room, surveying the best of the NBA that Toronto had to offer, she had to admit that professional sports definitely had a few attractive features.

"Thank you, Sydney."

Sydney grinned and folded her arms as she considered her younger sister.

"For what?"

"For Christmas in October." Lissandra bit her lip. "Look at all those presents."

Sydney turned in the direction where Lissandra was staring, just in time to catch the burst of testosterone-laced eye candy that walked through the main doors. Tall, muscular, and irresistible, in every shade of chocolate a girl could dream of sampling. She was starting to have a new appreciation for basketball.

Sydney's eyebrows shot up. "Is that . . . ?"

"Yes, girl. And I would give anything to find him under our

Christmas tree," Lissandra said, as her eyes devoured the newest group of NBA stars to steal the spotlight. "I love this game."

Sydney laughed. "I don't think it's the game you love."

"You laugh now," Lissandra said, pulling her compact out of her purse. "But when that hot little dress I had to force you to wear gets you a date for next weekend, you'll thank me."

Sydney folded her arms across the bodice of the dangerously short boat-necked silver dress that fit her five-foot-nine frame almost perfectly. It was a bit more risqué than what Sydney would normally wear but seemed almost prudish compared to what the other women in the room were sporting. At least it wasn't too tight. And the cut of the dress exposed her long, elegant neck, which she had been told was one of her best features.

"I'm here to work, not to pick up men," Sydney reminded her sister.

"No, we're here to deliver a spectacular cake." Lissandra checked her lipstick in the tiny mirror discreetly. "And since that cake is sitting over there, our work is done. It's playtime."

"Focus, Lissa." Sydney tried to get her sister back on task with a hand on her upper arm. "Don't forget this is an amazing opportunity to make the kinds of contacts that will put us on the A-list. Once we do that, more events like this might be in our future."

"OK, fine," Lissandra huffed, dropping her compact back into her purse. "I'll talk to some people and give out a few business cards. But if a player tries to buy me a drink, you best believe I'm gonna take it."

Sydney smirked. "I wouldn't expect otherwise."

"Good." Lissandra's mouth turned up into a naughty grin. " 'Cause I see some potential business over there that has my name etched across his broad chest."

Sydney sighed. Why did she even bother? "Be good," she said, adding a serious big-sister tone to her voice.

"I will," Lissandra threw behind her. But since she didn't even bother to look back, Sydney didn't hope for much. She knew her sister, and she'd just lost her to a six-foot-six brother with dimples across the room.

Sydney eventually lost sight of her sister as the crowd thickened. She turned her attention back to their ticket into the exclusive Toronto Raptors NBA Season Opener event.

The cake.

Sydney stood back and admired her work again, loving the way the chandelier from above and the tiny lights around the edges of the table and underneath it lit up her creation. The marzipan gave the cream-colored square base of the cake a smooth, flawless finish, and the gold trim caught the light beautifully. The golden replica of an NBA championship trophy, which sat atop the base, was, however, the highlight.

She had to admit it was a sculpted work of art, and one of the best jobs she had done in years. It was also one of the most difficult. It had taken two days just to bake and decorate the thing. That didn't include the several concept meetings, the special-ordered baking molds, and multiple samples made to ensure that the cake tasted just as good as it looked. For the past month and a half, this cake job had consumed her life. But it was well worth it. Not only for the weight it put in her pocket, but also the weight it was likely to add to her client list. Once everyone at the event saw her creation, she was sure she would finally make it onto the city's pastry-chef A-list, and Decadent would be the go-to spot for wedding and special-event cakes.

She stood near the cake for a while, sucking up the oohs and aahs of passersby, before heading to the bathroom to check that she hadn't sweated out her curls carrying up the cake from downstairs. She took in her long, dark hair, which had been curled and pinned up for the night; her slightly rounded face; and plump, pinked lips; and was satisfied. She turned to the side to get a better view of her size six frame and smiled. Even though she had protested when Lissandra presented the dress, she knew she looked good. Normally she hated any kind of shimmer, but the slight sparkle from the dress was just enough to put Sydney in the party mood it inspired. OK, so Lissandra may have been right—she was there for business—but that didn't mean she couldn't have some fun, too.

* * *

By the time she reapplied her lipstick and headed back, the room was full.

She tried to mingle and did end up chatting with a few guests, but her maternal instincts were in full gear and it wasn't long before she found her way back to the cake. She was about to check for anything amiss when she felt gentle fingers on the back of her bare neck. She swung around on reflex.

"What do you think you're doing?" she said, slapping away the hand that had violated her personal space.

"Figuring out if I'm awake or dreaming."

Sydney's eyes slid all the way up the immaculately toned body of the six-foot-three man standing in front of her, to his strong jaw, full smirking lips, and coffee brown eyes. Her jaw dropped. And not just because of how ridiculously handsome he was.

"Dub?"

"Nini."

She cringed. "Wow. That's a name I never thought I would hear again."

"And that's a half tattoo I never thought I'd see again."

Sydney slapped her hand to the back of her neck self consciously. She had almost forgotten the thing was there. It would take the one person who had witnessed her chicken out on getting it finished to remind her about it.

Hayden Windsor. Now wasn't this a blast from the past, sure to get her into some present trouble.

She tossed a hand onto her hip and pursed her lips. "I thought Toronto was too small for you."

"It is."

"Then what are you doing here?"

"Right now?" His eyes flitted across her frame in answer.

"Stop that," Sydney said, her cheeks heating up as she caught his perusal.

"Stop what?" he asked with a laugh.

"You know what," she said. She shook her head. "You are still the same."

He shrugged in an attempt at innocence that only served to

draw Sydney's eyes to the muscles shifting under his slim-fitting jacket.

"I can't help it. I haven't seen you in almost ten years. What, you gonna beat me up like you did when you were seven?"

"Maybe."

"Bully."

"Jerk."

"How about we continue this argument over dinner?" he asked.

"They just served appetizers."

The corners of his lips drew up in a scandalous grin. "Come on, you know you're still hungry."

He was right. That finger food hadn't done anything for her—especially since working on the cake had kept her from eating all day. But she wasn't about to tell him that.

Sydney smirked. "Even if I was, I don't date guys who make over one hundred thousand dollars a year."

He raised a thick eyebrow. "That's a new one."

"Yes, well," she said, "it really is for your own good. This way you won't have to wonder if I was with you for your money."

"So how about we pretend like I don't have all that money," he said, a dangerous glint in his eyes. "We could pretend some other things, too—like we weren't just friends all those years ago."

"I'm not dating you, Hayden," Sydney said, despite the shiver that ran up her spine at his words.

"So you can ask me to marry you, but you won't date me?"

"I was seven years old!"

"And at nine years old, I took that very seriously," Hayden said, his brow furrowing.

Sydney laughed. "That would explain why you went wailing to your daddy right after."

He rested a hand on his rock-solid chest. "I'm an emotional kind of guy."

"Hayden! There you are. I've been looking all over for you!"

Sydney turned to where the voice was coming from and fought her gag reflex. A busty woman with too much blond hair sidled up to Hayden, slipping her arm around his.

"This place is so packed that I can barely find anyone." The woman suddenly seemed to notice Sydney.

"Sydney!"

"Samantha."

Samantha gave Sydney a constipated smile. "So good to see you."

Sydney didn't smile back. "Wish I could say the same."

Hayden snorted. Samantha dropped the smile, but not his arm.

Sydney glared at the woman in the red-feathered dress and wondered how many peacocks had to die to cover her Dolly Parton goods.

"So I guess you two know each other?" Hayden asked, breaking the silence that he seemed to find more amusing than awkward.

"Yes," Samantha volunteered. "Sydney's little bakery, Decadent, beat out Something Sweet for the cake job for this event. She was my main competition."

"I wouldn't call it a competition," Sydney said, thinking it was more like a slaughtering.

"How do *you* know each other?" Samantha probed.

Hayden grinned. "Sydney and I go way back. Right, Syd?"

Samantha raised an eyebrow questioningly and Sydney glared at her, daring her to ask another question. Samantha opted to keep her mouth shut.

"So this is where the party is," Lissandra said, joining the small circle. Sydney caught the flash of recognition in Lissandra's eyes when she saw who exactly made up their impromptu gathering.

"Hayden? Is that you?"

"The very same," Hayden said, pulling Lissandra into a half hug. "Good to see you, Lissandra."

"Back at you," Lissandra said. "Wow, it's been ages. I probably wouldn't recognize you except Sydney used to watch your games all the—oww!"

Lissandra groaned as Sydney's elbow connected with her side.

"Did she?" Hayden turned to Sydney again, a smug look in his eyes.

"Well, it was nice to see you all again," Samantha said, trying to navigate Hayden away from the group.

"Samantha, I can't believe you're here." Lissandra's barely concealed laughter was not lost on Sydney or Samantha. "I thought you would be busy cleaning up that business at Something Sweet."

Sydney bit back a smirk as a blush crept up Samantha's neck to her cheeks. Samantha went silent again.

"What business?" Hayden looked around at the three women, who obviously knew something he didn't.

"Nothing," Samantha said quickly.

"Just that business with the health inspector," Lissandra said, enjoying Samantha's discomfort. "Nothing major. I'm sure the week that you were closed was enough to get that sorted out."

Hayden raised an eyebrow. "The health inspector shut you down?"

"We were closed temporarily," Samantha corrected. "Just so that we could take care of a little issue. It wasn't that serious."

"Is that what the exterminator said?" Lissandra asked.

Sydney coughed loudly and Samantha's face went from red to purple.

"You know," Samantha said, anger in her eyes. "It's interesting. We have never had a problem at that location before now. It's funny how all of a sudden we needed to call an exterminator around the same time they were deciding who would get the job for tonight's event."

"Yes, life is full of coincidences," Sydney said dryly. "Like that little mix-up we had with the Art Gallery of Ontario event last month. But what can you do? The clients go where they feel confident."

"Guess that worked out for you this time around," Samantha said, glaring at Sydney and Lissandra.

"Guess so," Lissandra said smugly.

Sydney could feel Hayden eyeing her suspiciously, but she didn't dare look at him.

"Well, this was fun," Sydney said in a tone that said the exact opposite. "But I see some people I need to speak with."

Sydney excused herself from the group and made her way to the opposite side of the room toward the mayor's wife. She had only met the woman once, but Sydney had heard they had an anniversary coming up soon. It was time to get reacquainted, and get away from the one man who could make her forget what she really came here for.

By the time the hands on her watch were both sitting at eleven, Sydney was exhausted and completely out of business cards.

"Leaving already?" She was only steps from the door, and he was only steps in front of her.

"This was business, not pleasure."

Hayden's eyes sparkled with mischief. "All work and no play makes Sydney a dull girl."

This time her mouth turned up in a smile. "I think you know me better than that."

His grin widened in a way that assured her that he did. "Remind me."

She shook her head and pointed her tiny purse at him.

"I'm not doing this here with you, Dub."

He stepped closer and she felt the heat from his body surround her. "We can always go somewhere else. Like the Banjara a couple blocks away."

Sydney scowled. Him and his inside knowledge.

"If we leave now we can get there before it closes."

She folded her arms over her midsection. "I haven't changed my mind, Dub."

He grinned. "That's not what your stomach says."

Sydney glanced behind him, and he turned around to see that Samantha was only a few feet away and headed in his direction. Sydney wasn't sure what string of events had put Samantha and Hayden together that night. The woman was definitely not his type. Or at least she didn't think Samantha was.

"I think your date is coming to get you," Sydney said, her

voice dripping with amusement. "Maybe *she* wants to go for Indian food."

"How about I walk you to your car?"

Without waiting for a response, he put a hand on the small of her back and eased her out the large doors into the lobby and toward the elevator.

"What's the rush?" she teased.

"Still got that smart mouth, don't you."

"I thought that was what you liked about me," she said innocently, as he led her into the waiting elevator.

"See, that's what you always got wrong, Nini." He leaned toward her ear to whisper and she caught a whiff of his cologne. "It was never just one thing."

Sydney tried to play it off, but she couldn't help the way her breathing went shallow as her heart sped up. And she couldn't keep him from noticing it, either.

His eyes fell to her lips. "So what's it going to be, Syd? You, me, and something spicy?"

He was only inches away from her. So close that if she leaned in, she could . . .

"Hayden!"

A familiar voice in the distance triggered her good sense. Sydney stepped forward and placed her hands on his chest.

"I think you're a bit busy tonight."

She pushed him out of the elevator and hit the DOOR CLOSE button.

He grinned and shook his head as she waved at him through the gap between the closing doors.

"I'll see you soon, Nini."

For reasons she refused to think about, she hoped he kept that promise.

Prologue

Chloe scanned the incredibly packed sanctuary and groaned. The only seats available were in the balcony, and that just wouldn't do. Chloe wanted to kick herself for not gassing up her Benz the night before. That extra fourteen minutes at the gas station had probably made all the difference. Now, instead of sitting close enough to her next husband that he could smell her Chanel No. 5, she would be in the rafters with the nonimportant attendees . . . unless she could convince one of the ushers to seat her in front, where she so obviously belonged.

Chloe weighed her choices. One of the center aisles was being guarded by a white-haired woman with a body like a Baltimore Ravens lineman and a glare to match. Chloe immediately decided against her. She was likely immune to any of Chloe's charms and would probably have her removed from the sanctuary for trying to sidestep the rules.

The other center aisle was being handled by a distinguished and handsome man of about fifty years. Every few seconds he wiped tears from his eyes. He probably knew the recently departed Chandra Chambers personally. Had probably dined with the family in that gigantic mansion off West Paces Ferry Road, right smack in the middle of Atlanta's old money. He was, without question, Chloe's mark.

Chloe stumbled down the aisle, tears flowing freely, and soft sobs escaping every few seconds. The sensitive usher approached her and touched her arm.

"I'm so sorry, miss, but there are no more seats in the main sanctuary. You'll have to sit in the overflow."

Chloe nodded and placed one hand on her chest. As she'd hoped, the usher's gaze followed her hand to her slightly surgically enhanced, sufficiently heaving and bronzed bosom.

"I know," Chloe said in a throaty whisper, "but I just want to look at Chandra one more time. We were roommates at Spelman, and she was just like a sister to me."

The usher looked unsure, so Chloe went in for the kill. "When she was sick, she asked me to look after her babies for her. How can I do that from the balcony?"

This settled it for the usher. Chloe was sure he believed every word of her emotional speech. And why wouldn't he? Who would lie at a funeral about the wishes of the deceased?

Only a desperate person.

And as much as Chloe hated to admit it, she was desperate, and her socialite status was in severe jeopardy. She had just a couple hundred thousand dollars in the bank, which enabled her to strategize without getting a nine to five, but it wouldn't keep her in the society circles she'd infiltrated with her late fiancé. Walter had been a billionaire. She'd met him on the beach in St. Bart's one holiday. Although he was seventy-eight, Walter was spry and sexy, and he'd given Chloe everything her heart had desired. Well . . . almost everything. He'd never made her his bride, and when he died suddenly of an aneurysm, Walter's children unceremoniously threw Chloe out on her behind. All she had left was the sum of the gifts he'd given her—a fully furnished townhouse, several large diamonds and other jewels, and a car.

Chloe tried not to draw too much attention to herself as she followed the usher down to the front row. She wanted to be remembered by only one person—Quentin. The lineman usher scowled, but Chloe's friendly usher made room for her on the aisle. None of the family paid attention to the extra person in their pew. In fact, the family seemed to be in a tearful haze. Quentin looked especially hopeless, but even still, his incredible good looks made Chloe's heart skip a beat. His caramel skin seemed to glow as tears coursed down his face.

Chloe wanted to reach out and comfort him, pull him to her saline plumped breasts and caress his pain away.

Yes, Chloe did believe she would have her some of Quentin Chambers. And his millions.